The third
The Caterpill

ASYLUM

ADAM LONGDEN

Previously...

After watching his family home burn to the ground, a house littered with dead bodies, Jack, a teenage boy brought up in isolation, makes a dash for the English coast.

He is subsequently caught, but exonerated of any crimes. A deal is struck, and Jack is given a brand-new identity. For the first time in his life, he actually exists. Safety and anonymity are provided – a respite from the baying press – in the form of a flat, a safe house, on the North Norfolk coast.

This provides the opportunity for a fresh start for Jack and Daisy. New jobs. New friends. A new life.

But Peasgood, Jack's former boss, has other ideas. Hell-bent on saving his own skin, it seems he will stop at nothing to silence Jack and Daisy, sending his henchmen to find and terrorise them.

Seaside Skeletons closes with Jack and Daisy cornered by one of their relentless pursuers. Isolated, in the dark and frantically looking for escape...

CHAPTER 1

Quarry

Jack had heard the car on the lane. The angry sound, so at odds with the stillness, disturbed his reverie.

And then Daisy's blessed voice, her familiar shadow in the purple gloom.

The urgency of the situation.

'Follow me,' Jack said. They sprang from the cover of the back door and onto the drive.

A desperate glance to the right confirmed they wouldn't be leaving via the driveway. If at all. The driver of the car was already there, between them and their exit. His shape and attire were sickeningly familiar. It was one of Peasgood's men, the guy who had been in the back of the car that night, the night Jack was kidnapped. Worse still, despite the limited visibility, it was clear he was wielding some kind of weapon in his right hand.

Jack faltered, and Daisy slammed into his back. Not expecting to see anyone other than the girl, the man froze too. There was a brief standoff, about twenty yards apart. 'Yous!' the man cried in recognition, pointing his cosh at Jack, his thick Scottish accent causing a further chill. He began to lumber towards them.

'Quick!' Jack said, recovering. 'Follow me.'

At first, Jack had no idea how they were going to get away. He hadn't had time to think ahead, and didn't know what he was dealing with. But now his survival instincts kicked in. There were a hundred different hiding places on that rambling plot, all discovered when on the run from his father and the threat of another serious beating. The number of times he had hidden as a child – holding his breath as his heart clattered in his chest – as his father had crashed by, angrily cursing him. In chicken runs, outbuildings and sheds. On corrugated iron roofs. Up trees, in ditches, in hollows in hedges. All he could do was wait until his father gave up, retreating to get blind drunk, pass out and forget. Until the next time.

It was the orchard that Jack headed towards, sprinting across the driveway with Daisy in tow. Immediately, their pursuer veered towards them. There was a heart-stopping moment, accompanied by a squeal from Daisy, as they avoided the desperate lunge of a grasping hand by mere inches. Then they hit the long grass, charging up a slight incline past the incinerator. Despite not daring to look behind, Jack knew they were already putting some distance between themselves and their pursuer. They were both quick on their feet. Young, slim and nimble. 'Watch out for the swing!' he cried, swerving suddenly. Daisy followed Jack's course, homing in on the rucksack bobbing on his back, the long grass and darkness enveloping them as they went.

Before long, they reached the fruit trees, a waiting regiment, dormant and spindly. They heard a clang and a yelp from a fair distance behind. The swing. 'Stick close to me!' Jack cried, as they hurtled between the trees, the low branches brushing and clawing them. 'And when I say "jump", jump.'

'What? Why?' Daisy heaved, out of breath. 'I can't keep this up!'

'Not much further,' Jack panted over his shoulder. 'Are you ready?'

'Ready for what?'

'JUMP!'

Daisy saw Jack spring into the air, then land again. Before she knew it, she was upon it herself – a broad ditch or gully – cutting across their path through the trees. It was filled with broken branches and leaves; she wouldn't have had a clue it was there. She vaulted it and landed on the other side, jarring her ankle, but tried not to cry out in pain. 'Shit!' she said. 'How much further?'

'Nearly there.'

Jack slowed suddenly. Then, to Daisy's surprise, he threw himself onto his stomach in front of what appeared to be a large tree. 'What are you doing? We can't stop.' She cast a desperate glance behind her. 'Is this a dead end?'

'Get on your knees, and follow me,' he said over his shoulder.

'Where are you going? We can't both hide under there.' There were noises from behind, the snapping of branches and cursing. 'Shit! He's coming. Hurry up!' Daisy dropped to her knees. Jack began to wriggle forward on his stomach. 'Quick, Jack, quick!' Daisy cast another glance behind her as the noises got louder, closer. 'Shit, shit, shit!'

Jack grunted and groaned as his rucksack got wedged under a thick branch. Daisy frantically shoved with all her might, and it came free. A Scottish voice behind, getting angrier: 'Where the fuck are yers?'

'Shit!' Daisy threw herself after Jack. God knows where he was going; there seemed nothing but a dead end. But then he gradually began to disappear, as if being consumed by the hedge itself. Then his legs, until there were just his boots left. Daisy continued to wriggle after him, frantically. Where was he going? She found herself inside a dark tunnel, a gap between the hedges. It felt as if she was being eaten by a large boa constrictor, her chest and stomach crushed. Tiny branches like teeth dug into her, poking her in the ribs. Then it got lighter, and she was out the other side. Jack's pale hand in the gloom reached for her. She held out an arm and he pulled her through. Then they were both out. Breathing heavily. But where were they?

There was a loud shout and a crash. Louder than before. They looked at each other. The ditch had got him. Like Rambo, Daisy thought.

'Come on,' said Jack, pleased.

Daisy jumped to her feet. They were in a field beyond the top end of the garden. Jack dashed for the gate, and Daisy followed him. They vaulted it, and were on the pot-holed lane that led down to the main road – and their escape.

As they ran, the canisters of ashes in Jack's rucksack clinked about. The thug, still pulling himself out of the ditch, covered in leaves and mud, stopped and turned towards the lane. They were passing him in the opposite direction. 'Yer bastards!' he shouted again. 'I'll get yous.'

Jack and Daisy sprinted down the lane, Jack in front. Ahead of them, their pursuer's abandoned car was taking up most of the width of the lane. It looked empty. 'Where the hell's your van?' Jack called over his shoulder.

'It's on the main road, but it's run out of petrol.' She winced as she said it, feeling stupid.

'What?' Jack cried, pulling up. 'How are we meant to get back home?'

'Sorry, I didn't have a chance to tell you.' Daisy stopped too, breathing heavily. 'We'll have to leg it.'

'Where? To get petrol? It's miles. He'll catch us. We'll have to go cross-country.'

'Not to get petrol – there's nowhere open. Back to Mum's.'

'I'm not going back to your mum's. She…'

'Wait! Maybe there's keys in the car.' Daisy cupped her hands to the window and peered inside. 'Damn.' No key in the ignition. After checking the back seat, she tried the driver's door. It was unlocked. She looked at Jack, then pulled the door open.

'What are you doing? We haven't got time for this. He'll be coming.' Daisy was bent over, rooting around inside. The passenger seat, the dashboard, the footwell, the door. 'Come on!'

'Shit! What about the handbrake?' she said, turning to him. 'Let's crash his car.' Jack pictured the car picking up speed down the lane's considerable slope, then hurtling out across the main road. What if a car was passing at the same time? It would be a disaster. He couldn't have that on his conscience. Daisy appeared to read his thoughts. 'Yeah, stupid idea.'

'Let's go,' Jack said, resigned to the fact that Daisy's mum's was their only option – if she would let him in. 'Come on, we can't stay here.' He set off for the meadow opposite his house. His cross-country route to the village and Daisy's home.

'Wait, just a second,' said Daisy, stopping him. And she dashed to the back of the car.

'What now? We need to go.'

'The reg plate. I want the number.' She crouched down behind the car, her nose practically touching it. The number plate was filthy and hard to make out in the dark. She gave it a rub with her sleeve, then read the digits out loud. 'Got it!' she said.

'Come on then.' They bounded into the meadow and headed for the spinney. Jack had taken this route so many times, but not Daisy. She followed his lead, trusting he knew where he was going. All the while, she repeated the car's registration number in her head; surely it had to be traceable.

Meanwhile, Peasgood's henchman had extricated himself from the ditch and, cursing and muttering, was retracing his steps – a little more gingerly – through the garden. He'd taken quite a tumble, and was limping. Not for the first time, he thought that he was getting too old for this shit.

He reached his car as quickly as his body would allow, but most of the chase had gone out of him. The kids were nowhere to be seen. He gave one last glance behind him. He couldn't imagine they'd gone back in the house. All around was nothing but darkness, save for a lamp post at the bottom of the lane, illuminating the main road. He thought of the girl's van. His best bet now. Had they reached it? She'd appeared to have run out of petrol earlier, otherwise why would she have abandoned it? But he didn't know for sure. He sighed and got into his car, tossing his cosh onto the passenger seat. He needed to find a phone box. The old bastard would be waiting for an update. Fuck 'im, he thought. He can wait. This job wasn't worth the risks.

Jack and Daisy crouched in the ditch between the meadow and the spinney. If their pursuer tried to find them in the spinney, he wouldn't stand a chance in hell: Jack knew the place like the back of his hand. The thought gave him some comfort and, strangely, a sense of pride. He felt safe. Or safer, at least. Unless the guy was desperate and was willing to wait until it was light – then it would be a different story.

They listened, still breathing heavily, for any sound of pursuit. Through the sparse hedge that separated the meadow from the main road, Jack noticed the faint blinking of hazard lights, signalling the location of Daisy's van. Then the sound of a car starting up carried across the meadow, and headlights lit up the lane. Jack and Daisy looked at each other. He must be leaving. Daisy reached for Jack's hand and squeezed it. They watched the headlights make their way slowly up the lane. He was searching for somewhere to turn around. Reversing into the driveway wasn't an option, not with the barrier there.

'He'll have to use the field entrance,' said Jack.

'No guessing who "he" is,' said Daisy.

'No. He was the one in the back of the car that night.'

Sure enough, they saw the car stop, reverse, then make its

way slowly back down the lane, as if the man was searching for them. It was a creepy feeling.

The car halted briefly, then pulled onto the main road. Then, to their surprise, it stopped and appeared to pull over onto the grass verge. The handbrake creaked on and their stomachs dropped. Despite being the other side of a tall hedge, their pursuer was only about fifty yards away. And that hedge was easy to slip through. They hunkered down.

'What's he doing?' whispered Jack. 'Why isn't he going away?'

'The van. I think he's going to check the van.'

They heard the car's suspension groan as the man got out, and the door slammed. The sounds were so loud. So near. They waited as the car idled.

'Did you lock the doors?' asked Jack.

'I can't remember. I was in such a state.' Daisy suddenly panicked and reached for her pocket. The bump of her keys was a relief.

As if to answer Jack's question, a door creaked open. She hadn't locked the van. It made her feel violated, the thought of that man invading her personal space and rummaging around like a burglar. The fact that she'd just done the same to him didn't enter her head. Instead, her mind raced to remember anything important or precious that he might see. All she could think of were cassette tapes.

After what seemed an age, during which the other doors opened and closed, a sudden hiss and a whoosh, followed by a groan from the van's suspension, made them jump. What was he doing? A few moments later, there it was again, with another protestation from the van, this time more violent, as if the brakes were struggling to hold it. 'The tyres. He's slashing the tyres!' said Daisy.

She gulped, trying to swallow, but her mouth was too dry. There was something so menacing and unnecessary about the man's actions. Vindictive. Not for the first time, she couldn't believe that such violence, such a threat, had visited their lives. He must have had his reasons for going to such lengths, but surely he realised she'd run out of petrol? It wasn't as though she could get anywhere without finding a garage. At this time of night, on New Year's Day...

The sudden pop and whooshing sound happened again, and Daisy squeezed Jack's hand tighter. Their palms were slick with sweat. She thought of the weapon the man was using, and the fact that he had one. A knife? A screwdriver? Would he have used it on them? They waited again, Daisy's eyes screwed shut as she anticipated the sound of the last tyre being slashed. The final insult...

But it didn't happen.

They waited a bit longer, then Daisy cautiously opened her eyes again. They heard the man get back in his car. Why would he leave one tyre intact? It didn't make sense. After a few moments, the car crunched into gear, then squealed quickly away.

Jack and Daisy both stood up to watch the car's red tail lights disappearing over the brow of the hill, near the council houses. And then it was gone.

But where?

CHAPTER 2

Enough is Enough

Once they felt it was safe enough, they made their way to Daisy's van. It was looking very sorry for itself, listing at an ungainly angle with all but the rear driver's side tyre slashed. It made Daisy want to cry. The van had been her parents' pride and joy, bringer of many fun-packed trips, family holidays and nostalgic memories. For the umpteenth time, she wished her dad was there. Still in her life. What would he have made of all this? What would he have done? He would have refused to be bullied, she knew that much. He would have taken action, but in his own quiet, resolute and clever way. She fought back a tear and her bottom lip trembled. But the thoughts strengthened her resolve. Enough was enough.

They set off cross-country for the village, Jack leading the way. Once through the spinney, they felt cold, damp and exposed. But at least they were far enough from the road not to be seen. Every time a car's lights appeared in the distance, they thought the same thing. It was Jack who voiced it first. 'What if he's waiting for us? At the house?'

'I know. I was thinking the same thing.'

'Was he there before? Did he follow you from home?'

'I don't know, I honestly don't. I left in such a rush.'

'We can slip round the back, through the patio doors.'

'They'll be locked and I don't have a key. We'll have to knock Mum up. We haven't got a choice. We can't risk the front, no way.' It was the first time Daisy had really thought of her mum since she'd left the house. Guilt flooded in. Had she noticed she'd gone? Had she tried to follow her? She couldn't have: she would have found the van. Perhaps she thought Daisy had headed back to Norfolk. She'd be worried sick.

Jack's heart sank at the prospect of being at the mercy of Daisy's mum. He'd been hoping they could slip in unnoticed and sit it out till morning. Indignation flared up in him at the way she had treated him, the way she had refused point-blank to hear his story or to let him see Daisy.

As if reading his thoughts, Daisy said, 'We've got to tell her. Everything. This has gone on long enough. That man had a weapon: I swear he wanted to kill us. Peasgood needs to be stopped.'

Jack said nothing, but he knew she was right.

They trudged on, Daisy repeating the car's registration number in her head.

*****

They arrived at Daisy's home without incident. Both of them felt nervous. Light from the kitchen illuminated them as they stood on the decking: two teenage kids, damp, shivering and cold with their hair clinging to them, eager for warmth and safety. Sanctuary.

Mum must still be up, Daisy surmised. She never went to bed and left downstairs lights on. And she wouldn't be able to sleep until she knew where Daisy was. Guilt again. Daisy reached out a pale hand, numb from the cold, and tried the door handle, just in case. As she had guessed, it was locked. Probably best, considering who was out there. The thought came to her suddenly. What if he'd come straight back here and knocked on the door, and she'd let him in? He could have said anything to trick or persuade her; she could be naïve sometimes, far too trusting. That man seemed capable of anything. He could be holding her right now, tied to a chair in this very house, inside these very walls…

Daisy panicked and rapped sharply on the patio door. She looked at Jack, whose face was a picture of apprehension. They waited for thirty seconds or more. She'd better not have the bloody telly on too loud, Daisy thought. She rapped again, louder, and tried to quell her rising panic – that thug had got her rattled. Moving to the kitchen window to see down the hall more clearly, she put her forehead to the glass.

Almost immediately, her mum appeared from the lounge, her movements familiar and quick as she entered the kitchen, a strained, worried look on her face. It was such a relief to see her unharmed, but her eyes were red-rimmed and swollen under the harsh striplight, as if she'd been crying. Then Carol saw Daisy peering in. The unexpected sight startled her, and she stumbled backwards, clutching her hands to her chest. She shook her head at Daisy, almost angrily, at the fright she had been given. Or maybe because of how her daughter had left.

Carol got another fright when she opened the patio door to find Jack standing there, wraith-like, pale and bedraggled. 'Oh my Lord!' she exclaimed, clutching her hands to her chest again. Was there no end to this? She *was* angry now.

Daisy nudged Jack aside. 'Mum, let us in: it's freezing out here.'

To Daisy's surprise and dismay, her mum paused, as if considering this. 'What's he doing here?' she said. 'And why can't you use the front door like any normal human being?'

Daisy couldn't believe it. If only her mum knew what they'd been going through – she'd be sorry when she did. 'Mum, seriously, let us in – I'll explain everything in a minute.'

Carol paused briefly again, then stood aside to let them in, giving Jack a purposeful stare. She still hadn't forgiven him for getting her daughter pregnant – on top of everything else. The way she saw it, he was trouble. Not good enough. Jack, as always, averted his gaze. 'Look at the state of you both, you'll catch your deaths out there. Where have you been? I thought you'd cleared off back to Norfolk! And where's the van?'

'I'll explain in a minute,' Daisy said, locking the door behind them, then marching straight through the kitchen and out into the hall. 'Where's Lily?'

'In bed. Last night's caught up with her. Where are you going? Where's she going?' she said, turning to Jack.

Jack shrugged. And then he cottoned on.

They followed Daisy, Carol leading the way. They found her in the living room, peering cautiously round a curtain and out of a front window. It was hard to see anything and she cupped a hand round her eye, rubbing the glass. There didn't appear to be a car out there, not that she could see anyway, but that didn't mean anything; he could have parked anywhere. 'Is the porch door locked?' she said.

Carol and Jack went after her into the hall. 'Yes. I locked all the doors after you left,' Carol said. 'Like I said, I thought you'd gone for good, and I didn't want you sneaking back in again – not without me knowing anyway. What's going on?' Daisy was checking the front door for good measure, but didn't venture out into the porch in case she was seen.

'Nearly done,' she said, then bolted upstairs for a better view out to the front.

'Daisy!' Carol called after her, then she huffed in exasperation. 'I give up. I'm putting the kettle on; I'm not following her around all night.' She waved her arm in Daisy's direction, but appeared to be addressing Jack without looking at him. Not wanting to stand awkwardly with him as they waited for Daisy (he was so taciturn, and she hadn't a thing to say to him), Carol stomped off back to the kitchen.

Jack peered up the stairs, lost without Daisy and jigging

from one foot to the other as usual, his rucksack still on his back. Soon she reappeared, descending the stairs quickly. 'I can't see anything. I think he might have gone.' She paused to kiss Jack quickly on the lips, then continued to the kitchen. The kiss surprised him, but felt good. It had seemed so long since they'd kissed, or hugged, or done anything like that. So much had happened. Had New Year's Eve really only been last night? Before following her, Jack was momentarily rooted to the spot, cherishing the ghost of Daisy's lips on his. Such a brief gesture had conveyed so much: that he was forgiven, and that Daisy was feeling a little safer, a little more relaxed, now that they were indoors and the immediate threat had passed.

The three of them sat at the kitchen table, all nursing mugs of tea. Carol seemed to have temporarily put her antagonism towards Jack to one side. She wanted to know what had been going on. Why the look of fear on their faces when they arrived? Where was the van? And why all the cloak and dagger stuff?

'Right. I'm going to start from the beginning,' Daisy said.

'Please do,' Carol said, a little impatiently.

Daisy told the story of Peasgood, concentrating on the stuff her mother didn't know: the kidnapping in Norfolk, one of the men following her to the house, the pursuit through the garden, the slashing of the tyres. She spoke as quickly and matter-of-factly as she could. It wasn't the time for prevarication; Daisy wanted to contact Haslam and the police as soon as possible.

Carol turned angry pink then deathly pale as Daisy spoke, tapping her fingernails on the table in agitation. On hearing what had happened that very evening – her own daughter being stalked in a car, then chased and threatened by a weapon-wielding thug – she'd got up to call the police immediately, unable to hold her outrage in any longer. But Daisy urged her to wait: she hadn't finished. So Carol sat there, thin-lipped, hands shaking, clutching her mug. Those vile men weren't the sole source of her anger; it was Jack too. If Daisy had never met him, none of this would have happened. And why hadn't they told the police sooner?

'Now can I call the police?' Carol said, as Daisy finished. 'This isn't going on a second longer.' She got up from the table again.

'Yes, I want to too,' Daisy said in return. She instinctively reached for Jack's hand, knowing the anxiety this would cause him. 'But will there be anyone there?'

'There's always someone there. Maybe not at East Leake – but definitely West Bridgford, big station like that. They have to keep someone on the desk.'

'West Bridgford? That's Haslam's station.'

'I know. So much the better. At least he knows the history of this thing – or most of it.' She couldn't resist the dig.

'Shit – sorry, Mum – if only we had his direct number on us. Jack, I don't suppose…' Daisy turned to him, but he shook his head.

'I'm calling anyway. I want action. Besides,' Carol added over her shoulder, 'your Haslam will be in bed, no doubt.' She still wasn't convinced by the detective and his methods – someone else she hadn't forgiven for their part in her daughter's predicament.

Daisy got up to follow her. 'Don't you think it's best I phone? It's me all this has happened to, after all. Us, I mean. Me and Jack. They'll need to know the details.'

'We'll cross that bridge if we come to it. Where's the phone book?'

Daisy sat on the stairs next to Jack, rolling her eyes occasionally, whilst Carol bumbled her way through what had happened. It wasn't long before the phone was handed over to her. She gave her mum a look, as if to say 'I told you so.' It was Carol's turn to roll her eyes. Daisy clarified a few points to the officer on duty. Then she asked for Haslam's number, explaining they hadn't got it with them, or at least for the detective to be notified.

The officer said he wouldn't hand out a DCI's personal phone number to a stranger without checking the ins and outs first. And he also wouldn't be calling an off-duty DCI at this time of night on New Year's Day either, unless it was urgent.

'Trust me, he'd want to know,' said Daisy.

Daisy was assured that the incident(s) had been logged and would be looked into as a matter of urgency. But given the time of night and that they were now safe, nothing would happen until the morning. 'Having said that,' the officer said, 'a car will be sent out to check the exact location of the broken-down vehicle. Sounds like it's in a dangerous spot, and that's my immediate concern.'

Great, thought Daisy. Talk about priorities. To add insult to injury, she had to promise she'd arrange for the van to be towed to a garage first thing in the morning – at her own expense.

'I'll instruct the patrol officer to swing by your house on the way back as well, purely to do a quick recce and for your own peace of mind. We've got your address. In the meantime, if there are any further incidents or threats, then you're to notify us immediately. Don't go outside again tonight, or open the door to anyone under any circumstances. I suggest you check the house is secure again and go to bed.'

So they did as the officer said.

*****

Despite an uneventful night, no one in the Jones household slept properly. Except Lily, of course, who was oblivious to the whole situation. Daisy was awake and up and about at the crack of dawn, agitated. She wanted to phone the garage in East Leake the second it opened. She couldn't stand the thought of being in trouble with the police hanging over her head. Carol was up and about early too. She had been awake most of the night, stewing over the fact that Daisy had kept all this from her – and from the police. It was hard not to take it out on her daughter, so she was trying to keep busy. Daisy knew her mum was pissed off at her – and Jack – which made the situation worse. That and the guilt.

Daisy entered the kitchen. The smell of fried animal fat made her feel queasy. She wrinkled her nose and tried to hold her breath.

'It's just boiled,' Carol said, indicating the kettle.

'Do you want another one?'

'No. Thank you.'

Daisy refilled her mug and a got a fresh one for Jack. He was still in bed.

'There's bacon here if you want it. And Jack. A butty or something.'

Daisy cast a sideways glance into the wok her mother had taken to using as a frying pan. There were eight rashers of bacon in it. All undercooked. Pale pink and lolling about in a sea of clear fatty liquid. They reminded Daisy of dogs' tongues. Her stomach churned again. 'No thanks, I'm vegetarian.'

'Since when?' Carol turned to her.

'Since now.'

'You're kidding me, right?'

'No. I'm not.'

'You've just decided you're vegetarian now. Right this second.'

'I've been thinking about it for a while. It's a New Year's resolution. Morrisey's vegetarian. Meat is murder.'

'Don't be ridiculous. You've always loved your meat, especially a fry-up.'

Looks more like a boil-up, thought Daisy. 'I've gone off it, the smell and that.'

'Well you could have told me that before I cooked all this bloody bacon!'

'I didn't know. You didn't ask. Sorry. Jack'll have some – and Lily.' Just then, the phone in the hall rang, startling them. They looked at each other, then up at the kitchen clock. It had just turned eight.

'That's early,' said Carol.

'Bet it's Haslam,' Daisy said. 'I'll get it.' Before Carol could stop her, she was on her way.

Daisy was right. It was strangely comforting to hear Haslam's voice. But he sounded serious, agitated, not his usual jovial self. Clearly this had escalated to a whole new level. He wanted to know everything, from the start. Especially what Jack had to say. But not over the phone: he was coming round to the house at nine. They were to make sure they were in and ready for him.

This suited Daisy. It would give her plenty of time to phone the garage. After telling her mum, she took Jack a cup of tea and a bacon butty. He was already sitting up in bed, a worried look on his face. 'Was that the police?' he asked.

'Yeah. Haslam.'

'What did he say? Have we got to go to the station?'

'No. He's coming round here at nine o'clock.' She passed him his plate and put the tea on the bedside table. He accepted the sandwich gratefully; he was starving.

'Thanks. You had yours already?' Jack asked, a little put out at the thought of her eating without him; he liked them to eat together. He liked them to do everything together.

'No. I'm not hungry. Besides, I'm vegetarian now.' She sat down on the bed.

Jack snorted, thinking she was joking, and set about his sandwich, his hunger getting the better of him.

'So, yes, nine o'clock. He wants to know everything.' Jack looked worried again and paused momentarily. Big scared rabbit eyes bulging over the top of his sandwich. 'It'll be OK.' She put her hand on his leg through the duvet. 'This needs to be done. We just need to make sure we're ready. So finish your sandwich, then get dressed. I've got to phone the garage. I'll be downstairs.'

'What, you're not coming back up?'

'Maybe. I don't know how long I'll be on the phone. You'll be OK.' She kissed his head and got up to leave.

'Daisy?'

'Yes,' she said, turning.

'I love you. And I'm sorry. About … you know…' He looked forlorn, a smudge of ketchup at the side of his mouth, the half-eaten sandwich floppy in his hand.

Oh, that other stuff, thought Daisy. Jeanie. Strangely, with everything that had happened since, it had been pushed to the back of her mind; she certainly hadn't been dwelling on it. But Jack's apology was a reminder, and it stung again. She had a very sudden, very clear vision of that slender bare back and shoulder, the fine blonde down on it. The way her hand had been resting on Jack's chest, that fancy fucking nail polish. She suddenly felt sick. 'It's OK,' she said, swallowing the feeling and banishing the image. 'Love you too.'

CHAPTER 3

Action

Daisy explained to the garage the urgency of the situation. They said they would deal with the van as a priority. They were a family business. Her dad had always used them: everybody did locally. Daisy didn't even have to be there: just pop the keys into the garage first and they'd send the lorry out. The tyres needed to be ordered, as they didn't have them in stock. This might take a day or two. All this was OK, and essentially good news, but it raised two problems.

First was money. The recovery was going to cost forty-five quid alone. 'Sorry I can't do it any cheaper, duck, but that's the minimum callout charge for the lorry.' He didn't know the price of the tyres until he'd called the supplier. Daisy was going to have to ask her mum if she could lend her some money, which she hated the thought of. She had her grandma's Christmas money left and a little of her own, totalling about a hundred pounds. But she was going to need more than that. She had her building society savings of course, around five hundred pounds – perhaps now was the time to use this. And Jack had his money from Haslam too. But that was his money. His savings. He'd been waiting so long for it. There was no way she was going to dip into that.

She explained all this to her mum, leaving out any mention

of Jack's money. Carol begrudgingly said she would help out, figuring that Daisy might need her savings, as the van wasn't going to last much longer. She suggested Daisy should ring her insurers to see if slashed tyres were covered; three new ones weren't going to be cheap.

The second problem was leaving the house to drop the keys off. What if that man was still out there somewhere? What if he *did* know where they lived? He must do, Daisy figured. Or how would he have known when she had set off in the van? The obvious thing would be for her mum to go. Or Lily. But what if he saw them leave the house? What if he followed *them*? None of them could be on their own. It was too risky, too dangerous. But Jack and her mum going together didn't seem an option either. If only her dad was there. Daisy gave herself a talking to. She wasn't going to be bullied, remember? Or live in fear. Sod it, it was broad daylight out there. What could happen?

Carol was furious about the whole situation. 'First it was those reporters, and now it's some thug on our doorstep, menacing us, making our lives a misery,' she said. 'I'm selling up. I don't want to live here any more.' Daisy had to calm her down, but the commotion woke Lily up. Carol quickly filled her in, whilst Daisy told Jack that she and her mum were going to the garage. It was Jack's turn to be angry. He refused point blank. No way was she going out without him: he would have to go too. After some discussion, they decided this made sense.

They put their plan into action. First, Carol ventured cautiously out to the end of the driveway to look up and down their road. Jack and Daisy kept a close eye on her from the porch. Lily stood behind them. Jack was holding a stout and heavy piece of wood that Daisy's dad had kept under his bed: he'd called it his 'burglar stick'. It had never been moved, just lay there in the dust. It had been Carol's idea to grab it. There was no sign of the guy or his car. Carol wrapped her coat around her, then ventured out further to be sure. 'Mum, be careful,' said Lily.

'Wait!' said Daisy. 'Come on, Jack.' They sidled up to the end of the driveway where Carol had stood. They looked both ways, paying most attention to the end of the close, only fifty yards or so away, where it joined Main Street. They felt alarmingly vulnerable, knowing that man could screech round the corner at any moment. It was horrible.

Knowing Jack and Daisy were watching, Carol did a cautious check of the cul-de-sac. All seemed clear. Lily went back to bed, having been instructed under no circumstances to answer the door. After defrosting the Montego, then locking the house, they set off. Jack took the stick with him.

The garage was only a two-minute drive, but they kept a lookout the whole way, behind them and down side roads. They reached their destination without incident, and Daisy ran in alone – she insisted – whilst Jack and Carol kept watch from the locked car. As she handed the keys over, the garage's owner inadvertently shed some light on the car insurance situation. 'Who's got it in for you, duck?' he asked. 'Must have been a nasty piece of work.'

'Sorry?' said Daisy, distracted.

'You said only three tyres were slashed on the phone. Insurers sometimes only pay out if all four have been done. Always seems a bit cruel to me…'

'Bastard,' said Daisy, unable to help herself. 'Sorry.'

The man chuckled, surprised at the fruity language. She was a sweet girl, attractive. Lovely hair. But she seemed in a rush. 'I'm sorry. I shouldn't have laughed. Ex-boyfriend, maybe? You broken some poor young fella's heart?'

'No. No, I just ran out of petrol, then found it like that when I went back.'

*****

Haslam's hair had grown since Daisy had seen him last. It needed trimming. His silver-grey sideburns were like unruly clumps of wire wool. He'd also put on a fair bit of weight. To Jack's dismay, the detective had another officer with him in proper uniform: Sergeant Nichols from the station. It gave a heightened sense of gravity to the situation. The familiar Haslam was almost like an old family friend now, and always in plain clothes.

New Year greetings dealt with and hot drinks dished out, they got down to business, sitting round the kitchen table – Carol included. Jack struggled at first. He felt shy and reserved talking to adults at the best of times, but in front of Daisy's mother and an unfamiliar police officer it was even harder. The black spot on his eye pulsed and throbbed just out of sight. His leg tapped under the table. He kept faltering, losing his train of thought, watching the officers' pens flick back and forth as they scribbled notes. Haslam was used to Jack's tics and manner by now. The new guy wasn't, and Jack became aware of his scrutiny. It made him feel like a 'special case' again. Not normal. He hadn't felt like that for a while.

Daisy helped Jack out, more so than was necessary, as usual. Reminding him of things, backing him up and prompting him. Again, Haslam was used to this dynamic. Nichols wasn't. Bit by bit, though, the youngsters made their statements to the best of their knowledge, including timings and descriptions of the two men. Haslam's patience was increasingly tested, and his exasperation began to show when he found out about the kidnapping. He sighed and ran his fingers through his thinning hair, threw down his pen and sat back in his seat. 'Jack, I asked you if there was anything else, anything at all. I asked you over and over. He could be in custody by now – and this wouldn't have escalated.' Jack bowed his head, shame-faced.

'I knew too,' Daisy said. 'Not just Jack. We were scared. Both of us were. They threatened me. Jack was protecting me by not telling the police. What would you have done if it had been your family, detective, your wife? This was two men in the dark in a car in the middle of nowhere, one of them with their hands round Jack's throat.' She was angry, and she had a point. Even Carol could see why they hadn't said anything. They'd been terrified.

At this inopportune juncture, Lily wandered into the kitchen. 'Oh, sorry,' she said, acting surprised. The policemen looked at Carol.

'Sorry, this is my other daughter, Lily.'

'Lily,' said Haslam. They'd met briefly once before. Sergeant Nichols nodded his head.

Lily smiled broadly, batted her lashes, and said hello. She had a full face of make-up on. 'Would anyone like another cup of tea?' she asked, reaching for the kettle. Daisy groaned. She knew damn well Lily knew about the interview – and that she had a thing for men in uniform. And she never, ever, offered to make anyone a hot drink. She was as subtle as a chainsaw.

Haslam coughed awkwardly, keen to carry on with the meeting. In private. He looked at Carol again.

'Lily, do you mind waiting in the lounge for a bit, sweetheart?' Carol said.

Lily wanted to protest, but knew she'd come across like a stroppy child. She put the kettle down, trying not to slam it. 'Yes, no worries,' she said calmly, smiling again, but thinking she wouldn't even be able to eavesdrop now. 'I'll get some juice if that's OK.'

'Yes, of course,' said Carol. 'Thank you.'

Lily helped herself to a glass of orange juice from the jug in the fridge, taking her time. Then she sashayed off to the lounge, humming to herself. Daisy shook her head again.

'Sorry about that,' said Carol. 'Where were we?'

The meeting went on. When Daisy unexpectedly proffered the car's registration plate, the policemen stopped writing and looked at each other with raised eyebrows. The significance of this information couldn't be overstated; it could make all the difference. It tied the men to the scene. There were already police up there (Jack's favourite, Sergeant Brewster, amongst others), combing the vicinity for any further evidence: tyre tracks, footprints… Not only did this new development, this priceless nugget, help to diffuse Haslam's frustration, but he was also decidedly impressed. Given the circumstances, to have that foresight… The girl would make a good detective herself one day, he reckoned. Softening, he told Daisy so. She blushed, but felt proud, and looked at Jack. He smiled. She was so clever and amazing. And she was his.

Haslam wrapped up the interview, keen to get off and put that number plate into the system to see what came up. He already had a hunch: some of Peasgood's associates from the Glasgow area. He just hoped it wasn't a false plate. His gut told him they'd be back up north by now, across the border. Long gone. He couldn't imagine Peasgood risking any physical contact with the men, especially as he was already under investigation. But it was impossible to say. They could be holed up somewhere locally, waiting. They seemed determined. Peasgood, it seemed, wasn't going to let this go; not without a fight anyway. For this reason, he decided to send a regular patrol car past the close.

Before leaving, Haslam said, 'You'll still need to come into the station quite soon. There's probably no point in heading back to the coast just yet. And being in the area means we can keep an eye on you until those scum are off the streets.' Jack's stomach sank. This was a blow, and made him think of his job. He'd not called in sick; just not turned up. And it'd been New Year's Day lunch. They'd have been rammed. He'd got some serious explaining to do… Haslam reiterated that they were not to go anywhere alone, especially after dark. It was like being under house arrest all over again. 'We've got your number here now,' he said. 'Which reminds me, Jack, Verity Storm's people have been in touch with your estate administrator again. Fishing for information, and contact details for you. They know you exist now, must have been doing some digging, but they still don't know who you are – your connection to the family – or *where* you are. Just proves we did a good job with that!'

Before Jack could reply, Carol cut in. 'Hold on. Who's this? What are we talking about?'

'Oh. Sorry, I thought Daisy would have told you,' said Haslam.

'No. Daisy?' Carol turned to her daughter.

'Sorry, Mum. It happened after we left – the day after Boxing Day.'

'What? What happened?'

'This woman, Verity Storm or whatever, Carla's sister – the woman Jack thought was his mother…'

'Yes, yes, I remember who Carla is. Go on.'

'All right,' said Daisy. The policemen shifted awkwardly. Haslam was wishing he hadn't said anything. He'd got more pressing issues to deal with. 'Well, apparently she reckons she's got some sort of claim on Jack's old house, the land and that. That's right, isn't it, detective?' He nodded. 'Now that everyone's de– passed away. Sorry, Jack.' She touched his arm, then added, 'Except Jack, of course.'

'Really?' said Carol, her interest piqued. 'Well, there's a turn-up – and unlucky for you, Jack: that place could have been yours.'

'It still is!' said Daisy.

'Not if there's a will or deeds that say otherwise,' said Carol.

'That's what I reckon,' said Haslam. 'I've been looking into it a bit myself – nothing better to do over the Christmas period, enquiring mind and all that – and, like you say, Daisy, she's from the mother's side, right? Well, Jack's father was the last one alive, so the property would already presumably be his – unless something legal said otherwise. And then, in turn, it would have gone on to be one of his children's – the only one still living being Jack. But that's another issue. Jack never existed as a Hemsley, remember? Not on paper. He hasn't got a birth certificate.' Jack and Daisy looked at each other, alarmed. It was another blow, and so much to take in. 'You can see it's complicated,' Haslam continued, 'but not the end of the world. We'd have to prove he was the man's son or something – they're doing some amazing stuff with DNA testing these days, paternity testing. It's called RFLP – I won't bore you with the details – anyway, we're getting ahead of ourselves… Even if we couldn't prove Jack was next in line, or he actually wasn't – just saying. You never know.' He held his hand up in defence. 'Unless there's a will saying otherwise, the estate will go to Jack's father's extended family anyway. It's called intestacy. But, going back to my original point, without a will, she doesn't have a leg to stand on.' The detective let out a deep breath, then mopped his brow.

Jack and Daisy looked at each other again. There was so much riding on this. The money at stake could change Jack's life.

'Well I never,' said Carol.

'Yeah,' said Haslam, sighing. 'I'll put 'em off for as long as possible, but what you need is a solicitor, someone professional on your side to fight your corner. To look into it from a legal standpoint.'

'We've got a family solicitor he could use,' said Carol. Daisy was surprised, and pleased. She squeezed Jack's hand.

'Good,' said Haslam. 'Get them on board and fill them in. By the sounds of it, this woman reckons she's got a rightful claim to that property – unless you prove otherwise, Jack. The solicitors too, otherwise it wouldn't have got this far. They wouldn't have made contact. Looks like she's ready for a fight.'

'Yeah, and so are we,' said Daisy.

CHAPTER 4

Developments

Jack had to deal with work. Fortunately, he wasn't due back until the next day, Wednesday, but that didn't help with the fact he hadn't turned up on New Year's Day. It was so unlike him – or anyone in the kitchen brigade for that matter. They didn't just not turn up, or call in sick, 'put their mates in the shit' as it was called.

'You could say you got food poisoning,' Daisy suggested. 'Some dodgy buffet stuff on New Year's Eve at the Sailor.'

Jack's hopes were raised for a moment. That was a good idea. But then he thought it through more. 'But what about everyone else? Why would I be the only one who got food poisoning? Everyone at work knew we were going there, all of us. Pretty much everyone from work was there too.'

'Yeah, that's true. Aitch practically ate half the buffet on his own.'

Jack afforded himself a brief smile at the thought of Aitch – the first time he had thought about the gang since the Jeanie incident. He was such a character, and Jack missed him. He missed all of them.

'Well, what if you say you were hungover? I mean, really hungover and couldn't stop throwing up. That'll be believable after New Year's Eve, and I'm sure the gang'll back you up if you ask them.'

This was more believable, thought Jack. 'But what about the fact I didn't call in sick?'

'Because you *were* sick, ninny. You were too poorly to go to the phone. This is it. It's totally believable. Just really grovel to Chef, say how sorry you are…'

'But wouldn't I have got you to call in for me? I would have done.'

'Maybe I was dying too. Don't worry so much. What d'you think he's gonna do, sack you? You've been his golden boy by the sound of it; everyone was saying so the other night.' Daisy poked him in the ribs, but he grabbed her hand. He wasn't in the mood.

All this was depressing. Jack *had* been in Chef's good books lately; he'd been doing well and progressing quickly. He hated letting Chef down, or the thought of him thinking he was a wuss, someone who wouldn't turn up just because of a hangover. He'd soon lose faith in him. Chefs were a tough lot; Jack had learned that much already. They worked hard and played hard; it was part of the culture. Rolling into work in the morning with a hangover was standard: they couldn't start drinking until they got home late from work.

Besides, there was something Daisy seemed to be overlooking: Haslam wanted them to hang around till further notice. Could he even demand that? They hadn't committed a crime themselves. Or was it just a recommendation? If they had to come back again, surely it was their problem, not Haslam's. 'Shit, Daisy, we're forgetting about the van!' It had just occurred to him they couldn't go anywhere until it was fixed.

'Shit, I'd forgotten about that.' And it was her turn to feel a little glum. It was as if their lives were in limbo, put on hold – and all because of effing Peasgood. It couldn't go on indefinitely. 'Perhaps we have to come clean,' she said. 'Not properly – but maybe explain there's a police or family matter that needs dealing with, so it's out of our hands. It'll take the pressure off a bit… I dunno, maybe it *is* time to explain about our pasts a bit – shit! That reminds me, I haven't told you, have I?'

'Told me what?'

'Alison. She knows.'

'Knows what?'

'About us. Who we are. Well, me anyway. And you, I guess.'

'What? How? How the hell did she find out?' Jack was horrified.

'The staff personnel book at work. It happened that day she rang up here, New Year's Day, after… you know… That's where she got Mum's number from: my emergency contact from the staff book. She'd already remembered the name from the papers, then put two and two together, I guess.'

'What, she just came out and asked you – and you said yes?'

'No, I didn't say anything, I don't think. My head was in a right state at the time 'cause of – you know … so it's hard to remember exactly. But it had to happen sooner or later – it was national news for a while. I'm surprised it hasn't happened before, to be honest, like when we started working there. I know your name wasn't in the papers, but mine was. It was all over them. But maybe this is the way to go, Jack. The cat's out of the bag anyway. It'll buy us some time.'

'But what about Haslam? What about everyone knowing who we are? The whole reason for moving out there was to remain anonymous. What if the newspapers get hold of it?'

'This is true,' said Daisy. 'Well, we can always tell them to keep it quiet. At the restaurant, I mean. It's not like they're gonna sell the story to *The Sun*, is it? They're a good lot – especially the gang; they'll probably like the fact they have these friends who are secretly famous, the intrigue and that and keeping it a secret – except *her*, of course – I wouldn't put it past *her* to go blabbing…'

In the end, Daisy phoned the Crab's Claw for both of them; she was so much better at these things. But she only spoke to Hilary, thinking it was simpler that way. She was the manager after all. Jack was uneasy, knowing how much Chef would hate his authority being bypassed. Daisy explained to Hilary that a family matter back home had involved the police, and they had got to hang around for a while to give witness statements. Hilary didn't press her: it would have been disrespectful to pry at a sensitive time.

To stop Jack stressing about Chef, Daisy relayed his concerns. Hilary joked, 'Tell Jack not to worry, I'll deal with Chef. I'm sure he can re-jig the rota: it goes dead after New Year anyway. Jack would have probably been doing more cleaning than anything, so he's got out of that one. We'll treat it as paid holiday for you both if you like. Have the week off. Like I say, it's a quiet time.'

Daisy couldn't thank Hilary enough. It was a big relief, and they could relax a little now. It bought them some time – and getting paid was a bonus. They were probably safer here for the time being: who would keep an eye on them out there on the coast? Those guys could easily follow them again.

*****

There was a knock on the bedroom door. It woke Daisy up. Then her mum's voice. 'Can I come in for a second?' Daisy and Jack had been dozing, snuggled up on her bed.

Shit, Mum, Daisy thought. Her mum rarely came in her room, and had certainly never asked to when Jack was there. Before she could answer there was another knock. 'Daisy?'

'Yes, yes, just wait a minute. Jack, wake up!' She shook him. 'What?'

'Wake up. Mum wants to come in.'

This was enough to startle him into sitting up. 'What? Why?' Daisy sat up too, as Jack rubbed his eyes, pale-faced at the shock of being wrenched from sleep.

'Sshh, I don't know. You ready?' Jack nodded, pulling a face and yawning at the same time. 'Come in,' Daisy said.

The door opened. 'Sorry, I hope I didn't wake you,' Carol said, figuring she had by their somewhat dishevelled look.

'No, it's OK. We were watching a film and nodded off. All the stress, I guess. You OK? Carol looked as if she'd been crying. Again.

'Yes, I'm OK. I just spoke to Kerry, that's all, the solicitor.'

'Oh, right.' Daisy brightened; she hadn't expected her mum to get onto it so soon. 'Any good? What did she say?'

'Yes, no. Good news really… It just brought back memories, that's all. You know, Dad and that… We had a bit of a chat. She was asking how we all are.'

'Oh yes, course, they dealt with it all. She was nice.' Daisy didn't know if that was what her mum wanted to talk about, so she waited.

'Anyway,' said Carol, pulling herself together. 'The good news is – about this will thing – she's willing to look into it, to represent Jack if necessary.'

'Oh, wicked,' said Daisy, turning to Jack excitedly. He gave a worried smile. He was so far out of his depth with all this stuff, and it scared him. Solicitors seemed like the authorities to him. Legal stuff. Serious stuff. Trouble.

'Yes – providing there's a case, that is. She was keen to stress that. It all costs money, you see, contested wills and all that. Frightening, really. She said she'd do some initial digging free of charge – once Jack's spoken to her and given her some background info. Which was good of her, actually, some solicitors won't – you can't even speak to them without the meter running – but we've always used them as you know, for Dad's business as well. It's not what you know, but who you know, as they say. To be honest, it sounded like she was a bit intrigued by it all, something out of the ordinary to get stuck into. But if Jack *does* have a case, it's obviously going to cost money to prove it and see them off, so to speak.'

'Well, how much?' said Daisy. She looked worried.

'I've got my money off Haslam,' said Jack, finding his voice.

Bless him, thought Daisy. It was going to cost more than two hundred quid. Even she knew that.

'Who knows?' said Carol, shrugging. 'That's the dilemma. But the good news is, if it's contested in court and Jack wins, it won't cost him a penny – *they* have to pay for it. And Kerry stressed that if it's an open and shut case – if the property's legally hers, because it says so in a will or something – they won't go any further with it. There'd be no point. So it's not all doom and gloom. She was very honest and open about it; we can trust her. Oh, and she said not to talk to anyone in the meantime, Jack, their solicitors or anything: let her deal with it. The less they know from our side the better at the minute, keeps 'em in the dark and us one step ahead, she said.' Daisy noted how her mum had slipped into saying 'our' and 'we': she liked that.

'So, what now?' said Daisy.

'Jack's got to phone her tomorrow morning. She's in the office all day, she said, and hasn't got any meetings. They're still settling back in after New Year. But morning would be best, after nine o'clock. You're both around tomorrow, aren't you? Did you get hold of work?'

'Yes, all sorted. We've got some time off. And we're getting paid!'

'Oh good. Silver linings and all that. Let's just hope all this horrible business gets wrapped up quickly. I don't think it will, though. And what about the van? Was that the garage that phoned earlier?'

'Yep, getting sorted, too,' said Daisy. 'They're putting four new tyres on instead of three, though. The remaining one was shot and needed changing anyway. So that's more money, but they didn't cost as much as I was expecting, which is good. Said it should all be ready tomorrow afternoon.'

*****

The following morning, Jack spoke to Kerry, the solicitor. He was nervous as hell, but she seemed really nice, which helped to relax him. Like Haslam, she said she had already been doing a bit of research – studying the newspaper articles about the so-called 'fire-house murders', and, also looking into intestacy; that word the detective had used. She was keen to hear the story from Jack's point of view and for him to fill in the blanks. Of which there were many. And they were huge. Especially how he fitted into it all. There was little or nothing out there on his identity or background. As Haslam had said, they had done a good job keeping it under wraps.

'I know some of this is going to be hard, Jack,' Kerry said. 'I apologise in advance for that, but I need to know everything pertinent to the case. Your connection to the property, the people who lived there, your relationship to those people, especially Jacob Hemsley.' Jack shuddered at the name. 'The more information you can give me the better, and it's imperative you tell the truth as well as you can remember it. So, are you ready?'

Jack gulped. It was one of the hardest things he had ever done, revealing some of his story to a complete stranger – or to anyone for that matter. From birth it had been instilled in him not to – and he was still only coming to terms with some of it himself. It made him sift through memories, past events, feelings – junk, bad, black junk – that he had boxed up and ferreted away, relegated to the attic of his mind to gather dust. But his overriding emotion was shame. It always had been. Shame at where he'd come from.

As for Kerry, she was tactful and professional, but privately shocked. And she jotted all Jack's answers down. The whole thing took longer than everyone was expecting. When it was done, Jack felt drained, but the solicitor said he had done amazingly well. 'The sticking point, I'm afraid, is that you haven't got a birth certificate. This is going to be a problem.

But it's not the end of the world. There are ways round it…' This didn't sound good to Jack. But there was something reassuring about Kerry, to know that you had a professional on your side. After asking what station Haslam was based at, so she could get hold of him, she said she had everything she needed for now and would be in touch.

Daisy gave Jack a big hug. 'Well done, baby.'

After lunch the garage rang: the van was ready to collect. They went together to pick it up, and Daisy handed over a painful amount of cash to the garage owner. 'We've stuck a good squirt of petrol in it for you, on the house,' he said. 'You were lucky not to have dragged up debris from the bottom of the fuel tank, to be honest. So try not to run out again: you might not be so lucky next time.' The mild ticking off made Daisy feel like a foolish little girl, but it was good to have the van back. Its four smart new tyres were almost comically out of keeping with the rest of the vehicle. They reminded her of liquorice wheels. The van's other striking new addition was a shouty orange 'POLICE AWARE' sticker on the windscreen. Daisy removed this when they got back, again a bit embarrassed. But not enough that she wasn't going to keep it and paste it in her diary to document the incident.

Talking of the police, a very excitable Haslam phoned up during the afternoon with some significant news. It turned out the car's registration plate was genuine, and had been successfully traced back to a Malcolm 'X' O'Donnell, brother of Danny 'Danno' O'Donnell, Peasgood's known associates from the Glasgow area, and dangerous characters by all accounts. Carol shuddered at the sound of them. Furthermore, some near-immaculate fresh tyre tread impressions and footprints had been found at the property. Both could help to incriminate at least one of the men if they could get a successful match. 'The net's closing in,' Haslam said. 'Which, in turn, means it's closing in on Peasgood, the puppet master in all this. The evidence connected to him is growing by the day. He's up to his neck and drowning in it. As we speak, the boys up north should be paying a surprise visit to the two brothers, complete with a search warrant. This is serious stuff, mind – they'll go in armed – but if all goes well, a jam sandwich with two handcuffed and arrested O'Donnells in it as extra filling will be heading back down the motorway to the East Midlands, so the men can be interrogated.' It was frightening but exhilarating stuff.

CHAPTER 5

A Rogues' Gallery

The rest of the week was a whirlwind. Kerry got back in touch with some significant news. It turned out that the title deeds to the property did indeed belong solely to Jacob Hemsley at the time of his death. More importantly, although he didn't leave a will himself, his wife, Carla, had done. This had now come into play, bringing Verity Storm into the mix. 'Don't worry,' Kerry said. 'We've just got to prove who you are, that's all. Looks as though you'll have to do a DNA test – you might have had to anyway to claim the property. I'm not sure of the exact ins and outs of the procedure, but it all sounds pretty routine. Just a quick blood sample, I think…' Blood sample, thought Jack. It sounded terrifying; he'd still never even been to a doctor's. The solicitor signed off by saying he would receive a letter confirming everything, along with a copy of the will, for his perusal and records.

This was all a great shock. A bombshell. 'Well, it doesn't change a thing,' Daisy said, trying her best to sound calm. 'We just need to prove who you are, that's all. Like Kerry said.'

And then Haslam called again with another update. The brothers had been successfully arrested without serious incident and were being interrogated. It was all going well. They would probably be charged by the end of the day. He then came up with an unexpected and somewhat daunting request. 'I want you both to come in at ten a.m. tomorrow morning to act as witnesses. And separately – not together – pick out the men, or man, you saw at the kidnapping and up on the hill in an identity parade. I appreciate it was dark on both these occasions, but you're to do your best. It's really important. Oh, and it's at Meadows police station in town, not Bridgford.'

'But won't they see us?' Jack said, panicking. 'What if they come after us?'

'Don't worry, they can't see you – it's one-way glass. And, trust me, these guys aren't going anywhere, except to jail for a bit. This is just the final nail in the coffin.'

Despite Haslam's reassurances, they were all extremely concerned. Of course the men were going to know who was picking them out and making the accusations. Who else was it going to be? 'Let's hope to God he's right,' said Carol, speaking for all of them.

In another twist, Alison from the Crab's Claw phoned out of the blue for a catch-up. She and Daisy hadn't spoken since New Year's Day, and as Daisy and Jack weren't back at work yet, she and the rest of the gang were getting a bit worried. Someone had overheard Chef and Hilary talking, so a few rumours were circulating. She said everyone missed them, which was sweet. 'We're all here, in fact,' she said, and there were shouts and hollers in the background.

Daisy smiled. 'Wait a minute. Let me call Jack.'

Jack came down and sat on the stairs. He looked slightly comical and was feeling foolish, wearing some of Daisy's dad's clothes as his were in the wash. Some hellos and we miss yous were exchanged, which cheered Jack up. It was a welcome bit of light relief. Daisy heard Aitch call them 'Bonnie and Clyde' and Alison hissed at him to shut up. So they all knew… It felt strange.

'Sorry, Daisy. Don't worry, we haven't told anyone else,' Alison said. 'I've sworn them all to secrecy.' Yeah, wonder how long that's gonna last, Daisy thought. Especially with Jeanie. Talking of whom, Daisy heard her voice for the first time in the background. It made her feel a bit sick, her stomach churn. 'Is this all connected to that other stuff? Why you're not at work,' Alison said.

'In a way,' Daisy said. She gave a brief version of events, explaining how they had been followed and terrorised by two thugs, and that it related to Jack's previous employer. And that now they had to pick them out in an identity parade.

Alison couldn't believe it. 'God, Daisy, it all sounds terrifying. It's like something from *The Bill*.' When Daisy said the two men in question were Scottish, Alison cut in. 'Hold on, wait a minute. Did you say Scottish?'

'Yes, why?'

'Hold on a minute.' The sound became muffled as Alison put her hand over the receiver. Daisy held the phone away from her ear for a moment and shrugged at Jack.

'What's going on?' he said.

'Don't know. She's talking to the rest of them, I think. She went funny when she heard that the men were Scottish.' Jack moved in closer, so he could listen properly.

Alison came back on. 'Sorry, Daisy, hold on.' Then the sound went muffled again. 'Let me put Aitch on. He wants to explain it to you. It could be important.'

'Hey, babes.' It was Aitch. 'How you doing?'

'Get on with it. This is my mum's phone bill. She'll kill me,' Alison said in the background.

'All right, don't get your tie-dyed knickers in a twist.'

'I'm fine, thanks,' Daisy laughed, despite the situation. Jack did too. 'Hold on. Aitch, let me put Jack on – speak to him.' She thought it was the right thing to do, Aitch was Jack's friend after all – and she didn't want him to feel left out.

Jack, a little reluctantly, took the receiver from Daisy. He felt a bit shy, and still wasn't used to talking on a phone. 'Hello.'

'Jackeroo! How you doing buddy? We miss you in the kitchen. Word of warning, though. Chef says he's gonna make your arse look like the Japanese flag when he gets hold of you.' And he burst out laughing. Jack had no idea what Aitch meant, but didn't like the sound of it.

'Aitch, get on with it! This is serious.' Alison again.

'All right. Bloody 'ell. Women!' he said. 'Anyway, down to business. These guys that were after you – sorry about that by the way, buddy, that's some serious shit … and the other stuff. Anyway, Alison said they were Jocks.'

'Jocks?' said Jack.

'Scottish,' said Daisy.

'Oh. Yeah, they are. Both of them.'

'Right, well, is one of them, how can I put this, kind of fat with a bald head? You know, shaved?' Jack's blood ran cold. Danno, the one who was driving that first time.

'Er, yes. Why?'

'Fuck,' said Aitch, sounding more serious all of a sudden. Seeing the worried look on Jack's face, Daisy leaned in to listen more closely. 'You're not gonna believe this. The morning you guys left, sorry, when me and Jeanie left and you were still in the flat and Daisy had already gone, New Year's Day morning?'

'Yeah…' How could he forget?

'Well, just as we were leaving, crossing the street from the flat, a guy collared us on the other side, sitting in his car. Jesus, it gives me the creeps thinking about it now… Anyway, he asked if – shit, I can't remember exactly, I was still battered – if we knew you and Daisy, or if we'd just come from the flat. Something like that. He spoke about Daisy more than you from what I can remember, asking where she was, but definitely mentioned both of you. Shit,' – he spoke away from the phone – 'What did he say, Jeanie?'

'You're not talking to her,' Daisy hissed, putting her hand over the receiver. 'Give me the phone.'

'Wait!' said Jack, wrestling the phone back and holding it out of her reach. 'He's just *talking* to her.' Daisy scowled and waited.

'Yeah, that's right,' Aitch answered Jeanie. Then he spoke to Jack again: 'He was asking if Daisy had gone to work yet. Saying it was a bit early. Acting like he knew you both really well. That was it. He said he was family, and was down for the New Year.'

'You're joking,' said Jack.

'No. And I remember his Scottish accent clearly. It was a good un, really thick. I thought he was taking the piss at first 'cause I was still wearing my kilt after New Year. And a Scottish accent in Cromer – especially in the off season, well, it sticks out like a sore thumb.'

'Ask him what car he was in,' said Daisy to Jack.

'Not sure exactly. It was black, though, I remember that, wasn't it, Jeanie? The car, it was black. Yeah. A Beemer or Merc or something…'

'Yeah, that's it,' said Daisy.

'So, how was it left?' said Jack. 'Did he just drive away or what?'

'No, he was still sitting there. I thought it was a bit odd at the time, looking back. Jeanie said Daisy might have headed to Daisy's parents, I think, that's how it ended. Shit! I hope that didn't get you guys in trouble. Ow!' Aitch let out a yelp – Jeanie had hit him. 'She didn't mean to, she was just trying to be helpful. Ow, that hurt!'

'Give me the phone,' said Daisy, grabbing it. This was getting silly. And she didn't want to talk to Jeanie. 'Aitch, it's Daisy again. Listen. Would you be able to pick this guy out, in a line-up or something if you saw him again?'

'Dunno. I reckon so. He was an ugly git, bit of a bruiser.'

'Good. It might be important. Keep in touch – actually, give us your number. I might need to get someone to call you.'

Daisy took his number and they all said their goodbyes. 'What are you thinking?' asked Jack.

'That we need to speak to Haslam. This could be really significant. More proof. If Aitch could pick him out – Jeanie too, come to think of it – it just adds more weight to the case. More witnesses. This is just another incident where they were stalking us, planning to kidnap us again or whatever. They were right outside our bloody house!' She was right, thought Jack.

Daisy rang Haslam right away. He was thrilled with this new information, confirming its significance. 'Logistically, it's not ideal,' he said. 'I can't really expect these kids to make the two-and-a-half-hour trip over here for a line-up… But there are other ways. Give me some contact details. There's more than one way to skin a cat.'

And that's how the gang got involved. It was crazy, really. That very same day, Aitch and Jeanie were both called into Cromer police station and separately shown faxed photographs of ten different men. They were asked to pick out the one they had spoken to. All the men looked pretty similar, two of them especially. But there was no mistaking him. They both picked out Danno.

Then it was Jack and Daisy's turn. They were both nervous when they arrived at the Meadows police station, Jack more so than Daisy. The station was nearer the centre of town: bigger, busier, more daunting. Adding to their unease was the sudden and very real thought that those two men were somewhere inside the building. Carol made the trip with them – she had never expected to visit so many police stations – and waited whilst they took it in turn.

Jack was up first. Killing two birds with one stone, the brothers were placed in the same line-up of ten men. All of them looked generally alike. Same builds, more or less, same haircuts – shaved heads or crewcuts. A proper rogues' gallery. When Jack was first confronted with the viewing window, he shrank back in fear and retreated. He felt exposed and on view, as if all the men were looking straight at him. Brewster was there too, which didn't help. 'It's OK,' Haslam said. 'They can't see you. Trust me, it's one-way glass: it just looks like a mirror on their side.' Jack couldn't get his head round this, and practically had to be dragged back to the window. When he clapped eyes on the two men, his heart and the black spot pulsed in unison. The men were staring straight ahead. Menacing but aloof. There was no mistaking them. Even the fatter one, Danno: Jack had seen just enough of his face in the moonlight when he turned round in the car. The speed and certainty with which Jack picked them out pleased Haslam no end. He looked at Brewster, and the two policemen nodded and smiled.

Daisy's experience was pretty similar to Jack's, except she only had to pick out one man, the man on the hill. Malcolm. She hadn't seen Danno. Unlike Jack, Daisy was familiar with the concept of one-way glass – she'd seen enough police shows and films growing up. It didn't make it any less unnerving, though: the feeling of being stared straight at by a man you had been terrorised by and were dobbing in. But, like Jack, she picked out the accused straightaway. No hesitation. No messing. From start to finish it took no longer than half an hour.

CHAPTER 6

Back Home

With their duty done, Daisy and Jack were free to return to Norfolk. They were keen to get back the same day before dark. Haslam said he would keep them updated, and seemed positive and upbeat. He was confident the two thugs were going to be off the streets for a bit, and that if they gave him what he needed, Peasgood's days were numbered: he was going to be behind bars for a long time. Haslam told them not to worry about the men in the interim: if all went according to plan, they would be in custody until sentencing.

Carol was sad to see the teenagers go. Her stance towards Jack had softened. Spending more time with him and Daisy, experiencing their worry and fright, she realised that bad luck had befallen him the minute he was born. He didn't look for trouble; trouble found him. And, unfortunately, so had her daughter. After waving them off, she locked the porch door behind her. It would be a while before she felt safe in her own home again.

The familiar journey was uneventful, just a bit of a drag as usual. The flat landscape. The strange, almost creepy place names: Guyhirn, March, Crowland, Eye. The isolated barns, marooned in seemingly infinite fields, reminding Daisy of the book cover of *Nathaniel*, an American horror novel she'd read as a child. The unfortunately named River Great Ouse, which looked as dirty and unappealing as it sounded… Jack and Daisy were both fairly quiet, lost in their own thoughts. As with Carol, there was a shared, unspoken feeling of not being able to relax, not until all these men, Peasgood included, were, as Haslam had said, 'off the streets' and 'behind bars'. Nothing felt over. Far from it. They found themselves nervously looking in the van's rear-view mirror from time to time, fearful of a black car tailing them. The fact that one of those men had been waiting outside their flat that morning was on their minds as they turned into their street. He must have missed them by a matter of minutes. They quickly headed inside.

*****

It was Saturday morning, the day after they had got back to Cromer. The flat was arctic as usual, such a shock after Daisy's mum's house, especially Daisy's warm bedroom. The cupboards were bare and the fridge was empty. Jack and Daisy decided to go into town for food shopping and to buy a heater: they'd got the whole weekend to themselves, along with the early part of the next week, and Daisy was determined they weren't going to spend it freezing their bloody arses off. Jack was glad they had this unexpected time off; he wasn't ready to go back into the kitchen and face Chef just yet. Aitch's comment about Jack's arse and the Japanese flag had put the frighteners on him. Whatever it meant. He'd heard stories of chefs being carried out the back and dumped into the stinking skips before.

Daisy was a little distracted too. She'd had a strange dream that had left her feeling shaken and disturbed. It had been about Jack – and Jeanie. In the dream, they had got it on with each other that night. Daisy had been woken by the sound of them. Drawn from her bed and down the corridor to the lounge. The nearer she got, the more she could hear. Especially her. A high-pitched, regular moan and her urgent cries, 'Fuck me, fuck me.' Heart racing, stomach spinning, Daisy had pushed open the lounge door and seen them. The light was still on. She was riding him, bucking backwards and forwards rhythmically, as if on one of those playground rocking horse seesaws at school. 'Fuck me, fuck me.' Jack was reaching up, his hands on her tits. It had been sickening. But possibly more disturbing than this, it had turned Daisy on. She'd woken up tingling, as if she was experiencing it, as if she was being fucked, and she wanted to touch herself. This confused the hell out of her. It was similar to how she had felt with Jack looking at those women in that dirty magazine. But more so. She didn't understand it. How could her greatest fear turn her on?

It took a while for Daisy to shake the dream. She was grumpy with Jack first thing, hurt, as if he really had done it. She hated him for it. Perhaps it was simmering resentment that anything had happened at all, that he'd been so stupid. Perhaps it was being back at the flat again, the scene of the crime. Or maybe it was hearing Jeanie's voice yesterday that had triggered something. Stop thinking about it, she told herself. 'I want to go to the library,' she said.

'The library? What for?' asked Jack.

'I want to find a book on paternity testing, this DNA stuff and that. See what's involved. I want us to be prepared if it happens.'

'Us? Me, you mean,' Jack said glumly. Having no real idea about what it entailed, his imagination had been running away with him. Men in white coats in a laboratory, with him being prodded and experimented on. Naked even. Like in a bad dream. Giant mazes and hamster wheels, needles and bags of blood. His blood.

'Yes, well, you know what I mean. I want us to be ready. This Storm woman's got a storm coming to *her*.'

This raised a smile. Jack knew what Daisy was like when

she got the bit between her teeth; how she loved fighting for justice and being the underdog. He felt lucky to have her. 'Well, it might not get that far,' he said. 'Not if she's got a will or something.'

'We'll see,' said Daisy.

Warily opening the front door of the flat, a grimy day in the bowels of a seaside winter greeted them. An icy squall growled and pressed at them, briny-tasting, seaweed-smelling and mist-damp; taking their breath away, blasting their hair back. Daisy felt like retreating back indoors, shutting the door on the morning, letting it rage and sulk and wear itself out. But they had things to do… That's the thing with New Year: nothing actually changes. All the earnest resolutions are made in vain. The vices and procrastination remain. Like Daisy's intentions to finally address her college situation – where she was going in life. Even her mum had stopped badgering her about it, what with all the stuff that had been going on. But there's no magic wand with New Year. No new world order. January's just another month.

With the wind still buffeting them and shaking its fists, they made their way to the shop that sold heaters. Thankfully, it was open. After a chat with the owner, Daisy stuck with her original idea of getting a small portable fan heater. The owner suggested an oil heater for cheaper running costs, but they were a lot bigger, bulkier and a damn sight more expensive to buy. 'We just won't leave it on for long,' said Daisy, leaving the shop with their purchase. 'And it might be best if we stick to the bedroom more for the time being. The lounge is the coldest room in the house – and hardest to heat: it's those bloody windows.'

As they approached the library, the gunmetal-grey sky cracked open, releasing an onslaught of pebble-sized hail. Using their heater as a shield from the ricocheting ice-bullets, Jack and Daisy ducked inside the building. A wincing librarian accepted Daisy's request to join, as they fought to be heard over the insanely loud hammering on the skylights. Daisy tried to talk Jack into joining too, but he wasn't bothered. The hail disappeared as quickly as it had come and the library fell quiet again. Daisy spent the next ten minutes or so browsing until she found what she was looking for; a newish volume containing the history of genetic testing, including up-to-date methods. Pleased with herself, she took the book to the front desk. She hadn't borrowed a book from a library since school, even though she had loved visiting as a kid: the smell of the place, the furniture polish and all the books. Even the silence, broken by the too-loud squeak and clop of echoing footsteps.

The librarian's stamp made a satisfying thump as she marked the front of the book. Daisy was only the second person to have borrowed it. 'Interesting choice,' the librarian remarked.

'Yeah, I'm studying to be a police detective,' Daisy said. Jack looked at her.

'Ah, good for you,' the lady said, handing the book over with a jangle of bracelets and a warm smile. 'A female detective.'

*****

The following few days were a time of waiting. Of still feeling on edge. Hoping the phone would ring, or the letterbox would pop with a letter. The only time they had a phone call it was Carol, asking if there had been any news. They watched films. Got stoned. Ate. Drank. Made love. Despite missing the gang, they didn't make contact with them, and were careful not to walk past the restaurant. No one knew they were back. The thought of it was too exhausting. And as for Daisy, she wanted to put off seeing Jeanie again for as long as possible. Jack just hoped his paltry stash of gear would last until Wednesday when he was back at work.

Come Tuesday, the solicitor's letter arrived, as promised. Jack and Daisy opened it together, feeling nervous. There were two sheets enclosed. One, a formal typed letter on the solicitors' fancy headed paper. The other, a photocopy of a somewhat crumpled-looking will.

It turned out that Verity Storm, Carla's estranged and only sibling, had in her possession several tear-stained letters from her sister dating from 1966 – around the time Carla knew her cancer was serious – begging for reconciliation. None of which Verity had replied to. But more importantly, in a letter she wrote in 1967 – a desperate last olive branch – Carla had informed her sister that she had amended her will. In the event of Carla's husband passing away without remarrying or siring more children and, heaven forbid, the two girls passing away childless, Verity would inherit the property on the hill. A copy of the amended will was enclosed.

At the time, Verity had dismissed this for what it pretty much was: a hollow 'grand gesture'. And also a strange thing to do. It smacked of desperation. Carla had reiterated how desperate she was to see her sister before she died. She couldn't come to her, so please, please would she visit. Jacob didn't have to be there. She would make sure of it.

There was no possible way in which the will would come into effect – therefore rendering it worthless. Unable to help herself, and breaking her silence, Verity had said as much in a curt letter: it was the medication and guilt talking, Carla's attempt to even up the score, to clear her conscience, as she had benefited financially far more than Verity from their parents' demise – and, furthermore, she hadn't the slightest interest in the infernal property.

Verity secretly hoped this reply had gone up in smoke. Not that it mattered, because she still had in her possession a copy of that twenty-two-year-old will. She'd come so close to sending it back at the time – enclosing it in her reply – but at the last minute something had stopped her.

After reading the solicitor's letter and examining the will

again, Jack and Daisy looked at each other. It had been strange seeing it all laid out and confirmed. Really brought it home. 'So, are you willing to do this test then?' Daisy said. She had that look on her face, a look that Jack was becoming familiar with. Her fighting face.

Jack gulped. Then, after a moment's hesitation, he nodded.

Chapter 7

Caramel Run-Outs

Rather than writing back to the solicitor, wasting time, Daisy got Jack to ring her, giving the go-ahead for a DNA test. 'Whatever it takes,' Daisy had told him to add.

'Great,' the solicitor said. 'Just to warn you, though, this won't happen overnight. You'll get a letter in the post with a date. And also it costs, unfortunately…'

'Hold on, let me put Daisy on,' said Jack. It was all getting too much for him.

'That's fine,' Daisy said, after a short conversation. 'We've got savings, and Mum will help out if necessary.' She sounded confident. The way she saw it, it would all come back to them – fingers crossed, anyway. And she was so protective of Jack that this had become personal.

Jack was a bag of nerves walking to work on Wednesday; he was on his own, as Daisy wasn't due in until later. The first person he saw was Whizz, smoking at the table out the back. ''Ere 'e is,' he cried. 'Old part-time Pete. Hope you've got over that hangover. Must have been a blinder to last a whole week.' Jack was hoping this had been forgotten about. He'd also forgotten how strong Whizz's Norfolk accent was; it really stood out after being around people from the East Midlands.

'Hi, Whizz.'

'Hope you're ready for action. We've got the owners in at lunch. Big table. Their daughter's twenty-first. Set menu.'

Jack's heart sank; it was all he needed after being off. The stress, the pressure. He was out of practice and had been hoping for a quiet lunch to ease himself back in. Just his luck. 'What, is Chef in?'

'Yep.' Jack's heart plummeted further. 'So, just a heads up, I'd try and stay out of his way a bit this morning if I were you – but keep on yer toes; he's in a mood, stressed 'cause of this table…' Jack felt like crying.

He got changed in the familiar stale-fried stench of the changing rooms. He hadn't missed that at all. Nor the smell of his chef's clothes. They'd been left at work this whole time, in and on top of his bag. Even the unused and clean jackets smelt tainted. He pulled out the freshest one and proceeded to get changed.

Taking a deep breath, Jack pulled back the fly screen to the kitchen. The heat, sounds and smells hit him straightaway – like a different world, a whole different environment. It was going to take some getting used to again. The other chefs seemed pleased enough to see him and asked how he was doing, which was nice. But they seemed a little subdued and serious. On edge. Jack could sense the tension in the air; it didn't seem a normal day. And there was Chef. At the stoves, which was rare.

Chef ignored Jack as he nervously approached. That bypassing of his authority had clearly stung him. Jack cast a quick glance over to the potwash area, praying that Aitch was in, a familiar friendly face. He wasn't. It was some new kid Jack didn't recognise. Great. Could this day get any worse?

'Ah, nice of you to join us finally,' Chef said, still not looking up as Jack stopped in front of him. He was pouring alcohol into a pan to deglaze it, his fat thumb over the end of the bottle. Brightly coloured flames shot up as he shook the pan, then quickly died again. He was sweating as usual. 'Not too hungover today? Sure you don't need a sit down?' He finally looked at Jack, or rather glared.

'No. Sorry, Chef.' Some of the other chefs watched nervously to see how this was going to pan out.

'You're on veg prep today, I don't want you on service, fucking things up. I'm on Sauce, Whizz is plating up and helping Steve on Larder. Billy's on Fish and Rash is on Garnish – you might need to help if he gets in the shit.' So, Jack wasn't on his normal section then, cooking and dishing up the veg. He wasn't on any section at all – as if he'd been demoted, his worst fears come true. He hoped it was just for today, because of this table.

'Yes, Chef,' he said quietly.

'Sorry? I can't hear you.'

'Yes, Chef!'

'And then I want you to hang around and help Baz on desserts, have a look at the pastry section, see what's going on.' This surprised Jack and had its pros and cons. Pastry was one of the hardest sections to work in a big kitchen because of the long hours. It was also one of the most important, requiring specialist skills. Most pastry chefs were therefore a bit psychotic and self-important, and Baz was no exception. On the plus side, it suggested Chef still had faith in and plans for Jack.

'Yes, Chef.'

'Right, get a sack of spuds peeled. Then there's a load of spinach needs picking.' All the good jobs, thought Jack.

He hadn't peeled a sack of spuds – or 'fed the monkey' – for a while. Hadn't had to: the pot washers generally did it. Jack guessed it was Chef's way of punishing him. This didn't bother him, though: as Whizz had advised, it would keep him out of Chef's way and off his radar for a bit. He scurried to the veg store and carried a sack of potatoes back on his shoulder, enjoying the weight of it, the physical effort required. He had missed that.

As Jack worked, he kept an eye on the clock, waiting for eleven o'clock when Daisy was due in. At five minutes to, she appeared. It was good to see her. She looked amazing in her uniform, so pretty. He couldn't help but smile as she searched the kitchen for him, a confused look on her face. She spotted him and waved, then shrugged as if to ask, 'What's going on?' Then looked a little sad and angry when she figured it out. It was frustrating they couldn't talk. Tom came in too, a few minutes after Daisy. She had clearly told him what had happened, as he looked over at Jack straightaway, smiled sympathetically and waved. It was really good to see him too. Jack felt better just having them there.

Service started, and the tension built as the serving of the big table approached. Even the front of house staff seemed on edge. 'Five minutes, Chef. Just waiting for two more!' said a breathless Dan, Hilary's second in command.

'What, to arrive or sit down?'

'Sit down.'

'Fuck's sake,' said Chef. 'Get them fucking sat.'

'Trying our best, Chef.'

Hilary appeared, taking more of an active role than usual, overseeing things as the food was finally taken out. 'Everyone at the pass, all hands on deck. Birthday girl first, then the ladies,' she said. Daisy lined up with Tom and the rest of the waiting staff, Alison was there too. Jack felt a bit out of it, watching from the veg prep station. Chef continued to bark orders and instil fear. Whizz was the only one who seemed immune to it all. Despite being a bit of a nutter, he was good under pressure – and this helped keep the other chefs calm. Chef was the complete opposite as he shouted and sweated.

All went smoothly, though – fucking things up wasn't an option that day – and only once was Jack called into action to help on the garnish section. But he was pleased to do it, to get back into the swing of things and work his way back into Chef's good books.

Once the mains had gone, Jack was told to go into the pastry section, which was separate from the main kitchen. He'd never worked with Baz before, and had always been a bit wary of him. He was quite a scary character. Despite only being in his mid-twenties, he had bad teeth and his head was as bald and smooth as an egg, not a single hair on it. Shiny too. And now wasn't the best time to be thrown into the pastry section with him. The pressure was on Baz to get everything ready and timed perfectly to go out. 'What the fuck are you doing in here?' he said, looking up from what he was doing and scowling.

'Chef told me to come in, to help I think.'

'Fuck's sake,' he cursed. 'That's all I need. Well, don't get in my way, there's not much space in here.'

Great, thought Jack. What was he supposed to do? Where was he supposed to stand? Baz was right, there wasn't much room. Jack loitered awkwardly, watching. Baz was busy piping a vivid scarlet sauce out of a plastic squeezy bottle onto dozens of plates, lined up on his pass. He did it carefully but with amazing speed, his tongue protruding and licking his discoloured teeth in concentration as he repeated each pattern to perfection. Five red dots of ever-decreasing sizes in an arc. Jack noticed he had an impressive number of striped burns on his arms and some on his hands.

When he had done the last plate, he became aware of Jack again. 'Well, don't just stand there, Numbnuts. Make yourself useful. Here, pick some of this mint. Twenty-four bits, and stick 'em in some cold water.' He shoved a cellophane pack of fresh mint at Jack. A vibrant, clean green smell wafted up to Jack's nose as he clutched it. It was lovely.

'What do you mean, pick it?' he said.

'Fuck's sake, the spears. Pick the spears. Look.' He grabbed the pack and threw it on a counter. He pulled out a sprig of the fragrant mint, then proceeded to quickly pinch off the end and side shoots of attractively bunched smaller leaves. 'Spears, that's a spear,' he said, holding one up for inspection between a yellow, nicotine-stained thumb and forefinger. 'We garnish the desserts with it.'

'Got it,' said Jack. He quickly set about his task. 'Finished,' he said before long.

'Well, stick them in some cold water then, grab a tub or something.' Dan passed by. 'How long?' Baz called to him.

'At least ten till clearing yet. Most are still eating.'

'Done,' said Jack.

'Right, here's your big moment, Numbnuts. Come here and watch. I'll only show you this twice.' He pulled a wooden skewer, a thin pointy stick, out of a gaggle of them that were stuck in a half-pint glass on his counter like pencils. Jack went and stood next to him. 'Pull this through the second biggest dot – not the biggest one – and through the others like this.' He drew the pointed end of the stick through the dots, and as he did so they made pleasing perfect heart-shapes, four of them in an arc getting smaller, joined together by thin tails. Jack was impressed. It looked cool. 'Here, I'll show you again.' He repeated the operation, wiped the end of the stick with his thumb and finger, then passed it to Jack. 'Keep the end of it clean, and if you fuck it up I'll stick it up yer arse. Got it?' Jack nodded. 'Good. Right, let's see you.'

Jack was terrified as he moved into position, hunched over with his skewer poised. He didn't want to mess it up: Baz had made it look so easy. Jack could feel his hand shaking. He took the plunge and did it, slowly and carefully. Amazingly, it worked. He was thrilled. 'Again,' said Baz. 'A bit quicker this time. The slower you do it, the way your hands are shaking it makes it worse.' Jack did as he was told. This one was noticeably better.

'Again,' said Baz, removing the first plate and replacing it. Jack did another. 'Good. Right, carry on till they're all done.' Jack had never concentrated so much in his life.

Next, he was instructed to place a small, delicate basket – a sweet tuille basket, perfectly formed – gently onto the largest pool of sauce, or 'coulis' as Baz called it. The tuille baskets were neatly stacked in a tub, lined with kitchen paper. 'Do not, *whatever* you do, bash these about or knock the fucking tub off the side. They're delicate as fuck and will smash to pieces. I swear to God, I'll kill you if you do. I've only got a few spares.'

No pressure then, thought Jack, gulping. He began doing as he was told, carefully nestling the baskets into the larger pools of untampered sauce, making them spread slightly.

'How we doing, girls?' a voice said. It was Whizz.

Jack looked up, but only briefly. 'OK, thanks,' he said, then went back to concentrating.

'Jesus, what the fuck is this today, Piccadilly Circus? Why don't you invite the whole kitchen in 'ere?'

Whizz laughed. 'Just keeping you on yer toes, Bazza-Boy, making your day a little more interesting. Nice work, Jack. Looking good.' Whizz was watching, making Jack more nervous.

'Yeah, well, I don't need it today, I tell yer. How long? Any word?' said Baz.

'Nah, they haven't started clearing yet. How's he doing?' Whizz nodded at Jack.

'Who, Numbnuts? I haven't had to kill him yet, put it that way. But there's time…'

Whizz laughed again. 'If you need a hand, though, seriously, just give us a shout.'

'What, to put twenty-four slabs of chocolate tart and a ball of ice cream on a plate? I think I can handle that.'

The chocolate tart portions looked amazing. Perfect triangles all exactly the same size; dark, indulgent and rich, with an impossibly thin sand-coloured pastry casing. Baz positioned them on the plates so that the arc of red hearts curled round them. Clearly, he didn't trust anyone else with this job, so Jack had to stand and watch. 'Whilst you're waiting, fish that picked mint out again and let it dry on some kitchen paper. Give it a shake,' Baz said. Jack did as he was told. He noticed for the first time a sort of rubber mat on a marbled counter. On it were some elongated oval shapes, held together in spirals, made out of hard glassy toffee or something. They looked amazing, but again very fragile.

'Right, raspberries,' said Baz. He gave Jack a small punnet and kept one for himself, popping a raspberry into his mouth and squishing it. 'Four on each plate,' he said. 'On top of each tart. Watch.' He placed three raspberries in a triangle as a base, then one on top to form a pyramid.

'Got it,' said Jack.

'Clearing,' said Dan, popping his head round the corner.

'Fuck!' said Baz. 'Right, hurry up, but do it neatly. Don't fuck it up.' Jack had no intention of doing so.

'Clearing,' Tom said, popping his head round the counter. He smiled at Jack, eager to see him.

'I know yer fucking clearing,' Baz shouted.

'Clearing,' Tom said again in a high-pitched voice, taking the mickey, then ducking out the way, knowing from past experience he could get something thrown at him.

'Swear to God, when I get hold of you, Queerboy,' Baz threatened. Tom disappeared, laughing. Jack tried his hardest to suppress his grin.

'Right, start doing the mint,' Baz said. 'I'll finish these, yer taking too long. A sprig on each on top of the raspberries.'

Jack did as he was told. 'Like this?' he said.

'Yep, spot on.' Once the mint and raspberries had been done, Baz placed an ice cream scoop under a hot tap. He left the tap running. Then he poked his head out of the pastry-parapet. 'Ice creams going on,' he shouted. 'Five minutes, yeah?'

'Chef!' someone replied. Baz slid back the glass of an ice cream counter next to the pass and pulled out a tub. The ice creams and sorbets looked amazing all lined up, a rainbow of different colours. Jack had seen similar set-ups at the ice cream parlours in town. The ice cream Baz had chosen was a creamy ivory colour.

'Vanilla?' Jack asked, trying to impress.

'Nope. White chocolate. Vanilla's the one with the black specks in it.' Damn, thought Jack. White chocolate ice cream sounded delicious, though. 'Right, they'd better be ready,' Baz said. As Jack watched, he ran the hot scoop across the surface of the ice cream to form a perfect, glistening, creamy ball. Then he placed it gently but quickly into a waiting basket. He repeated this process over and over, intermittently dipping the scoop into the hot water. It was mesmerising. When the plates were nearly two-thirds done, some of the waiting staff began to hover. 'Ready when you are, chef,' Dan said.

'Yeah, yeah,' said Baz. Jack felt the pressure on him. Urgency. Nerves.

When the ice cream balls were all in situ, Baz began placing the toffee swirls onto the plates, propping them at an angle between the baskets and the tart, so that they stood to attention. 'Give us a hand,' he said to Jack. 'But be careful, don't fucking drop any.' Nervously, Jack helped until they were all done. Then Hilary arrived.

'We ready? Which one's the birthday girl's? I've got a candle,' she said.

'Nearly, just got to dust. Take your pick,' said Baz.

'Here, you do it,' Hilary said, passing Baz the candle. 'I don't want to mess it up.'

A candle was placed in one of the desserts and lit, then, before they were sent, each plate was dusted with a gentle cascade of icing sugar, dispensed via a battered metal tin. 'Service!' Baz shouted out of habit, even though the staff were already standing there in front of him. Then he stood back, mopping his brow. 'Phew,' he said. His face, like his bald head, was shiny, but glowing. Clearly, he had loved the buzz of it. Daisy appeared, joining the rest of the staff, to take the desserts out. She smiled proudly at Jack. Tom had told her he was in the pastry section.

'These look amazing,' she said, taking two plates.

Jack had been blown away by it all, by what was involved. He'd never before appreciated the effort that went into presenting one of the desserts. He loved how it had been built up in stages, bit by bit.

''Ere, get yer gnashers round this,' Baz said, dumping a left-over portion of tart into a bowl and plonking a generous ball of ice cream on it, followed by a scattering of raspberries. 'You got a spoon?'

'Of course,' said Jack, fishing it from his back pocket.

Baz reached for a broken left-over toffee swirl, crumbling it on top of the tart for good measure. 'What are those things?' Jack asked.

'Caramel run-outs. Just water and sugar, cooked till it caramelises. But you have to stop the cooking process by putting the base of the pan in cold water. Then you have to shape them before the mixture sets up too much. They're tricky, but worth it.' They tucked into the pudding. It was like no dessert Jack had ever tasted. The combination was mind-blowing. 'You did okay, Numbnuts,' Baz said.

*****

And that's how it went on. Jack was given all the crappy prep jobs to do, then sent into the pastry section towards the back-end of service. This meant he had to stay at work longer for the same amount of money, sometimes way past three o'clock.

As he had to be back in for five-thirty, it made for a long day. It was the same with the evening service. Even Baz started taking advantage of the situation. He didn't trust Jack with preparing desserts for customers, but he was more than happy to clear off and leave him to clean down. He thought the new arrangement was great.

But if Chef thought all this was going to break Jack or make him give up, he was sorely mistaken. Work was all Jack had ever known – especially as a form of punishment. Prepping vegetables and cleaning a kitchen were a breeze compared with some of the tedious, back-breaking stuff he'd had to put up with growing up – and he was getting paid for it. Being in the pastry section, he was also learning new skills. He slowly built up a rapport with Baz, who stopped calling him Numbnuts. Baz was impressed – and Jack was useful.

Amongst other things, mainly pastry items, Jack had been taught how to measure out and prepare the sorbet and ice cream mixes. The ice cream mixes were like a home-made custard, cooked until they thickened, then cooled before being frozen. He found it fascinating that flavours could be introduced to a neutral base – vanilla, chocolate, pistachio, raspberry ripple… It was the same with the sorbets, but these were made from a basic sugar syrup base – just boiled sugar and water – that was then mixed with fruit purees, such as raspberry, blackcurrant, passion fruit or even melon. The citrus flavours – pink-grapefruit, lemon, lime – were infused with the zest and juice of the fruits. Some of the smells were intoxicating.

Jack couldn't stop talking to Daisy about it all when he got home. In direct contrast, Daisy's hours had been reduced since Christmas. It was hard having to wait up even longer for him, but she always did, sometimes barely able to keep her eyes open. But Daisy loved hearing about his day, especially the ice cream stuff. She found it fascinating too, and it only served to fuel her desire that they should make and sell their own ice cream at music festivals. They talked about this long into the night, coming back to it and getting carried away by it over and over again.

*****

Haslam rang with some truly amazing news. Things had moved quickly and significantly. The two men had confessed to pretty much everything; enough to put them behind bars anyway. The charge list had been almost endless… Kidnap. Affray. ABH. Criminal damage. Possession of an offensive weapon. Haslam could have thrown the book at them, but then he wouldn't have got what he *really* wanted – Peasgood. When they were told some of the charges would be dropped in return for everything they knew about Peasgood, along with all their dealings with him, they didn't think twice. Couldn't believe their luck, in fact. So much for honour amongst thieves. They pleaded guilty and were sentenced to eighteen months.

With regard to Peasgood himself, the police had wasted no time in bringing him in. He was questioned and charged for orchestrating most of his associates' crimes, and then there were all the crimes from the original investigation: tax evasion, utilising illegal workers, perverting the course of justice. 'The arrogant bastard, 'scuse my French, is finally shaking in his boots and currently out on conditional bail for a not-inconsiderable sum,' Haslam said. 'There's gonna be no leniency where he's concerned – he's going to be made an example of.'

Jack and Daisy were delighted to have the two thugs off the streets and convicted. Even though Peasgood was – as Haslam had said – the orchestrator, he didn't pose an actual physical threat. They wanted him brought to justice, but more than anything, they wanted Jack's money back. The money he had rightfully earned. His savings. That was all Jack had *ever* wanted from all this.

Although equally thrilled and relieved that the two men had been sentenced, Carol didn't quite share the youngsters' point of view. Until Peasgood was put away, what was to stop him paying someone else to terrorise Jack and Daisy? And then there were those reduced sentences. Those men could be back on the streets in a year. A year! Maybe less. Men like that didn't forget. What if they wanted revenge? The thought of it chilled her. She seriously considered selling up and moving. She thought Jack and Daisy ought to move too – whilst those men were still in prison. Or how would they ever feel truly safe again?

The gang insisted on celebrating, of course. They organised a party – at Jack and Daisy's flat (they weren't really given a choice in it). They brought any left-over booze they had from the festive period (in some cases raiding their parent's drink cupboards) and partied until the early hours. Drinking, getting stoned and listening to music. It was like New Year's Eve all over again – without its shitty culmination. Daisy was adamant she was never going to drop her guard, to let something like that happen again, so she didn't drink anything near as much as the others. She was slowly coming round to forgiving Jeanie, who had not only delivered a tearful, heartfelt apology to Daisy, but had also been on her best behaviour since. It was almost as if the incident had needed to happen so she would back off. Jack was Daisy's, and that was that.

CHAPTER 8

Birdhouse in Your Soul

The day after the party was a Sunday, so fortunately Jack and Daisy had the day off. The rest of the gang weren't so lucky: most of them were at work, the poor sods. Despite being plastered, stoned or both, they'd all managed to drag themselves home in the wee small hours.

It was mid-morning. Jack and Daisy were still dozing in bed when the phone rang out from the lounge, startling them. Daisy stirred, but was too tired to go and answer it. And it was so cosy and warm in their room; that heater had been a godsend. The phone kept on ringing. 'Fuck's sake,' she groaned. 'Who the hell's that?' It had best not be one of them lot, she thought.

'Uh?' uttered Jack, still half-asleep.

'The phone,' said Daisy.

'Who is it?' said Jack.

'I don't bloody know. I haven't answered it, have I?'

Still drunk, Jack emitted a muffled guffaw into the mattress. Daisy hit him.

The phone rang off. 'Shit,' said Daisy. 'What if it was important? What if it was work – or Mum or something?'

'What day is it?' mumbled Jack.

'Sunday.'

'More likely to be your mum, then… Unless one of the guys has called in sick. Ugh,' he groaned and rolled over.

The phone rang again. They tutted, then Daisy made to get up. 'Leave it,' said Jack. 'Don't answer it.'

'I can't. It must be important for them to ring back.' She clambered out of bed, wrapping a blanket around her and wishing there was a phone socket in the bedroom. Jack was privately bemoaning the fact that Daisy had her winter pyjamas on, so he didn't get a flash of her bum. 'I'll put the kettle on,' she said as she left.

'If it's work, I'm not going in,' Jack called.

He listened for Daisy's voice, trying to make out the phone conversation. But it was too far away, too muffled – until Daisy said loudly, 'Dead? You're joking!' Jack quickly sat up, straining his ears. 'Oh my God. I can't believe it. When?… That's awful… Wait, I've got to tell Jack. Wait a minute, Mum.' Jack's heart began to pound. Thoughts clattered and bumped round his hungover-head, like trainers in a washing machine. Who was dead? Surely not her grandma or Lily – Daisy would be distraught; she didn't sound distraught, just shocked. He heard Daisy padding quickly down the hall. 'Jack! Jack, you're not gonna believe this.' She appeared breathless in the bedroom. 'Peasgood's dead.'

'What?'

'I know! Killed himself.'

'Jesus. When?'

'Last night, apparently. It's made the news this morning – over that way anyway. He hung himself.'

Jack suddenly felt sick. It was so shocking, so violent. That man – even though he was a monster – was dead. Jack had known him. Worked for him. Sat in his office. And he'd hung himself – a horrible drawn-out death by all accounts. The colour drained from Jack's face.

'Sorry,' said Daisy, not even knowing why she was saying it. She went to hug Jack, and they embraced. 'It's awful, isn't it?'

Jack felt sick again, thinking about it. He kept picturing the scene, Peasgood hanging from the ceiling: bulging eyes, lolling tongue, purple face. He shut his eyes to make it go away. But the gruesome image was replaced by another horrible thought. What if it was their fault? Because they'd got him arrested and he was going to jail? Probably for years and years. What if it was the thought of that that made him do it? 'Come on,' Daisy said, pulling away and interrupting his thoughts. 'Mum's still on the phone. Come and put the telly on, see if it's on there.'

'OK,' Jack said distractedly. 'I'll be there in a minute.'

A few minutes later, a fully dressed Jack joined Daisy in the lounge. She was deep in conversation with her mum, but gestured to the TV. Jack put it on. As he flicked through the channels, searching for some news, he still couldn't quite fathom that Peasgood was dead. It didn't seem real.

There wasn't any news on. It was the wrong time of day. 'No, there's nothing...' said Daisy to her mum. 'It'll be one o'clock now.'

It was an anxious wait for the lunchtime news. Neither of them could eat; they didn't feel hungry. The sombre thoughts wouldn't leave Jack's head. He was quiet. Pensive. 'You OK?' said Daisy.

Reluctantly, Jack voiced his fears. 'What if it was our fault, Daisy? Peasgood?'

'What do you mean? Him killing himself?'

'Yeah.'

'How's it our fault? Don't be silly.'

'But he's dead. Probably because he was going to go to jail.'

'We didn't make him kill himself. And it was Haslam who wanted him behind bars, not us; and he was just doing his job, representing the law. That's what it's there for. To provide justice – and to protect people. People like us.' Daisy had also been feeling awful about the bombshell that had been dropped, but talking about it was helping. 'Think what he did, Jack, from start to finish. Think how he treated you, denying you ever worked there, getting your money taken off you. And then getting those men to terrorise us, to kidnap you. Threatening me. What if they'd got hold of us again? Me *or* you? It was only by chance they didn't. He was paying them to hurt us, seriously hurt us. That guy had weapons. A knife probably. *And* he slashed my tyres. We've been terrorised for months by them, and all because of Peasgood…'

'OK,' cut in Jack. He'd heard enough. Daisy was right, but it didn't help.

The news finally came on. The story had made the national headlines. It turned out Peasgood's factory had been temporarily closed whilst the investigation had been going on, affecting dozens and dozens of workers. On top of that, once the extent of his crimes and subsequent charges thereof had been revealed, his considerably younger second wife had walked out on him and filed for divorce. This was apparently what had finished him off.

'See,' said Daisy, taking Jack's hand. 'That should make you feel better. It does me. That's what pushed him over the edge: his wife leaving.'

It did make Jack feel a little better. But only slightly.

*****

Surprisingly, they didn't hear from Haslam until the next day. 'I take it you've heard the news then?' he said. 'Shocking really, but there you go…' He sounded serious again, matter of fact, and by no means disturbed by the outcome.

'Yeah,' said Jack.

He must have sounded sad, as Haslam said, 'I wouldn't dwell on it, son. These things happen. He clearly couldn't face a long stretch behind bars – some can't – that's where he should have been, though, so he's got away with it really. It's the workers I feel sorry for…' It turned out the factory was still closed and would remain so until new buyers took over.

If anyone took over at all. Again, as if reading Jack's mind, Haslam added, 'Don't worry, you'll still get your money back – I'll make sure of that. Minus the two hundred quid you owe me, of course…'

True to Haslam's word, a fat envelope arrived in the post a few days later. There was a knock on the door, and Jack had to sign for the delivery. Inside the bubble-wrapped package was a wad of notes. The very same notes that had been handed to him by Peasgood's gnarly hand. It was a creepy feeling and all Jack needed – the prospect of inviting another apparition into the flat, another ghost of a dead enemy visiting him to add to his father's – like Jacob Marley, dragging his chains. What with his dead sister's ashes lurking there as well, it was becoming like *Rent-A-Bloody-Ghost*. Jack didn't even want to touch the money to count it. He didn't have to. There was a handwritten note from Haslam: 'Here is the remainder of your confiscated money. £850. I have already taken back my cut. Don't spend it all at once.' It also said that apart from a few last possible queries, their connection with the Peasgood matter was pretty much wrapped up. Unless they wanted to take it any further, of course – compensation or anything… They didn't.

Daisy was thrilled Jack had got his money back at last, and she insisted he open a bank account with it to earn a bit of interest. This took some talking. 'I've only just got my hands on it again, and you want me to hand it over to a bank?' he said. 'What if the bank gets robbed and my money gets stolen?' He wanted to put it back in his tin, under the bed, where he could keep an eye on it. But eventually he gave in. And feeling slightly reassured after visiting the bank, Jack had to admit it was a nice feeling to have an account, to get his own little account book. It made him feel grown up.

'You ought to start putting some of your wages regularly in there, too,' Daisy said. 'To see it accumulate. It's harder to spend money once it's in a bank.'

*****

Slowly but surely – despite their nervous wait for the DNA test – the end of January saw things begin to settle down; unlike the weather. A violent storm battered the UK, tragically killing dozens of people, including schoolchildren: it was later labelled the 'Burns' Day Storm'. But for Jack and Daisy, routines and normal life, whatever that was, resumed. There was the sense of a huge weight lifted, what with their tormentors being behind bars and Peasgood – well – dead. For the first time in a while, Daisy went back to her old habits. She indulged in her weekly fix of *NME*, devouring the music news and checking out the new releases. Sinead O'Connor's 'Nothing Compares 2 U' single was the first big one of the year. She'd got a new album coming out soon. Daisy thought the song was OK, but it was quickly overplayed in her opinion and she went off it. But it did make her replay Sinead's debut album, which she had been crazy about a couple of summers earlier. Another current song Daisy couldn't get out of her head, as it was everywhere, was 'Birdhouse in Your Soul' by an unfamiliar American band called They Might Be Giants. She was forever humming and singing it – especially to Jack – imploring him to say she was the only bee in his bonnet.

The first big album release of 1990 for Daisy was The Sundays' *Reading, Writing and Arithmetic*. She had loved their debut single 'Can't Be Sure' – she had put it on Jack's last tape – and *NME* had given the album 10/10. She was dying to get her hands on it. There were a handful of indie singles she wanted as well, including the insanely infectious 'Bikini Girls with Machine Guns' by The Cramps. Daisy loved Poison Ivy and Lux from the band. They were so cool – and married to each other, which was sweet. Sort of a rock 'n' roll equivalent of Morticia and Gomez Addams.

The problem with all this new 'alternative' music was that Daisy had nowhere to buy it locally. Woolworths was OK for more mainstream Top 40 stuff, but that didn't really interest her. And the Town Hall was good for vintage second-hand bargains (if she was lucky), but she missed her beloved record shops at home. Like the Left-Legged Pineapple. She bemoaned her frustrations to Jack and the gang.

'There's a little independent record shop in Holt,' said Tom in response. 'That's where me and Ali get our tunes from.'

'Yeah,' said Alison. 'It's OK, but some stuff you still have to order. If you want a big selection, like HMV, you'll have to go to Norwich.'

'Oh my God! Why didn't you tell me?' said Daisy.

'Dunno. You never asked, I guess,' said Alison.

Daisy thought about this for a second. She probably hadn't. She hadn't bought a new record in ages, and hadn't even been keeping up with the current scene – there had been too much else going on. Well, not any more. She was going to make a list.

'So, where's Holt?' she asked.

It turned out that Holt was a little market town about twenty minutes west down the coast, but further inland. It had somehow passed Daisy by: she couldn't remember her family ever taking her there. They made the journey in the van on their next day off together, intending to make a bit of a day of it. The weather was a little kinder, and it was nice to see a different part of the local area.

The town was lovely, slightly bigger than Daisy was expecting, but not so big they couldn't find the record shop without too much trouble (Tom and Alison had given them instructions). The Vault of Holt, it was called. Quite cleverly, Daisy thought. They walked in, Daisy clutching her handwritten list:

Birdhouse in Your Soul 7in single – They Might be Giants
Bikini Girls with Machine Guns 7in single – The Cramps
Sleep With Me 7in single – Birdland
Ride EP – Ride
Reading, Writing and Arithmetic LP – The Sundays

It was a small shop, just one room of new and second-hand records. Jack followed Daisy around as usual, feeling a little lost. Daisy managed to find four out of her five items, which she was pleased with. Bearing in mind what Alison had said about being able to order stuff, she did just that with the missing Ride EP.

Afterwards, they visited one of the many pubs in Holt, the King's Head. It looked welcoming and there was a fire going. It was a weekday lunchtime in the off season, so they pretty much had the place to themselves, and they sat near the fire. They ordered some food and some pints. Daisy had a cheese cob, moaning it was the only vegetarian thing on offer. Jack tutted in his head, but refrained from saying anything. He hadn't thought she would keep this vegetarian thing up for so long. He was enjoying doing most of the cooking at home now, the practice and the experimenting, especially as he wasn't doing so much savoury cooking at work lately. But having to prepare two different meals, one for him and one for Daisy, was a pain.

Daisy went through her records. It felt nice, like old times. But she was feeling a little guilty that Jack hadn't bought anything – he didn't seem to want anything – and this reminded her of something. 'Jack?' she said, looking up. 'Isn't it your birthday soon?'

'Huh,' he said.

'Your birthday. Didn't you say it was in February?'

Jack looked sad suddenly, and sipped his cider. He'd never had his birthday celebrated, not properly; he didn't even know the exact date. And that, in turn, reminded him of his sister and their upbringing.

'Sorry, baby,' Daisy said. 'I didn't mean to make you sad, that was the last thing I wanted. But you did say it was in February, didn't you?'

'Yeah, suppose,'

'Well, when in February? The beginning? The end? The middle? Can you remember? Didn't you say your sister made you some special pudding or something at dinner?'

She had. Angel Delight, strawberry flavour, his favourite. She hadn't dared make anything more. His father had liked it, too, so she could get away with it. He'd never cottoned on; was normally too drunk. 'I honestly don't know.' This sad fact irked Daisy, really irked her. She would hate it if she didn't know her birthday. Or more to the point, her birth *date*. It was criminal that something that important, that significant, wasn't registered – and now no one would ever know for sure. It sickened her.

'Well, not the middle, surely – that's near Valentine's Day.'

'What's Valentine's Day?'

'You don't know what Valentine's Day is?' This was starting to feel like when they'd first met. It was crazy there was so much he still didn't know. Sometimes she forgot.

'No.'

'It's the most romantic day of the year – supposedly – when people send each other cards and gifts and that. We always used to send them at school, 'love from your secret admirer'… She trailed off. Of course he wouldn't know what Valentine's Day was. Why would he? 'Never mind.' She reached for his hand. 'But we *are* celebrating it. And your birthday.' She began to get excited. 'Our first Valentine's Day and your first birthday celebration, all in one month. Imagine!' She kissed him. 'So we can't make them near each other, that would be rubbish – like celebrating Christmas and your birthday on the same day.' She thought for a moment. It was weird, but there *was* an upside to all this. They could, in effect, make his birthday whatever day they chose. Who was to say or prove anything otherwise? It was a strange feeling, deciding when someone's birthday should be. Especially when he was about to turn seventeen. 'How about the end of February? That way it gives us plenty of time to organise – hey, we could even get the gang involved; have another party.' Jack noticeably brightened at this. But Daisy immediately had reservations. That meant *she* would be there again. What if she tried to kiss Jack because it was his birthday? 'Anyway, what about the end of Feb? But not right at the end, just in case it's a leap year – you don't want to miss your birthday for another four years now we've finally started celebrating it,' she laughed.

'What's a Leap—'

'Don't even say it,' she said, holding the palm of her hand out.

*****

They were on the way back home. 'Come on, there must be *something* you want for your birthday?' Daisy said. She'd already asked him at the pub, but got nothing useful in return.

Jack had been racking his brains since and reckoned he'd come up with something. Ever since the kidnapping, he hadn't been able to shake how vulnerable those men had made him feel, and he never wanted to feel like that again. He wanted to be able to protect himself better – and Daisy. Against anybody. Somehow, he'd slipped out of the habit of doing his exercise routine, his press-ups and that, and wanted to get back into it again. But more so – to really build up his strength. He'd been 'curling' the sacks of potatoes in the veg store at work when no one else was about.

'I wouldn't mind some weights,' he said.

'Weights?' said Daisy. 'What, like scales or something for recipes?'

'No,' Jack said. 'Proper weights, you know, heavy ones for exercising with.' He felt embarrassed saying it.

'Oh,' said Daisy. 'Sorry. What, you planning on being the next Arnold Schwarzenegger or something?' she laughed.

Jack blushed even more. 'No,' he said, put out. 'Forget it.'

'No! I'm sorry, honey, honestly. I just wasn't expecting that, that's all. I didn't think you were into that stuff.'

'What stuff?'

'Weightlifting and that.'

'Aitch has got some,' Jack said in defence.

'Really?' said Daisy. 'Not that you'd know!'

'Yeah, he got them from Argos.'

Daisy couldn't believe Jack had even been talking about this stuff. It was strange, something she didn't know about him. She wondered what else he talked about with the boys. Not girls, she hoped. 'Well, yeah, we can try and get you some then. Good idea. I'll look into it!' They were silent for a bit, but Jack was secretly pleased. 'Just for the record,' Daisy said, 'you're not gonna get all muscly, are you? Like one of those body builders? I hate guys like that: it's gross.'

CHAPTER 9

Festeggiato

Valentine's Day arrived, and Jack and Daisy exchanged cards for the very first time. Jack also bought Daisy some flowers – red roses, no less (he was feeling flush): Aitch had talked him into it. He'd felt foolish and self-conscious buying them, but Aitch had said, 'Birds love that stuff.' Jack had taken his advice, despite the fact that by all accounts Aitch had never had a girlfriend himself. Daisy was thrilled. She'd never had a bunch of flowers bought for her before.

And then it was Jack's birthday. Being practical as well as meticulous in her planning, Daisy talked Jack into choosing the 25th of February. It was a Sunday, so they could spend the whole day celebrating without having to worry about work, and all the gang could be off in the evening for some sort of party. They could also stay up getting drunk the night before for when it struck twelve o'clock – officially the start of his birthday – without worrying about waking up with a hangover.

Daisy really went to town, making sure it was a day Jack would never forget. Imagine being seventeen years old and never having celebrated your own birthday... She made sure her mum and Lily and all the gang knew about it, so Jack received plenty of cards. He'd never received a birthday card in the post before. Even Grandma sent him one with a tenner in it – and a football scene on the front cover, bless her.

It was all a bit overwhelming for Jack, but he did have one of the best, most memorable days of his young life so far. Daisy had bought him a set of weights – a barbell, two dumbbells and about fifty kilos. She had no idea how much weight he would need or want, but it all came as part of a set. The boys – Tom and Aitch – had to secretly help to collect it from the store, drive it back to the flat, then carry it upstairs. It almost killed them, Daisy could tell. But Aitch was showing off, of course, pretending it was no big deal. The set didn't come cheap, so there weren't too many other presents from Daisy, just bits and bobs, most noticeably a good quality kitchen knife. But Jack was thrilled with the weights. Daisy wanted him to try them out straightaway so she could watch, but Jack was too embarrassed to try until he got the hang of it.

The gang made up for any lack in quantity of presents on Daisy's part by all contributing with their own gifts and cards. They all met up at The Sailor for a drink, before heading to a local Italian restaurant in town. Everyone was in high spirits as Jack's presents were handed over and opened at the pub. Even Mike, the landlord, bought Jack a pint. Jack felt spoilt rotten; it was the strangest feeling. Aitch had bought Jack a board game from Woolworths – Scrabble – and handed it over with a mischievous look on his face, winking and saying they were going to have some fun with it later. Daisy had apparently mentioned at some point – she couldn't remember when – that she and Jack played Scrabble together when they were stoned, and that their battered set had some letters missing. 'I have also, Jackeroo, baked you a cake,' said Aitch, plonking a plastic Tupperware tub on top of his Scrabble board.

'A cake?' said Jack.

'Oh, I've bought him a cake already,' said Daisy. 'We're having it at the restaurant.'

'Oh, this is a *special* birthday cake,' said Aitch. 'Go on, open it up, but be quick.'

Intrigued, Jack prised off the turquoise lid and peeked inside. There were cubes of what looked like chocolate cake cut up, and a faint but familiar smell. Marijuana.

'Hash brownies,' said Aitch. 'Made them myself. Quick, close the lid. Their powers will escape! We'll 'ave some later.'

Everyone thought it was hilarious. 'Unbelievable,' said Tom.

Daisy was more interested in what Jeanie had bought Jack, but she had played it safe with a four-pack of cider. Her card did say 'Love from Jeanie', though, with a kiss – but then Alison's did, too. Both girls gave Jack a birthday hug and a kiss, so there was little Daisy could complain about. Jeanie was a little tartily dressed for Daisy's liking, in a short sparkly party dress and heels that showed off her figure; she made looking sexy so effortless. When Daisy snuggled into Jack, to re-establish her claim on him, he smelt of Jeanie's perfume. The tart.

They'd chosen the restaurant as it did lovely authentic pizzas, including vegetarian options for Daisy. The boys ribbed her about this during the meal, but both the girls said they admired her for it and wanted to try it themselves. Towards the end of the meal, Daisy shyly asked one of the waiters if he didn't mind if they had their own birthday cake for dessert, and portioning it up for them. She gestured to it on her lap. 'We can do better than that, Bella,' he said in his thick Italian accent. '*Festegiatta* or *Festegiatto*?' He surveyed the table, sweeping with his arm, a bit of a showman.

'No, I think it was Frascati, actually,' said Aitch, not to be outdone, and everyone laughed hysterically. They'd sunk two bottles of it between them during the meal.

'Sorry, I don't understand,' said Daisy, blushing and still laughing.

The waiter leant down and whispered in her ear, 'Birthday boy or birthday girl?'

'Oh,' said Daisy blushing further and giggling again. Jack was beginning to take more notice. If the waiter was a few years younger, he might have been jealous. 'Birthday boy,' she said and pointed to Jack, who was sitting opposite her. '*My* Birthday boy.'

'Molto bene, grazie, Bella.' He whisked the cake away.

'What was all that about?' said Alison.

'No idea,' Daisy shrugged.

'I reckon he fancies Daisy. Reckon you've got some competition there, Jackeroo,' teased Aitch, nudging him.

'Oh, shut up,' said Daisy. She knew Jack didn't like stuff like that. He was already scowling. She stroked his leg with her foot under the table.

About five minutes later, the lights in the restaurant went dim, so it was only lit by the candles on the tables. Everyone gasped. 'What is it, a power cut?' slurred Jeanie. Before anyone could answer, some strange old-fashioned music began to play, filling the restaurant. It was the strains of 'Happy Birthday'. Before they knew it, other tables had begun to sing: 'Happy Birthday to you...' The gang joined in as the waiter slowly walked over with the cake, which was crowned with a glowing halo of candles. Jack wanted to die when he realised what was happening. He sank down in his chair, and Daisy felt for him. She'd never expected all this fuss to be made. After an excruciating amount of time, the song finally ended and the cake was put in front of Jack. Everyone cheered and clapped.

'Blow out the candles,' said Alison.

'Make a wish,' said Jeanie.

Still red and dying of embarrassment, Jack blew out the candles on his cake. Thank God it was dark. Seventeen years old, and the first time he had ever blown candles out on a birthday cake. Or even had one.

'Well done, babe,' said Daisy, leaning over and squeezing his hand. She knew it must be emotional for him. Especially without his sister. Jack was just relieved when the lights came back on and the attention left him.

By the time they headed back to the flat in a pungent cloud of garlic, enough to ward off every vampire in Cromer, everyone was pissed, stuffed and dying for a smoke.

Aitch and Jack both started rolling, whilst the girls sorted the drinks and Tom sorted the tunes, starting of course with a Sisters of Mercy number, 'This Corrosion'. Then Aitch cried, 'Strip Scrabble!' This was met with a volley of disapproval.

'Er, gross,' said Alison.

'Pervert,' said Tom. 'Just 'cause you haven't got a girlfriend.'

'How do you even play Strip Scrabble?' said Jeanie.

'We're not playing it anyway,' said Daisy, nipping it in the bud, her face flushed and heart pounding at the prospect. The last thing she needed or wanted was Jeanie removing clothes. Or her or Jack for that matter.

'Yeah, but how?' Jeanie persisted.

'Easy,' said Aitch. 'You just–'

'We're not playing it,' said Daisy.

'How about rude word Scrabble instead?' Alison suggested, sensing the tension building.

'Yeah,' said Tom. 'Wicked idea. Crack open the board.'

Jack and Daisy exchanged relieved glances. The new board was set up and tiles were divvied out, added to with Daisy's old set, so there were enough to go round. The game began, but none of them were quite prepared for just how hilarious a game of rude word Scrabble could be, especially when everyone was drunk and stoned. Nor for some of the vulgar and downright bizarre expressions that were used. And the girls were the worst: well, Alison and Jeanie anyway. Daisy was a little more reserved. Jack had never heard of half the expressions and struggled to come up with many of his own. But that made them all the more hilarious; they were so innocent in comparison.

Despite spending most of the game either scoffing his hash brownie or trying to force it on other people, rather than concentrating, Aitch was declared the winner. He was fortunate enough to end up with the letter 'z' from both Scrabble sets; and despite his inebriated state, somehow had the wherewithal to not only come up with the word 'jizz', but also to have the ingenuity to place it on a triple-word score, giving him a grand total of 87 points. The last four-letter word of many. This blew everyone else out of the water, and the game ended with a descent into chaos and a squabble over whether 'jizz' was spelt with one or two 'z's. Having a competitive streak, Daisy was a little peeved at not winning, and blamed the letters she kept getting stuck with. Unsurprisingly, Jack came last.

*****

All the talk over the next few days was of the severe gale that had hit the Norfolk coast (as if the UK needed another one), so bad it had totally destroyed the pier's amusement arcade. Some of the gang were gutted about this, and went to look at the damage and take photos. The amusement arcade had been there since they were born, a feature of the scenery of their hometown, and held strong childhood memories for them.

Winter gradually melted into spring; but still the DNA test letter hadn't arrived. Jack became addicted to doing his weights in the afternoons between shifts. It became a routine, and helped pass that restless, graveyard period as he waited to go back to work. He'd tidied and cleared space in the spare room for his new hobby, so he could work out in private. He even dragged the coffee table from the lounge in there, so he could lie on his back and do some bench-pressing; Aitch had lent him a training manual with all the exercises in it. Jack was still embarrassed and shy about Daisy watching him. More was the pity, thought Daisy. Sometimes she crept down the hall and listened outside the door to him groaning from within, wondering what was going on in there. For some reason it turned her on. Her favourite bit was when he walked bare-chested through the kitchen to the bathroom afterwards to look in the mirror. He always did it. Daisy would pretend she was busy, but would always watch him. He secretly knew she was watching and liked it. Then he would put his T-shirt or jumper back on in front of her, hoping for a comment. He was getting stronger and his body was changing. He loved it.

Jack's new exercise regime spurred Daisy into dusting off the Jane Fonda video again. She was determined to become leaner. Not that she was in any way fat; but she was sick of being around Jeanie, who was so skinny (she had had another of those sexual dreams about her and Jack), and was sick of the few extra pounds she had gained that seemed impossible to shift. She thought being vegetarian was meant to help you lose weight. It hadn't in her case. She blamed it on all the extra cheese she was eating to replace the meat.

Jack didn't help in this respect. Not only did he have an infuriatingly high metabolism, seemingly able to scoff anything he could lay his hands on without gaining a single ounce of fat, but he had also taken to making puddings and desserts on his days off – influenced by working in the pastry section. Baz had started to let him make some of the desserts now, along with the ice cream and sorbet mixes. Everything was prepared in an almost scientific way, to eliminate inconsistencies and the waste of expensive ingredients. Baz had a plastic box that contained all the recipes and methods neatly written out on index cards. This seemed out of keeping with the rest of his personality and appearance, but it worked. Jack enjoyed plucking out a card, weighing the ingredients and following a recipe. He had his own notebook now – something all the junior chefs were encouraged to do – and when Baz left at the end of lunch service, Jack copied as many recipes as he could, including all the ice cream ones.

Poor old Daisy was on the receiving end of it all. 'Oh, I'm just going to knock up a bread and butter pudding,' or 'Oh, just try this chocolate brownie…'. She didn't stand a chance.

Jack had never had a sweet tooth, although he seemed to be developing one, but Daisy had. It was a bit of a weakness from childhood. Especially in the colder months, when a comfort pudding or two was just what they needed – and also when they were stoned.

The one thing Jack couldn't make at home was ice cream. And this was getting more and more frustrating as the weather started to warm up. The middle of March had seen an unseasonably warm spell, with temperatures in the twenties. The beach had been packed – and everybody was eating ice cream. Jack was dying to try some out, and they started to look into getting a decent machine for the flat. Something similar to the one at work, but maybe smaller. Baz had said there was no point in skimping on price if you wanted a quality result, and the machines weren't cheap, a couple of hundred quid at least. But Jack had money sitting in the bank. And, as Daisy kept reminding him, fingers crossed there would be more on the way, a lot more.

CHAPTER 10

Flavour of the Month

The ongoing debate over the purchase of an ice cream machine was finally decided by an announcement in the music press...

'Oh my God, Jack! The Cure are headlining Glastonbury,' Daisy squealed, looking up briefly from the *NME*. She continued to scan the details. 'Jesus Jones, Happy Mondays, James...' Her voice was getting gradually louder. 'SINEAD O'CONNOR!' At this point Daisy dropped the paper, stood up, and began to jump up and down in excitement. Literally jump up and down. 'Oh my God, Jack. We've got to go. We've got to.' She had been working her way through Sinead's new album *I Do Not Want What I Haven't Got*, and she loved it. It was good, really good. But softer than the first album. Not so raw.

Jack, who was used by now to Daisy getting carried away by anything music-based, hadn't seen her this excited and animated in a while. And he broke into a grin at the sight of her. 'OK...' he laughed. 'When is it? What day? I might have to book it off.'

'It's not a day, you donkey, it's a whole weekend – three days of music. You camp there.'

'Camp?'

'Yeah,' Daisy said, out of breath; she had stopped jumping up and down. 'In tents – or we could take the camper van.

Actually, we wouldn't be able to sleep in it, thinking about it – unless we took a mattress. Hold on, that's just given me an idea.'

'What?'

'The ice creams – we could sell them out of the back of the camper van. Well, the side of it anyway – like a hotdog van. Oh my God, it's genius. It would save us getting a cart or something. What d'you reckon, Jack? This is it. Shall we do it?' She grabbed hold of him and shook him, staring right into his face. Her excitement bubbling again. It was infectious, but almost scary. 'Shall we? Shall we do it?'

'OK,' said Jack, with no idea what he was letting himself in for.

'Oh my God!' Daisy squealed again and threw her arms around him, practically cutting off his windpipe in a fragrant chokehold. 'Thank you, thank you.'

As if she was gonna take no for an answer, thought Jack. 'Woah, I can barely breathe.' He toppled backwards under the sheer force of her enthusiasm, and she ended up on top of him, straddling him, both of them laughing.

'Oh God, I've really needed something like this, Jack. Something to look forward to and plan for. I've been so bored – not bored, but, you know, everything that's been going on – and what with you and your cooking and your weights – I need something for me. Just think, you, me, a tent – selling ice creams by day, watching gigs by night, then getting all snuggled up in sleeping bags…' She entwined her hands in his and began to gyrate gently on his groin.

'Hey, what about the gang?' said Jack. 'What if we all go? Shall we ask them?'

This statement instantly sobered Daisy, snapped her out of her moment. She sat up straight and tucked her hair behind her ears. She hadn't even considered this. It had been an adventure for her and Jack. Just the two of them. 'Er …we *could* ask them, I suppose,' she said.

'You don't sound too sure,' Jack said. 'It would be a laugh, though, wouldn't it? All of us. Camping and that? Imagine!' He put his hands on her legs.

'Yeah, I guess.'

'You still don't sound sure…' He stroked her thighs.

'Yeah, I just hadn't thought that far ahead, that's all. We've only just decided ourselves.'

'You're sure?' he smiled, pulling her onto him.

'Yeah, it's cool.' She lay on his chest with her heart thumping against him.

'Cool, I'll mention it to them at work.'

Daisy brooded about this for some time afterwards. It wasn't that she didn't enjoy being with the gang; she did. But not as much as Jack appeared to. Especially lately. He seemed to be loving his 'boy time' more and more, probably because he had never had it growing up. But doing things with the gang always seemed to involve *her*. Jeanie. She always had to tag along. Daisy still saw her as a threat. It was her body, no question (certainly not her mind), the clothes she wore, that made Daisy feel insecure. Made her feel as if she had to compete, so she couldn't quite relax. Those dreams weren't helping. Why couldn't Jeanie get a boyfriend? Or get fat? Or have spots?

Jack mentioned the Glastonbury idea to Tom and Aitch as soon as he got the chance; and they told Alison and Jeanie. They all thought it was a fab idea. Aitch, uncharacteristically, was the least enthusiastic; he normally jumped at a chance to get wasted with his friends. But he was feeling a little narked at everyone's excitement, given that he had spent the previous month or so trying to talk them into going to the Stone Roses gig at Spike Island in May. Along with the Happy Mondays, they were his favourite band; he had really embraced the whole Madchester scene, complete with flares and a Reni hat. But everyone had their own reasons for their lacklustre responses, most of them musical. Tom and Alison were diehard goths for a start, not baggies.

As for Daisy, it was more than that. The upcoming Stone Roses gig had caused much conflict in her head ever since being announced. It reminded her of the tickets her dad had bought her, which she still had tucked in her diary, and the fiasco of the missed concert. She'd always thought she would want to see the band again, the first chance she got, but when she heard about Spike Island, despite an initial jolt of excitement, she just felt sad. The band would always be connected with her dad. She realised she'd almost stopped listening to them – and hadn't been a big fan of their latest single, 'Fools Gold'. Seeing them at a huge outdoor concert felt like something she'd feel detached from. It was complicated. Almost as if she was betraying her dad's memory, given she'd foolishly wasted the tickets he bought her. The last thing he ever bought her.

So it was decided, and they all forked out for Glastonbury tickets. Aitch a little begrudgingly. 'Fine. I'll go and see the Roses with me bro, then,' he said. The tickets were thirty-eight quid. A lot of money. It was the festival's twentieth anniversary, marked by a change of name to the Glastonbury Festival of Contemporary Performing Arts – but Daisy, didn't care what it was called, or that tickets were ten quid more than the previous year. She was going to see The Cure and Sinead O'Connor – and not just at a gig, but a festival.

And then there was the ice cream business to organise… Daisy and Jack started planning, Daisy writing everything down. The more they thought about the details, the more daunting it became, but they were determined to do it. First, they would have to buy the machine and make the ice cream. Lots of it. Loads of different flavours. Not just the classics, but unusual ones too. That could be their forte, their selling point. 'Jack and Daisy's Ice Creams – the weird and the wonderful'; something like that, anyway. They began to make a list of flavours, which was fun. Even the gang got involved, pitching in with increasingly far-out ideas. They thought it was a great plan and couldn't wait to help out.

To store all this ice cream, they would need some sort of freezer, something that was big enough to hold plenty of tubs but would also fit in the back of the van. Then they would need something to power it with. Daisy knew just the thing: a portable camping generator they had in the garage back home. The plan was taking shape. All of it was going to cost money, of course, but it was an investment, Daisy assured Jack. An initial outlay to make *more* money. Lots of it. If it worked, they could roll it out all summer. And forever. Jack loved it when Daisy was in full flow like this. She was awe-inspiring. He knew he'd be too scared to do anything without her.

They finally tracked down a suitable ice cream machine at a wholesale catering outlet Daisy had found in the *Yellow Pages*. They'd decided to go all out and get the same make and model as the one at the restaurant. This was a huge and scary decision, and a big investment, but they wanted to do it right. A smaller machine wouldn't be able to cope with the volume. They split the cost fifty-fifty, both using their savings. It was the first time Daisy had dipped into hers, but she thought her dad would approve. She was finally doing something with her life. Starting a business…

It was an auspicious moment when they carried the machine back up to the flat and unpacked it. The thing weighed a ton – about the size of a microwave, but a damn sight heavier. Brand new. Gleaming with silver chrome. Daisy had never bought or received anything like it in her life, certainly nothing so expensive. But she was surprised and disappointed at how small the freezing compartment was – the bowl you poured the mix into. She voiced her concerns to Jack. 'It produces two litres,' he said. 'The mix increases in volume as the blade churns and freezes it. You'll be surprised.'

'Yes, chef,' she said. 'Or shall I call you Uncle Jack? Aren't all ice cream men called Uncle something?'

Uncle Jack couldn't wait to set to work, but they needed ingredients. Daisy had thought about this, and decided to wait until they had the machine. They needed to buy in bulk, and as cheaply as possible, to save costs. Sugar, cream, milk, chocolate… They didn't come cheap. But she knew just the place: the cash and carry. Her parents had an account at the one in Nottingham; it was registered to her dad's business. They'd used it for office catering goods and cleaning products, and also whenever they'd wanted to buy anything in bulk for the house, especially for parties. Alcohol, mainly. Daisy rang her mum. 'Mum, can you send me your Makro card, please?'

'What on earth for?' Daisy explained their plans. Carol thought they were bonkers, and said so.

'It's too late,' said Daisy. 'We've already bought the machine.'

'Honestly, you and your hare-brained schemes,' Carol tutted. 'God knows what your dad would say.'

'He'd be pleased at my entrepreneurial spirit. His daughter following in his footsteps…'

'When are you coming back over here, anyway? It's Mother's Day this Sunday in case you'd forgotten.'

'I hadn't forgotten.' She had. 'I don't know, Mum, we've got a fair bit going on…' This was true, but she felt bad.

'Yes, sounds like it.'

'Why don't you come over here instead?'

'And sleep where? And you know I don't drive long distances any more. Lily would have to bring me – and she'll have to sleep somewhere too.'

'Well, just come for the day, or book yourselves in somewhere. The town's teeming with B and Bs, especially at this time of year. It's not like you can't afford it.'

'That's not the point.'

'Then what is? We've been here, what, nine months or

so now and you haven't visited us once – which is ironic, considering we used to come to Norfolk pretty much every year.'

'Yeah, but that was when Dad was alive.'

'You're just making excuses, Mum. Just being stubborn.'

'No, I'm not.' She was. Daisy knew her mum too well. She wore her pride like a crown; she never believed Daisy would make it out in Cromer on her own. 'Maybe when the weather warms up properly,' she said. 'I'll send you that card anyway – if I can find it. It's been a while since it's been used…'

'Thanks, Mum. I'll send you a card too.'

Simply dying to try the machine out, Jack couldn't wait for the cash and carry. The supermarket would do for now, just for a couple of trial mixes. There was a brief debate over what flavour to make first, and they quickly decided on vanilla: it would probably be the most popular flavour in the long run. And Jack had a recipe for it.

Setting about his first ever solo mix was beyond exciting, as if they were on the verge of a great adventure, the start of something big. Daisy watched him, increasing the pressure. Preparing an ice cream custard was no mean feat. There was a crucial point during the cooking process when the warmed egg yolks gradually thickened the mix to the perfect consistency and temperature; once this was reached, you had to quickly take it off the heat and pass it through a sieve to cool. A couple of seconds too long and you ended up with sweet scrambled eggs and a ruined split mix.

But Jack pulled it off with aplomb, breathing a sigh of relief. Then they had to wait for the mix to chill properly before freezing it, which took hours. Pouring the ice cream custard into the machine, ready to be churned, was another significant moment. They'd bought a cheap bottle of fizz, and they bumped it against the side of the machine first, as if it was a ship being launched. Then Jack turned the dial. The machine whirred into life, the blade slicing through the mix, creating a continuous wave. It was louder than Daisy had expected, quite noisy in fact. Then they cracked open the bottle and drank. And watched, and waited, Jack with his tea towel slung over his shoulder. It was silly, really, as it took around half an hour for an ice cream mix to churn, but they couldn't help it.

Slowly but surely, the mix thickened and grew in volume until it started to resemble ice cream. The process was fascinating. Although Jack had seen it all before, it was so satisfying to be in charge. Finally, it was ready. The result was nothing short of a revelation. Daisy had only ever had her mum's home-made ice cream. Because she'd just put the mix in a tub in the freezer and whisked it occasionally, it had been slightly grainy in texture with tiny ice particles. Jack's mix was velvety smooth. Creamy, sweet and rich with an intense flavour. A Rolls-Royce of vanilla ice creams.

'Darling, you're a genius,' Daisy declared, dipping her finger into the mix for the third time. 'This machine will pay for itself in no time.' Jack blushed, brimming with pride. It was one of his greatest ever achievements. 'Well, there goes my waistline,' Daisy said, devouring another huge dollop and sucking her finger.

*****

'Christ, have you seen this?' The morning news was on. There'd been riots in London the previous day; it looked like carnage. Fires and everything. What looked like thousands and thousands of people.

'What's the matter with them?' asked Jack. 'What are they so angry about?'

'It's all this Poll Tax nonsense again. We had something sent through about it. I ignored it. I didn't understand it.' It was the sort of thing she would have asked her dad to explain. Jack was oblivious to stuff like this: it was up to Daisy to deal with it.

'Well, it must be important if it's caused all this trouble. Maybe we should check…'

'You mean maybe *I* should check…'

'Yeah, you check,' he said cheekily. 'Oh, Daisy.'

'What?' She was trying to watch the news. There was some crazy footage.

'I've quit my job.'

'WHAT?' she said, tearing herself away from the screen.

'I've quit my job, so we can do the ice cream thing. I can't do both…'

'Jack, you're joking. Please tell me you're not serious. How are we going to pay the rent? How are we going to afford the ingredients? I mean, we haven't even started the business yet.' She was running her hands through her hair, thinking of the implications.

'Ha! Got you!' he said, breaking into a grin.

'Hey?'

'April Fool!'

'What?' Daisy was dumbfounded. 'How do you even know what April Fool's Day is?'

'Aitch told me.'

'Oh, he did, did he? Come here, you!'

Jack began to run off, cackling at his trick, chuffed to bits. 'I got you,' he called.

'I'll get *you*!' said Daisy, chasing after him.

They ended up on the bed in a playfight. Jack overpowered her quickly as usual. He sat on her, pinning her down. Eventually he rolled off, and they breathed heavily side by side, still laughing.

'I love you,' Daisy said.

'I love you too.' It felt nice.

'Hey, I've been thinking. We ought to do a dummy run with the ice creams.'

'How do you mean?'

'Like a practice. See if we can pull it off on a smaller scale.'

'How? Where?'

'There's a car boot sale, a huge one, at East Runton. Same place the fair was. On Easter Monday, the bank holiday. They have one once a month.'

'What's a car boot sale?'

'What it says. People sell things out of their car boots – and from tables and stalls as well. They're becoming really popular. There'll be hundreds, maybe thousands, of people to sell ice creams to. It's perfect.'

Great, thought Jack. On show in front of thousands of people. The thought made his head spin. He still wasn't used to people and hated crowds. Now that it came to it, he wasn't sure if he could do it. He wanted to make the ice cream, sure, but the reality of selling it to the public… 'When is it?' he said.

'A couple of weeks' time.'

'Well, we haven't even got a freezer yet. Or the generator. And your mum still hasn't sent that cash and carry card.' He sat up on his elbow, a panicked look on his face.

'I know, but we can get them. We just need to get our arses in gear. And I've no idea why Mum hasn't sent the card yet, it's been a week. I'll call her. I reckon she's forgotten.'

Jack threw himself onto his back, breathing heavily, his mind whirring, thoughts scudding. He ran his fingers through his hair. 'It's too soon, Daisy. It's … it's too soon.'

'Hey, calm down. You're not getting cold feet, are you?' She leant into him, putting her hand on his chest. His thumping heart answered for him. Bless him, she thought. 'God, sorry, baby. I didn't mean to pressure you. It's OK, we can wait a bit, get used to the idea. There'll be another one in May.' In her enthusiasm and impatience, she'd totally forgotten how daunting something like that, crowds and the public, would be for Jack. It would be for her too, but she hadn't really thought about the reality of it. Just got carried away by the romanticism of it all.

'I think it would be best to wait a bit,' said Jack. 'Give us more time to get organised and make all the ice cream. It's hard with working as well…'

'Yeah, you're right. We'll wait. Aim for the May bank holiday. It'll take the pressure off. Like you say, give us more time to get organised.'

It turned out Daisy didn't need to call her mum. The card arrived in the post the very next day, along with a note. 'Sorry about delay. Couldn't find the thing.' This immediately prompted them to make a shopping list, based on the ice cream flavours they had chosen: green food colouring, dark chocolate drops, white chocolate drops, rum flavouring, raisins, crystallised ginger, liquorice, lemon curd, frozen strawberries and raspberries…

They set off early on their next day off to visit the cash and carry in Norwich, and also to purchase a freezer: a good-sized domestic one that would fit in the van. It was going to be an expensive day. The plan was to hit the stores bang on opening time, so they could get back and start making the ice cream as soon as possible. The biggest problem they faced, a bit of a gamble in fact, was storing the milk and cream. And their fridge at home wasn't the biggest.

The guy at Currys was incredibly helpful, and allayed Daisy's fears about transporting the ice cream. A freezer's contents could stay frozen for up to forty-eight hours if the door remained closed. The fuller it was, the better, he said. Perfect. A trip to Glastonbury without power wouldn't be a problem. The cash and carry was a huge warehouse. You name it, it was there – all in huge receptacles, and cheap. Jack wandered around, mouth open, eyes wide. They bought plastic two-litre tubs to store the ice cream in. Each of them would hold one batch perfectly. And they also picked up some cooking equipment – plastic measuring jugs and bowls, and a much larger, better quality, heavy-bottomed saucepan for Jack to cook with. This meant he would be able to double up some of the mixes.

By the time they'd lugged everything upstairs, they were exhausted. And starving. But there was no time to waste, as the sooner the ice cream mixes were made, the sooner they could be chilled. And that milk and cream wasn't going to stay fresh for ever. The freezer had to be left to settle for an hour or so before being turned on; they had to plug it in in the lounge as there wasn't room in the kitchen. After organising his stock and washing his hands, Jack set to work. Daisy helped as much as she could, weighing ingredients, cracking and separating eggs. She enjoyed being his assistant.

That day, Jack managed to prepare and cook seven different ice cream mixes, some of them double batches. To start off with, he stuck to the basic flavours to gain confidence. Vanilla, chocolate, strawberry: he'd got the exact recipes for them. But even some of these, with Daisy's input and encouragement, were given his own little twist. And this was the really time-consuming bit. A simple chocolate ice cream had chocolate brownie chunks added to it. Strawberry became 'double strawberry' – a strawberry ice cream with an intense strawberry ripple. The most adventurous two flavours of the day were lemon curd and ginger and one of Jack's inventions, white chocolate and raspberry ripple. He'd got the inspiration for this from work, remembering how well the raspberries had gone with that white chocolate ice cream. Although Jack worked late into the evening, not all of the mixes were frozen that day. They simply ran out of time: the machine could only produce so many litres per hour, and you had to be careful not to burn it out. But they had got through enough of the cream and milk that the remainder, along with the unfrozen mixes, could be stored in the fridge. This took the pressure off and the need for such haste. They still had weeks to go.

They dropped into bed utterly exhausted. As Jack drifted

off to sleep, his head was still whirling round like the ice cream machine with weird and wonderful ice cream flavours. He needed to write them all down so he didn't forget them, but was too tired. Tutti frutti, cappuccino, peanut butter, rhubarb and custard, chocolate orange, blueberry, honeycomb…

CHAPTER 11

A Trip Down Memory Lane

The middle of April saw Jack and Daisy make a trip back home to the East Midlands. They needed to pick up the generator: the final piece of the puzzle. Carol had confirmed it was buried in the garage somewhere. Whether it still worked or not was another matter. Daisy prayed it did. There was still time to sort something if it didn't, but they could do without any more big outlays. They had checked out the car boot sale in East Runton the previous day, during Jack's split. It looked perfect. Far too busy for Jack, though. Despite the weather not being the best (typical bank holiday), there were other ice cream vans there. Competition. Something Daisy hadn't considered.

There was another reason for making the journey back. Jack had been increasingly missing his home countryside. He'd been talking about it more and more, sadly and wistfully, when he'd been stoned. He didn't miss the house itself, which was gone anyway, but his old haunts. The stile, the spinney. Bunny Wood. Oh God, Bunny Wood. How he missed that place. It must have been the time of year, spring in full flow. It stirred something in him; like a migrating bird that has to fly south in winter. His internal body clock was telling him something. He knew the bluebells would be out in Bunny Wood round about now. The weather had been warm. As long as he could remember, he had never missed them. 'Let's do it,' Daisy said. 'I'll take the camera. We can even go to the pubs.'

The morning they set off, they discovered a letter on their porch floor as they were leaving. It looked official. Important. It was the long-awaited appointment date for the DNA test. Jack gulped and his hands shook as he slowly read the letter. The black spot on his eye skirted across the typed words like a mechanical rabbit, just out of reach, luring a greyhound. 'Finally,' Daisy said. 'At least we know when now.'

'All right for you,' said Jack morosely. 'You're not the one that's got to have it done.'

'It'll be fine, honey,' she said, pecking him on the cheek. 'I promise. Over in a jiffy.' The date was still a few weeks away, more was the pity; it meant Jack would have it hanging over his head. But at least he could mentally prepare now. He re-read the letter in the van, clutching it for the first part of the journey. He'd been so excited about going back home, and visiting Bunny Wood, but now his mood was dampened.

'Put that letter down and cheer up, you,' Daisy said. She'd also been looking forward to the trip, and she wasn't going to let the letter spoil things. Getting that date was good: a chance to shut that woman up once and for all. 'You know what's just occurred to me,' she said, trying to take Jack's mind off it. 'It's got to be about a year since we first met, hasn't it?'

'Don't know. I hadn't really thought about it.'

'Yeah, it's got to be. I wonder when our first-year anniversary date should be? It's got to be our first kiss at the brook, surely. That's when we started going out properly. God, I wish I had my diary with me, that would have all the dates in it. How annoying!'

'What, did you write them all down?'

'Not the dates, but what we did on the days things happened. Like us first talking on the bus. You were all I wrote about after that.'

'Really?' said Jack, sitting up in his seat. For some reason, he found this fascinating. Intriguing and flattering. 'What did you say?'

'I'm not telling you that,' said Daisy, blushing. 'It's embarrassing – a girl's diary is private.'

'Ohhh,' said Jack, disappointed. 'I'll just find it and look anyway.'

'You bloody won't,' she laughed.

'I will.'

'It'll only be cringeworthy stuff, soppy stuff, saying how much I loved you and fancied you. Anyway, like I say, it's got to be this time of year we first met...'

'Yes, it must be,' said Jack. 'Bloody hell...' This had taken his mind off the letter. Could it really be a year ago? Such a magical time. Getting to know each other, and all the stuff they did. 'Remember camping?'

'God, yes. How could I forget? I can't believe we did that now. Disappearing off into a wood overnight. We barely knew each other, looking back. You could have been a madman. You *are* a madman,' she joked, smacking him on the leg and making him laugh. 'Oh God, and our trip to town. Remember you fainting?' Jack groaned with embarrassment and covered his face with his hands. What an idiot. He'd come such a long way since. 'And going to the Red Lion afterwards for our first pint... I can't wait to go there today, actually. It'll be nice. We can sit outside – on the same bench – if it's still there. Mum said it had changed hands, didn't she? Good thing, considering you were barred.' Jack couldn't forget that either, punching that guy. 'Yes, I'm looking forward to this today, a little trip down memory lane.' Daisy turned the stereo up. The Cramps' new album, *Stay Sick!*. She was mad about it. 'Pass me my sunglasses, baby.'

They arrived just before midday: traffic had been slow. Carol was pleased to see them. 'Here, stick this in the freezer before it gets any softer,' Daisy said. 'Mint and choc chip. Your favourite.' She'd brought her mum a smallish tub, wrapped in a carrier bag. She was dying to show off their product, to get some feedback.

'Ooh, lovely,' said Carol. 'We can have it for dessert. Thank you, love. It's a shame Grandma's not here.'

Lunch was home-made quiche, salad and new potatoes. Lily wafted in from work for the occasion, all perfume and make-up, wearing her Boots outfit. 'Ooh, you been pumping iron, Jack?' she remarked. Daisy scowled. Trust her to notice. They all sat down to eat. The food was delicious, and they got stuck in. Peasgood was the first topic of conversation, how awful and shocking everything had been, and how it had caused quite a stir locally. Then Daisy told them about the DNA test; and Carol, like Daisy, thought this was good news. 'Quite exciting, really,' she said.

'God, imagine if it turns out they're not actually related,' said Lily.

'Lily!' said Carol.

'What? They *might* not be…'

'Jack's here, you know, he's not invisible,' said Daisy. Jack went red.

'Yes, don't be so insensitive, please, Lily. Sorry, Jack.' This was a first, Carol protecting him like that. Jack went redder.

'God, you can't say anything round here any more,' said Lily, spearing a Jersey Royal and stuffing it in her mouth.

Carol sighed. 'Anyway, tell me all about this ice cream malarkey,' she said, changing the subject. 'Sounds interesting.' Daisy excitedly filled her in on their plans, including Glastonbury. At which point Carol casually dropped a bombshell. 'I think you might need to book a trade spot for that, love. Have you asked?'

'No,' said Daisy, mid-chew. 'What do you mean?'

'Well, a pitch. You know, a trade pitch. In the trade area. Especially if you're planning on using the van.'

'We were just planning on doing it on the campsite. I didn't even know there *was* a trade area.'

Lily snorted. Daisy glared at her.

'Well, yes. Course there is. Burgers. Hot dogs. Beer tents. I imagine it'll be stricter than ever now. Glastonbury's big business these days. It used to be just a few thousand of us hippies hanging around in a field, smoking pot.'

Normally Daisy would have laughed at this, but it was no laughing matter. It could ruin everything. She looked at Jack. He'd stopped eating and was staring pensively back at her. He didn't understand what was going on, but figured it was serious.

'Well, how do you book one of these trade spots?'

'I've no idea. Ring up, I guess.'

'Ring who?'

'I don't know. The organisers?'

Daisy was gutted. She wouldn't be able to stop fretting about this until she knew. And that wouldn't happen until they got back home. Maybe there was a number on the back of the tickets or something. It wasn't like you could look in the phonebook or the *Yellow Pages* for Glastonbury Festival. And the tickets had been booked through an agency. She felt foolish. They'd spent so much money. But how could she have known? She'd never been to a festival before, and she'd certainly never sold ice cream. Why did everything have to be so complicated these days? Not for the first time, she wished she lived in medieval times. Or the seventies, at least. Bet they didn't need bloody trade pitches then.

Things went a bit quiet after that. Daisy kept noticing Lily glancing at Jack's arms, which were looking quite defined in his T-shirt. It started to wind her up. But Lily also had some parsley stuck in her front teeth from the potatoes, which looked decidedly unattractive, therefore evening things up. Then the ice cream was dished out. 'Oh, my word,' said Carol. 'This is absolutely delicious.'

'Told you,' said Daisy, cheering up a little. 'Jack made it. He makes all of them.'

'Clever boy,' said Carol. 'It really is good. So smooth. And the flavour! So fresh.'

'That's the fresh mint. You infuse it.' Daisy had got this term from Jack.

'What do you think, Lily?' Daisy asked. Lily hadn't said a word, but her bowl was empty. Probably jealous.

'Yeah, it's good,' she said, licking her spoon. 'Right, some of us have got to go back to work.' She got up from the table.

'We're gonna go out for a bit too, if that's OK, Mum.'

'Oh,' said Carol, put out. 'You've not long got here.'

'I know, but we want to go for a walk in Bunny Wood, see the bluebells and that.'

'Oh. I wouldn't mind a quick walk actually...'

'We weren't sort of planning anything quick. We were going to have a nosey up at the house too, Jack's old house, see what state it's in.' This was news to Jack. His heart jolted and he looked at Daisy, but didn't say anything.

'Whatever for?' said Carol. 'It's just rubble, I'm presuming.'

'Because it's going to be Jack's rubble soon. We might build a new house there.'

'Yeah, righto. Go on then,' Carol sighed. 'I know when I'm not wanted.'

'Thanks, Mum,' Daisy said, unexpectedly giving Carol a hug and kiss. 'We'll have a game of cards later when we get back.' Carol's hands were full with empty bowls, so she couldn't reciprocate, but she let out a pleased squeak.

They headed straight to Bunny Wood, passing the house on the hill on the way. Or where it had stood. This gave Jack mixed feelings. A knot of dread in the pit of his stomach at the memories the place held. But now some time had passed, there was a curiosity, a desire, to see it again in broad daylight.

Reaching Bunny Wood was another emotional wrench. Just

the sight of it. They parked at the front gate, the one Jack had rarely used. The gate that Daisy had sat on when she was waiting for him on their first outing together. Their first date. This brought back some memories, like Jack inadvertently creeping up on Daisy from behind and making her jump. Daisy got her camera out, and they took photos of each other sitting on the gate.

Inside the wood, the nostalgia was even stronger for Jack. Overwhelming. It felt like coming home. Comforting. Welcoming. The sounds, the smells, the light. It had rained recently, and everything was stirred up in a potpourri of scents. Wet leaves. Damp earth. Sweet pine. Sawn wood. They walked to where the bluebells always grew, and Jack was right: they were already abundant, as magical and enchanting as ever. A sweeping haze of purple-blue jewels amongst the trees. This backdrop provided more photo opportunities.

Next, they wandered down to the mine and sat on the ledge above the entrance, just as they had before. The drop still gave Jack that spinny-tummy feeling. The strange smell that emanated from within was still unnerving. Jack lit up a ready-rolled joint, wishing they had brought some cider too. He was thirsty. They shared the joint and reminisced some more. 'I used to sit up here and dream and dream about America,' said Jack. 'About running away to live there.'

'I know. I remember you telling me that on our first date, sitting right here.'

'Did I?'

'Yes. Just as the sun was setting. You made it sound so appealing. But I didn't think you were being serious.'

Jack was quiet for a moment. 'I still want to,' he said.

'Really?'

'Yeah.'

'What, even leaving all the guys in Norfolk behind, our friends, wouldn't that bother you?'

'Not with you by my side.' He leant into her. 'No, it would. Course it would, but there's just something about it. America. It's like it's my dream, my destiny. The house I want to live in. White wood, with a veranda and porch swing. Imagine. Me and you…'

'It does sound romantic. I just don't know whether I could leave Mum. And what about jobs? What would we do for work?'

'Sell ice cream?' Jack joked.

'Yes, that's got off to a good start, hasn't it? Come on, we'd best be getting along. We've got so much to do. Mum will be waiting. And I want a pint.'

They stopped off at the house next. Jack wasn't prepared for how traumatic this would be. The power the place still wielded. The feelings it stirred up. Seeing it all in the cold light of day: the layout of the rooms, burnt remnants of beds still in them. The stone steps to the basement. It reminded Jack of Anne so much. The caustic tank where he had found her was still in the yard. Rustier now. Jack couldn't go and look at it; it was too painful. The bitter taste returned to his mouth and throat. The anger and resentment towards his father. Anne had been his mother. She had raised him. And now she was gone. He missed her terribly, and he began to sob. Daisy cried too, at his reaction.

They ventured up the garden and into the orchard. The grass was waist-high, the swing still there. Jack sat on it sadly, and rocked to and fro. 'I could never live here again, Daisy. Not ever.'

'I know, honey. I was only joking about building a house.' She stood in front of him, pulled him to her and stroked his hair. She bit her lip, feeling guilty. Perhaps they shouldn't have gone up there. But with all this will stuff going on, she'd wanted to see the place properly, the land. What was at stake. 'Come on, let's go and get that pint.'

They did everything they'd set out to do that day – a sort of 'Jack and Daisy's Courting Locations Tour' – save for the 'kiss at the brook scene', because they ran out of time. By the time they'd had a couple of pints and done the rest of their sightseeing, they were both feeling a whole lot better. Especially Jack. And they returned to Carol's feeling generally content with their trip down memory lane.

It was whilst they were playing cards, as promised, that Carol surprised Daisy by saying she'd been looking at houses. 'Really?' said Daisy.

'Yeah, she's kicking me out,' said Lily.

'I'm not kicking you out at all; you know you're welcome wherever I go. But I've been thinking about it a lot – since Dad passed away – and what with you moving out, and then all this horrible business with those men...' She shuddered at the thought of them. 'It makes me feel uneasy. Them knowing where we live. Knowing they'll be out of prison before long.'

'God. Sorry, Mum.' Daisy said. She felt awful. Guilty that her life, her actions, meant her mum wanted to sell their family home.

'God, no. It's not your fault. Not your fault at all. It's just another factor, really. This place reminds me of your dad too much. It always will. I see him everywhere. I see him sitting on that sofa there, watching telly.' She gestured with her arm and her top lip began to wobble. She'd had a couple of G and Ts. 'And with you girls all grown up now and doing your own things, we've got four rooms here with two of them sitting empty. And the garden's too big for me to manage on my own. I could downsize, go travelling – I'd love to visit my brother in the States. I've never been. Your dad never wanted to.'

'Uncle Phil?' said Daisy. Her mum's older brother and eldest sibling. He'd emigrated before Daisy was born and only visited once that she could remember. He'd brought his family with him – Daisy's cousins and his wife, Trish. His children were quite a bit older than Daisy and Lily: both girls. Daisy must have been around six or seven at the time and his kids were already teenagers. Or at least one of them was. They'd seemed huge and had braces. It had been a big occasion. The whole family had been there. They'd had a roast turkey dinner in Phil's honour, and Daisy couldn't understand why they were celebrating Christmas in November. She hadn't thought about Uncle Phil in years. 'That's funny, me and Jack were only talking about America earlier.' She gave him a quick glance.

'Yes. I'd love to fly out there and see him. He and your dad never really got along. Sad, really. It's about the only thing we ever fell out about.'

That *was* sad, thought Daisy. 'Where would you move to? In the UK, I mean – if you moved?'

'I don't know. Maybe nearer Grandma. She's not getting any younger. I could be of some use. It'd keep me busy. I've got all this money sitting in the bank, but nothing to do with it – or anyone to do it with.'

Then it was time to go home. After a coffee to liven Daisy up for the drive, they retrieved the generator from the garage. Daisy also spotted a decent-sized foldaway camping table they could borrow. It would be ideal to set out as a stall to serve customers from. Then they said their goodbyes, and set off. 'Good luck with the ice creams,' Carol said as a parting shot. 'I'm sure it'll all work out fine.'

All the way home, Daisy fretted about the trade pass.

CHAPTER 12

Poppyland

The next morning, after a restless night, Daisy finally got hold of a Glastonbury Festival representative. Carol was right. You *did* need to apply for a trade spot to sell food there. But that wasn't the worst of it. 'Sorry, love,' the lady said. 'All the pitches got snapped up in record time this year, months ago, in fact, what with it being such a big year for us…'

Daisy thanked her and hung up. Then she burst into tears: she'd never handled disappointment well. And this was a huge blow. It broke Jack's heart, and he hugged her close to console her. It had been Daisy's dream since they'd moved to Norfolk to sell ice creams at a music festival – and especially since getting the Glastonbury tickets. Jack tried desperately to think of something to cheer her up.

'We can still do the car boot sale,' he said.

'The car boot sale? How does that compare to Glastonbury?' she wailed. That worked well, thought Jack.

'I don't know… But we're still going, aren't we? To Glastonbury? We've still got tickets.'

'Of course we're still going, but it won't be the same. I loved the thought of us selling ice creams there. It was so romantic. I had it all planned out, decorating the van and that. Getting it all decked out and some signs done. Everybody pitching in and helping. Taking photos of it all…'

'Well, there'll be next year. We can do it then. Or other festivals, surely? Didn't you say there was another big music one?'

'Reading,' she said, calming down a little.

'Yeah, when's that?'

'August, I think. We could do that, I suppose…'

'See? Then we can just enjoy Glastonbury, not have to worry or stress. I *was* a bit stressed about it all, to be honest. We can just concentrate on having a good time now, us and the gang. The music, the camping…'

'Suppose so,' she said, wiping her nose on her sleeve. 'But what about the ice creams? What about our machine? All your hard work. It seems such a bloody waste.'

'We can still do the car boot sale, like I say. And didn't you say there was one every month? We can do them all. We'll soon get rid of all that ice cream, I bet. And then there's Carnival Week. What about that? Remember how busy it was last year? We could still get the van done up.' Daisy stopped sniffling and looked at him. 'What?' he said.

'Jack. You're a genius.'

'Am I?'

'Yes. A fucking genius.'

'Well, you know…'

'Carnival Week. Imagine! The busiest week of the whole year – especially if the weather's good. But not only that, the tourist season. All summer long. We'd make a killing.'

'But how? Where?'

'I don't know – everywhere. The car boot sales, the fair, the car parks – like the one by the pitch and putt in town – the quayside at Wells. We need to look into this. I bet you need bloody licences or trade passes for some of this, too. And we're not missing out again.' She stood up. 'We're never gonna miss out again because of some stupid paperwork or red tape. We need to get organised. Approach this professionally. We're going to turn this disappointment into energy. Into a success.'

Jack looked up at her, trying to keep up. She was like that prime minister lady on the telly, giving one of her rousing speeches. He was in awe as usual. It was inspiring. She made him believe anything was possible. 'Put the kettle on, baby. I've got some phone calls to make, and we've both got work soon.'

Daisy rang the council first; it seemed the most sensible port of call. And it was the right decision. They were incredibly helpful, and gave her all the information she needed. It turned out there was more to selling ice creams than met the eye. Especially *where* you could sell them. But nothing was the end of the world: it was just a few different bits of paperwork, the most important being a trader's licence if they wanted to sell anywhere that wasn't private land. This came with a small fee, but was nothing compared with the fines if you tried to park somewhere and sell without it. She was so glad she had made the call. Now they could just get on with the selling of ice creams without worrying about getting into trouble. It was a big weight off her mind. A negative had been turned into a positive. Roll on the May bank holiday.

Pretty much everything in the run-up took a back seat, including work – which was just something that got in the way. The only thing that didn't was music. There was a steady stream of releases Daisy was interested in, including fantastic new singles by Morrisey and James. But, more significantly, there was a new album by Nick Cave and The Bad Seeds called *The Good Son*. She had already been seduced by the single 'Ship Song', an absolute beauty, and the album had more of the same. Stirring ballads. She loved it, and it provided the soundtrack for their ice cream preparation. It made her want to make a new compilation tape to document it all.

Daisy transferred some of her ideas for Glastonbury to the car boot sale. She bought some bunting and signage for the van, which had its best clean in years, if not decades. It looked OK, considering its age. They also fashioned a very basic wooden housing for the generator, which was a little noisier than they would have liked. The drawers from the freezer were removed to maximise space, and the ice cream tubs were neatly stacked inside, labelled with black marker pen. There was room to spare.

The one thing they couldn't decide on for their fledgling ice cream company was a name. 'Jack and Daisy's Ice Cream' was too boring. 'Hokey Pokey' was considered, the title of a risqué Richard and Linda Thompson song from the seventies Daisy had grown up with. The song was about a flavour of ice cream that made everyone feel, well, 'frisky'. It wasn't until Daisy was older that she understood all the double-entendres in the lyrics, lines such as 'Feels so good when you put it in your mouth'. Daisy loved the idea of this, but it didn't exactly promote the right image for their ice cream company. They decided they'd make their own Hokey Pokey ice cream instead.

As with most things, the name came about purely by chance, and in a moment of inspiration. The days leading up to the bank holiday, the first days in May, were absolutely sweltering. Some of the hottest on record for the time of year. It was a proper mini-heatwave. This, coupled with the unusually warm spring, caused some of the bright red poppies, native to the area, to spring up almost a month early. The earliest anyone could remember. They were everywhere – at the base of walls by roadsides and in the fields. There was even a feature on the local news about it, which mentioned that the stretch of coastline they lived on was referred to affectionately as 'Poppyland'. The origin of this was some boring old nineteenth-century poet who stumbled upon the area and was struck by all the pretty red flowers. So much so that he'd written a poem about them.

Daisy loved this. Poppyland Ice Cream. It was perfect. Quirky, bright, summery – and connected to the local area. People would love that, locals and tourists alike. This gave her another idea. She'd been thinking of decorating the freezer as it would be on show. Something colourful and exciting. Having tracked down some specialist paints at a craft shop in town, she set to work, using her dormant artistic skills. The main motif was bright red poppies and a logo she had designed. She spent a lot of time on it, sometimes working late into the night. The flat had gone from freezing to sweltering. When Jack came home from work late he'd find her still at it, with all the big windows open. He would hear her singing along to Nick Cave's rich deep voice, and this would make him smile. She'd be covered in paint, shiny with sweat, and wearing nothing but her denim shorts and a bra. One of the sexiest things Jack had ever seen. And as for the freezer, it looked amazing: colourful swirls and ice cream cones and bright red poppies all over it.

Then the big day arrived. Typically, the weather had turned. It wasn't raining, thank God, but it was considerably cooler and nothing like the preceding week. Having barely slept because of nerves and tension, they got up early. There was so much to organise and remember. The van needed to be loaded. Ice cream scoops, two of them. Napkins. Cash box and bags of change. Blackboard. Signs and bunting. A full petrol can for the generator. A stereo. Daisy was going to need a stereo. Logistically, the hardest thing to deal with was the freezer. They roped the boys in to help to move it. They whinged at how early it was, and that they'd both got work later.

At the site, they found somewhere to park – amazed at how many people were already getting set up, and how organised it was. There were parking staff, and you even had to pay for a ticket. It had been billed as a May Day fete, a celebratory event, rather than a standard car boot sale. There was a bouncy castle, a maypole and a whole raft of entertainment planned: jugglers, balloon-blowers, face-painters… And there was music playing over speakers.

'Right, let's get set up,' said Daisy. She was nervous, but

ridiculously excited, her stomach almost giddy with it. She hadn't managed to eat a thing for breakfast. This was one of the most exciting things she had ever done. Jack was plain nervous. He wanted a drink and a spliff, but Daisy had banned him. She said he had to have his wits about him. She was counting on it. 'Can you boys get the generator set up the other side of the van with the big hole in the box facing away from us? And feed the lead through the window, but don't plug it in yet.'

'Yes, ma'am,' said Aitch, saluting her. 'Is she always this bossy?' he joked to Jack, digging him in the ribs. 'Come on, buddy, lighten up! We'll get shit-faced when this is all over. At least you haven't got to work today.' Jack forced a smile.

By nine-thirty, they were all set up and ready to go, except for turning the freezer back on; it needed to settle first – and it would also mean starting the generator up, and Daisy figured it would guzzle petrol.

They all stood back to admire their work. 'Looks amazing,' said Tom. Aitch agreed.

'Thanks,' said Daisy. It did: really professional and organised, but bright and eye-catching too. She was chuffed to bits with it and cursed herself for forgetting to bring her camera. 'And thanks for your help boys. Really.'

'No probs,' said Tom.

'Ay, no worries,' said Aitch. 'Right, I'm gonna go and get me some scran before work.'

'Yeah, me too,' said Tom.

'You *are* coming back later, aren't you?' said Jack. He'd been quiet and was looking pale.

'Yeah, course,' said Aitch. I want my free ice cream for helping you guys out. A double scoop. Just got to decide what flavour… Hey, you know what flavour you should make? Hash brownie. Imagine that? I'll provide my secret recipe – for a cut of the profits, of course…' They all laughed.

'Come on, idiot, let's go,' said Tom, dragging him away.

'What? I think that's a genius idea…'

'What, getting kids stoned?' They were still discussing it as they walked away.

Jack and Daisy looked at each other, shaking their heads, still smiling. Jack was going to miss them. The banter. The moral support. They took his mind off the day ahead.

Meanwhile, the site was getting busier and busier. It pleased Daisy to see how basic some of the other pitches were in comparison, nothing more than a seller sitting in a foldaway chair next to their car. 'OK, let's get that genny fired up,' Daisy said.

It kicked out a fair bit of smoke at first as it hadn't been used properly for a while, but then it settled down. Despite its housing, it sounded loud, but once they were back on the other side of the van it wasn't so bad. And putting the stereo on helped to drown it out. Soon, it just blended into the noise of the place. Especially with the loudspeakers blaring music as well; it sounded like a live local radio show was being broadcast, with a female DJ talking between songs.

*****

By eleven-thirty, they hadn't sold a single ice cream. Not one. Daisy, who had been trying to remain positive and smiley, was getting more and more down. People kept passing by slowly, having a nosey, then carrying on; it was really starting to get to her. She blamed the weather, which was still cloudy and overcast. 'Jesus, surely somebody's got to want a bloody ice cream,' she said to Jack. He was lurking near the van, still dying for a smoke or drink. He just wanted to get the first sale over and done with; he couldn't stand the tension. And he was getting hungry. This was the one thing they had forgotten to bring: their own food and drink. The smell of hot dogs and fried onions was killing him. And in the last quarter of an hour or so, two ice cream vans had turned up about ten minutes apart. Perhaps they knew something Jack and Daisy didn't. Perhaps people didn't eat ice creams before midday? Their appearance worsened Daisy's mood. Competition wasn't going to help sales.

Then Alison turned up. She had agreed to come and help out if it got crazy-busy, as she wasn't working that day. It was nice to see a familiar face, but Daisy felt foolish at their lack of customers, what with their big plans and all the effort they had put in. Alison's face lit up; it had taken a while to spot them. 'Oh my God! This looks amazing. You sold many?'

'Nope. Not one,' said Daisy.

'You're *joking*!'

'Nope.' Daisy looked forlorn, about to cry. Disappointment again.

'Oh, babes. Come here.' She gave Daisy a big hug. 'Well, we're gonna fix that straightaway,' she said. 'I'm going to order one right now. I've been dying to. Maybe that will encourage others. What have we got?' She consulted the list of flavours taped to the table.

'They're on the blackboard too,' Daisy said.

'Oh yes, cool. Erm…'

'You know I'm not letting you buy one,' said Daisy. 'It's free for you.'

'Don't be silly,' said Alison. 'That defeats the object.'

'Nope. We wouldn't dream of it.'

'No, I insist.' This went on, back and forth, but in the end Alison relented. She had, as Daisy pointed out, offered to work for them for free.

She decided on chocolate brownie flavour. Immediately Daisy got a little thrill in her stomach. 'OK, baby, this is your big moment. One chocolate brownie please for the young lady here.'

Jack had already got the door open. 'Chocolate brownie, chocolate brownie…' He looked up and down the tubs, feeling under pressure. This wasn't helping him to read the writing on them.

'Bottom shelf, sweetheart, first row,' Daisy said, spotting it. She shared a glance with Alison and they giggled. He passed the tub to Daisy. 'You're meant to be dishing it out, remember? I'm taking the orders and sorting the money.'

'Oh, yeah.' He took the tub back, put it on the table and peeled off the lid. Daisy passed him a cone. The ice cream was harder than expected, as the freezer had been on full and hadn't been opened for hours It was a real pain to scoop, but they figured this would get better as the day went on. Jack fought with the ice cream and eventually managed to fashion a decent scoop out of it, plonking it on the cone. He passed it to Daisy and mopped his brow. It had made him sweat. Daisy wrapped the cone in a napkin and passed it to Alison. 'There you go.'

'Mmm, lovely, thank you.'

Jack went to put the tub back. He'd left the freezer door open. Perhaps that wasn't a bad thing; he didn't want to have to struggle like that again. But he had to remember to close it when they were busy. It had all been good practice. But they wanted more. Alison's ordering an ice cream and the act of serving it had been like a shot of adrenaline, a little ray of hope that things would get better. It felt good.

'Oh God, this is amazing,' said Alison, licking away.

It was good timing. A couple with a small child walked by and stopped.

'Do you want an ice cream, honey?' the lady said to the child. The girl nodded, shyly.

'What flavour, darling?' The little girl thought for a moment, then pointed to Alison's ice cream, again shyly and sweetly. They all laughed.

'Chocolate brownie,' Alison said. 'It's incredible.'

'One chocolate brownie flavour, please. Do you want one?' She turned to her husband.

'No, I'm fine.'

'Oh gosh, they all sound so good. And unusual. Give me a lemon curd and ginger as well, please. Sounds delicious.'

Daisy got that thrill-ripple of excitement in her belly again. 'Coming right up. That's two pounds, please.'

Jack set about his task, determined to get it right, and done as quickly as possible. He was so glad they had already served Alison: it had settled his nerves a little and helped him to perfect his routine. He got the ice creams dished out pretty sharpish, remembering to close the freezer door.

'What do you say?' the lady said to the girl, bending down.

'Thank you.'

'Aah, you're welcome, sweetie,' said Daisy.

'Thank you.' The family walked away, licking their ice creams.

Daisy let out a little squeal. Their first customers. Their first sale. It had been such a buzz. Daisy gave Jack a quick peck on the cheek. 'Thanks, Alison,' she said. 'That was your doing, I reckon.'

'Don't be silly,' Alison said. 'Soon they'll be queuing up. Hey, you're good with the customers too.'

A couple of hours passed, and they still weren't queuing up; just dribs and drabs, every fifteen minutes or so. But it was something at least, albeit nowhere near what they needed or wanted. They'd only taken fifteen pounds all day, and they'd spent some of that on food and drink for themselves: Alison had gone to grab something for them. The maddening thing was that there were so many people about. The place was teeming. What was even more galling was that quite a few families were walking past with Mr Whippy ice creams. Perhaps the other vans were in a better spot, or perhaps people didn't like normal ice cream. But they did. Daisy knew they did. The parlours in town always had queues.

Then the rest of the gang turned up: Aitch, Tom and Jeanie.

It had been an unusually quiet lunch at work, as there was lots of other stuff going on in the area. It wasn't exactly seafront weather either. 'Christ, cheer up, you lot. You ain't gonna sell many ice creams with those faces,' Tom said. 'Hi, gorgeous.' He gave Alison a kiss. They all exchanged hellos. 'What's going on then? Not a lot, I'm guessing?'

'It's been a bit quiet,' said Alison, trying to be tactful. But it was getting to her too. She so wanted it to work out for Daisy and Jack, and it was fun serving the ice creams. She'd had a go whilst Daisy was scoffing her cheese cob.

'Really? It's heaving here.'

'You should be serving Mr Whippy,' said Aitch. 'They're queuing up for that.'

'Aitch!' said Alison.

'Yeah, thanks, Aitch. That makes us feel a whole lot better,' said Daisy.

'Ha ha! Only joking.' Jack reckoned Aitch was stoned. Probably just had a post-shift spliff. And Tom. It made him jealous. 'We can't have this, though. We need something to drum up business…' Aitch looked round.

Just then, two things happened at once. The sun finally came out and a group of local lads the Cromer lot had known from school walked past. Four of them. 'Ice cream, boys?' Jeanie said, catching their attention.

'Ah, 'ey up, you lot,' one of them said. 'Aitch,' he nodded. 'How you doing, buddy?'

'Sound, sound.' Aitch had suddenly developed a Manc accent. These lads knew him, a lot of people did. Fellow baggies. Aitch 'sorted them out'.

'What's going on 'ere, then?' The lads strolled over and surveyed the set-up. 'Nice.' They, too, seemed to have developed the Manc swagger. There was some shaking of hands and fist pumps. Daisy smiled, hoping for a sale. Jack skulked in the background, feeling shy and foolish. Selling ice creams wasn't exactly cool, and he didn't know the lads. 'You going to see the Roses?' one of them asked Aitch.

'Ay. Can't wait.'

'Yeah, it's gonna be a mad one.'

'You gonna buy an ice cream or not?' Jeanie said, slipping behind the table and taking off her denim jacket, chucking it under the table. Underneath, she was wearing skimpy shorts and a tight T-shirt. Daisy rolled her eyes.

'I am if you're gonna keep taking your clothes off,' the lads' apparent leader said. All his mates laughed.

'Order one and we'll see,' she said, leaning on the table. Daisy couldn't believe this was happening. It was turning into a scene from bloody *Grease*. All the lad needed to do was get out a comb and run it through his hair.

There was a brief silence whilst the two of them eyeballed each other, and the lad considered if Jeanie was being serious or not. 'What flavours ya got?' he said finally.

'They're all on the board there.' She nodded her head in its direction.

'Ice cream, lads?' he said to the group, the spell broken.

'Chocolate brownie's good,' said Alison. 'I can vouch for that.'

The lads all shifted to consult the board. 'Ay, go on then. Chocolate brownie sounds good to me.'

'Make that two,' another lad said. Jack couldn't believe it, and immediately cracked open the freezer.

'I'll have the strawberry,' another one said.

'White chocolate and raspberry ripple for me,' said the fourth. 'Sounds wicked.'

It was the first time four ice creams had been sold in one go all day. As they were dished up, Alison mucking in too, a family of five stopped by to look. Seeing the ice creams, they made appreciative noises and consulted the board. 'Mmm, local ice creams... Sorry, what's that one?' a lady asked, pointing to one of the lads. 'Looks amazing.'

'White chocolate and raspberry ripple,' said Daisy, finding her voice again. Jeanie had briefly knocked her confidence. She had almost forgotten for a second this was her and Jack's gig. 'All home-made.'

'Mmm, sounds delicious. I'll have one of those please. Kiddies?' All five ordered ice creams.

The lads disappeared, licking their ice creams. And after being served, so did the family. They all looked at each other and laughed. They'd nearly doubled their day's take in the space of five minutes. 'It's a rush, isn't it?' said Alison. They all agreed.

'Now that, my friends, is where business creates business – as my old man always says,' said Aitch. They all looked at him. 'It's true. People see a queue and get interested, want a piece of the action. Look at the chippies in town. Which is the busiest one? The one on Garden Street that you have to practically queue to Sheringham for in high season. Seriously, the idiots'll queue for hours when they could just order from the one over the road. But they don't. It's crazy. They figure the busiest one is the best. Must drive the other chippies mad.'

Everyone thought about this for a second. It made total sense It was probably the most sensible thing he had ever said. 'So, with that in mind,' he continued, 'Jeanie, get your arse back out front and keep your jacket off. I'll be back in a minute. I've got another idea.' He pulled out his car keys.

'But it's cold when the clouds go in,' said Jeanie.

'Tough. And if you see any more lads, reel 'em in. But only lads – don't go harassing the general public. And dirty old men. Lick an ice cream suggestively or something.'

Daisy had heard enough. 'For Christ's sake,' she said. 'What is this, a brothel?'

Everyone burst out laughing, but she was serious.

'Hey, it worked, didn't it?' said Aitch, beginning to jog off. 'Back in a minute.'

Jeanie took her place out front again, standing with her hand on her hip. Daisy tutted. She looked like a teenage hooker on a street corner, trying to drum up business. This really wasn't how Daisy had planned on promoting her business. The funny thing was, Jeanie didn't seem to mind being used as a sex object: she just enjoyed the attention. Daisy looked at Jack to make sure he wasn't looking at her arse. He'd better not be. He quickly set about wiping down his freezer door handle. It had chocolate ice cream smudges on it.

It wasn't long at all before Jeanie spotted some more victims – or customers – there were so many people milling past. Again, these were kids she knew from school. Girls as well this time. 'Hi, guys. Fancy an ice cream?' she said, gesturing with both hands to the stand. She was brazen, Daisy would give her that.

'Oh, hi, Jeanie. How you doing?'

'OK, thanks.'

'Hi, Ali. Didn't see you there.'

'Hey, Dawn.'

'Mmm, what we got here then? Is this your guy's business?' She came over to the table.

'No, it's Daisy's,' Alison was quick to point out. 'Daisy's and Jack's.' They smiled and said hello.

'You on commission or something, Jeanie?' one of the boys asked her. They were hanging around her, what was that expression, thought Daisy, like flies round…?

'Something like that. So… What yer having?'

'Dunno. We haven't looked yet.'

'The flavours are on the board,' she nodded. 'And on the table. All home-made.' She'd heard Daisy say it.

'Really?' said the girl, Dawn. She studied the list. The rest of the group moved over to the board. Lo and behold, another group, four pensioners this time, hovering to see what all the fuss was about, joined them.

Both groups ordered ice creams. Whilst they were being served, Aitch returned. He was clutching two sheets of cardboard, like flattened boxes, some string and what looked like three soft juggling balls. God only knew where he had got the stuff from.

'Bloomin' 'ell,' he said, seeing the queue and jinking behind the table. 'Business is looking up. All right if I nip behind the van?' he said.

They were trying to concentrate and no one answered. 'Cheers!' He disappeared, then popped back. 'Sorry, folks.' He leant over the table and grabbed Daisy's marker pen, which she had brought to cross through ice cream flavours when they ran out. Needless to say, it hadn't been used yet. But if the chocolate brownie continued to sell so well…

'Aitch, mind out the way,' said Alison, nudging him with her hip. She was helping Jack on ice cream scoop duty; that was the time-consuming bit.

'I've got to see what he's up to,' said Tom, heading for the back of the van. He was the only one who felt like a bit of a spare part. He didn't quite have the guts to nip behind the table and muck in – and as he'd had a smoke he'd probably mess things up. He'd got to hand it to his buddy Jackeroo, though; he didn't think he had it in him.

Ten minutes later, there was some giggling from behind, and both Tom and Aitch reappeared. Aitch was sporting a makeshift sandwich board, tied with string and fashioned out of his two sheets of cardboard. On the front and back in large black lettering were the words **I SCREAM**. As he shimmied sideways, looking like a thrown-together Knave of Hearts from *Alice in Wonderland* and clutching his juggling balls, he said, 'What? That's how you spell it, innit?'

Daisy looked up briefly from what she was doing, mouth agape, but too busy to say anything or to stop him. She didn't know what to say anyway. She was perturbed at the prospect of their business being turned into a laughing stock, and also trying not to burst out laughing. The few customers they had seemed to think it was hilarious. 'Oh, that's brilliant,' one of them said. And it was. This helped Daisy to keep her mouth shut to see how it panned out.

Aitch proceeded to set himself up out front, off to the right of the stall, opposite Jeanie, who was standing to the left. The two apparent 'fronts' of the business: Beauty and the Beast. Then, to everyone's surprise and amazement, Aitch began to juggle. He was a dab hand at it, the possessor of a hidden talent. 'Roll up, Roll up. Come and get your ice cream,' he called, not breaking his throw for a second. 'Norfolk ice creams, all home-made!' People stopped to watch and stare; to point at the 'I scream' slogan in stitches. He was a hit. Some people even took photos. But it worked. Attention on Aitch turned into attention on the ice creams. Jeanie pouted and posed. Aitch juggled and hollered. A crowd formed and the punters rolled in. It went crazy. A large queue formed.

'Tom, you're gonna have to help,' called Alison. He was skulking round the back of the van, rolling a fag 'Tom!' He only just heard her over the generator, and popped his head round with a roll-up hanging from his mouth. Then he saw the sea of people.

'Holy shit,' he said, gulping and ditching his fag.

'Unpack the cones, and get them lined up and ready. It's taking too long to get them out,' said Alison.

'I'm gonna need more change. I'm nearly out. This is crazy! Everyone's paying with fivers,' said Daisy.

'What do you want me to do?' said Alison.

'I don't know. Ask Jeanie. She's bloody doing nothing. Get her to go to another stall and see if they'll give us some change or something – a bag of fifties or pounds. Here.' She handed Alison some notes. The cash box was filling up with them. 'Tell her to get twenty quids' worth if she can.'

'You OK, buddy?' Tom said to Jack, whose face was as white as a sheet. 'Jackeroo?'

Jack turned to look at him, sweating, and looking as if he'd been woken from a trance. His eyes were wide and wired. He'd been in the zone, as they called it at work. It was the only way to stave off the panic and blot out all the people and the stress. Busy services in the kitchen had stood him in good stead: he would never have survived otherwise. Not for a second. He nodded briefly, then carried on.

There was another moment of panic when the generator ran out of fuel, and only Daisy knew how to put more petrol in it. This was the worst part of the whole day, worse than not selling anything and waiting around. The stall was rammed, and they couldn't leave the generator off, not with the freezer door being opened constantly. Everything went noticeably quieter without the background noise. 'Sorry folks,' Daisy apologised. 'Back in a second.' She dealt with the problem swiftly and they carried on. Almost like a pitstop.

Slowly but surely, they started to run out of ice cream flavours. Chocolate brownie was the first to go. Daisy did her best to keep people informed, but as they were already deciding their flavours whilst queuing up, there were a few disappointed customers. She began to call out to Aitch when a flavour had gone, so he could rub it off the blackboard. This only appeared to add to the drama, and to the buzz and appeal of the stall: 'White chocolate gone!' 'Strawberry gone!'

Then there was possibly the most remarkable moment on that remarkable day. A lady who had appeared with a microphone and a tape recorder, accompanied by a photographer, was talking to Jeanie. Daisy tried to listen to what was being said, but only got snatches. When things finally died down a bit, she noticed Jeanie pointing at her, and the lady nodding then coming over. 'Hi. Daisy, is it?' She held out her hand.

'Erm, yes.'

'Rachael Sumner, BBC Radio Norfolk.'

'Oh gosh, hi,' said Daisy, blushing.

'Hi. What a fab set-up you've got here. Amazing. And your friend there, Jeanie, says this is literally your first time selling? This is all new to you, right?'

'Yeah,' said Daisy. She felt tongue-tied.

'Wow. That's remarkable. We couldn't believe the crowds earlier. People were even talking about you guys and your ice creams over at the radio tent. And your resident juggler,' she laughed. 'You must be thrilled.'

'Erm, yes. It's been amazing,' Daisy giggled.

'And this is Jack, is it?' she said pointing. 'Your partner in crime – and *partner*, from what I hear? The chef in this operation?'

'Erm, yes,' Daisy blushed.

'Can we get a word with Jack too?'

'Oh, I don't know, he's pretty shy,' said Daisy. She gestured for him to come over, but he shook his head. 'Sorry,' she said.

'Now listen, Daisy. Would you mind if we do a little interview live on air? It would make such a great story. And it would appear in the local papers, too…'

'Oh gosh, I don't know,' said Daisy. It was so daunting. And so much for keeping a low profile.

'It would be great if you could. Think what it could do for your business. Poppyland, isn't it? Love the name, by the way. We can take a picture of you guys for the paper, the stall and everything, even the juggler.'

'Oh, he might not always be here,' Daisy laughed.

'What?' cried Aitch, overhearing.

'And what's your name, young man?'

'Aitch. Well, Harry. But everyone calls me Aitch.'

'And would you like to be on the radio and in the papers, Aitch?'

'Absolutely.'

She looked at Daisy. 'Come on,' Aitch said.

Alison joined in. It would be fun to get their picture in the paper, a memento of the day.

'I'll keep on serving,' said Tom. He was getting used to it now; it wasn't that much different from being a waiter.

'Oh, go on then…' Daisy succumbed, and they all cheered.

'Fab! Now don't worry. There's no need to be nervous. I'll just ask you questions like I just did. Just think of that as a dummy run. You'll be fine. And no swearing, kids. Remember. We're going live on the radio and you'll get me shot!'

The interview began. It was strange because it could be heard on the public address system of the fete as it was happening. Quite unnerving.

'And I'm here with Daisy…' she pointed the microphone at Daisy for her surname.

Under pressure and nerves, it just came out. 'Jones.' Oops, she thought.

'Daisy Jones and her boyfriend Jack, two local young entrepreneurs who have set up a home-made ice cream business…' The interview went on.

Unable to drag Jack to the microphone, the interviewer telling everyone he was 'a bit shy', Aitch was roped into talking. He was a natural, explaining the wording on his costume. He said it had just come to him, and that being dyslexic had helped. The interviewer laughed awkwardly, not knowing if he was being serious or not. She changed the subject by asking if he thought he would be able to juggle live on air and still talk. A crowd had gathered round, and they all egged him on. Aitch pulled it off famously and the crowd cheered. Then even Jeanie took her turn at the microphone for her five minutes of fame.

Finally it was over, and they had their photograph taken. The whole gang, including Tom. They all lined up, Jeanie to the left, Aitch to the right and the rest of them behind the table. Aitch was asked to juggle again for the photo. They looked a motley crew, but it was a fitting souvenir for a truly unforgettable day.

CHAPTER 13
Taking Stock

D espite being absolutely shattered by the physical and mental strain of the day, the gang got shit-faced to celebrate, true to Aitch's prophecy. Jack and Daisy supplied the refreshments, including a cheap bottle of fizz and an ice cream apiece – something everybody had been hankering after. It was the least they could do after the contribution everyone had made. The buzz and glow lasted for days, longer than their hangovers the next morning. The local radio station's involvement and promised newspaper article were the icing on the cake.

The following day, Jack and Daisy took stock. This brought its own satisfaction and rewards. Daisy hadn't envisaged how much she would enjoy this part of it, the analysing of the figures. They'd sold a grand total of a hundred and sixty-five ice creams at a pound a pop. A hundred and sixty-five quid! They'd paid for the freezer already. And that was even though the day hadn't got going very early. Judging by what was left in the freezer, they estimated they had used around two-thirds of their stock, and the freezer had only been about two-thirds full.

Daisy was certainly no maths whizz – she had only just scraped a C in her GCSE – nor was she a businesswoman. But by her scribbled estimations, she reckoned they could hold nearly four hundred quid's worth of ice cream. The only way to know for sure would be to calculate exactly how many scoops you got from each tub (why hadn't they done that?) and how many tubs fitted in the freezer. They needed more tubs, that was for sure. It was interesting analysing what flavours had sold too. The chocolate brownie had been the runaway winner, followed by the strawberry, then white chocolate and raspberry ripple. Surprisingly, they hadn't sold much vanilla at all.

This left a lot to think about for next time. It was all so exciting. Daisy had never felt like this about anything before – except her music and Jack. She thought her dad would be so proud of her. It killed her that he couldn't see it.

*****

The newspaper article was a peach. It appeared in the *North Norfolk News* on the Thursday following the bank holiday. Despite everyone's own personal embarrassments at how they looked in the photo, they all agreed it was a nice shot that really captured the day. The article was the talk of the Crab's Claw. The restaurant got a mention, what with all the gang working there. "Local entrepreneurs', eh?' said Hilary. That line got the most comments and ribbing. Jack was called a 'dark horse' by a few of the other chefs. Being a private person, none of them had a clue what he got up to in his spare time.

Baz was impressed, although he did say, 'You better not have been nicking my fucking recipes.' Jack kept quiet. Most of the gang had never had their picture in the paper before, and they all bought extra copies for family members and for posterity. Daisy got one for her mum. A copy of the paper was kept on show out front at the restaurant; this kind of publicity was good for business. The article was also stuck up on the corkboard in the changing room.

Another topic of conversation in the kitchen was Jack's impending DNA test. He hadn't been able to keep it entirely to himself. He'd had to ask Chef for the day off and word had spread. Chef had softened his stance towards Jack of late. He couldn't knock the lad's work ethic, even if he was alarmingly wet behind the ears sometimes. And he was able to pick things up quickly. Jack had been moved back into the main kitchen again, his 'punishment' in the pastry section apparently over. It was a shame: he had enjoyed the work and learned heaps. But it was back to his old section again, which was a bit stressful at first. The timing of cooking and preparing hot food to order, table after table. But there was talk that once he had mastered the garnish section, he would be having a go on larder next: the starter section.

The day of the DNA test arrived, and Jack and Daisy made the trip to the specialist clinic in Norwich. 'We can have a bit of a wander round for a change when we're done,' said Daisy. 'It's supposed to be lovely.' This didn't help Jack's mood. He didn't want to 'wander round the town'. He just wanted to get the thing done and get back home.

The clinic was on the outskirts of the city and a bugger to find. Jack's map reading skills were more or less useless, so they arrived late. By then, Daisy was feeling stressed too. They'd waited so long for this and it was of the utmost importance. But she tried to push her own anxieties to the side for Jack's sake, dealing with the parking and finding the right entrance to the building. Jack was a mess. Barely speaking. He'd withdrawn into himself, just as he used to. To blot it all out. It was his way of dealing with a frightening new environment and situation. The building. The smell. The people in uniforms. The squeak of their shoes. The endless corridors. But most of all, what was about to be done to him.

Daisy showed the appointment letter at reception and they were given directions to the correct department. There they were met by a nurse and guided to a waiting room to sit and wait. The nurse was black. Jack had never seen a black person up close before, or been spoken to by one. He was scared, but fascinated. She was plump. The whites of her eyes looked yellowish, but her teeth looked very white. Her skin was shiny and pimpled. Her hair was impossibly frizzy.

After about ten minutes, he was called in. 'Am I OK to come in with him?' Daisy asked. 'He's a bit nervous.'

'Yeah, of course. Bless him,' the nurse said. 'Follow me. There's no need to be nervous. It's pretty routine and painless,' she addressed Jack over her shoulder. 'You never had blood taken before, honey?' Jack shook his head. He felt sick and the black spot had made an opportune appearance.

'No, he hasn't,' said Daisy.

They were shown into a small cubicle with a bed, two chairs and a stand with medical paraphernalia on it. A female Indian doctor in a white coat was waiting for them. Jack pulled up abruptly at the sight of it all. The doctor smiled and said hello. Daisy said hello back. 'We've got a nervous one,' the nurse said.

'Ah, I see… Well, nothing to be nervous about, I assure you,' the doctor said. 'It's very routine. Take a seat, Jack, and I'll talk you through it.' Daisy pushed Jack towards the spare seat, then stood behind him. 'Firstly, have you got some identification for me?'

'We've got these,' Daisy said. She handed over Jack's national insurance card, a bill with their address on it and a copy of Jack's new identity deal that had been set out by Haslam. 'We don't have a birth certificate or passport, I'm afraid. But he's getting a passport soon.' Jack nodded. 'It says so in the letter there. And Detective Haslam – of Nottinghamshire Constabulary – can vouch for Jack. He sorted it all out. He's a chief inspector there. We can give you his number…'

'No, no. These should be fine…' The doctor examined the documents. 'I've been reading through the notes and have been in touch with the inspector. It is an unusual case, but these will suffice for now.' She looked up and smiled reassuringly. 'OK, Jack. Today, we're going to take a blood sample from you. Two samples actually. We locate a vein, usually in the arm, here', she placed two brown fingers on the crook of her elbow, 'and take two small vials' worth, that's all – so it's not like when you're giving blood. You'll just feel a small prick and a bit of discomfort as the needle goes in, but that's it. It's all over in a matter of minutes. Is that all OK?'

Jack gulped and nodded. 'Good boy,' she said, getting up. 'Right, if you could wheel your chair a bit closer to the bed for me, please, then roll up your T-shirt sleeve a bit further and rest your arm on the bed, we can begin.'

It was nowhere near as bad as Jack had expected. Uncomfortable, yes. And scary and slightly painful as the needle went in – the doctor had tried to distract him from it, commenting on how good and prominent his veins were. But overall, it was a strange sensation and experience; especially seeing the blood, his bright, dark-red blood, filling the little tubes. And then it was over. The needle was removed from his arm and he was told to keep the swab of cotton gauze pressed tightly against his vein for a while.

It was good to be back outside in the fresh air. But Jack was still quiet. 'You OK, baby? It's over now.' Daisy gave him a kiss. 'You did really well. So brave. I was cringing at the needle going in. Ugh! It looked horrible.'

'It was OK,' Jack said, trying to sound brave. But he still felt a bit traumatised by the whole thing, a bit violated. 'Can we get a drink?'

They headed into Norwich city centre and found a car park. Open-air rather than a multi-storey, for Jack's sake. He'd already been through enough trauma without reliving that one.

Norwich reminded Daisy of York, which she'd been to on a school trip. There were so many different things to see. Waterways, canals and bridges. Pastel-coloured houses. An ancient quarter. Cobbled streets, lined with timbered buildings. Then, to top it all off, a castle and a huge and stunning cathedral. They'd never seen anything like it. Daisy rued not having her camera with her.

On one of the many cobbled streets, they stumbled across an intriguing-looking pub, one of the oldest in the city, called The Murderers. The pub sign had a fantastic illustration on it of two sinister men in dark, old-fashioned capes and hats, both carrying weapons dripping with blood. Jack and Daisy couldn't resist, and they ducked inside for a much-needed pint. The welcoming landlord filled them in on the pub's gruesome history and how it got its name.

Two pints later, Jack felt a whole lot better. They explored the town further, finally discovering the huge market square. The sun was out and something caught Daisy's eye. It was an ice cream seller, but not in an ice cream van; he had a cart instead, small and compact. A man wearing a boater and a white apron was behind it, busily serving a long queue. 'Look, Jack. An ice cream cart. Let's go and check it out.'

They wandered over and loitered nearby, so they could watch. The cart was a box on wheels with an attractive roof attached. A logo was painted across the front: 'Toni's Ices'. Why were they always called Toni or Carlo? Next to it was a blackboard with the flavours on it, but more like an A-board with legs. It looked great. The whole set-up was really eye-catching; slick and professional. It made their operation look clumsy and amateur, Daisy thought – and a lot of hassle. Not to mention the noise. Where was this guy's generator? And how were the ice creams served? How did he store them? How did he get the cart there? Daisy needed these questions answered. Feeling brazen after a couple of drinks, she decided she was going to. 'Come on, let's get an ice cream.'

'I don't want an ice cream,' said Jack. He wanted another drink.

'Neither do I, but I want to see this thing close up, how it works. It's amazing. Don't you think?'

'Yeah, it looks good.'

They joined the queue. As they waited, they looked at the cart more closely. The serving counter was made of sliding glass, like the ice cream freezers in shops. Underneath was a row of ice cream tubs. It reminded Jack of the freezer counter at the restaurant. Next to the glass were three purpose-built holes that the cones sat in, stacked up. Everything was to hand. It was so much quicker. So much easier. There was no toing and froing. No messy removing of lids.

They reached the front of the queue. 'Yes, young lady, what can I get you?' The man had a strong Italian accent.

'Erm … I'll try the banana, please.' They hadn't tried making a banana ice cream. It sounded nice.

'One banana coming right up.'

Daisy looked behind her. No one else had joined the queue. This was her chance. 'Erm, excuse me, how much does this ice cream cart hold? In litres.'

The man paused, surprised, his eyes narrowing slightly. 'You in the game?'

'What game?'

'The ice cream game. *Gelato,*' he added with a flourish.

'Kind of,' said Daisy, blushing. 'We're just starting out.'

'You local?' The man narrowed his eyes further.

'No. Well, not really. Cromer.'

'Ah,' The man appeared to relax. 'This baby holds ninety-eight litres. Underneath here is your back-up.' He patted the side of the cart. 'Plenty of room.'

Ah, thought Daisy. Clever. So the back-up tubs were stored underneath. 'Ninety-eight litres,' she said. The booze had bamboozled her a bit, but she reckoned their freezer was eighty-five litres. This was bigger, although it didn't look it. 'And how do you power it?'

'Battery. Twelve volts. You charge it up in advance and it runs all day – or for ten hours at least.'

'Wow,' said Daisy. 'And how do you get it here, into town, I mean.'

'You can stick it in a trailer or in the back of a van. Or you can tow it. Look, a tow bar.' He pointed. 'I got it converted. Just make sure you park your vehicle somewhere you don't have to pay,' he added.

'And how much does it cost for one of these things – if you don't mind me asking?'

'A lot of questions, young lady… I lease this one; it's about twenty quid a month. But you *can* buy them … not cheap.' He passed her an ice cream. 'And for the young man?'

'Jack?' Daisy turned to him.

'No, I'm fine, thanks.'

'That will be one-ten, then, thank you kindly.'

'No, thank *you*.' She handed over the money. 'Thank you so much for your help.'

'You are welcome, Signorina. Good luck. And enjoy your ice.'

They walked away. Daisy's brain was whirling. 'This is it, Jack. This is the future,' she said. 'An ice cream cart. What do you reckon? No more lugging a generator around. No more noise and petrol. We could get our logo written on the front professionally. Poppyland Ice Cream. Imagine! Easy to serve. Easy to transport. I reckon one of those would fit in the back of the van, easy. If not, we'll tow it. Imagine the car boot sales. We'd just pull up and set the cart up in front of the van…'

Jack's thoughts were racing, too. It made sense. It was impressive. And so much easier to serve the ice creams from. That's what he liked the most. 'But what about the cost?' he said. 'He said those things weren't cheap. We've already spent a fortune. And what about the freezer we've already bought?'

'It's all just start-up costs. An investment.'

'You keep saying that.'

'But it's true. Once we're up and running, that's it. This would streamline our business. Take us onto a whole new level. A professional one. And as for the freezer, we've already got our money back for it, and it can just be used as our home freezer. We need one anyway. The poxy one at the top of the fridge is useless; we're always having to go to the shops. Or we could use it as a back-up freezer. We'd need one anyway for storing the ice creams.'

Jack thought for a moment. 'We could always – what was it he said? – lease one. Pay for it monthly.'

'We're not leasing one. Never lease *anything*. Dad always said that.'

'But where would we get the money from?'

'We've got savings still. Some anyway. And I bet Mum would lend us the money if we could convince her how serious we were. We'd soon be able to pay her back. Look how much we made on that first day. And don't forget, you could be coming into some money yourself soon. Lots of it.' Jack looked at her. 'What?' she said. 'Sorry, but it's true. You could be.'

'I wouldn't count on it.' He still refused to acknowledge this might happen. Nothing good ever happened to him. Except Daisy.

'Shit!' Daisy said. Her ice cream was melting and dripping onto her hand. She hadn't even touched it. She gave it a good giraffe-like lick and then her fingers. 'Hmm… not sure about that one. What do you reckon?' She offered it to Jack.

He tried it. 'It tastes too fake. Like banana flavouring, rather than real banana.' He took another lick, then handed it back, unimpressed.

Daisy took another lick. 'Yeah, know what you mean.'

'And it needs something else. Chocolate. That would work. Chocolate ripple running through it.'

'Oh, God. Yes! Now, that *would* work. Banana and chocolate

ripple. We need to remember that one. You're so good at this, Jack. The best. See? That's why we deserve that cart.'

They discussed the possible purchase all the way back home. Daisy, as always, was so excited she wanted to dive straight in. But Jack was more reserved. It was strange how he was the more sensible one when it came to things like this. He didn't like risks; they never worked out for him. By the time they'd got back, he'd managed to convince Daisy they should wait a while. See how their next few sales days went first. How much ice cream they sold and how much money they took. Their first day might have been a one-off. And they could save more money towards a cart this way. 'Let's not try to walk before we can run,' he added.

Daisy burst out laughing. '*Run* before we can *walk*. You nana,' she said.

'Oh,' said Jack, blushing.' He'd got the expression from Chef at work. 'Well, you know what I mean.'

'I do. God, I love you.' She leant across and kissed him. They'd just pulled up at home. And now the alcohol was wearing off a bit, she begrudgingly accepted he was right. An ice cream cart was a great idea. Undoubtedly the way forward. A natural progression for their business if things went right. But, yes, let's try not to walk before we can run… She chuckled again. Then she looked up at the flat and something occurred to her. Where would they store an ice cream cart?

Chapter 14

Madness

The next morning, Daisy was leaving the flat when a man collared her. He was in his early thirties by the look of it. She'd noticed him loitering when she'd opened the front door, and thought he was waiting to cross the road. 'Excuse me, Miss. Daisy isn't it? Daisy Jones?'

This took Daisy by surprise and she took a step back. She'd been lost in her own thoughts and was running late. Jack was already at work. 'Er, who wants to know?' she said, looking the man up and down. He was wearing a lightweight beige sports jacket, a shirt and trousers. Clean-shaven with glasses.

'I saw your article in the *North Norfolk News*, Poppyland Ice Cream, right? Love the name!'

'Oh. Yes,' said Daisy, brightening. 'Yes, I'm Daisy.'

'Thought so.' Then the man's face changed. 'Daisy, have you got any comment on the recent suicide of Jeremiah Peasgood, former proprietor of Peasgood's Meats, Nottingham? You knew the man, didn't you? You were involved in the case?'

Daisy's blood ran cold. She hadn't been expecting this. 'I've nothing to say about that,' she said, beginning to walk off. But the man followed her.

'What about your boyfriend, Jack? Will he have anything to say?'

'Get lost!'

The man kept up with her. 'He was the mystery boy, wasn't he? He worked for Peasgood.'

Daisy stopped and turned on him. 'Where are you from? I'll report you for harassment.'

A couple walking their dog on the other side of the street looked over at the commotion. The man backed off. 'Gerald Belcher, *Cromer Herald*. Here, take my card.'

'I don't want your card. Belch off.' She knocked it out of his hand and walked away again. Quickly. This time the man didn't follow. He crouched to pick up his card.

'It's a story that needs to be told, Daisy,' he called. 'There's money in it for you if you change your mind. For both of you.'

When Daisy got to work, she found Jack straightaway and asked to have a word with him in private. Fortunately, Chef wasn't there. 'Go on,' nodded Whizz.

They went through the fly strip and into the corridor. As soon as they were out of sight, Daisy flopped against Jack's chef's jacket and cried. For some reason, the incident had got to her. It had made her feel vulnerable again. Exposed. She thought they'd finally put all the Peasgood stuff behind them. This had stirred it all up again. Reminded her of those men. Why couldn't people just leave them alone?

'What is it?' said Jack, stroking her hair. 'What's wrong? What's happened?' He feared the worst again. Grandma dying.

'They've found us, Jack.'

'Who? Who's found us?' Suddenly a penny dropped. The wrong one. 'Not Peasgood's men?' He suddenly panicked and jolted her away from him to look at her properly. 'They didn't hurt you? Tell me they didn't touch you.'

'No. No, not Peasgood's men. I'm fine. Reporters. *About* Peasgood.'

'You're joking.' But he was somewhat relieved. 'How?' he said as it sank in. 'And how many?'

'Just one, but he was a creep. He tricked me, the bastard, talking about ice creams, and then he wouldn't leave me alone.' This made Jack's anger boil again. 'It must have been the article, the newspaper article . He'd seen it. It said we all worked here, didn't it? Someone must have said something.'

'Not one of the gang. None of them would have said anything…'

'No, they wouldn't. But maybe someone else out front. That guy might have been hanging around here, asking questions.'

'Well, at least it was just one. Hopefully he'll go away.'

'Yeah, for now. But what if another one turns up? And then another? They're like bloody parasites.'

'I know. But the main thing for now is you're safe. I thought someone had hurt you. I thought it was them again.' He held her close.

His jacket smelt. 'I'm going to stink of chips,' she said. But it felt nice. She was calming down. It had just been a shock, a bolt from the blue. She already regretted losing her temper with the guy and flipping out. What if it affected their ice cream business locally? But so would being associated with all that business back home. Things had been going so nicely as well. It seemed that trouble – or more specifically their past – never seemed very far away. Why had she agreed to do that article? And why had she said her name?

When they got home after lunch service, the man's card was on their porch floor. He must have posted it through. 'Cheeky bastard,' said Daisy. On the back, handwritten, it said, 'In case you change your mind. Both of you'.

*****

The spring bank holiday rolled round. The next ice cream day. Jack and Daisy had been busy in the run-up again, with another trip to the cash and carry and making all the ice creams. It was a lot of work on top of their normal jobs, especially for Jack. But under his instruction, Daisy had been learning how to make ice cream too. After a few early (and costly) disasters involving overcooked mixes, she was now able to pitch in. They'd come up with some new flavours that they were really excited about – a cappuccino one that looked and tasted amazing – coffee and vanilla flavours, gently folded with a sweet coffee syrup, and Jack's banana and chocolate ripple idea. This was the part they enjoyed the most: coming up with new and interesting flavours, then producing them.

They'd ummed and aahed whether to do the car boot sale again. It looked as though it was going to be a sunny bank holiday for once, so, would they be better nearer the beaches? Or even in one of the busy car parks in town? It was a big decision. Get it wrong, and it could dent their day's take considerably. In the end, they opted for the car boot sale. Stick to what they knew. It was a good site to cut their teeth at, and Daisy had come to the conclusion there was no immediate rush. They didn't have to make a million overnight. They didn't rely on their ice cream takings to pay their rent, so it was just a bonus. And none of the gang were able to help them out this time: they were all working, except for Aitch. He was away on his Spike Island pilgrimage and hadn't a clue what time he would be back on the Monday. 'If I come back at all,' he had said. 'Gonna get off me tits!' So they didn't even have their resident juggler.

They had to learn to stand on their own two feet anyway, Daisy figured. If people had to wait, so be it. Even Aitch had said that a queue was a good thing. It generated business. Once they'd got a cart, there wouldn't be room for more than two servers anyway. But what about *two* ice cream carts down the line? Or three? A whole fleet of them. Now that was something to think about…

The morning arrived, and Tom pitched in with transporting the freezer again. Then he left them to it. Lugging the freezer about, especially up and down the stairs, was already becoming a pain, but Daisy came up with a solution that would help a little; there was just enough room to keep the freezer in the porch. They'd have to put up with an extension lead permanently trailing up the stairs, but that wasn't the end of the world.

The day was a success. Hot and sunny weather clearly meant more sales – and from earlier on in the day. Customers started ordering at around ten-thirty this time. And a lot of them were mentioning the newspaper article: it appeared to be making a difference. Some of them even asked where the juggler was. From mid-morning onwards, there was a fairly steady stream, reaching its peak at around two o'clock when the weather was at its hottest. A big queue formed and things got decidedly hairy, but Jack and Daisy got through it by the skin of their teeth. They had a broader spread of ice cream flavours to sell this time, and the cappuccino one had gone down a storm – especially with the ladies, for some reason. And the kids seemed to like the banana and chocolate. A few people asked if they did tubs as well as cones. It was something to think about.

By the end of the day Jack and Daisy were shattered; starving and lightheaded. They'd stupidly forgotten to bring food again, and they hadn't had a chance to go and get anything. So, apart from a can of cider they'd shared secretly round the back of the van throughout the day, they'd had nothing. They pushed the freezer further into the van, then plonked themselves down in front of it with their legs dangling over the side. Daisy put her head on Jack's shoulder. 'What a day.' Jack put his arm around her and kissed her head. He was dying for a spliff and another drink. Daisy was clutching onto the cash box. 'Feel the weight of that,' she said, passing it over. 'Isn't that the most satisfying feeling ever?'

'Jesus,' he said, opening it up. It was bulging and heavy with cash.

Aware that she shouldn't really be doing so in public, Daisy pulled out the notes to count them. 'That's two hundred quid in notes alone,' she said. 'I thought there would be more, actually. But there must be another fifty or so in change on top of the float.'

'Me too. It was more spread out this time, though, wasn't it? And we were on our own, so it probably seemed busier than it was.'

'I guess. Beats last time, though.'

'Yep.'

'And we did it on our own. I'm proud of that. We coped. Hey, did you see that ice cream van pull up earlier to look? Must have been around three or four o'clock. Uncle Lorenzo, or something.'

'No.'

'No, you probably wouldn't have done at the back. Anyway, he just pulled up in his van. Sort of leant over and stared for a bit – or rather glared, then sped off.'

'Really? said Jack. 'Probably 'cause we're stealing his business. Whoops.'

'Yeah. Well, sod 'im. There's no law against it.'

'Come on, let's pack up and get off,' said Jack. 'I'm dying for a drink. And I'm starving.'

Daisy let out a groan. 'I don't think I can budge an inch. But I'm ready to put my feet up.'

'Me too. At the pub.'

'Really? Can't we just have a night in? I'm knackered. I want a bath.'

'Oh, come on. I feel like celebrating again. We've had a good day. We can get some grub there too. Invite the gang. Aitch must be back from the Stone Roses concert by now. Don't you want to hear how he got on?'

'You and the bloody gang! We can't celebrate every time we sell ice creams, you know, and spend all our profits.'

'Why not?' he grinned.

'Because we can't.' She shoved him, but they laughed. It did seem a nice routine. Work your socks off, then have a few drinks afterwards to celebrate.

'Pleeeaase.' He leant into her.

'Fine. But as long as I get my bath afterwards. And you can massage my feet. They're killing me.'

'It will be my pleasure,' said Jack. 'I love your feet.'

'Really? God, I hate them. They're so small and stumpy.'

'They're not. They're lovely. I imagine you doing things to me with them.' He put his hand over his eyes and reddened. It had just come out.

'Things like what?' He never normally admitted anything like that.

'I don't know. Just things…' he blushed further.

'Oh my God. You pervert,' she laughed, smacking him again. 'Well, I'd better make sure they're clean then, hadn't I? Come on, let's get packed up.'

*****

They all met at The Sailor. The restaurant closed on bank holiday Monday evenings, so everyone was pleased to be out. It was like a bonus night off. They were all starving too, so they ordered a variety of baskets for the table to share. Fried chicken, scampi, fries, garlic bread. They all got stuck in.

Through mouthfuls of food, everyone asked Aitch what the Stone Roses gig was like. It had been a big deal in the news, promoted as a legendary, era-defining event. To have actually been there… Even Mike the landlord was leaning on the bar to listen. Aitch was in a dishevelled state, wired-looking; he'd only woken up about an hour or so before, and wouldn't have got up at all if it wasn't for meeting up with everybody. But he was revelling in the attention. He felt worldly wise, as if he'd been places, seen a thing or two… 'Madness,' he said. 'Absolute fucking madness. I've never seen *anything* like it.' He paused to grab another fistful of fries, munching on them with his mouth open, then taking a swallow of lager. 'Just madness…'

'Stop saying "madness", you knobhead,' said Tom. 'Tell us what it was like. I bet it wasn't as good as The Sisters at the Albert Hall in '85. Now *that* was legendary.'

'Don't talk to me about what is or isn't legendary, Thomas, my friend, especially if you haven't witnessed it. You weren't even at the Sisters gig. You were only about ten.' He let out a big burp of disdain to emphasise the point. Everyone laughed.

'Prick,' said Tom.

'Just tell us about the concert,' said Jeanie.

'It was madness, I'm telling you.' Everyone groaned. 'OK, OK…' He splayed his hands out in front of him, as if picturing a scene. 'Imagine getting on for thirty-thousand people descending on one place. One island. *One love…*'

'There weren't that many,' snorted Tom. 'And it isn't a *real* island.'

'There fucking was, I'm telling yer. You couldn't bloody move.'

'Volume, Aitch,' said Mike.

'Sorry, boss. And it *is* an island: we had to get to it by bridges and everything. It was surrounded by water. The tide was coming in, getting higher and higher. We all nearly drowned.'

'Bollocks,' said Tom.

'We did. We didn't know about this till later, of course. We were too off our tits. But anyway, there was this huge security fence round the place, you couldn't even find the way in. And then when you did, they were taking our cans off us, saying you had to buy them inside, and some lads even had their scran taken off them and they were kicking off. There were fights breaking out, dealers everywhere, people pissing and being sick…'

'Sounds revolting,' said Alison.

'Yeah,' agreed Jeanie. 'Gross.'

'But what about the band?' said Daisy. She wanted to know, but didn't. She still felt funny about the whole thing. The missing out.

'Yeah, they were sound.'

'Just *sound*?' said Daisy.

'Some say he can't cut it live,' said Alison. 'His voice goes.'

'No, more than sound. They were banging. I don't want to do them an injustice. It was just the sound was a bit shit, that's all. The PA system. You just couldn't hear them enough.'

'Ah, I hate it when that happens,' said Tom. 'It ruins it.'

'Yeah, the wind was blowing across the place, which didn't help. There was this red dust swirling everywhere, getting in people's eyes, people coughing. Some were saying it was chemicals from the factory next door…'

'Jesus, you're really not painting a good picture 'ere, Aitch,' said Mike. 'Sounds like bloody Chernobyl.' Everyone laughed again.

'Nah, nah, I can't explain it.' Aitch looked a bit deflated, a bit tired now. 'It was wicked, Absolutely wicked. The event itself, the whole spectacle, to be part of it all… There was music from three o'clock, DJs, it was a whole day thing, everyone was dancing, totally off their tits … which perhaps didn't help… By the time the Roses came on, we were absolutely spannered. But, no, it was wicked…'

'Well, roll on Glastonbury, I say,' said Tom. And they all cheered and raised their glasses. Jack joined in, but he'd been very quiet, taking it all in. If Glastonbury was anything like that, he didn't want to go. It sounded terrifying.

CHAPTER 15

A Storm in a Teacup

As before, the second lot of ice cream money – just over two hundred and fifty pounds – was deposited in the bank. Jack's account. Now it could earn a bit of interest. Rates were amazing for savers – and had been for some time – but were crippling for borrowers. Jack didn't understand any of this stuff; he just went along with what Daisy said. She had her sights set on that ice cream cart.

June was a busy time for them. There was always something going on, what with work and the ice cream-making and Jack working out. There were also the preparations for Glastonbury, buying equipment and camping stuff. Daisy was in her element making lists and a compilation tape for the trip. The days were getting longer and excitement was building for everyone. The World Cup had started, Italia '90, and there were high hopes for the England team, which was adding to the furore. There was even a decent tune for the lads for a change: New Order's 'World in Motion'. There was something in the air. A buzz. It felt good to be young and by the coast in the summer of 1990. The fields were a pure sandy gold, like the beaches, almost glowing when the sun shone and sprayed with a fine mist of red poppies. On top of all this, Aitch had his eighteenth birthday coming up.

Then another significant missive plopped through the door,

to be discovered when Jack and Daisy returned home from work one afternoon. It was from the clinic. The test result. Jack couldn't open the letter; that morning they'd had a visit from another reporter about the Peasgood story, and that had burst their bubble of excitement. They didn't need any more bad news. He went pale and his hands shook. It was as if the reality of it all had suddenly hit him. Come crashing down on him. What if the man he had been raised by wasn't his father? He had hated him, but the certainty of who he was had been something he was anchored to. It had never been in question. His mother's identity, yes – and for Jack's whole life. But not his father's. And then there was the property. Could he really become the rightful owner of that place?

'Here, you open it.' Jack passed the letter to Daisy.

'No, don't be silly. It's your letter. Your future. You should open it.' She was feeling nervous, too. Incredibly so. Her heart was racing. She tried to pass the letter back.

'No, I don't want to.'

'Jack, take it.'

'No.'

'Jack!'

'I'm going to skin up.'

'Please don't. Not in the afternoon. You never do in the afternoon these days. You've got your workout to do, remember. You'll regret it. Come on, open the letter. The suspense is killing me.'

'I can't.' He couldn't shake the fear of being cast adrift again. Of not belonging. Not knowing where he'd come from. That sickening, dizzy, lost feeling he'd got when he'd found out Carla wasn't his mother. 'I want you to do it. Please. Just tell me what it says.'

'Is it the money? If it is, don't worry about it. We don't need the money. You never miss what you've never had.' She searched his anguished face.

Jack shook his head.

'The other thing?'

He nodded.

'Come on, let's sit down.' She took his hand and led him into the lounge. They sat down on the sofa. She held the letter out in front of her. It suddenly seemed heavy in her hands. He'd put doubts in her mind. 'You sure you want me to do this?'

'Yeah. Just tell me what it says.' Jack sat back on the sofa and closed his eyes in anticipation, took in a deep breath, then let it out again. Daisy turned the envelope over, stuck her thumb in one side of the flap, and began to rip it open. She pulled out the letter and slowly opened it. She began to read, her eyes devouring the words. Then she turned to Jack. He still had his eyes closed.

'Jack.' He screwed his eyes shut tighter. 'Jack, look at me.' He gingerly turned to look at her.

She threw herself at him. 'It's positive! The test is positive! He's your father!' She showered his face with kisses, the letter still clutched in her hand. Jack was speechless. He felt relief. Overwhelming relief. He broke down and cried. He'd spent his whole life wishing that man wasn't his father, and now he was crying because he was. It was so confusing. 'Oh, baby,' she said. 'I'm so pleased for you. For everything. That property is yours. All yours. *Fuck you*, Verity Storm!' she said, sticking her middle finger up at the letter. '*Fuck you*!' This took Jack by surprise. It surprised her too. All the pent-up tension – this had been going on for months – was finally released. Another thing over. But it was also the enormity of what that woman had been trying to take from Jack. It wasn't her home, never had been. She'd probably barely set foot there. It was Jack's home, what was left of it anyway, to do with what he pleased. And there was nothing *she* could do about it.

At Daisy's suggestion, Jack phoned Kerry immediately, so she could pass on the news to the estate's administrator. Kerry was delighted, and congratulated them, but now there was a new issue to deal with. Under UK law, a person under the age of eighteen could not legally inherit. Jack and Daisy were stunned: Jack wasn't eighteen for another eight months. And they had to sell the property. 'It's not the end of the world,' Kerry said, 'that's why I haven't mentioned it before. In a case such as this, a trustee can be appointed to hold any monies or property until the relevant party turns eighteen. This trustee can advance, on request, capital to the beneficiary – at the trustee's discretion, of course. Their word is final. Obviously, if the administrator deals with the sale of the property, it'll speed things up for you. Do you know anyone who could take on a trustee's role?'

Daisy had been listening, and Jack looked at her totally lost; all of this was way beyond him. 'Mum,' Daisy said. 'Tell her, she'll do it.'

Daisy wasted no time in asking her mum, almost giving her no choice in the matter. Carol agreed, even though she was fearful it would cause problems down the line: she knew only too well how wilful Daisy could be. But who else was Jack going to ask?

Thrilled and very appreciative, Daisy passed this news on to Kerry, also confirming that the administrator could go ahead with selling the property. 'The sooner the better,' Daisy said.

*****

The result of the DNA test coincided with the weekend of Aitch's birthday. A double celebration was organised for the Sunday night, when everyone was off: a pub crawl around town, then back to the Shack for a smoke. Jack and Daisy finally got round to making their first batch of Hokey Pokey ice cream in aid of the occasion. They devised the recipe between them and really went to town on it. There was a bit of everything in it. Vanilla and strawberry ice cream bases, with sprinkles of tiny marshmallows, honeycomb and Smarties. Chocolate *and* raspberry ripples – and of course, the all-important magical ingredient, little chunks of hash brownie. This one strictly wasn't for the customers; despite the entertainment value it would give. It had the feel of something magical about it: a little bit 'Willie Wonka'. Everyone was blown away by it. And there were murmurs of appreciation as they dived in with spoons. Waiting for the Hokey Pokey to take effect, conversation turned to what flavour ice cream everyone would have if they could create any in the world. 'This! Just this! Every time!' Aitch cried.

Ice cream (and football) aside, the main topic of the night was the XR2 Aitch had been bought for his birthday by his parents and grandparents. Second-hand, of course. White with black and red trim. Aitch was thrilled to bits with it. He and Tom spent most of their time sitting in it and admiring it. It was a warm night and everybody was sitting outside the Shack on foldaway chairs, rather than inside. It got so smoky in there. Jeanie seemed impressed with the car too, and couldn't wait for Aitch to take her for a spin in it. Aitch thought this was a great idea, to have a pretty girl in his new sports car, and would have driven her round town there and then. Windows down, music thumping, everyone thinking she was his girlfriend… ''Ere, listen to these speakers,' he said, turning the stereo on, forgetting how late it was. Music suddenly blared out, making them jump. Aitch quickly switched it off, but too late. A bedroom window opened, and there was his bare-chested father, hair sticking up at all angles. 'Do that again, and I'll come down there and whip yer bare arse in front of all yer friends. I don't care if it is yer eighteenth birthday. And the car goes back too!'

'All right,' said Aitch, feeling brave in his inebriety. 'Keep yer 'air on. I didn't mean to do it.' His father glared for a moment, then began to close the window. 'Pervert,' Aitch muttered, and everyone stifled laughter.

The window opened again. 'I 'eard that, you little shit. I'm warning you. If I 'ave to come down there!' Then Aitch's mum appeared.

'Aitch, keep the noise down. Your father's got work in the morning. Inside the Shack or your friends go home. It's late. You won't be 'aving them round again! Come on, love, come back to bed...' She shepherded her husband away from the window.

'All right, all right... Love you, Mum.' His mum slammed the window. Everybody laughed again. Except Jack. Aitch's father had reminded him of his own father a bit. He would never have dared to speak to him like that. 'Come on. Let's go inside before they start kicking off again.'

They continued to talk about the car, and then driving in general and driving lessons. Jack felt a bit detached from it all. Cars, driving lessons... He was the only one who hadn't had any. Everyone else had passed their test, except Jeanie, and she was having lessons. This was picked up on. 'Hey, that's a point,' said Daisy. 'Driving lessons. You could learn to drive now, Jack. You're seventeen. You could get one of those block-booking things. It's cheaper.'

Driving. What a terrifying prospect, he thought.

CHAPTER 16

Glastonbury: Day One

'Right. Tent,' said Daisy.

'Err… yes,' said Jack, yawning.

'Just say "check".'

'Why? I just did.'

'Did what?'

'Check. It was there. Why would I ask *you* to check?'

'You're not asking me to check – it's just what you say: "check".'

'Why?'

'It doesn't matter why. OK, forget it. We'll be here all day. Just say "yes". Let's start again… Tent.'

'Check.'

'Swear to God, Jack, I'm gonna kill you.'

It was early morning on the day they were setting off to Glastonbury. The day after the Summer Solstice. Neither of them had had much sleep. They'd been too excited, and it had only been dark for a few hours. They were both standing on the street outside the flat, next to the open boot of the family Montego. Daisy had her notebook and a pen in her hand. Carol had suggested taking the Montego to Glastonbury during a phone call; she hadn't liked the thought of them travelling all that way in the camper van: it was a five-and-a-half-hour drive. This had sown a seed with Daisy. Breaking down on the way would be a total disaster. But it did seem a shame to be using the van for day-to-day stuff, then leaving it behind when they went on a camping trip to a festival. It would have fitted in nicely: photo opportunities for a start. But getting there safely was the main thing. So Daisy had got insured on the Montego for a week. They'd had to go and collect it, which was a pain; but this gave them the opportunity to grab the old tent too, rather than buying a new one. It also gave them the opportunity to take Carol a bunch of flowers and say thank you properly for agreeing to the trustee business.

The rest of the gang were travelling to the festival by coach: they'd paid extra for 'tickets with travel' when booking. Jack and Daisy hadn't been able to because they'd thought they were doing the ice cream thing. They'd had mixed feelings about this since: on the one hand regret, as it would have been fun to set off on the coach together, and a slight sense of missing out (more so for Jack than Daisy); but on the other hand it was nice to be doing their own thing. They were travelling in comfort, listening to music and stopping as and when they liked. Even Jack conceded that the prospect of five and a half hours on a coach with Aitch – never mind a horde of stinking, noisy revellers – sounded like a trying experience.

So, all in all, they were both feeling pretty OK when they finally set off. Better than OK. Daisy had quickly got used to driving the Montego: it was a damn sight more comfortable to drive than the van and she felt grown up in the driver's seat. She felt like the adult of the trip, the mother of the outing – packing things for the journey her parents would have remembered. Sweets. Snacks. Drinks. Tissues. Puzzle books.

The Montego's stereo was better too, and Daisy couldn't wait to stick on her newly finished compilation tape. Although she'd been trying to kid herself that this was for Jack again, to continue his musical education, it was primarily an attempt to define the musical year so far and to provide a soundtrack for their Glastonbury trip. She'd had to use a special 120-minute cassette to include all the songs she wanted:

SIDE ONE
Feels So Different – Sinead O'Connor
How Was it For You – James
What's Inside a Girl? – The Cramps
Birdhouse in Your Soul – They Might be Giants
November Spawned a Monster – Morrisey
Lips Like Sugar – Echo and the Bunnymen
Sleep With Me – Birdland
Yellow Walls – Jackson. C. Frank
Here's Where the Story Ends – The Sundays
Chelsea Girl – Ride
Hey Venus – That Petrol Emotion
Love Street – World Party
The Ship Song – Nick Cave

SIDE TWO
Sight of You – Pale Saints
Sit Down – James
Three Babies – Sinead O'Connor
Bikini Girls with Machine Guns – The Cramps
Happy When it Rains – The Jesus and Mary Chain
The Weeping Song – Nick Cave
Untitled – REM
Boots of Spanish Leather – Bob Dylan
Stand Guard – Bob Mould
Ceremony – Galaxie 500
Talkin' Bout a Revolution – Tracy Chapman
Land: Horses/Land of a Thousand Dances/
La Mer – Patti Smith

Jack, hunkered down on the passenger seat, was especially excited about the whole weekend. It had occurred to him that this was their first proper trip away together. His first proper holiday of any kind. He felt a childish thrill at the prospect of seeing a bit more of the world, and at the prospect of spending a whole weekend with the gang. He'd brought a good lump of hash with him. All the boys had: Aitch had planned well in advance for this. Jack had wanted to have a smoke on the way, but Daisy had strictly forbidden it because of the smell of smoke and the possibility of hot-rock burns in the car upholstery. Her mum would go spare.

The journey seemed to take forever: around six hours including stops. They didn't envy the guys on the coach at all. The nearer they got to the site, the narrower the lanes became and the slower their progress. There were tailbacks for miles: cars, vans, camper vans, coaches, all heading for Worthy Farm. To add to the hold-ups, the weather was rubbish, with rain on and off for the whole journey. They were so close, could even see the entrance up ahead, but the traffic was barely moving. It was lucky they weren't in the van: it would surely have overheated. 'Oh, come on. I'm busting for a wee,' said Daisy, wriggling in her seat, then resting her head on the steering wheel. 'I can't believe the weather. I hope it's not like this all weekend. Camping in the rain isn't fun. Nor is setting up a tent.'

'I'm sure it'll clear up,' said Jack. He was trying to remain positive, but was getting increasingly nervous. Through the droplets on the van window, he got his first glimpse of tents in the distance. There seemed to be hundreds of them. Blurred dabs of colour, like flapping flags, on the grey-green canvas of the horizon.

'It had better.'

Finally they reached the entrance, where attendants were stopping each vehicle. Daisy showed their tickets and they were given pale blue wristbands with Glastonbury '90 written on them. Seeing these gave Daisy a little thrill; they would make a nice memento. She passed them to Jack, then followed the man's directions, which seemed a little unnecessary: all they had to do was follow the wagon-trail of campers ahead of them. But now they were in. Daisy kept her window down, and as they edged slowly forwards, she heard music for the first time. The sheer size and scale of the place quickly became apparent – a sea of vehicles and tents as far as the eye could see. Jack gulped. 'Oh. My. God!' said Daisy. There were fields and fields. And not just small fields: huge ones.

They were stopped again by an animated attendant, wearing a cagoule and wellies. All the staff were wearing wellies. The ground looked a little churned up already. Fortunately, they had wellies too – Carol's suggestion. 'Cock-Mill Meadow. Head for Cock-Mill Meadow. Field after next,' the man said. 'Park up, pitch up, then return the car to the main car park. Follow the signs.'

'Thanks,' said Daisy. The car slid slightly on the greasy ground. 'Oops! Jesus, if it's like this now, what's it going to be like by Monday?' She followed the trail of vehicles through a large gap in a hedge, to be met by another huge field of tents. It was intimidating. 'Right, look out for Cock-Mill Meadow... Jack?' He didn't answer; he was shutting down again. 'Jack, don't go quiet on me now. I need you. This is stressful enough as it is.'

He snapped himself out of it and sat up straight. 'Sorry.'

She put her hand on his leg. 'We'll be OK as soon as we find our field. We'll find the loos, then get set up. Then we can park the car and get our bearings a bit. Shit, Jack.'

'What?' he groaned. Not more stress.

'Something's just occurred to me.'

'What?'

'How on earth are the guys going to find us?'

'Shit,' he said. She was right.

'I mean, we could be put in any field, and so could they. We could wander around the festival for the whole weekend and never bump into them.'

Jack was horrified at the prospect of this. It could ruin everything. Why hadn't they thought of this? 'Well, what are we gonna do?'

'I don't know; we'll think of something. Here it is,' she said, spotting a sign on a stick. 'Let's find a spot.' Further into the field, the vehicles and tents gradually thinned out. Daisy picked a spot by a hedge away from everybody else, and deliberately pulled up sideways at an awkward angle. She wanted there to be enough space for the other guys' tents too. If they found them. It would be rubbish if they had to camp apart. Then she turned off the engine and let out a huge sigh of relief. 'Thank God for that,' she said, speaking for both of them. 'What a journey…'

They sat there for a moment, watching everybody else. Some battling with their tents. Some already sitting drinking under awnings. Jack thought the cans of beer and cider looked good. Daisy thought the steaming hot drinks looked good. It was amazing – and surprising – the sheer number of people who were already there and set up. It was as if the festival was already established and in full swing. People must have arrived at the crack of dawn. Or yesterday. Or even earlier in the week. Daisy hadn't known that was even possible. It was something to think about for next year – if there was a next year…

'We're gonna have to get out and face the music,' Daisy said. 'I'm busting for the loo. Ooh, that's a point, I must fish the loo roll out…' But they sat there for a moment longer. It didn't look very appealing – a bit of a damp squib. Just a wet field full of tents. A giant campsite, miles from the action. If only the sun would come out… Everything looked different when the sun came out. But at least it wasn't exactly ice cream weather, Daisy thought. Thank the Lord for small mercies. 'Come on,' she sighed.

As they got out of the car, they heard the live music again. It was exciting, made it seem more like a festival, but was quite far away. After finding the loo roll and donning their wristbands, they set off in search of toilets. Before long, they spotted some, typically on the other side of the field. A row of portaloos. Daisy hadn't been expecting that. She didn't really know what she'd been expecting, but maybe some purpose-built concrete loos? A shower block? The problem of meeting the gang reared its ugly head again. Jack was quiet, stressing about it. 'What time did they say they were setting off?' said Daisy, as if reading his thoughts.

'About nine, I think. Why?'

'You know what? I reckon our best bet is to try and meet them off the bus. There's got to be a designated drop-off point somewhere, like a bus car park. Once they're in, they could be lost for good. What do you reckon?'

Jack brightened. 'Yeah, it could work. But what if we miss them? Or can't find them?'

'Well, what time is it now?' She checked her wrist, glad to have brought her watch with her. 'Nearly two-thirty. I reckon they're gonna take at least an hour longer than us with stops and traffic. So if they set off at nine…' She tried to think, but the pain in her bladder was stopping her. 'Oh, God, I'm dying for a wee. I'll think about it on the loo. Or you work it out.'

'Me?' said Jack, trotting after her. 'I need the loo, too.'

They reached the loos. 'Do you need loo roll?' Daisy said.

'No,' he said, reddening. Then under his breath, 'Won't there be any?' He hadn't thought about the toilets and how it was all public; people knowing what you were doing. Imagine going in there, clutching toilet roll. It was all right for the girls…

'I don't know. See you in a minute.'

It wasn't all right for the girls. It wasn't all right for either of them. The toilets were basic, dark, already littered and stinking. And there wasn't any loo roll provided…

They came out, looking traumatised.

'Err, that was gross,' said Daisy. 'At least you can stand up. I had to hover with my knickers round my ankles.' Jack pictured this for a second. Why did it always turn him on, the thought of Daisy weeing? What was he, some sort of pervert? 'Where do you even wash your hands?' They looked around and spotted what looked like a water point. A woman was filling a large, plastic tub with a screw-lid. Why hadn't they thought of that? At least they knew where the water was now. And the toilets. They were getting their bearings. Now all they needed to do was locate the bus drop-off point. They waited for the woman to finish. Daisy said, 'Excuse me, I don't suppose you know if there's a bus drop-off point somewhere, do you?'

'No, sorry, darl, I don't. We always come in the van. Your first time 'ere?' She paused to relight her roll-up, sucking on it to get it going again. The sweet, pungent smell was achingly familiar.

'Yeah.'

'Bless yer. I remember my first time. Nothing like this. Must be a bit daunting for you young uns. Even I'm worried about getting lost this year – and I've been most years. Place seems twice the size. Lost a bit of its spirit, if you ask me… Anyway, listen to me waffling on… Yer best bet is one of the information centres. There's usually a couple of 'em dotted about, especially in the main bit. They'll be able to point you in the right direction.'

'Oh, thank you,' said Daisy. 'That's a great help.'

'Yer welcome, darl. Enjoy the festival, the pair of you. And word of warning, lock up yer tent.' She toddled off, carrying her water, puffing away.

Jack and Daisy looked at each other. The woman's warning had seemed a little ominous, and they didn't have a lock. They rinsed their hands, thinking about this. 'Well, she seemed nice,' said Daisy. 'Helpful.'

'I can't believe she was openly smoking in front of us.'

'I know. But they'll all be at it here, I bet. Even Mum used to "toke" at Glastonbury, remember?' she laughed.

The main centre was in the opposite direction to their camping spot. 'What about the tent?' asked Jack, as Daisy set off towards it. 'And taking the car back?'

'It'll have to wait. This is more important. Once we know where the bus depot is, and how far from our camp – I mean, it could be anywhere on site, miles away – *then* we can decide if we've got enough time to set the tent up or not. I reckon they'll be getting here about three-thirty, and it's two-fifteen now.'

Heading into the centre of the festival was a jaw-dropping experience: they knew they were there when they passed under a huge hand-painted banner, saying 'Welcome'. It got busier. And louder. And madder. And muddier. They hadn't donned their wellies either. It was too late to go back now. There were people everywhere. Stalls and hawkers selling their wares. Fires burning in oil drums. Jugglers. Acrobats. Buskers and revellers playing various instruments. If it wasn't for the far-out fashions and hairstyles on show, it would have been like stepping back into the middle ages. Hippies, punks, dyed hair, shaved hair, mohicans, dreadlocks, crusties, goths, baggies, metalheads. Mostly in groups or couples, like different tribes. There were even people in fancy dress. A trio of men were dressed as policemen, truncheons and all – clearly fake. There was a guy dressed as a Dalek with sawn-up pool cues taped to his head. A lot of people looked wide-eyed and spaced out. No wonder. A man up ahead sporting a bin liner as a tunic, with cut-out arm and head holes, was blatantly calling, 'Hash for cash!' at passers-by. 'Hash for cash!' he said to Jack and Daisy as they passed; it wasn't the last time they would hear this.

Families with kids were selling jewellery and tie-dye T-shirts. People were plaiting and beading hair. There were food and drink stalls and tents. Circus tents. God-knows-what tents. Hand-painted signs and art everywhere. Most of them were wacky and humorous. They passed one stuck in the mud that said 'COSMIC INFORMATION STATION' with a pointing arrow. Perhaps that was where they were heading. There were bins painted with flowers. Bunting and huge flagpoles *everywhere*. There were animals wandering about – not just dogs, but chickens, goats… And all the while, the thumping background music.

It was all mind-boggling, enough to make the devil dizzy. Daisy held onto Jack, and they tried to stick to the edges, away from the muddier main thoroughfares and on the wooden boards haphazardly dotted about. Eventually, they found an information centre and breathed huge sighs of relief. They stepped inside. 'Helloo, campers, what can we do for you?' A man behind a table greeted them jovially, as if all the chaos was the most normal thing in the world.

'Hi,' said Daisy. I don't suppose you can tell us if there's a designated bus drop-off place, can you?'

'There surely is.' Jack and Daisy looked at each other. 'Let me see…' He picked up an eye-catching festival programme from his desk, a flaming sun, a moon and a triangle on the cover. He leafed through until he found a map of the site. 'Let me see…', he said again. 'Bus station… Here we go, I knew it wasn't far from here. Out of the tent, straight ahead, first right before the camping field, next left, then straight up to the main exit. You can't miss it.'

'Great,' said Daisy. 'Thank you so much.' It was such a relief. She picked up one of the programmes – the twentieth anniversary souvenir edition, with that all-important map. She had to have one.

With Daisy proudly clutching the precious programme, they joined the madness again and made their way to the bus station. They spotted a medical centre, a phone point and a police compound on the way. The organisers had created a temporary town here. Daisy was impressed.

To their surprise, the path they took skirted the top of the field they were camping in. Daisy thought things were looking familiar, and then she spotted their car in the distance. They were literally just one field from the exit and the bus station. The place was disorientating. Daisy got out the map. 'Look,' she said. 'The bus station's only up there. We can't miss it.' She checked her watch. Two-thirty. 'Sod it,' she said. 'Let's risk it. We don't need to go and see it now. It's no more than ten minutes away. We've got an hour – or three-quarters anyway with walking. Let's get the tent set up.'

'OK,' said Jack. 'But if it gets to quarter past and we haven't finished, we'll have to leave it.'

'Agreed.'

*****

Erecting the tent was relatively stress-free. A couple of cans of cider and some music helped, rather than hindered. There was no time for messing about. The only thing they didn't get to finish was pegging the guy-ropes. But that could wait. Remembering the pot-lady's words of warning, they left anything valuable locked in the car. They hadn't time to take the car back, and hoped they didn't get into trouble. Then, taking another can of cider each in case they had to wait a while, they headed for the bus station. Daisy took her programme with her. The day had been a write-off when it came to seeing bands, so she needed to make an itinerary for the weekend.

They made it to the bus station for half-past three. Seeing an empty coach leave as they approached made them panic – what if they'd already missed the gang? 'Keep your eyes peeled,' said Daisy, slightly out of breath. 'Excuse me,' she said to a group of stragglers. 'Where have you just come from?'

'Birmingham,' a girl said.

'Phew,' said Daisy. 'Thanks.'

Whilst Jack and Daisy were looking for somewhere to sit and wait, they spotted what looked like an arrivals hut and rest place for the drivers. 'I'm going to see if I can find anything out,' she said. 'Are you OK waiting here, just in case?'

'Yep.'

A few minutes later Daisy came back out. She looked forlorn, downcast, and Jack's heart sank. 'What?' he said. 'Don't tell me we missed them.'

'Their bus was due in at three. Half a bloody hour ago. I'm sorry, Jack.' She put her hand on his shoulder.

'You're joking. But how? I thought you did the calculations.'

'I did. It must be closer from Norwich. I had no idea.'

Jack was distraught. He looked around him, at the huge festival, the sea of tents. The whole weekend was in tatters. 'But how…' He could barely even say it. 'How are we going to find them?'

'Dunno. When their bus pulls up, I guess.'

'What do you mean, when their bus pulls up? We missed it. We were half an hour late.'

'No we weren't. It hasn't arrived yet.'

'What?' Jack cried.

Daisy's face cracked into a grin, and she did a little jig. 'Ha ha ha! Got you!' she said. 'That'll teach you for your little April Fool's day trick. Their bus hasn't arrived yet – thank God. It's running late. I got you back, finally. Good and proper!'

'Oh, you bloody cow,' he said in disbelief. 'That's not funny.'

'Oh it is,' she said. She couldn't stop laughing. 'Your face!'

Jack rushed her, and rugby-tackled her to the floor. They rolled about on a damp, grass slope, laughing. 'Oh, I'm gonna get you back for that good and proper, Daisy *Lonicera* Jones,' he said. 'Just you wait.' They were still rolling about when a loud horn honked, making them jump out of their skin. Another coach had just pulled in, and they were in danger of getting run over. They quickly jumped to their feet, brushing themselves off.

'Idiot,' said Daisy, still chuckling.

'You're the idiot,' he said.

The coach swung past them, and there was a sudden loud rapping on a window, startling them again. They looked up, trying to see in. And lo and behold, there was the gang. The whole stupid, bloody lot of them, banging on the windows and waving and grinning like mad people. Aitch was pulling faces. Tom knocked his hat off, then Aitch got him in a stranglehold and started punching him. Jack and Daisy burst into fits of laughter at the sight of them. It was such a relief.

The second the girls disembarked, they ran up to Daisy, screaming and throwing their arms around her. They jumped up and down, Daisy and Jeanie included, which was a turn-up for the books. Both Alison and Jeanie smelt of cider. The boys just sidled up to each other, coolly. 'How you doin', buddy?' said Aitch, holding out his hand. Jack shook it.

'Jackeroo,' said Tom, giving him one of his fancy handshakes, which Jack was getting used to by now. 'You settling in?'

'Just about. How was the journey?'

'Dunno. I slept most of the way. Had a bangin' hangover,' said Aitch. Jack laughed.

'This place is huge,' said Tom.

'I know.'

There was an awkward silence for a moment

'Bloody splitties,' Aitch said, acknowledging the girls, then rolling his eyes. 'Embarrassing.' This expression was bandied about a lot in the kitchen, when the chefs referred to waitresses. Short for 'split-arses', apparently – whatever that meant.

'*We're* embarrassing?' said Alison, breaking up the group hug. 'What about these two, rolling around in the mud? What on earth were you doing?'

'What, was that you two the coach driver was honking at?' said Jeanie.

''Fraid so,' said Daisy, laughing. 'Long story.' Jack blushed.

'Yeah, save that stuff for your tent, will you?' said Tom, and everyone laughed.

'You'd better not be shagging all weekend,' said Aitch. 'I 'aven't brought my earplugs.'

Alison tutted. 'Always has to take it too far…'

'Come on. We'd better queue up for our stuff,' said Jeanie. 'He'll be giving it to someone else.'

'Yeah, we wouldn't want anyone else getting hold of your knickers, would we, Jeanie? Wink, wink. You'd have to go commando for the whole festival. And we wouldn't want that,' said Aitch.

'Pervert,' Jeanie said.

'Yeah, I've got me stash in there too,' said Tom. 'Didn't want it stinking out the bus. Let's hurry up.'

*****

'Here we are,' said Daisy. They'd arrived back at the campsite.

'Cock-Mill Meadow? What sort of name's that?' said Aitch. 'Better not be a bummers' hangout.' They all burst out laughing. Trust Aitch. Daisy and Jack had privately noted the name too, but had refrained from saying anything. It was a relief to get it out in the open.

'Honestly,' said Alison.

'Plenty of room, anyway,' said Tom.

'Yeah, wonder why,' said Aitch.

'Well, there will be once we've taken the car back,' said Daisy. 'We'd better get that done, Jack, before we get drunk.'

'Talking of which…' said Aitch, unshouldering his rucksack, 'where's my beer?'

'Hadn't we better get set up first?' said Alison. 'Or shall we have a cup of tea? I've got a kettle – and water. And milk.'

'Sod that! I'm cracking open a can,' said Aitch. 'And I'm not setting up a thing until I've had a smoke. I've just spent six hours on a bloody bus. And I'm at Glastonbury *fucking* Festival.' Everyone cheered.

'Good point,' said Tom. 'Let's have a smoke first – we deserve it – then we'll get set up.'

'Can someone help me with my tent, please?' said Jeanie. 'When we get set up. I haven't a clue how to do it.'

'Ah, I thought we were sharing,' said Aitch.

'You wish,' she laughed.

Jack and Daisy left them to it and went to park the car. When they returned, everyone was sitting around on chairs, drinking and smoking.

'Well, if you lot are just sitting around, I'm going to look at my programme for a while,' said Daisy, brandishing it. 'See who's playing when.' She and Jack sat down.

'Oh, wow,' Alison said. 'Where did you get that from?'

'The main centre, an information tent,' said Daisy.

'What, you already been down there? What time did you arrive?' said Tom.

'About two. And, yes, it's mad isn't it?' Jack nodded.

'You seen any bands yet? Jesus Jones are on today, I think,' said Jeanie.

'And the mighty Mondays tonight,' cried Aitch.

'No, we haven't. More's the pity. I'm getting itchy feet. I didn't pay all this money just to camp with you lot,' said Daisy. 'No offence.' She began to peruse her programme, whilst Jack rolled a spliff. 'Wow! This is amazing. There's articles on all the bands.'

'Yeah, looks it,' said Alison. 'I'm gonna get one.'

'Never mind the bleedin' articles, what time are the Mondays playing?' said Aitch, blowing out smoke.

'Hold on, I haven't got to the schedules yet...' Daisy flicked ahead. 'Ah, here we are. Pyramid Stage. Friday. Happy

Mondays. Nine-thirty tonight, apparently – and Jesus Jones are on before them at seven-thirty. Yes!'

'Perfect,' said Aitch. 'That gives us plenty of time to get set up and wasted beforehand.'

'Yeah, great,' said Tom sarcastically. 'Can't wait.' Neither of these bands were really his scene. He was there for The Cure on Saturday night.

'Well, if you're doing some reading, then so am I,' said Aitch. 'Whilst I enjoy my spliff.' He pulled a rolled-up newspaper out of his rucksack and laid it out on his lap, immediately turning to page three. It was *The Sun*. 'Look at the knockers on that,' he commented.

'Jesus,' said Alison. 'Why are boys such filthy pigs?'

Jack was embarrassed, and concentrated on building his spliff. Daisy felt uncomfortable too.

'Yeah, how would you like it if it was men with their bits out?' said Jeanie. Jack and Daisy said nothing. The conversation was getting way too graphic for them.

'Well, Tom would probably like it,' said Aitch.

'Screw you,' said Tom. 'I'm not looking anyway, so don't tar me with *his* brush.' He covered his eyes with his hands.

'Yeah, you were on the bus. I saw you sneaking a peek,' said Alison. She shoved him.

'I wasn't.'

'What's wrong with it anyway?' said Aitch. 'A guy can find two girls attractive at the same time. It's just human nature – like the animal kingdom…'

'Yeah, like you'd know anything about it, virgin,' said Tom.

'What was that on the front page anyway?' said Daisy, keen to change the subject – and for that image to disappear. 'The headline.'

Aitch flicked back. 'Ah, something about an earthquake. Iran or somewhere. Tens of thousands dead, apparently.'

'God, that's awful,' said Alison.

'Yeah. But on a brighter note, England got their first win last night.' He immediately turned to the back page to read the match report.

Everyone groaned and tutted. 'Typical,' said Alison.

'What? It's about time. They needed it. Drawn their first two matches.'

'Is that why you were so hungover this morning?' said Jack, finally joining in. He'd finished rolling his spliff.

'Yeah. Celebrated a bit too hard.'

'I thought you were Scottish,' said Tom.

'Nah, that's just my ancestry. Dad supports them until they get knocked out. But I'm English born and bred. What chance have Scotland got in the World Cup anyway?'

*****

The night was a bit of a blur. After partaking of beer, cider and marijuana, setting up the tents became a bit drawn out. It didn't help that they were trying to set up three tents at once. Jack and Daisy ended up helping Jeanie with hers. Daisy didn't mind; Jeanie was wearing hardly any make-up and baggy clothes for once. It made her seem more human, a mere mortal. Daisy liked that. She was still naturally pretty, though, her skin annoyingly flawless.

They just about reached the gig on time, negotiating the mayhem on their way to the infamous Pyramid Stage. None of them could believe what they had witnessed and there wasn't time to discuss it. They kept on looking at each other in shock and amazement, and stumbled on. The crowd for the band was huge. Daunting. Aitch had experienced Spike Island, so he wasn't fazed, but the others had never seen anything like it. Daisy held onto Jack's hand, squeezing it, knowing how intimidated he must be. It was for her too. Everyone seemed so much taller, and it was hard to see. In the end, they made their way to the fringes, where the crowd was sparser – but near a beer tent, which was a bonus. Although they were a fair way back, the view was better and it was nice to get a breather.

'Jesus Christ,' said Jeanie. 'This place is bonkers.'

'Isn't it?' said Alison.

'There were more at Spike Island,' said Aitch, trying to be cool.

'Yes, but this is only Jesus bloody Jones. They're not even headliners,' said Tom. 'Imagine what it's gonna be like for The Cure tomorrow night. I heard one of the staff say they were expecting seventy thousand people this weekend.'

'I meant the whole thing,' said Jeanie. 'There are people *everywhere*.'

'Yeah, and all off their tits,' said Tom.

'No wonder,' said Alison. 'I saw a tent selling magic mushrooms.'

'Oh my God, we need to find that again,' said Aitch. 'I'm definitely having some mushrooms whilst I'm here. We've all got to.'

'Did you see those guys sawing up that huge tree, whilst people sat around playing hillbilly music? What the hell was that about? It was like something from *Deliverance*,' said Daisy.

'I think I saw a live pig,' said Tom. They all burst out laughing.

'And did you hear that guy selling umbrellas? "Don't be a wally, buy a fucking brolly!" It had me in stitches,' said Aitch.

'You OK?' Daisy said to Jack. He was quiet, but smiling at least.

'Yeah.' And he did feel OK, surprisingly. The crowds at Cromer had slowly got him used to hordes of people, albeit nothing like this. The drink and smoke helped. He felt in a bit of a daze, a bit out of it, but surprisingly chilled.

As they were queuing for drinks, the band came on stage to a huge cheer from the crowd. It was so loud when they began playing, and the crowd went mental. Especially all those at the front. Jesus Jones were amazing. Their energy, the catchy songs… They got the whole crowd dancing; even Tom and Alison were nodding and bopping away. Daisy and Jack had a little dance too, mainly Daisy – she knew all the songs – bumping and gyrating into him. Jack swayed awkwardly, clutching his slopping pint – and Daisy when he could. By the end, despite the fairly cool evening, they were wet with perspiration, their coats or jumpers tied round their waists. They'd taken it in turns to get the drinks in and passed around a couple of spliffs.

But that was the high point of the evening. Everyone got a little too carried away with the 'festivities', so by the time the Happy Mondays came out – late – everyone was wasted. They'd forgotten to eat. Jeanie was the worst, barely able to stand up, and she kept on saying she was going to be sick. The headline act were a huge disappointment, even for Aitch, who was a massive fan. After a couple of particularly shambolic and sloppy numbers, the majority of the crowd seemed to become restless. People began to leave in droves. It didn't help that it had started to rain again.

'I think we need to get Jeanie back to the tent,' said Alison. 'She's had it.'

'Well, you're not going on your own,' said Tom. 'No way. How are we even going to find the way back?'

'I've no idea, to be honest,' said Alison. It was getting dark.

'We'll come too,' said Daisy. 'I know the way.' She wasn't really enjoying the band either and was ready for bed.

'Aitch. You coming?' said Tom.

'What? You're all going?' Aitch stopped dancing; he was the only one still watching the band.

'Yeah. Jeanie's fucked and the band are shit.'

'But it's the Mondays!'

'I know. They're shit.'

'Well, I'm staying.'

'You can't. You'll never find your way back in the dark. We don't want to lose you on the first night. We've got the whole weekend. Come on back to the tent, and we'll have a smoke.'

This nearly persuaded him. 'Nah, fuck it. I'm staying. The boys need some support. And they haven't played "Step On" yet.'

'Fuck it,' said Tom, giving up. 'Be careful!' He left Aitch doing his Bez dance and rejoined the group.

'What's happening?' said Alison. 'Where's Aitch?'

'He's staying, the twat.'

'What?' said Alison and Daisy together.

'I know.'

'But he'll never find his way back,' said Alison.

'That's what I told him. But you know how stubborn he gets when he's wasted. And this is the highlight for him, I guess. It's like us leaving during The Cure.'

'I want to go home...' Jeanie groaned again. It was a dilemma.

'Hold on,' said Daisy. 'I'll talk to him.'

'I'll come too,' said Jack. He was probably the most worried, as he couldn't think of anything worse than trying to find your way back in the dark to a single tent amongst thousands. He didn't want to lose his friend.

But Aitch wouldn't listen: he was feeling brave and boisterous. The best Daisy could do was give him all the directions and instructions she could. The name of the camping field, as if he'd forget. Where the medical and information tents were. If the worst came to the worst, where the police compound was.

Jeanie threw up twice on the way back, then started crying and saying she wanted to go home. People were stumbling about arm in arm. Singing and shouting and swearing. Impromptu sing-alongs of 'World in Motion' filled the air. Men were urinating in hedges. It was a relief to reach the camping field, which was now dotted with the glow and smoke of fires.

The gang piled into their respective tents, shattered by the day's trials. But it was impossible to sleep properly. All around them, the noise and partying went on. All kinds of music was playing, and there was thumping dance music coming from somewhere on site. Everyone seemed to be having a better time than them. Some first night, they all thought. Not even midnight and they were in bed.

CHAPTER 17

Glastonbury: Day Two

'Jack… Jack,' Daisy whispered. 'You awake?'

Jack groaned, coming to. Where was he? Why was it so hot? Why did he feel trapped? And why was the bed so hard? Then it came back to him. He was in a sleeping bag in a tent. In a field, surrounded by tens of thousands of other people. Ugh…

'Jack. You awake?'

'Yes. Unfortunately. What time is it?'

'Early. Just six.'

'Why aren't you asleep?'

'I can't. I've been awake for hours. I'm dying for a wee, but daren't go on my own.' Jack groaned again. 'Will you come with me?'

'Really?'

'Yes. Please.' The thought of it was horrendous, but he needed a pee himself. At least they'd managed to both make it through the night. And at least that was all he needed. Daisy rolled nearer to him and put her arm round him. 'I'll make it worth your while…' She tried to manoeuvre her hand into his sleeping bag, but it was impossible. 'Bloody sleeping bags,' she said. 'I can't get near you to cuddle properly. I missed it last night. I had to cuddle Denim instead. Look.' She pulled her threadbare teddy bear out of her sleeping bag. 'Morning, Jack,' Daisy said in a high-pitched voice, waving one of his paws. 'I slept between Daisy's legs.'

'Give him here,' Jack said, trying to grab the bear. He'd always been jealous of her teddy, and now she wound him up about it. Daisy laughed and rolled away, stuffing the bear back into her sleeping bag. 'No. He likes it down there. You'll have to come and get him.'

'Fine. That fleabag can go to the toilet with you instead then.'

Daisy burst out laughing again.

'Will you two shut up!' came a voice from nearby. It was Tom. Oops.

'Sorry,' called Daisy, giggling again. 'You've woken them up,' she whispered.

'*You* have,' he said. 'You and your bloody teddy bear. I'm going to chuck him on a fire later.'

'You wouldn't dare, you horrible sod. I'd never forgive you.'

'I would.'

'Hey, I wonder if Aitch made it back all right. Did you hear anything?'

'No, I didn't.'

'Me neither. Hope he's OK…'

Wincing at the light and on all fours, Daisy (clutching the loo roll), then Jack, emerged from their tent. They were already wearing their clothes, as they had slept in them, and had donned their wellies. The day looked finer, brighter, which was something at least. They stood up, aching and stretching, trying not to groan too loudly. It was so strange to see all the tents. It was nice and quiet, with barely anyone about at all. The air smelt fresh, but with an undercurrent of lingering smoke from the fires. The grass was wet and sparkling under a pale-lemon sun, large and low, hovering above the fields. They looked over at Aitch's tent for any sign that he had returned, any movement, but there wasn't any. It was zipped up. They looked at each other, shrugged a little, then set off. As they did, a long, loud flatulent explosion from behind startled them. It had come from Aitch's tent, signifying an end to any debate over his whereabouts. They looked at each other, shocked – they never did anything like that in front of each other – then laughed. 'Well, at least we know he's back,' Daisy said.

They carried on walking, taking in the morning sights of a festival campsite. 'You know what day it is today, Jack?'

'Er… Saturday?' said Jack.

'Yes, I know it's Saturday, clever clogs, but do you know what *day* it actually is? It's Midsummer's Eve. The best night of the whole summer. The night me and you first… you know… In the summerhouse.'

Bloomin' hell, thought Jack. That was a year ago? He pondered this for a moment. Then his thoughts turned darker. It was a significant night for another reason. 'Yeah,' he said. 'It was also the last night I saw Anne.'

'Oh, God. Yes. It would have been wouldn't it? I hadn't made that connection. Sorry, honey. That's so sad.' She reached out for his hand as they walked.

'It's OK.' But it was going to be a tough day now that this had got into his head. He hadn't really thought about it at all before. But now he knew, Midsummer's Eve was always going to be bittersweet.

The toilets were worse than before. Smellier. Disgusting, in fact; partially blocked and piled high with used toilet paper. They did what they had to do, holding their breath, trying not to look, and exiting as quick as they could, letting out deep breaths and inhaling the fresh air.

'Oh my God, that was revolting,' said Daisy.

They headed over to the water point to rinse their hands. 'Shit. We forgot the water bottle for tea,' Daisy said. 'Bloody hell. I hope Alison's got some left, or we'll have to come back again. My throat's parched. We really need our own bottle. We'd better sort that today.'

Jack agreed. They headed back to the tent and Daisy tried to wake Alison up, feeling guilty. It was still early and the water bottle was in her and Tom's tent. But getting back to sleep seemed out of the question. They were up for the day.

After a few moans of protestation, Alison and Tom's tent unzipped and Alison's black nail-varnished hand appeared, holding out the water bottle. Fortunately, it was still half-full. Daisy thanked her and promised to fill it back up. The hand retreated and the tent was rezipped. Then someone from inside broke wind. 'Tom. You pig!' said Alison.

'Sorry,' he chuckled.

Jack and Daisy set about making a cup of tea. Both being hungry, they had a bowl of cereal whilst waiting for the kettle to boil, which took forever on the small camping stove. Daisy consulted her programme again, earmarking the bands she wanted to see that day. There were plenty to choose from, including James, whom she loved, at four that afternoon. But most significantly – the highlight of the festival, for Daisy at least – was Sinead O'Connor at six-thirty and The Cure that night. What a day to look forward to. On Midsummer's Eve no less.

As they sat and warmed themselves with their tea, the sun rose in the sky and all around them the campsite stirred into life. It made such a difference that it wasn't raining: the whole place looked different. Jack and Daisy looked at each other and smiled. It was nice to have a bit of peace and quiet to themselves before the gang woke up, and it was interesting to watch other people going about their business. Women mainly, some with little ones, getting up first and making the dreaded trip to the toilet or water point, clutching loo roll and in some cases shower bags. There must be some on site somewhere. Daisy felt like a shower. But if they were anything like the toilets, forget it. She consulted the site map. 'Hot showers', marked with an '**S**'. Yes! She wouldn't be able to go the whole festival without one.

Jack considered rolling a spliff, but it was early, even for him. He still felt rough from the previous night. But it wouldn't hurt to roll a few for later whilst he was just sitting about. He could get ahead with them. He was on his third when there was movement and rustling from Alison and Tom's tent. Alison popped her head out, wincing at the light. 'Morning,' she said gingerly.

'Morning,' they said.

'Bit early for that, isn't it?' Alison said, noticing Jack at work.

'Just rolling for later,' he said.

'I feel rough,' said Alison. 'Why on earth are you guys up so early? Are you mad?'

'Couldn't sleep,' said Daisy. 'And I needed the loo.'

'Yeah, I know what you mean,' said Alison. 'People seemed to be partying all bloody night. And what with him snoring like a bloody rhinoceros…' They all laughed.

'Oh, Aitch is back – safe and sound by the way,' said Daisy. Alison had reminded her. 'Or at least we think he is, judging by the "dawn chorus" coming from his tent first thing.'

'Oh God, Tom's as bad. What is it with boys?'

'Ahem,' said Jack in protest.

*****

Intermittently, the whole gang hatched from their tents. Tom was next. Then Jeanie – their talking had woken her up. Her hair was all over the place, and she looked pale and younger. It was strange for all of them to see her without make-up on and in such a dishevelled state. 'Oh, God, don't look at me,' she groaned. 'I feel as rough as a badger's arse.' She shuffled over to join them, still cocooned in her sleeping bag. Aitch was the last to surface. It was mid-morning by then and Daisy was getting restless, keen to get on with the day. Explore some more of the site, and maybe see some bands. But it didn't look as if anyone was going anywhere quickly, especially now Aitch had appeared – and proceeded to crack open a beer. 'Hair of the dog,' he said, taking a swig, and everyone groaned in disbelief.

Eventually Daisy had had enough, and asked Jack if he fancied a wander. To a bout of heckling, as no one else was fussed about venturing out, they set off on their own. Jack wasn't fussed either – he just wanted to relax with the boys – but he didn't want to let Daisy down. The site was vast, and there was all manner of bizarre entertainment going on, not just music. Circus acts, bungee jumping from a crane, rock-sculpting (cleverly called The Heavy Rock Festival). Daisy had her camera with her and took lots of photos. The food tents were varied and endless – some of them specialising in vegetarian food, which was an unexpected bonus. Both Daisy and Jack got something to eat, washed down with their first cider of the day. But best of all for Daisy was a tent that sold bootleg tapes of live performances from previous years and other festivals. There were hundreds of cassettes lined up: REM, The Smiths, The Cure, you name it… Amazingly, Daisy found the Jesus Jones performance from the previous night. How did they do that so quickly? She snapped it up. Another memento. It was cool to think she could listen to a concert that she was actually at.

With no bands on that Daisy wanted to see, they returned to camp. The gang were already on their way to getting wasted and were in high spirits, drinking and smoking and listening to music. Jeanie was the only one who wasn't partaking yet, still feeling a bit tender from last night. They all cheered when Jack and Daisy arrived. Daisy waved her cassette. 'Look what I've got,' she said. 'The Jesus Jones gig on bootleg from last night.'

'No way,' they all cried.

'Wicked! Stick it on,' said Aitch.

Soon they were all nodding their heads to Jesus Jones and reliving the gig.

'We've come up with a plan for today while you guys have been out,' said Aitch over the music.

'*You* have, you mean,' said Alison.

'Nah, nah, you were happy with it, too.'

'What?' said Daisy, intrigued. 'What plan?'

'He wants the boys to watch the football later,' said Alison.

'Not just the football.'

'Yes, you do.'

'What football, anyway?' said Daisy. 'And where? England aren't playing, are they?'

'No, but the team that we'll play next are – if we win. It's the first knockout match between Cameroon and Columbia. There's a cinema screen where they show films. I met these lads last night – Scousers – and they reckoned the match'll be shown this afternoon.'

'Well, what time?' said Daisy.

'Four o'clock.'

'That's the same time as James,' said Daisy. 'I'm not missing them.'

'You don't have to. That's the idea. Me and Jack and Tom can watch the footy, and you and the girls can have a bit of girlie time and watch the gig. What d'you reckon?'

'I don't know.' Daisy looked at Jack. He looked non-committal and shrugged. 'Seems a shame to split up.' She didn't really want to leave Jack.

'It's only for a couple of hours,' said Aitch. 'Surely you can do without Loverboy for a couple of hours?'

'I reckon it'll be fun,' said Jeanie. 'A bit of girlie time. Get away from this 'orrible, stinking lot for a bit.'

'Yeah,' agreed Alison. 'And we've got all night and the rest of the weekend.'

Aitch grinned. He knew he was winning.

Daisy still wasn't sure, but it seemed everyone else was. She'd really wanted Jack to see the band. But she knew if she put pressure on him, she'd run the risk of him getting stick from the lads. Both of them would. They still had the most important bands that night, she supposed. She wasn't going to watch them without him. 'We'll discuss it and let you know,' she said.

'I told you he was under the thumb,' said Aitch.

*****

Jack didn't seem fussed either way when they retreated to their tent to talk in private. Daisy had wanted to make sure. So, it was a case of going with the majority. Daisy still wasn't used to this new Jack, the one who was happy to spend time away from her. He used to be so dependent on her, following her around like a lost lamb. She missed that old Jack somehow.

Before starting the day proper – even though it was already afternoon – the girls decided they were going to go for a shower to freshen up. None of the lads were bothered. The girls returned around half an hour later, clutching their towels and washbags. 'Nice shower, ladies? Did you have one together?' teased Aitch.

'Does it look like we've had a shower?' snapped Jeanie. 'We're bone dry.'

'Oh. Thought there might be hairdryers or something.'

'Hairdryers? At this place?' said Jeanie.

'Where have you been then?' asked Tom. 'Couldn't you find them?'

'Yes, we found them,' said Daisy, coming to stand by Jack. 'But they were communal.'

'Communal?' said Tom.

'Yeah. And unisex,' said Alison.

'Urr, grey growlers everywhere, I bet,' said Aitch, bursting out laughing.

182

'So, what did you do? How did you find out?' asked Tom, taking more of an interest. Even he didn't like the thought of Alison showering with a load of naked men.

By now, Jack was cottoning on, and he didn't like the sound of it either. He looked at Daisy. 'We didn't go in,' she reassured him.

'It was gross,' said Jeanie. 'We had to queue up for ages – men and women – and this miserable guy was in charge, letting people in in groups and turning the showers on and off for a certain time. You get like five minutes or whatever, regardless of whether you've finished or not – you could hear people moaning inside about it – it was like Auschwitz. Anyway, when it was our turn – we figured there were cubicles – I walked in first…'

'She saw a guy totally naked,' Alison cut in.

'It was gross,' said Jeanie. 'He was towelling himself, and he was old and hairy and fat. Ugh!' she shuddered. 'But at least it was a bit steamy in there.'

'I didn't see anything,' Daisy said to Jack. He was looking horrified.

'What did you do?' asked Tom again.

'We walked straight back out,' said Alison, laughing.

None of the lads could believe it. The concept of naked men and women openly showering together. 'I bet you get some right dirty old gits in there,' said Aitch. 'perving over all the girls. I might go up there.'

'You'd never dare,' said Tom. 'You'd be stark-bollock naked yourself.'

'I'd keep me boxers on – like in *Weird Science*.'

'That explains why loads of people were in swimming costumes,' said Alison. 'Men and women. I did wonder why when we were queuing up.'

'Yeah, me too,' said Alison. 'I thought perhaps they were just a bit shy.'

'I don't mind showering with women,' said Jeanie. 'But not men.' Both the girls agreed.

'Me, too,' said Aitch. 'I'm just picturing it actually…' He had a dreamy, faraway look on his face.

'Pervert,' said Alison.

Jack kept quiet. He felt a bit traumatised by it all – and what a near miss it was for Daisy. He could barely shower on his own, never mind in public. With men *or* women.

*****

By the time they finally headed out, the site had got even muddier, especially the main walkways. People were ankle-deep in sludge, sometimes even losing their boots and shoes. Some were covered head to toe in the stuff. It was crazy. As three o'clock arrived, they decided to split up, as Daisy wanted to get a good spot near the front. She wished Jack was going too, and they were sad to leave each other when it came to it. After another pint of cider apiece, they were both a bit tipsy. 'Be good,' said Daisy, kissing Jack, her arms around his neck. 'No talking to strange ladies – and stay away from those showers.' She was joking, but was also fully aware of the influence Aitch could have. It was all right for Aitch; he was answerable to no one.

'You be careful too.' Jack didn't like to think of Daisy in the crush of a large crowd without him there to protect her. There were a lot of drunken, drugged-up and dubious characters about. Someone had just offered them acid. Jack and Daisy waved at each other until the girls were swallowed up in the throng.

'Right, we've got about forty-five minutes to kill, lads. Back to the beer tent,' said Aitch.

It felt strange for Jack; it was a novelty to be on his own with the lads. They had another pint and a burger each, then made their way to the big screen for the match. But when they got there, a film was showing, and there weren't that many people about. 'Strange,' said Aitch. 'I thought they'd be showing the build-up by now.'

'Yeah, me too,' said Tom.

'There's still time yet. Maybe they begin just as the match starts. Ah, I know this crappy film – my mum's always watching it. *Dirty Dancing*. I'm sure this is only about halfway through…'

'You must know it very well,' said Tom. 'Secret fan, eh?'

'Get lost. It's a load of shit. Splitties' stuff.'

Four o'clock came and went. There was no sign of the match coming on, nor of the lads Aitch had befriended the previous evening. 'I reckon they were 'aving you on,' said Tom. 'Pulling yer pisser.'

'No, they were straight up. Perhaps they'd heard it from someone else who'd got it wrong, or made it up. It's definitely today. Four o'clock today.'

'Hate to say this, buddy, but it doesn't look like it's coming on.'

'Yeah,' agreed Jack. He wasn't fussed about watching the football, and was feeling pretty wasted. And he was missing Daisy.

Aitch looked around. There was no one to ask, just girls and loved-up couples watching the film. 'Fuck's sake,' he said. 'I was looking forward to that to pass a few hours.'

'Yeah, me too,' said Tom. 'Oh well, let's split. There's got to be other stuff to do around here. We could find a band to watch, or even try and find the girls.'

'Nah, it'll all be hippy acoustic shit at this time of day. Besides, this is lad's time, remember.'

Heading back to one of the main thoroughfares, they spotted a tent selling firewood and bought a net of it for later, splitting the costs. 'The girls can pay for the next lot,' said Aitch, as they set off again. In a while, they passed a tattoo stall with two women and a mirror behind it, one doing Henna tattoos and one doing transfers. The boys stood to watch for a moment. A goth girl was having one of the transfers done. The goths were out in force that day, more than any other tribe, what with The Cure being on that night. The woman pulled back the transfer paper to reveal a stars and moon constellation design on the back of the girl's neck. It looked incredibly real. The woman held another mirror at an angle behind the girl's neck – as they do at the barber's – to show her. 'Lads. I've got a cracking idea,' said Aitch. 'Let's get fake tattoos done and pretend they're real. The girls'll go nuts. Especially your two!'

'Oh my God. Yeah,' said Tom. 'Matching ones. Something really stupid or girly. They'll go spare!'

Jack broke into a grin. Being half-pissed, he liked the idea. It would get Daisy back for the bus trick. 'Excuse me, how long do these fake ones last?' slurred Aitch.

'About a week on average,' the woman said. 'Depends where you have it done and how you look after it. If you try to wash it off, it'll go within a few days. Keep it dry and clean and in a hair-free spot, and it can last up to two weeks.'

'Spot on,' said Aitch. 'They'll last for the festival.'

'Considering you don't wash, yours'll last longer than that,' said Tom. The woman laughed.

They looked excitedly through the designs on offer, trying to find something stupid that would freak the girls out, but not so stupid that they wouldn't believe it was real.

'That one,' said Jack, determined to take part more.

'Yes,' said Tom.

'Perfect,' said Aitch, slapping Jack on the back, 'Nice one, Jackeroo!'

It was a tiger's head design. Fairly big; about the size of a rose. 'But where?' said Tom. 'We don't want them to see them straightaway. We want a big reveal. Or see how long we can go without them knowing.' The woman was smiling, getting carried away with their idea. Her hair was beaded in corn-rows.

'A design like that would work at the top of your arm, here, near your shoulder.' She pulled her T-shirt sleeve up to show them.

'Yes. Perfect,' said Aitch. 'Three tigers then, please.'

'Let's hope I've got three of them.'

Aitch went first. Sitting down in the chair and whistling, casual as you like. It didn't take long to do all three; they weren't able to stop chuckling. They thanked the woman and paid her, and she wished them good luck. They rolled up their sleeves to compare. The tattoos all looked real, Jack's the best, the lads begrudgingly agreed. It actually suited him. 'All right, stop flexing your biceps, muscle-boy,' said Tom.

Pleased with themselves, they wandered off, still grinning in anticipation of tricking the girls. Before long, they stumbled across another tent that caught their eye. The magic mushroom tent. 'Oh my God,' cried Aitch. 'Yes! We've got to get some of these for tonight, we've got to.' He was buzzing.

'What's so magic about them?' said Jack. He didn't even like mushrooms.

'What's so magic about them? Oh, Jackeroo, did you crawl out from under a rock? Don't tell me you've never heard of magic mushrooms.'

'Nope. Only poisonous ones.'

'These are not poisonous, trust me.'

'Unless you have a bad trip,' said Tom.

'You done 'em?' said Aitch.

'Nah. But a lad at college I knew did. He had a bad trip. Went bonkers apparently and never came back. But he was always a bit tapped anyway.'

'Really?' said Aitch. 'That was unlucky. Depends who yer with and where. I've done 'em twice and they were amazing. Never a bad trip.'

'What's a trip?' asked Jack.

Aitch looked at him open-mouthed. 'Are you simple or

something? A trip. Like an acid trip. It's like getting high, but about fifty times more powerful. You see stuff. It's mental. And you feel horny.'

'Really?' said Tom.

'Yeah. You get all loved up. Want to shag everyone: that's why the hippies love 'em.'

Tom laughed. 'Are they even legal? Selling them like this?' he said.

'They must be. Hold on. 'Scuse me, mate. Not being funny, but are these legal? Like if we get caught with 'em?'

'Yes, my friend, perfectly legal. As long as you buy them raw. I can't sell them dried or ready prepared,' the man said.

'Ah, spot on. And what's the best way to have 'em, fresh like this? I've only ever had dried ones before.'

'You can eat them raw or make tea out of them. I prefer the tea. Raw, they don't taste the best and they take longer to kick in – up to two hours rather than half an hour. The trip lasts longer if you eat them, sometimes up to six to eight hours, and not everybody wants that.'

'Sound,' said Aitch. They bought a bag and split the cost.

'Enjoy, lads. And you don't get your money back for a bad trip,' the man said, as they walked off.

Jack didn't like the sound of this 'bad trip' stuff. He'd have to ask Daisy about it.

'Well, considering we missed out on the match, boys, we haven't done badly,' said Aitch. 'Firewood, tattoos and a bag of shrooms for tonight. Not bad going, eh?'

'Yeah, apart from I'm gonna be skint at this rate,' said Tom.

'We'll head back to the tent now,' said Aitch. 'I could do with an afternoon snooze anyway. Sleep off some of this booze. We've got a big night ahead of us.'

This suited Jack. He was feeling decidedly woozy. An afternoon nap in the tent sounded like heaven.

*****

The next thing Jack was aware of was being kissed and nuzzled. He came round, a little disorientated and too hot. He could smell Daisy's perfume and feel her hair. She must have snuck in while he was out for the count. He groaned contentedly, pretending to be asleep, as Daisy wrapped herself round him. He'd been sleeping on top of the sleeping bags. 'Hey, sexy, hope you've been a good boy,' she said. She had cider on her breath and sounded drunk. Jack continued to pretend to be asleep, and they dozed off together…

*****

'Shit, Jack! Wake up! It's nearly six o'clock.'

'What?'

'Wake up, it's nearly six o'clock. Sinead's on in half an hour. I can't believe we've slept this long.'

'Shit.' He felt fuzzy-headed and disorientated again. His mouth was dry.

Outside, some of the gang were talking. Or squabbling. It sounded as if they were preparing the fire. Daisy was ferreting around, trying to find things, fresh clothes and her make-up bag. She and the girls had agreed to dress up a bit, to make a bit of an effort relatively speaking: it was the festival's big night – and Midsummer's Eve. Daisy was regretting it now: they were short of time and Jeanie was probably all dolled up already. It had been nice seeing her without make-up, and Daisy couldn't deny that they had bonded during the festival, especially that afternoon. Jeanie didn't seem to have an agenda any more, Daisy didn't feel so threatened by her.

Eventually, they emerged from the tent. 'Ah, here they are,' said Aitch, placing another stick on the fire they had built. 'The lovebirds. What have you two been doing in there, shagging?' Chance would be a fine thing, thought Jack. He'd just had to watch Daisy wriggling about half-naked and squeezing into a fresh top and jeans. It had been quite a sight and he was feeling amorous.

Everyone was sitting round the unlit fire in a circle. As predicted, Jeanie was putting some finishing touches to her make-up. She'd gone for a goth style to fit in, and was wearing dark clothes. The look suited her: she looked vampish. Slim. Alluring. Alison had gone all out for the occasion, hair backcombed and face painted with heavy purple eyeshadow and black lipstick. She and Tom were both wearing The Cure T-shirts. It made Daisy wish she had one: she loved the band too, and couldn't wait. But no one seemed in a rush or to understand the urgency.

'Why didn't you wake us?' said Daisy. 'Have you seen the time? We need to go.'

'Ah, there's time yet,' said Aitch.

'No, there isn't,' said Daisy. She was feeling a little grouchy and stressed having just woken up. 'We need to go. She's on at six-thirty and the crowd's going to be massive.'

'I wouldn't count on it,' said Tom. 'And the bands always start late.'

'Come on, you lot. Get off your arses,' said Alison; she knew how important the gig was to Daisy.

'Fine…' Tom sighed, getting up.

'Hold on. We've got something to show you first, haven't we, boys?' said Aitch. He winked at Jack. Jack was befuddled at first, then he remembered. He smiled. It was lucky Daisy hadn't seen his tattoo whilst he'd been sleeping.

'Well, can't it wait?' said Daisy, putting a bit of lipstick on in the mirror of her make-up bag; she didn't want to be outdone by Jeanie.

'Nope,' said Aitch. Daisy groaned. 'It won't take long.'

'Well, hurry up then.'

'Over here, boys, line up with me,' said Aitch. 'Are you ready? Daisy, are you looking? You'll want to see this. Won't she, Jack?'

Jack blushed, feeling a bit sheepish and self-conscious in front of the girls now that the alcohol had worn off.

'What are you going to do? Strip for us?' laughed Jeanie.

'Oh, it's better than that,' said Aitch.

'That wouldn't be hard,' said Jeanie.

'Promise you won't be cross, Ali?' said Tom, playing the part.

'Cross about what?'

'Just get on with it,' said Daisy.

'Are you ready, boys? Assume the position…' They all turned sideways, facing the same direction. 'One, two, three…' They rolled their T-shirt sleeves up and tensed their biceps. The girls all laughed, then their jaws dropped in unison when they saw the matching tattoos, three coloured ink tigers all in a row. The boys were all grinning.

'They are *not* real,' said Alison.

'Yep,' said Tom.

'Oh. My. God!' said Jeanie. 'You're joking.'

'Nope,' said Aitch. 'We got 'em done today as a reminder of the festival. Twenty quid a pop.'

'You absolute *idiots*,' said Alison, no longer smiling.

Suddenly, there was a distressed noise from Daisy. She dropped her make-up bag, spilling the contents everywhere, and dashed into the tent in tears.

'Daisy,' cried Jack, mortified. 'Shit.' He ran after her.

'Idiot!' said Alison again, addressing Tom. 'Look what you've gone and done now. We leave you alone for five minutes and that's what you do. How would you like it if we did that? If *I* got a tattoo – a matching one without telling you first – they're forever, you know? That'll never fucking come off. I'm going to have to look at it forever.'

Meanwhile, inside the tent, Jack was desperately trying to console Daisy. She'd flung herself on her front and was curled up in the corner, bawling her eyes out. 'Daisy, it's not real. I promise you. It's not real.'

'Get away from me!' She shrugged him off violently. 'I hate you.'

'It's not real. I promise you, look.' He rolled up his sleeve again and tried to show her, scratching at it, but she wouldn't look up.

'Go away. I hate you.'

'Daisy, it's not real. It's a transfer. It was just a joke.' He was nearly in tears, seeing her so upset. He'd hardly ever seen her so angry with him. 'It was just a joke. A stupid joke. It was Aitch's idea. I'm sorry.' He tried to hug her again, clinging onto her shaking back. He'd never expected this violent a reaction from her, not in a million years.

Daisy gradually began to calm down. 'Promise me it's not real – not that I believe a word you say any more. You're cruel.'

'I'm not. I'm sorry. And, yes, it's fake, I promise. It comes off in a couple of days…'

'I hate you,' she said again, but Jack knew she was softening now. 'Why would you do such a thing? Trick me like that? How could you be so cruel?'

'It was Aitch's idea. I'm sorry. We got carried away.'

'So if Aitch told you to jump into a fire, would you?'

'No.'

'Well then.'

'I'm sorry.'

'I thought it was real. I really did. I don't think I would ever have forgiven you.'

'Why?' he said, softly stroking her hair. She'd made her eyeliner run. 'Why did it upset you so much?'

'I don't know,' said Daisy, sniffling. 'A million reasons. It's like … it's your body. It's precious. And you'd stained and tarnished it forever. There'd be no changing it back or getting rid of it. Your body's my body in a way. I love looking at it, holding it, kissing it. And you'd changed it. Changed your character even. I didn't like it. It wasn't you, didn't suit you. And you didn't even ask me first or warn me. You'd feel the same if it was me. You'd hate it. *And* they were matching. Like you'd somehow bonded yourself to those boys. Not to me. If you were ever going to do something like that, I'd want it to be with me. We should have matching tattoos to signify our love – not those idiots. I think that really upset me too. That we'd never have a chance now; you'd already gone and done it.' It all made sense to Jack when she put it like this. He would feel the same. He hadn't thought it through. 'It wasn't just me,' she continued. 'Alison was pissed off too. I heard her shouting at Tom.'

'Yeah,' said Jack, trying to make her feel better. 'I'm sorry.'

'Let me look at the stupid thing again,' she said. She could bring herself to now she knew it wasn't real. Jack rolled up his sleeve. 'It's so pathetic,' Daisy laughed. 'A tiger, for Christ's sake. I think I would have disowned you if it was real.'

'I don't know. I kinda like it,' Jack joked. She smacked him.

They re-emerged from the tent. Daisy felt foolish. The girls had collected her make-up together and were looking sympathetic. The lads were looking sheepish, shuffling their feet.

'Sorry,' said Aitch, serious for once.

'Tom?' said Alison, as if to a child.

'Sorry,' said Tom.

'No. I'm sorry,' said Daisy. 'Guess I over-reacted a bit. Come on, let's get out. We're gonna miss Sinead at this rate – and that I *won't* forgive you for.'

'Hold on, can we have a quick photo first – of us all done up?' said Alison. 'Do you mind, Daisy?'

'Oh, bloody hell. I've been crying now, my make-up's gone everywhere. I look a right state.'

'No, you don't. Come here,' said Jeanie. 'I'll touch you up whilst Alison grabs the camera.'

'Oo aye,' said Aitch. 'Can you touch me up, too?'

'I meant her make-up.'

'Where's the camera, babes? In your tent?' said Alison.

'Yeah, at the bottom of my sleeping bag; the red one,' sniffed Daisy.

Alison headed into the tent, whilst Jeanie touched up Daisy's make-up. She'd never had a girl do this to her before. Then they all lined up for a photo. Tom stood in the middle and held the camera, as he had the longest arms. 'Everybody say shrooms,' said Aitch.

'Shrooms,' they all laughed.

It was a fine evening as they headed out, which was a blessing. The crowd for Sinead was huge, nearly double that for Jesus Jones. Determined that nothing else that evening was going to faze her, Daisy jostled her way towards the front. Jack helped to clear a path where necessary.

Sinead O'Connor was absolutely mesmerising for Daisy, and she felt starstruck for the first time in her life. She couldn't believe that *the* Sinead O'Connor, her great heroine and idol, was up there, in the flesh, on stage in front of her. She was sporting dark sunglasses, faded denim jeans and a black leather jacket, which she removed to reveal a 'Fat Slags' from *Viz* T-shirt. Her voice was amazing. That unique mix of fragility and raw punk venom negotiated a crowd-pleasing setlist of songs from both her albums. She finished with 'Nothing Compares 2 U', which the gang, along with the rest of the crowd, sang along to. Daisy was blown away – and possibly experiencing her first girl crush.

During the break, as they waited for The Cure, they headed to the beer tent. Whilst quaffing their much-needed pints, Aitch revealed to the girls that the night's plans involved a certain hallucinogenic fungus. The girls were a little shocked, but also a little giggly and excited. None of them had ever tried magic mushrooms before. But Daisy remembered her dad talking about his experiences 'back in the day'. 'I'm not letting you out with those two again,' she said to Jack in front of everyone. 'They're a bad influence. First tattoos, now magic mushrooms!'

'Under the thumb,' Aitch muttered under his breath, and they all laughed.

They drank their pints as something around them began to build. An atmosphere. Something in the air. Expectancy. The crowd began to swell. And swell. As a result, they felt themselves being pressed further to the side. They could still see the stage well enough, as they were about halfway back, but all around them, especially between them and the stage, people were tightly jammed in. And still they kept coming. There were a lot of goths and Rob Smith lookalikes, both boys and girls – all back-combed hair, eye shadow and smeared lipstick. It was an awesome sight to behold, but scary too. Suffocating. By the time the band finally appeared, the atmosphere was electric. Coloured lights illuminated the stage and the crowd. Flares went off. And then the band took their places, shrouded in the mist and hiss of dry ice. The crowd went ballistic. People were crying and holding their hands up, as if praising gods.

The sound of the music itself was like nothing Daisy and Jack had heard before in its clarity, clearness and volume. You could hear every note, every hypnotic drum beat: it built a wall of sound over which the vocals soared. It was as if Robert Smith was actually in your ears, singing only to you. People had their eyes closed. Daisy nudged Jack and gestured at Tom and Alison. He was standing behind her, holding her, both of them enraptured. It was a lovely sight. Not being big fans of the band, Jeanie and Aitch looked a little bemused by it all; the adoration, the fascination.

And then something strange happened. During the song 'Fascination Street', the band stopped playing unexpectedly, and Robert Smith told the crowd they were going to have to stop for a while: people were getting crushed at the front and someone was in a bad way. The music was replaced by a murmur that rippled through the crowd. There was a sense that panic could spread. Smith told everyone to step backwards and clear a space: a rescue helicopter was on its way. And then, a few minutes later, against the backdrop of red and amber smoke, it appeared, hovering over the crowd. Gasps went up. It was scary, but thrilling. People had come to see a rock concert, not to be bit-players in a disaster movie. 'Jesus Christ,' said Aitch. 'It's like *Apocalypse Now!*'

As the helicopter landed, in a field next to the stage, everyone waited with baited breath, craning their necks to see what was going on. Rob Smith asked everybody to take a couple of steps backwards again. After what seemed like an age, but was only about five minutes, the helicopter took off again. Everyone cheered as it disappeared into the Somerset night. What had they just witnessed? Something they would never forget, that was for sure. The band struck up again from where they had left off. But between songs, Rob still asked the audience to step back. It had shaken the band and the crowd.

Eventually, as the gig went on and the sun set behind the stage, the incident melted into a midsummer memory. The music hypnotised the crowd again. And as dusk fell, the coloured light show became even more breathtaking. The performance of 'A Forest' was a spectacle to behold, the crowd bathed in hues of vivid lime and deep woodland green, clapping in unison to the repetitive echoing bassline at the end of the song. Jack and Daisy looked at each other in wonder, knowing they were experiencing something they would never forget. It was one of those moments when you are aware a memory is being created. Something to cherish and never forget. A notch on the timeline of your life.

Everyone seemed a bit stunned afterwards, and not a lot was said as the gang joined the mass exodus back to the campsites. Jack and Daisy held hands, as did Alison and Tom. There was the usual drunken revelry across the festival site. People off their trolleys. Fires burning, with people jumping over them and hollering. Music was everywhere. Thumping music in the background. It always seemed to be there. Back at the tent, away from the bright lights of the stage, it seemed lighter, incredibly so for the time of day.

'Right, this is where the evening really begins,' said Aitch. He'd been looking forward to this all day. 'Let's get that fire started and put the kettle on.'

'Are we really going to do this?' said Alison.

'Yeah,' said Aitch.

'I'm looking forward to it,' said Tom.

Jack and Daisy looked at each other pensively. They weren't sure about it. It was a big step, even if it *was* a natural drug.

'It can't be that bad, surely,' said Jeanie. 'It's only mushrooms.'

'Oh, just you wait, Cupcake,' said Aitch. 'It's gonna blow your mind.'

'I've already had my mind blown tonight,' groaned Daisy.

The fire was lit. The music was put on. And so was the kettle. 'Jeanie, put the kettle on, Jeanie put the kettle on…' sang Aitch, as the stove was lit.

'Aitch, shut your fucking mouth, Aitch, shut your fucking mouth…' replied Tom, and everyone cracked up.

The fire was a revelation. Not a big one – you weren't allowed – but hot enough that they had to move their chairs back. It was a shame they hadn't had it the previous night. But it seemed apt, to Daisy at least, that they were having one on Midsummer's Eve, to carry on the parents' traditions. Her dad would be proud, looking down on her from somewhere up above, she thought sadly.

Jack and Tom rolled spliffs, and these were passed round whilst the kettle boiled. Aitch, meanwhile, began to prepare his magic tea, chopping up the mushrooms and whacking them into the largest pan they had. Sugar was dished out into six mugs. He kept on checking the kettle obsessively until the water was only just coming to the boil. Too hot and it could kill some of the mushrooms' effect, apparently. He poured the hot water into the mushroom pan and let them steep for a while, stirring them occasionally with a wooden spoon. When they were ready, he dispensed the potent water into the waiting mugs, using the pan lid as a makeshift sieve. 'It doesn't matter if you get some of the shrooms in there,' he said. 'Just pick 'em out or eat them. They're perfectly safe, but don't taste the best – and might give you a bit of stomach ache.'

'I think I'll pass,' said Alison. Everyone agreed.

They all sat back in their seats with their tea, but no one was allowed to try it without Aitch's go-ahead. They all had to have it at the same time apparently, so they 'came up' together. 'Right, bottoms up, then,' said Aitch, raising his mug aloft. 'Have a nice trip.'

'Yep. See you on the other side,' said Tom, doing the same.

They all raised their mugs. 'I'm scared,' said Jeanie.

'Me too,' giggled Alison nervously.

Jack and Daisy looked at each other. Both of them nervous, but not wanting to chicken out and curious to experience something new. Especially together. They all took a sip. 'Ugh,' that's bitter, said Daisy.

'Yeah, it's gross,' said Jeanie.

'Put some more sugar or some milk in it,' said Aitch.

'I think it's OK,' said Tom, picking out a bit of mushroom.

'Yeah, you've got about ten sugars in yours,' said Alison.

'Three actually,' said Tom.

'I don't know whether I'm going to be able to drink it all,' said Daisy. It was making her want to retch.

'Me neither,' said Jack.

'You've got to,' said Aitch. 'Stop being wusses. Just soldier on with it – like medicine – or some of us'll be trippin' and some won't.'

'How do we know when it's working?' said Alison.

'Oh, you'll know.'

'What should we be expecting?' said Jeanie.

'A ride. A wild ride. Like nothing you've experienced before. And if anyone's freaking out – having a bad trip – just give them some space and let them calm down, but don't leave them. It can be a lonely place. Give them some love and reassurance. Be there for them.'

'Jesus, what are you, a counsellor now?' said Tom.

'Yeah. Just call me the Love Doctor…'

Jack felt nervous again at the expression 'bad trip'. He didn't like it. It made him think of space. Black, infinite space. Travelling to a black hole and not being able to get back home. Just drifting.

They all sat back, waiting for the effect to kick in. Jack had the odd swig of cider to help wash down the grim-tasting liquid.

'How long's it gonna take?' asked Tom. He'd already necked two-thirds of his tea and wasn't feeling a thing. 'I reckon I'm immune to it. Like hypnotism. You couldn't hypnotise me if you tried.'

'Stop talking shit, Thomas,' said Aitch. 'It takes at least twenty minutes, sometimes longer, depending on how strong they are.'

'How do you know if they're magic? What if it was a con or something?' asked Jeanie.

'You don't, but they looked real. Liberty Caps, they're called.'

'We'll see,' said Tom.

Around fifteen minutes later, Tom and Aitch had both finished their tea. The others had given up, not able to finish the last quarter. They'd all been quiet, staring into the fire. Jack and Daisy were holding hands. 'How you feeling?' asked Daisy. Her voice was slurry. It seemed faraway to Jack.

'Nice. Stoned,' he said. His voice sounded faraway, too. It was an effort to speak. Daisy's hand felt nice in his. Kind of warm and tingly.

'Jesus, look at the sky,' said Tom. 'There's shooting stars. Thousands of 'em!'

''E's gone, cried Aitch. 'It's working.'

Everyone looked up. Tom was right. The sky was littered with shooting stars and comets.

And so it began…

'I feel sick,' said Jeanie. 'I can't look at them. It's making my head spin.'

'Me, too,' said Alison.

'It's just the shrooms kicking in,' said Aitch. 'It'll pass, just relax.'

'Look, my hands throbbing,' said Tom. 'It's huge. Look! It's going in and out. It's glowing.'

'Move it,' said Aitch. 'Look.' He waved his arm about. 'My arm's got a trail behind it, like a sparkler, like a light sabre.'

Jack and Daisy looked down at their free hands and waved them about. They were glowing too. Their other hands were still connected. It felt nice. Secure. But hot now. Aitch stood up and began circling the fire, brandishing his arm and making light sabre noises. 'Look, I'm Luke Skywalker.' Everyone began laughing. He looked such an idiot. 'Why are you laughing? I *am* Luke Skywalker.' He began lunging and swiping. This made them laugh even harder.

'Luke Skywanker, more like,' cried Tom.

'I am Luke Skywanker,' said Aitch, doing karate chops now. That was it. Everyone began howling with laughter until tears rolled down their faces. They held their stomachs in agony.

'I am Luke Skywanker,' cried Aitch, making obscene gestures.

'Stop!' cried Jeanie. 'Please, stop! I can't breathe. I'm going to wet myself.'

Tom was rocking back on his chair and slapping his knees so hard that all of a sudden, his chair gave way and he collapsed backwards. This took them onto a whole new level. No one could get control of themselves. All that could be heard was almost noiseless laughter, gasps and cries of agony. Every time someone tried to calm down, someone else would set them off again. This went on for what seemed like hours. Tom was rolling around on the floor. 'Ah, it feels nice,' he said, finally regaining control. 'It's cool down here. Feel the floor.' Aitch began rolling round, too.

'It's cool. It's like the sea,' he said.

'Look at the fire. It's so bright,' said Jeanie. 'It's got faces in it. Can anyone else see the faces? The lions' faces?'

'Aitch looks like the glowing man from *Scooby Doo*,' said Jack. He thought it, and it just came out.

'He does: the deep-sea diver,' said Alison.

'No, the Kelp Monster,' said Daisy.

'The Ready Brek kid,' said Jeanie.

'Can anyone see grids?' said Tom. 'I can see grids everywhere. It's like I'm in a computer game. Like *Tron*.'

'I need music,' said Daisy. 'I need to dance.' She got up, but too quickly. This was a mistake. The ground seemed uneven: as Aitch had said, a rolling sea. She reached out to Jack for sanctuary. His arm felt good. Safe and secure. The sea stopped rolling. She brushed his cheek with her hand. They locked eyes. It felt amazing. He looked amazing. Daisy dragged herself away to turn the music up. It was an indie mix; all the favourites. She began dancing, unabashed, and everyone joined in. They danced round the fire, hollering and throwing shapes like Red Indians. 'I am the Resurrection' by the Stone Roses came on and everyone cheered. 'Turn it up,' Aitch said. The song was a long one, about eight minutes or so, an epic. But it seemed to last for hours, days. Time became of no consequence. They became lost in their own worlds of shifting shapes and bright colours. Light and shadows. They jumped over the fire. A bottle of whisky appeared from somewhere, and they shared it, swigging from it and spitting it on the fire to make it flare. There was a lot of love and gratitude. Overwhelming affection. Everyone told everyone else they loved them. Then, as the hours slipped by, everyone disappeared down their own little *Alice in Wonderland* rabbit hole. They began to split up. Aitch seemed quite content to be on his own, still clutching his whisky bottle for dear life. He had become convinced that the floor and campsite were a sea: he was on a raft and couldn't fall in. All the other tents that were glowing in the dark were other ships, galleons, an armada. Alison and Tom seemed to stick together, lost in their own little trip. So did Jack and Daisy. Jeanie stuck with them, which was a surprise but seemed OK. She looked pretty. Beautiful to Daisy, and Daisy told her so. She told Daisy she was beautiful too. The two of them danced for an eternity. Jack stopped to watch them; to stare at the shapes and silhouettes and patterns. But Daisy couldn't stop. It was as if she had the red shoes on, from the film. Then 'Land: Horses/Land of a Thousand Dances…' by Patti Smith came on. Daisy was in her element. She became lost in the ebbs and flows of the song, in her own little world. A world of a thousand dances. She did them all, calling them out, as in the song. The Twist. The Mashed Potato. The Watusi. The Swim… Jeanie tried to keep up with Daisy, but struggled. Jack wanted to dance as well, but couldn't get up. Couldn't move. He was glued to his chair. Physically glued. A weight on him. Who'd done it and when? Was it Aitch? A trick? Eventually the music stopped, and in the silence he became aware of Tom trying to make Alison understand something. They were close by, but where had they been? He hadn't seen them for hours. Days. Tom was holding out his hand to Alison and trying to show her something in his palm. He was pointing. She was holding his hand. 'But how much have I got?' Tom said.

'You don't need to pay for it. Here, you can have it.' Alison was trying to pass him a bottle of water.

'No, I need to pay you for it. How much have I got?' He sounded angry, and kept pointing at the money in his hand.

'I don't know. I can't add it up. But you don't need to pay for it.'

'I do. How much have I got?'

Jack got up to go over to them. It was a real effort, but he didn't like Tom sounding angry and upset; he wanted to help them out, and to impress them with his counting skills.

'Jackeroo,' said Tom. 'God, I love you. Where have you been? Where have you been, buddy?'

'I've been right here.'

'I knew you wouldn't leave me. Help me out, buddy. I need to pay for this water. How much money have I got?'

'He doesn't need to pay for it, Jack. Tell him he doesn't,' said Alison.

'Don't listen to her, Jack. Listen to me. Have I got enough to pay for the water? I'm so thirsty.' Jack became confused. It became the most important thing in his life. The most important thing he had ever known: to be able to help his friend out, to be able to count the money.

But he couldn't. He simply couldn't. He stared and stared, but it made no sense. It was just metal shapes throbbing in the palm of Tom's hand like little planets. They had no meaning. No currency. Currency made no sense. It was of no value or importance. This made Jack scared and sad. Sad that he couldn't help his friend. Unexpectedly, he began to cry. 'I'm sorry, Tom, I don't know. I can't help you.' And once he'd started, he couldn't stop.

Daisy and Jeanie overheard and came over. 'Hey, what's wrong? Baby, what's wrong? Don't cry,' said Daisy.

'I couldn't help Tom,' said Jack. 'I couldn't help him count the money. He's thirsty.'

'It's OK.'

But it wasn't OK. He couldn't stop crying. Bad thoughts had

crept up to him, negative ones. His trip was turning, exactly what he had been dreading. He started to think of Anne and began to get confused. 'I couldn't help her, Daisy.'

'Who?'

'Anne. I wasn't there to help her. It's my fault she's dead. I want to die.' He was inconsolable.

'Oh, baby, don't say that. Come into the tent. Let me heal you. Me and Jeanie will heal you, won't we, Jeanie?'

'Yes. We're the healers,' said Jeanie. She really wanted to help.

'Come on,' said Daisy. They shepherded Jack into a tent, they weren't sure whose, and laid him down. He was still crying, still thinking black thoughts.

'Shush,' Daisy said. 'Shush, baby. Take his hand,' she said to Jeanie. They knelt either side of him, taking a hand each and stroking it. Immediately Jack began to calm down. It felt good. Warm. Tingly. 'See,' said Daisy. 'That's it. You just need to let us heal you.' They continued to stroke his hands. Daisy couldn't express how good it felt to touch his hand. Her man's hand. To heal him. It was the best thing she had ever felt. 'Can you feel that?' she said to Jeanie. 'It feels amazing.'

'Yeah, it does.' Jeanie had a dreamy look on her face. Daisy became aware she was slipping into a different phase. She felt overcome with the concept of physical love and beauty. Of physical connection. Of wanting to give and receive it. She wanted to touch more of Jack. She wanted Jeanie to touch more of Jack. To share him with her. To share the feeling.

'Let's take his top off,' said Daisy. 'He's hot.'

'He is hot. His hands are hot,' said Jeanie.

They pulled Jack's T-shirt over his head. He groaned quietly, but let them do it, barely aware of what was going on. Daisy shushed him as he lay there, bare-chested. He looked amazing. Like a young god. Daisy began to stroke his chest and his arms. The skin-on-skin contact was heavenly. Sensual.

She wanted Jeanie to experience it, too. 'Touch him,' she said. 'Feel his skin. I want you to.' Jeanie obeyed. It was if she was in a trance, under Daisy's spell. She touched Jack's bare chest and sighed unexpectedly in pleasure. It triggered something in Daisy. That sound. She'd heard it in her dreams. Those dreams about Jack and Jeanie. It was all getting confusing, wrapped up with those dreams. It made her feel amorous. Horny. She could make it happen. She could be the director of her own movie. Maybe that's what she needed. To sit there and watch. To rid herself of the thoughts. To stop them.

'Touch his arm,' Daisy said. 'Stroke it.' Jeanie did as she was asked, and sighed again. It was erotic. Addictive. Daisy began to kiss his chest. Light, seductive kisses. He began to respond for the first time, to moan. Jack reached for Daisy's hair and grabbed it, as if checking it was her. She ran her lips down his chest and stomach as Jeanie continued to sigh and stroke his arm and chest. It was as if Jack was Charles Manson and they were his disciples, his harem. Daisy felt overcome. That she could do this. Her inhibitions and insecurities were entirely gone. There was something empowering about it. To face your nemesis and demons. You only live once. You're only young once. She began to unbuckle his belt...

And that was when Jack became aware of what was happening. He felt for Daisy again, but found Jeanie instead. He sat bolt upright and cried, 'No!'

It shocked Daisy out of her lustful stupor. And Jeanie. They became aware of themselves, as if coming round. Aware of what was going on.

'What the hell are you doing?' Jack cried, shoving Daisy off. 'I'm sorry, Jack. I don't know...'

'You're not Daisy,' he said. 'None of you are. You're possessed. Get off me!' He pushed the girls out of the way, and, still bare-chested, burst out of the tent and into the night.

Jack ran and ran, not knowing where he was going or what

he was doing. Once, he tripped over a guy-rope and went sprawling. The people within hurled abuse. He got up and ran again, but had hurt his leg. He limped on, not knowing where he was going or what field he was in any more. Jack slowed down, searching for anything familiar. Up ahead, he noticed a pale shape, a blur in the darkness heading towards him. It was a person. A boy. The boy was getting closer and closer; his gait looked familiar. He was nearly upon Jack, as if he was going to career straight into him. Jack had to move quickly out of the way. As the boy sped past, Jack saw Aitch's face and mop of curly hair. His eyes were wide and manic, unseeing. His breath urgent. He was bare-chested too. His skin brushed Jack's, ever so briefly. It felt cold. And then he was gone. 'Aitch!' Jack called. The boy hadn't seen him, or recognised him. 'Aitch!' But he was gone, gone in the darkness. A vanishing ghost.

Jack felt sad again. Lost. He wanted it to go away now. This feeling. He wanted normality back. He wanted his friends back. He wanted Daisy.

'Jack!' Daisy, he thought. Was he imagining it? 'Jack!'

'Daisy?' He turned.

'Jack.' She ran up to him, breathless, and threw her arms around him. 'Jack, I'm sorry. I don't know what I was thinking. It's the mushrooms.' She bent and put her hands on her knees, as if she was going to retch.

Jack had almost forgotten what had happened. Scenes came and went so quickly. Only the current one was important. 'I saw Aitch,' he said. 'Did you see him?'

'Aitch? No. When?'

'Just now. I saw him.'

'Probably still tripping,' she said. But *she* wasn't: it was wearing off. She could sense reality coming back. Blessed reality. She wanted Jack back with her too. 'Jack,' she said, grabbing hold of his arms again. 'I'm sorry. I need you to understand.' She looked into his face, just visible in the dark. He still looked a bit out of it, his pupils dilated. 'I never would have done that. It was the drugs. I hate the thought of it already. It makes me feel sick. I'm sorry. I love you.' And she kissed his lips.

And as if by magic, that word 'love', as Aitch had said, love and understanding, brought Jack back round. Like the undoing of a spell. He was back; Daisy could see it in his face. 'It's OK, I love you, too,' he said. Daisy hugged him in relief.

'Come on, let's go and get some water,' she said.

They drank from the tap, gallons it seemed, their thirsts unquenchable. Jack let the cold water run over his head and hair. Then they sat on the breeze blocks at the base of the water point and looked around them. It was getting light. The glow of the sun, but not the sun itself, was changing the hue of the sky on the horizon. A few other people were milling about, stumbling around in the semi-darkness. Jack and Daisy looked at each other. Glad to be back to reality. 'Never again,' Daisy said.

CHAPTER 18

Glastonbury: Day Three

It was midday before Jack and Daisy woke, both of them with banging headaches and dry mouths, exacerbated by the heat of the tent.

Daisy ventured out first, saying she would put the kettle on. The weather was overcast again, and breezy. It looked like rain. A few tents had caved in and were sagging. Some were in total ruins. There was an abundance of litter blowing about. Some people, Daisy noticed, were packing up, while others had already gone; the scene resembled a semi-deserted battlefield. For the first time Daisy thought about going home early herself. She felt like shit, and seeing other people leaving gave her a twinge of envy, a longing for home comforts. A hot bath. Proper food. A decent night's sleep in a real bed. She'd seen all the bands she really wanted to see. Although World Party were playing later on, she wouldn't lose any sleep if she missed them.

In contrast to many of the other tents, theirs were intact and zipped up – which was surprising. Last night, Daisy thought, as things came back to her. Her stomach cartwheeled. How was she going to face Jeanie? Would things ever be the same again? As she put the kettle on, she noticed a spattering of vomit between two of their tents. Gross. Another reason to leave.

Daisy and Jack drank their tea in silence, lost in their own private thoughts. Alison emerged next, followed by Tom. They looked fragile and sheepish. Everyone was a little unsure, a little embarrassed, as if they'd made fools of themselves. It was all such a blur. There were so many blanks to fill in, and this took some effort. Mutual effort. Jeanie appeared next, quite a bit later, as if she'd been putting off facing everyone. Daisy found it hard to look her in the eye. No one was owning up to being sick yet. And there was only one person left to surface. Aitch. The medicine man, the shaman. And it was nearly two. 'Shall we wake him up?' said Tom. 'Teach him a lesson for doing this to us all?'

'Yeah. He gets us all off our trolleys, then lies low till the heat's off,' said Alison.

'I could just go back to sleep again,' said Jeanie.

'Shall we pack up and go home? Leave him here on his own?' said Daisy. She'd said it as a joke, but also wanted to gauge everyone's reaction to calling it a day. Sow the seed...

'Yeah, can you imagine?' said Tom, cracking up. 'He finally wakes up and we've all fucked off. That would be so funny.'

'Oh God, home,' said Jeanie. 'A proper bed. What I'd give for that.' Daisy brightened at this – a potential fellow-deserter. She looked at Jeanie properly for the first time that day. She looked young again. Pale and vulnerable. Daisy had no ill-will towards her at all. Last night had been her own doing. She felt a bit sorry for Jeanie. She seemed quite simple and vulnerable. No steady boyfriend and a bit pampered. She was probably who'd been sick. Again.

'Shall we do it?' said Tom. 'Shake his tent and wake him up?'

'Seems a bit cruel,' said Alison. 'I didn't see him go last night. He just seemed to vanish. God knows what time he went to bed.'

'I saw him,' said Jack. Only just remembering. Like a lot of other things about last night, he had totally forgotten. 'It was just before we went to bed, early morning. He ran past me in the field, but didn't see me.'

'Probably off his tits,' said Tom. 'Fuck it, I'm waking him up. Why should he get to lie in all day?' Tom got up and approached Aitch's tent. He began to circle it, pushing the canvas in and talking in a scary voice, 'Aitch, wake up. It's the mushroom police, we've come to arrest you.' Everyone laughed. 'Aitch, wake up.' He continued to push at the tent and rock it. 'The campsite's flooding. You were right.' There was no response. 'Aitch!' Tom shouted. 'Wake up, it's the filth.' Still there was nothing, not a snore, not a fart. 'Fuck it, I'm unzipping it. I know he can hear me.'

'Tom!' said Alison.

Everyone watched as Tom got down on all fours and unzipped the tent. 'Boo!' he shouted, thrusting his head in quickly. They all braced themselves for a retaliatory response. 'Oh,' came Tom's muffled voice instead. 'He's not here.' He withdrew his head and looked at everyone, quizzically. 'That's odd.'

'Perhaps he got lucky,' said Jeanie. 'Found himself a lady.'

'Aitch?' said Alison. 'A girl?'

'You never know – it's a festival. 'Free love' and all that,' said Jeanie. Then she wished she hadn't and looked guilty.

'Nah,' said Tom. 'It may be all he bangs on about, but when it comes down to it, he's more interested in getting wasted. If he fell into a barrel of tits, he'd come up sucking his thumb.'

'Tom!' said Alison again. 'I don't know what's got into you lately.' But everyone found it funny.

'Just quoting the great man himself. One of Aitch's favourite lines…'

'Well, where can he be?' said Jeanie. 'Anyone actually hear him come back last night? I mean, this morning?' They all shook their heads.

'Maybe he's gone for a wander,' said Daisy. 'Clear his head.'

'I can't see Aitch getting up before any of us,' said Tom.

'Well, what if he got lost last night? Couldn't find his way back?' said Alison.

'I don't see how that's possible – not when it's light anyway. There's enough information and staff about the place… He'll be back. He's not stupid – well, not totally. Maybe he's just sleeping it off somewhere. This place is huge. Or maybe's he's made some more mates. Like the night before. He'll talk to anyone. You know what he's like,' said Tom.

'Let's give it another hour,' said Daisy. 'Then maybe have a wander ourselves. With the map, we could do the whole site if we split up. But someone ought to stay here, just in case he comes back.'

'Good idea,' said Alison.

Jack nodded in agreement. He felt a little uneasy.

And so they waited.

*****

An hour later and Aitch still wasn't back. The day was getting on. But none of them had left the campsite, except for trips to the ever more revolting toilets. Until Aitch was accounted for, they didn't like doing anything, certainly not going to watch a band. And they all still felt a bit fragile: there had been a lot of staring into space going on.

They decided to search the site for Aitch, as planned. Tom, Alison, Jack and Daisy. Jeanie agreed to stay at the tents; she was feeling the worst, as usual. Alison had her copy of the festival programme, containing the site map, and Daisy had hers. But before separating, they decided to try the medical tent. This was Daisy's idea and seemed a good starting point.

Ducking inside, they were all feeling a little apprehensive – and foolish. What did they say? That they'd lost their friend? And then describe him, like ashamed and distraught parents describing a lost child? They half-expected – or hoped – to see Aitch sitting there, the silly sod – in a daze on one of the chairs, head or arm comically bandaged up, along with some other casualties. But he wasn't. Just two teenage girls, one of them in tears and clutching her stomach.

Daisy stepped up to the makeshift desk, where a couple of decidedly serious and stressed out-looking staff were sitting – very different from the information centre guy. 'Excuse me,' said Daisy. 'I know this might sound daft – but we appear to have lost our friend.' She laughed nervously.

The staff didn't laugh, just gave each other a look, then scrutinised Daisy. There seemed something odd about their reaction, and a sombre mood about the place in general. The gang picked up on it. Jack was jigging from one foot to the other, feeling stressed and claustrophobic. 'When did you see your friend last?' the man asked.

'Well, last night,' said Daisy. 'I mean, this morning – wasn't it, guys?' She turned to the rest of them for support. They shuffled forwards.

'Yeah,' said Tom, clearing his throat. 'This morning – not sure what time, though.'

'Approximately?' They all looked at each other and shrugged.

'Erm … well, Jack saw him last. It was getting light, but only just, so maybe around five? Sorry, it's hard to say…' Daisy felt guilty, as if everyone knew they'd been on mushrooms; as if they could read their minds.

'So, your friend is male?' the man said.

'Yeah. His name's Aitch,' said Alison. The staff looked at each other again.

'And how old is your friend? Same age as you guys?' the lady said.

'Yeah, he's eighteen. Just,' said Tom.

'And can you describe him for me?'

'Erm, yeah – but is there something going on here? Has something happened? Has Aitch been in?' said Tom.

'We don't want to concern you unnecessarily. We have dozens of young people come in here over the course of the festival. Can you just describe Aitch for me – if you don't mind? Hair colour, height, build etc…' The man was leaning forward.

'He's about, what, five-nine, I guess.' Tom held a flat hand to the side of his face, eye-level. 'Slim. Curly hair, sandy-brown…'

The man swallowed. 'And any distinguishing markings?'

'Like what?' said Daisy.

'You know, moles, scars, tattoos…'

The gang all looked at each other at the word 'tattoos'. They had the same look on their faces; acute anxiety, the sense that something was unfolding, something they couldn't stop.

'He's got a tattoo,' said Tom. 'Like this – it's only a temporary one.' He rolled up his sleeve and thrust his arm forwards. 'We got 'em done yesterday.'

The lady behind the desk let out a sob. 'Sorry.' She put her hand to her mouth, as a tear escaped her eye.

'What? What's going on here?' said Tom.

'You say you saw him this morning at about, what, five o'clockish? And you haven't seen him since?'

'Yes, about that,' said Daisy.

The man sat back in his chair. 'I think you all ought to take a seat.'

The hair on Daisy's scalp contracted – it reminded her of the phone call on the day her dad had died. Jack felt exactly the same: tiny spiders of dread crawling over his skin, arm-hairs standing on end. 'He's OK, isn't he?' said Alison, her voice wobbling slightly.

'Just take a seat over there. All of you. And we'll get someone to come and talk to you.' He gestured to a row of four empty seats.

'Just tell us what's going on, you fucking prick,' said Tom. It shocked everybody.

'Now there's no need for that, young man – aggressive behaviour won't be tolerated; it doesn't help anyone. Just take a seat over there. Mary, can you nip next door, please. You OK?' She nodded. 'Mary's going to fetch a police officer to talk to you.' The lady got up, still wiping her eyes. 'I'm sorry, I can't say any more,' the man said. 'Just take a seat and an officer will be with you.'

'He's OK, isn't he? At least tell us that. Where is he? In hospital?' said Alison.

'I'm sorry. A seat please.' The gang sat down, exasperated, distraught and confused. The man followed them. 'Would you like to move in here a moment, please,' he said to the waiting girls. 'Someone will be with you shortly.' He ushered them into one of two makeshift cubicles. He closed the curtain behind them.

Then, two police officers – not just normal bobbies – arrived. Mary pointed towards them. The officers looked serious. 'Have we got anywhere more private?' one of them asked.

'Erm, one of the cubicles?' the man said.

'Yes, that'll do. First,' he said, 'is anyone family? Related to your missing friend?' They all shook their heads. 'OK, bring your chairs in. Actually, you're probably all better on the bed; there isn't room. Are you OK standing outside, Dave?' he asked his colleague.

'Sarge,' he said in return. They all shuffled into the cubicle. The four of them sat on the bed. The man closed the curtain.

There was an expectant silence as the officer sat down and took off his hat. The enclosed space felt too warm and small for them all; it smelt funny too. The officer cleared his throat, looking terribly serious again. 'I regret to inform you that an as yet unidentified young man matching your description – Caucasian, medium height, slim, curly brown hair, tiger tattoo on his shoulder – was discovered on the festival site at around six-thirty a.m. near one of the water points.' They all held their breath. 'He was in a bad way and was taken to Yeovil District hospital around seven-thirty a.m…'

'But he's OK now?' cut in Alison. 'He's OK and being looked after?'

'I'm sorry to say,' the officer swallowed, 'that the young man didn't make it. The hospital staff did their utmost to save him, but he was pronounced dead at around eight-thirty of suspected drug-related complications. I'm very sorry.'

The girls let out sobs of disbelief. Jack gave an anguished howl. Tom burst into tears. 'I'm truly very sorry,' the officer repeated, bowing his head. He paused to give them time for it to sink in. Alison turned to Tom and Daisy to Jack – but Jack was staring straight ahead, seemingly in shock. She threw her arms around him. He was rigid, unyielding. 'Jack,' she said. He came to slowly and finally turned towards her, his mouth frozen in a bitter grimace. His eyes didn't follow his head. Then they caught up, his look vacant and empty. 'Jack,' she said again. Finally, he registered her properly, and another involuntary sound escaped his mouth. He butted his head against hers and they sat there, stunned. Surely this wasn't real? A bad dream or the aftermath of their trips? Jack became aware of Tom and Alison crying, close by but seemingly a world away. No tears would come for him.

The officer cleared his throat again. 'The unfortunate young man hasn't been formally identified yet – but it appears we're talking about the same person, what with the matching tattoo description. It's of the greatest significance that you've all come forward and declared him missing. So thank you and well done for that.' He paused for a moment. 'I'm sorry… I know this is tough, and a dreadful shock for you all, but in order to remove any doubt – for you and the boy's family, and so the relevant parties can be informed as soon as possible – could we start with one of you telling us your friend's full name?'

The rest of the conversation was a blur. Despite his tears, Tom bravely managed to deal with most of the officer's questions – he knew Aitch the best – his full name, date of birth, his parents' names and contact details. But they all pitched in where they could, all feeling responsible for Aitch and wanting to reunite him with his family. The conversation took an unexpected turn when the officer asked if any of them, including Aitch, had knowingly taken the drug ecstasy the previous evening. They all looked at each other, shocked, and said 'no'. Ecstasy? What was that all about? The officer went on to explain that early signs indicated the nature of Aitch's death was consistent with that of an ecstasy-related one. 'You sure?' he said. 'It's vitally important you tell the truth.' They were all scared, guilty at what they had been doing. They all shook their heads solemnly again.

The unexpected ecstasy conversation temporarily diverted the gang's thoughts from the awful reality. But a collective feeling of numbness and dread returned the second they left the confines of the tent: the feeling they were living a surreal nightmare that there was no waking up from. A member of staff from the welfare tent accompanied them back to the campsite; they still had to tell Jeanie. The prospect of this was awful beyond belief: to play the officer's part, to know you were going to ruin someone's life with words, with information, especially when you were still trying to deal with it yourself. The welfare person stayed with them throughout. Jeanie was utterly devastated, but characteristically handled it worse. Unlike Jack and Daisy, death had not previously visited her young life; and Tom and Alison were more level-headed. She was hysterical, refusing to believe it was true at first. Like Tom, Jeanie had gone to school with Aitch, both primary and secondary. School-mates and work colleagues didn't just die and disappear at the age of eighteen. Forever. Especially not in such a tragic, avoidable way. But was any death of a young person not tragic? Jeanie wanted her mum. She wanted to go home.

But they couldn't. Not yet. First, they had to pack up their tents, and then they had to make a horrific trip to the hospital to formally identify the body. None of them wanted to do this, and they were given the option not to; it was just a request. But again, out of respect for Aitch's family – and for Aitch himself, to speed up the process of him returning home – they agreed they wanted to do it. The police officer was relieved; for the best part of the day, they'd had the body of a dead boy on their hands with no leads as to who he was. It looked as though Tom was going to be the one burdened with the dreadful task.

Packing up the tents was a wretched affair. They all did Aitch's, and cried together. His rucksack was inside. His baccy tin. His clothes: his new Happy Mondays T-shirt, so white and clean; his England football shirt. His newspaper… It was heartbreaking. But they couldn't bear to leave anything behind. To leave a piece of him behind. They all kept on expecting him to pop up, hungover and grinning. The same reverence went out of the window for the rest of their gear: if something could be left or dumped it was, including a tent, a couple of ripped sleeping bags and all manner of food.

To Daisy's further desolation, the one thing she couldn't locate anywhere was her camera. It had vanished into thin air. This was all she needed; all any of them needed. They pulled their tents apart looking for it, even rifling through the dumped stuff, but it was nowhere to be found. Daisy was distraught, and broke down again as Jack comforted her. They all knew, without saying anything, that it wasn't merely the loss of the camera she was crying over: it was the photos it contained. The film included all their photos of the Glastonbury trip. Photos of Aitch, including the group picture they'd taken the previous evening. That's when the camera must have been stolen, whilst they were out. And what would that film mean to anyone else? To the bastards who'd stolen it? They'd have ripped it out and chucked it away without a thought.

Finally squashed into the Montego, with Jeanie still crying and Daisy still distraught, they made their way to the police compound to be escorted to the hospital. Driving past the remaining tents was a heart-wrenching experience. It was hard not to look out expectantly for Aitch, as if they were going to spot him in the crowds. It wasn't right that they were leaving without him. People were still enjoying the festival, drinking and laughing and dancing. And why shouldn't they be? Nothing had changed for them. Their worlds were still in perfect order, just as they should be. In comparison, the gang were leaving as different people, with something ripped out of them. Something decent and naive and good. They were leaving a man down; like an army corps, one short of their company. The self-appointed heart and soul. The joker, the carefree spirit. Corporal Harry 'Aitch' Prescott, RIP.

*****

By the time they'd got to the hospital, Tom was beside himself. In bits. He couldn't do the identification and hated himself for it. He couldn't bear to see his old buddy cold, still and lifeless. The anguish of this coupled with the missed opportunity and his desire to say goodbye was ripping him apart. It was awful to see. So Jack and Daisy did the decent thing: they left him with Alison, Jeanie and the welfare lady, and went to do the identification together.

It was the second time – in a relatively short time – that Jack and Daisy had had to go through this, to see the dead body of someone they were close to. For Jack, it couldn't have been more different an experience than identifying his father. This hit him like a truck. Shocked him. Daisy, too. They held each other and sobbed. Aitch was perfectly intact. The curly curtains on his pale forehead. His hands placed together on his chest. Familiar, fairly small and grubby. The nails bitten, and some of the fingers of his right hand tinged with yellow from nicotine.

But this was just a shell. Aitch was gone. The boy who was so full of life, always up to something. Never again would he grin at them, laugh that mischievous laugh, or say 'Jackeroo'. Jack recalled the first time he'd met Aitch in the corner of the kitchen, washing up. He'd smiled kindly at Jack. Welcomed him, as if he knew him. Given him advice and a spoon for the cottage pie. Settled him in. He was kind-hearted and knew what it felt like to be an outsider; he'd been there himself. And in time Aitch had become the best friend Jack had ever had. The person he loved the most in the world after Daisy and his sister. More like a brother. A blood-brother. And the painful sight of the tiger tattoo on his slight, freckled shoulder seemed to signify this. Jack wished their tattoos were real, so they would never fade and be forgotten. So that the memory of his friend, Aitch, would never fade and be forgotten.

CHAPTER 19

For Sale

The post mortem confirmed that Aitch had died from drug-related complications, specifically something called acute hyponatremia – a sometimes fatal condition triggered by the intake of ecstasy or MDMA combined with, somewhat bizarrely, drinking an excessive amount of water. Add everything else he had in his body into the mix, and he didn't stand a chance. This information was passed on to Aitch's distraught parents, who, in turn, passed it on to Tom and Alison. Alison relayed it over the phone to the rest of the gang.

Hearing about this was awful. Truly awful. And, despite the officer's early warning, they were all shocked and surprised at the discovery of ecstasy in Aitch's system. Ecstasy was something they were aware of and that was talked about, but not part of their world. Where on earth had Aitch got hold of it, and when? They felt guilty. Terribly guilty they hadn't kept an eye on him, looked after him. But they'd all been off their trolleys. No one except Jack could remember the last time they'd seen him, which haunted them. And had Jack really seen him? Or had he just been tripping? The water point Aitch had been found at was a long way from their tents. What if he'd got lost? Disorientated? The thought of this was unbearable. That he had been in such a bad way, lost and alone, without them. They felt a burning anger towards the bastard who had sold or given him the drug. The person who, in effect, had killed their friend.

The press, both locally and nationally, jumped on the story of Aitch's death. The acid house or rave scene, along with its supposed antisocial nature – large crowds, loud music and prolific illegal drug use – were already causing rumblings in the Houses of Parliament and the news. It was the latest threat to society and the corruption of young people, apparently. The press delighted in shining a spotlight on anything negative related to the scene, especially drug deaths. And poor old Aitch was no exception. A pawn in a much larger game. The tabloids were the worst; despite the coroner's official report not even being released, they led with sensation-grabbing headlines, such as 'Rave Teen' and 'Ecstasy Youth'. Aitch was neither of these things. He'd just dabbled one night, unfortunately and tragically. This misrepresentation was harrowing in itself for anyone who knew Aitch; especially his poor parents.

As for the local rags, which all covered the story, they soon made the connection between Aitch and the recent bank holiday ice cream article, and this became a story in its own right. None of this helped Jack and Daisy's mistrust of the press. Daisy had to have a difficult phone conversation with her mum about it all. Carol was angry and upset. 'Promise you won't ever be so stupid, Daisy,' she had tearfully said. 'Promise me!'

*****

Jack had been in a strange, black mood since they'd got back from the festival, unable to accept the unfairness of what had happened. He'd stopped smoking dope, never wanted to touch drugs again, and this affected his state of mind; he struggled with withdrawal symptoms, and with reality in general. On top of this, the rest of the gang had signed themselves off work indefinitely, unable to face going in. But Jack didn't have this luxury. He was needed in from the Wednesday regardless, for kitchen holiday cover – and it wasn't as if he hadn't had plenty of time off lately. Daisy, who didn't want to mope around at home without Jack, agreed to cover some of the other guys' shifts out front.

They were setting off to work one morning when a vaguely familiar voice – to Daisy – called them from behind. 'Jack, Daisy, can I have a quick word?' They turned. It was Belcher, the cockroach of a reporter, about ten yards behind. Where had he just appeared from? What did he do, lurk in doorways and wait? Daisy groaned. Jack stopped for a second, but Daisy grabbed his arm and encouraged him to keep walking.

'Just ignore him. He'll go away,' she said. They carried on walking, arm in arm.

'Can I have a word about Harry Prescott? Is there anything you'd like to say about your friend and that night? An insider's view...' Jack's blood boiled at hearing Aitch being called 'Harry', and being talked about for no other reason than to sell papers. He was simmering, Daisy could sense it. His teeth were gritted, his jaw protruding, his fists clenched.

'Fuck off,' Daisy said over her shoulder. 'How about that? Stick that in your paper.' She encouraged Jack to pick up the pace again, pulling him on.

The man continued to follow them. He wouldn't give up. 'Death seems to follow you two around, doesn't it? What with Bunny Hill and this...'

Jack spun round and marched towards the man, fists clenched, a look of murder on his face. Belcher, surprised and startled, tried to back-pedal, but too quickly. He lost his footing and fell backwards on his arse, his tape recorder and microphone clattering to the pavement with him. Jack reached down and grabbed him by his jacket collar, dragging him upright. In his anger, he felt he had the strength of ten men; had never felt so strong. He turned with Belcher in his grip and slammed him into a doorway, enough to shake the door in its frame. Belcher yelled out in surprise and pain, a look of terror on his face. 'Help!' he yelled. 'Help! I'm being assaulted!' But Jack didn't care; he'd got the red mist. He wanted someone to take his anger and pain out on, and this man was it.

He drew his fist back to put it through the man's face, to knock him into next week, when Daisy screamed, 'Jack! No!' in his ear and grabbed hold of his right arm. He tried to shake her off, practically swinging her about with her feet off the ground as she held on with both hands. 'Don't do it,' she said. 'Think of Haslam. Think of the deal. You'll ruin it all!'

Through his anger, Daisy's words suddenly became clear. Made sense. And trying to make sense of them tempered his anger and shifted his focus. She was right. 'Not so much as a scuffle…' Haslam had said. The deal. His passport. It would all be taken away. He was so close to it now. Mere months. He'd forgotten all about it. Blessed Daisy. His clever, level-headed saviour. He relaxed his right arm, lowered and unclenched his fist. But Daisy still held onto him, just in case. His other fist still had the collar of Belcher's jacket in it. And Belcher's terrified face was next to it. Jack gave him a last warning shove as he let go, glared at him, then turned away. 'Come on,' he said to Daisy.

'Wait,' she said.

Jack may be under some sort of restrictions, she thought. But she wasn't. And she slapped the unsuspecting Belcher round the face. It felt good. 'Now fuck off and leave us alone,' she hissed. Then turned and walked away.

'I'll sue you for that,' Belcher called after them, holding his smarting, red cheek. 'There were witnesses.'

'Bring it on,' said Daisy.

'And for my tape recorder. You'll pay for that if it's damaged. You pair of young thugs!' Jack broke his stride again, ready to go back and shut him up.

'Leave it,' said Daisy, pulling him on again.

They gave one last look behind them before they crossed the pedestrian crossing. Belcher was fiddling with his tape recorder and an elderly couple were talking to him.

'You don't think he'll do anything, do you?' said Jack, concerned.

'Not if he knows what's good for him,' said Daisy. 'Besides, let him sue. See where it gets him. We'll have money soon. Lots of it. Well, you will at least…'

*****

Somehow, they made it through the working week. Neither Jack nor Daisy had seen another member of the gang since Glastonbury. It was almost as if they had buried their heads in the sand and were putting off facing each other – maybe out of a shared, misplaced sense of guilt, or maybe because it was a reminder.

Alison finally called Daisy on the phone to discuss Aitch's funeral, which was another shock. How was this happening already? thought Daisy. It had been set for the following Wednesday, the 4th of July, and they were all invited. Alison said Tom was in a bad way, not handling things well at all. Neither was Jeanie, who had been round a couple of times. By the end of the phone call, both Alison and Daisy were in tears – and for Daisy, the talk of a funeral had brought back memories of her dad's. A dreadful day, not even a year before, that was etched indelibly on her memory.

On Sunday, Jack and Daisy made the trip back to the East Midlands to return the car. It was a distraction at least; a change of scene. They'd both had enough of Norfolk for the minute, and the restaurant. It was nothing but reminders. How many times that week had Jack looked across to the pot-wash area of the kitchen, expecting Aitch to be there? Towel slung over his shoulder, grubby apron tied round his waist with clingfilm, trousers hanging off him, whistling away. It was absolutely heart-breaking. The kitchen was so much quieter without him. No one bantered. No one wanted to.

'Oh, you poor things,' Carol exclaimed when they arrived. For once, she hugged them both. 'I'm so sorry about your friend. How awful. So tragic.' She ushered them inside. 'Car all in one piece, I hope?'

'Yeah, the car's fine,' said Daisy, taking off her shoes. Jack did the same.

'Come into the lounge. Sit down. I'll put the kettle on. You want a cup of tea both of you?'

'Yeah, OK,' said Daisy. None of them really did, but it was a ritual.

Carol returned a few minutes later and sat on the arm of a chair. 'It's just boiling. I'll make the tea, then you can tell me all about it properly – but only if you want to. I've got some news of my own as well,' she said, looking a little pleased with herself. She seemed a bit more animated than usual. More upbeat than she had been since Daisy's dad had passed.

'Something to do with that 'For Sale' sign out front, by any chance?' Daisy said. It was the first thing she'd noticed when she'd pulled up, but hadn't been able to get a word in edgeways about. The sign had been a shock and made her feel a bit sick. She knew her mum had talked about selling, but Daisy hadn't expected her to go through with it so quickly.

Carol looked a little guilty. 'Well, yes. That's one thing anyway. How do you feel about it? Are you OK with it?'

'Doesn't look like I've got much of a choice,' said Daisy. 'Looks like you've already decided. It's your house anyway…'

'Oh, don't be like that, darling.'

'I'm not being like anything. It's fine.' Jack shifted a little uncomfortably.

'It's just the right time for me, that's all. We did discuss it…'

'I know we did – briefly. I just wasn't expecting it so soon. Best make the most of the place whilst it's still here.'

'Oh, Daisy… It's a big wrench for all of us, I know. But you'll get used to it. It had to happen one day – you've got your own life now, and it's high time Lily got her own place too. I'll be in a position to help her with that…' Daisy didn't answer, brooding. 'I'll go and finish that tea…'

Jack gave Daisy a supportive smile, which she appreciated. She squeezed his hand in return. Then they sat in silence for a bit, save for the familiar, measured tick-tock of the hall clock. It was things like that, Daisy thought, that she was going to miss. Sure, her mum could take the clock with her, but it wouldn't be the same. It would never echo in exactly the same way as it did there…

Carol returned with the tea on a tray. 'The cat's about somewhere,' she said. 'I know you always like to fuss her, especially you, Jack.' Jack smiled in acknowledgement. 'There's some biscuits there if you want some. Now,' she said, settling in a chair, 'tell me all about this poor boy, exactly what happened…'

They spent the next twenty minutes or so talking about Aitch, Daisy mostly, and tentatively so at first. She was careful to leave some things out – the mushrooms and dope-smoking, for example. But it was the most they had talked about the actual event since it happened. Which was strange, and a little cathartic in a way. Daisy cried again, which nearly set Jack off, but he did his best to hold himself together. He still felt numb. 'You really have been through the wringer, you two, one way or another, I've never known anything like it. And God only knows what the poor parents are going through,' Carol concluded.

Next, they went onto her news. 'Now, without being disrespectful, I have some more … well … brighter news to discuss… You remember me mentioning Uncle Phil and the possibility of going out there to visit him?' She could barely contain her excitement. 'We've been writing to each other *and* spoken on the phone – but only once; it costs a bloody fortune. Anyway, we've arranged – or agreed at least – for me to go out and visit him – and see a bit of America.'

'Oh, that's fab,' said Daisy, feeling a little jealous. Jack was too.

'Well, don't sound too excited. Aren't you pleased for me?'

'Yes, course, it'll be nice for you. But won't you miss Dad, doing something like that on your own?' Carol's face changed, and she looked pained. Daisy felt bad: she'd taken the wind out of her mum's sails. She hadn't meant to, or at least she hoped she hadn't.

'Of course I'll miss your father,' Carol said sadly. 'I always do, whatever I do. But… life goes on. I've got to start doing things for myself. By myself. And it's been so long since I've seen my brother. Too long…'

'Well, what about Lily? Doesn't she want to go with you?'

Carol scoffed. 'I did ask, but she wasn't interested – said she wouldn't be able to get that long off work. Between you and me, I think it's 'cause she's got this new fella on the go – reckons this is "the one", but we've all heard that before. She's at his now, actually, having Sunday lunch with his family. Talking of which…'

'Hold on,' said Daisy. 'When you say "that long"… How long are you planning on going for?'

'Well, you can stay for up to three months with the right bits of paper.'

'Three months!' said Daisy.

'Yeah, what's wrong with that? I'm not saying I'm *going* to stay that long; I'm going to get a one-way ticket and see how I get on. Or if me and Phil get on. It's been so long. But I might as well make the most of it whilst I'm making the trip. Phil's retired already, and there's so much to see in that area – Niagara Falls, New York, Philadelphia, New England in the fall. Imagine that!' Daisy wanted her mum to stop talking now;

she was getting more and more envious. 'And it's not like I'm paying for the accommodation. Phil's house is huge – and just him and Aunt Trish there, now the girls have grown up and flown the nest. You remember the girls, don't you? Tara and Sue, your cousins?'

Tara was pronounced 'terror'. Daisy remembered finding that strange. 'Vaguely,' she said.

'They were a fair bit older than you: you'd only have been little when they came over that time. They must be well into their twenties now. Gosh … where does the time go?'

'Well, what about the house being sold?' said Daisy. 'Shouldn't you hold off for a bit? Seems odd timing to do both at the same time. Who's gonna show people round?'

'You're starting to sound as if you don't want me to go,' laughed Carol, almost enjoying the thought. 'The estate agents can show people round, that's no problem. Lily will be here too. I'll be glad not to have to put up with it all, to be honest. Just leave them to it. I thought about whether to wait, but I wanted to get the ball rolling before I changed my mind. And if we *are* lucky enough to sell quickly, which I doubt – these interest rates are killing the housing market – they can still contact me out there. Phil's got a fax machine. But I'm not going to let it ruin my holiday. I want a good month out there at least. I can tell any prospective buyers to wait, or I can even refuse the sale. They'll wait if they want the house. All people care about once the second half of the year hits is that they'll be in by Christmas – and that's no problem at all. I've got to find somewhere myself yet, and that's not going to happen overnight. No, this holiday's more important right now. I need it. It'd be Sod's Law if we did sell straightaway.'

She seemed to have it all planned out, thought Daisy. She wasn't used to this new, relaxed, confident mother. 'When are you thinking of going?' she asked.

'August, I think. No earlier than that – I want to be there when the trees start to change colour.'

August, thought Daisy, and looked at Jack. He looked back at her quizzically. What was she up to now? She looked back at her mum. 'Where does Uncle Phil live again?' she said.

'Pennsylvania. It's…'

'At the top,' cut in Jack, indicating upwards with his finger, then blushing.

'Yes… North,' said Carol. 'How did you know that?' She sounded surprised.

Jack looked at Daisy. 'He knows his states. He's always wanted to go there. Haven't you?' She squeezed his hand.

Jack nodded.

CHAPTER 20

Gazza's Tears

A itch's funeral wasn't like one of those you see on TV, where articulate, confident teenage friends or family members stand up to recite heartfelt eulogies. Everyone was too upset. Too shell-shocked – and not to mention too shy. So it was left to the priest. But it was a big family affair, including a considerable Scottish contingent who had travelled down to pay their respects. The gang sat near the back of the church, relatively unnoticed for the first part of the day. But as the wake, held at the Sailor, went on into the evening, it seemed that they drew more attention. And not altogether the most savoury kind. Aitch's immediate family had no problems; they were nothing but kind – united in their grief. It was the distant relatives, those who didn't know them from Adam. There were hushed conversations in huddled groups through scoffed mouthfuls of sausage rolls. Mistrustful glances cast their way over the top of pints and sherry glasses. So these were the bad influences, the ones who led our poor Aitch astray, got him into drugs, took him to a festival that he never came back from…

The day of the funeral had been chosen to coincide with England's crunch World Cup semi-final against West Germany, and the football match proved a welcome distraction. It was what Aitch's parents had planned, and what they thought Aitch would have wanted. His England shirt had been draped over the coffin during the service; the one the gang had brought back from Glastonbury. The sight of it had wrung out many tears. The match itself was England's biggest in twenty-four years, since the glory of '66; all the country had been talking about for weeks. Could this finally be their moment? The end of decades of hurt?

Mike projected the match onto a big screen. And as it progressed, there was barely a soul in the pub – men, women and children alike – not glued to the unfolding drama. England going 1–0 down. The bar erupting at Lineker's opportunistic and match-saving equaliser nine minutes from time. The cranking up of the tension as extra time arrived. Gazza's tears at the significance of his yellow card, meaning he would miss any potential final. Lineker's nod to the bench, caught and captured for eternity by the cameras. A disallowed goal for England that had the pub in momentary rapture, then despair. But all this was a sidenote to what followed – not just for England during the calamitous penalty shootout, but there in the Sailor at the wake…

An increasingly inebriated distant uncle of Aitch's, from his father's side – a staunch and proud Scot who had been brought up to hate the Sassenachs – had been heckling England for most of the match, including labelling Gazza, amongst other things, a 'sissy cry-baby' and 'English poofter'. And as Waddle blazed his crucial must-score penalty over the bar and into the Turin night, thus sealing England's fate, the Scot could not contain his glee, punching the air and roaring with laughter. This insensitive gesture – given the match was being shown in Aitch's honour – provoked uproar. With emotions running high, another pissed uncle, this one from Aitch's mum's side, forgot himself and flipped. He set about the heckler with flailing fists, calling him every name under the sun. Glasses were smashed and tables were knocked over as a drunken fight ensued. This escalated as the two sides of the family tried to intervene and break it up. Mike rang his last orders bell like a fire alarm, so hard that it fell off and crashed onto the bar; he then hollered that the bar was closed, and that if they didn't leave he would call the police.

Eventually this worked, and a mass exodus of shame-faced (and in some cases still angry) mourners spilled out onto the Cromer streets. It was a sour end to an already desperately sad day. Aitch's mum was in bits, shattered and disconsolate.

*****

Things in Norfolk weren't the same for Jack and Daisy after Aitch's death and funeral. It hit Jack the hardest. He had lost interest in everything. His job. Cooking. Working out. Smoking even. He just went through the motions, lost in thought and distracted. Daisy, also badly affected, was worried about him. She would find him in the bathtub, the water stone cold, sitting and staring into space.

Even the settling of his father's estate didn't cheer him up. The property finally sold at auction for the not too shabby sum of seventy thousand pounds – held in trust by Carol, of course. But the money meant nothing to Jack. Nothing. What was money? He couldn't buy his friend back with it. He would have swapped every last penny for that.

Jack was more concerned with the fact he would never again be able to step foot on that land, not without trespassing anyway. Trespassing on what had been his home, and also his prison, from birth to the age of sixteen. Now someone else would own it. What would they do with it? The house. The land. The orchard. The caustic tank. Would they even know what had happened up there?

The anniversary of Daisy's father's death was tough as well. Daisy had asked for a day off at fairly short notice; she just couldn't face going in. Jack had asked too, to support her, but

Chef wasn't having it. It was a Saturday, for a start. This caused resentment in Jack, and he was in a foul mood all day at work, which didn't go unnoticed. It made it even harder being there, missing Aitch and knowing Daisy was at home feeling sad. Carol had asked Daisy to come over for the day, so they could visit the grave together, reminisce and mark the day properly. But Daisy couldn't bear to do the trip without Jack, so it was arranged for the Sunday instead.

When Jack got home from work that Saturday night, Daisy was waiting up for him. She'd been looking forward to it all day, as she had so much to discuss. It had been a day for reflection. They cracked open a bottle of wine and snuggled up on the sofa. Then they talked. About everything. Daisy's dad. Aitch. The money. Work. How things felt different. Eventually Daisy brought up another topic that had been on her mind. 'Jack,' she said, pausing, not knowing quite how to word it. 'How would you feel about us going away to America with Mum?'

He nearly spat his wine out. 'America? What? On holiday?'

'Yeah. What else?'

'On a plane?'

'Er … yes, on a plane.'

'I don't know…' He hadn't thought about this at all, hadn't even dreamed that it could be a possibility – even though he had felt envious of Carol's plans. 'Would she even want us to go with her? And isn't she going for quite a long time? What about our jobs?'

'Yeah, she is. Maybe a couple of months. But even she doesn't know for sure how it's gonna pan out. That's why she's getting a one-way ticket. It's slightly more expensive that way, but she can afford it. And we could too.'

'But what about our jobs?' Jack asked again. 'Getting the time off. We've already had loads, I've used all my holiday up. Chef got arsey about me asking for today off, even though I would have swapped it, the twat.'

Daisy paused for a moment. She'd been thinking about this too. Their jobs. 'Well…' This one was even harder to broach.

'Oh dear,' said Jack. He knew that look on her face too well. She'd been planning something. 'Come on, spit it out,' he sighed.

'Well … like we were saying, things have been different lately – since Aitch died.' A pained look crossed Jack's face and Daisy squeezed his hand. 'See. That's what I mean. Things just aren't the same. Especially at work. *You're* not the same; it's like you've lost all interest. Not even wanting to be there sometimes…'

'I know, and it's 'cause Aitch isn't there any more,' he said sadly. 'Not just at work, but in general. I still can't believe he's gone. That he's never coming back. It's so fucked up.' Jack looked as if he was about to cry. He took a large gulp of wine.

'I know. It's a reminder. The whole gang feel it too. They haven't been the same either; we barely see them. But it's not just work, it's everything.' She sat back suddenly, sighed and ran her fingers through her hair. Jack watched her, waiting for her to speak. It seemed she needed to get something off her chest. 'It's like … I need a new start, I've been thinking about it so much, especially since, you know, Aitch… I'm going nowhere… Look at me, given up on college, a part-time waitress in a seaside restaurant … no qualifications or career prospects. Something occurred to me, just today. Hit me like a thunderbolt. We don't have to stay here any more – this freezing, flea-bitten flat owned by – well, I don't even know who. The government? The police? Imagine spending another freezing winter here. Or imagine, like Mum said, those bastards getting out of jail early and coming looking for us. We could put a deposit down on something, somewhere else. Anywhere we like. Even Mum's moving, giving up the old house. It's just like the timings right or something…'

'Well, what are you suggesting?' Despite being shocked and

daunted, Jack couldn't deny that his interest was piqued. His heartbeat had cranked up a couple of notches.

'OK.' She sat forward again, took a good glug of wine, then clasped his hands in hers. 'Here's the plan. We start with the holiday first, an open-ended holiday, to gather our thoughts and plan our next move. Where we want to live. What we want to do. No, scrap that. First we have to hand in our notices, especially you – you want to do it properly and not piss Chef off.'

'He's always pissed off. Especially with me.'

Daisy laughed. 'Yeah, but seriously, you might need a reference in future, so it's best to leave on good terms, to work your notice out, give them a chance to replace you…'

'I don't know what a reference *or* notice is.'

Daisy rolled her eyes. 'I'll tell you in a minute. But it's perfect – the timing. Think about it. We give a month's notice – warning, basically – tell Mum we want to go away with her. We could tell her tomorrow, actually. It's perfect. Shit, yes, it's best we do that before we go handing our notices in,' Daisy laughed.

'Yes,' said Jack. 'She might not even want us to go with her.'

'Mum?' said Daisy, taking another swallow of wine. 'She'll bloody love it, us spending all that time together. She's never forgiven me for moving out. Anyway, where was I? Oh, yes. We hand in our notices, timing it to coincide with you getting your passport – when was that? Early August? We need to chase that up with Haslam, maybe even ask him to hurry it along if necessary. So it's best we go away in late August to be safe. Hopefully Mum will be OK with that; she wasn't planning on going till nearer fall time anyway, was she? Hey! Maybe we could even fly out there for my birthday. God, can you imagine, Jack. America. Actually being there…' It was the first time she had let herself think about it properly. Jack too. And they were both silent for a while. A huge country, so far away… Jack's lifelong dream…

'How much do you think it'll all cost?' Jack asked.

'I've no idea. We'll have to find out. But here's the thing … a few things actually. The accommodation isn't going to cost us a penny, because we'll be staying at Uncle Phil's.'

'What? Won't he mind?'

'Well, we'd have to ask of course, but I can't see why not. Sounds like his place is huge – and practically empty. And here's the next part of my plan. You know what else is coming up soon, just before we'd go away?'

'What?' said Jack. Racking his brains to no avail.

'Carnival Week.'

'And? What's Carnival Week got to do with anything?'

'Ice creams. Carnival week and ice creams, remember? Tourists. We'd make a killing! Every day would be like a bank holiday, especially if the weather's good.' Jack's mind churned. It was funny, with everything that had been going on, they'd even forgotten about the ice cream; he hadn't had the enthusiasm for anything.

'OK…' he said, finally seeing where she was coming from.

'It's about the 11th to the 17th of August. I've checked. So we time it so we finish our jobs before that. Then we spend the whole week raking it in, enough to pay for the plane flights at least. We can knock Mum up for some of your money as well,' she put her hand on his leg, feeling bad for being presumptuous with his money, 'and then that's it. We bugger off on holiday for a month – or as long as we want. What do you reckon?'

Jack said nothing. He was too bowled over by the enormity of it all, the sheer audacity of what she was suggesting. But he liked the idea.

CHAPTER 21

Melting Chocolate and Wax Puddles

'Mum, we've got something to ask you,' Daisy said. 'A proposition.' It was Sunday at the Joneses' house. They were sitting at the dinner table: Carol, Daisy and Jack. The dishes had just been cleared away after a sumptuous Sunday roast in Jim's honour. Daisy had waited until Lily was out of the room; she'd gone to give 'the boyfriend' a quick ring before pudding. She'd only be a distraction, Daisy figured; she'd complicate things, act as if she was missing out on something – something she didn't even want to do.

'Hmm, this sounds serious,' said Carol. 'Pray tell, I'm all ears…' Such a 'Dad expression' thought Daisy; her mum did that a lot. Carol was a little bit tipsy, having washed down the lamb with a couple of glasses of red – again in Jim's honour. She was enjoying having the young ones around her, her family all together. The day had also been a celebration of Jack's estate finally being settled: it certainly hadn't been a dour affair.

Daisy squeezed Jack's leg under the table, as if to convey, 'Here goes, wish me luck.' She had all her hopes pinned on this. 'We were wondering, Jack and I, how you'd feel about us going to America with you.' She mentally crossed her fingers.

The look on Carol's face was priceless. Her eyebrows shot up in surprise and shock, and her mouth dropped open. There was a tense silence – for Daisy anyhow. 'Mind? I'd absolutely love it. But how? What about your jobs? The restaurant?'

Yes, thought Daisy. She squeezed Jack's thigh again, even harder this time; and he grimaced. But she knew she had to choose her words carefully: the whole plan could still backfire if her mum thought they were being cavalier with their futures, or just doing something on a whim. 'Well, the thing is … we've been doing some thinking, serious thinking, Jack and I' – why did she keep saying 'Jack and I'? She never said it normally; probably nerves – 'about our futures. Both our futures … and we've decided, or pretty much decided, that we're done with Norfolk.'

'Done with Norfolk?' Carol cut in, surprised again. 'Since when? This is news to me. I thought things were going really well for you, what with your jobs and the ice cream and everything.'

'I know,' said Daisy. 'We've only discussed this ourselves properly over the weekend. But it's been building for a while, ever since we came back from Glastonbury, ever since our friend, you know…'

'Oh yes, of course,' said Carol. 'Dreadful business. So sad…'

Go with that, thought Daisy. Her mum seemed to be empathising with her. 'Yeah, we were very close to him – especially Jack. And he used to work at the restaurant, in the kitchen, so it's been hard. For both of us – and for the rest of the gang: they went to school with him. It was his funeral this week.'

'Oh gosh, yes. How did that go?'

'Long story,' said Daisy. 'I'll explain in a bit.' She was keen to stay on track, for her mum not to get distracted. She went on to explain their vague plan, everything that she and Jack had discussed. Carol took it all in, nodding in the right places. 'So that's it really,' Daisy finished. 'What do you reckon? We'd love to go. Wouldn't we, Jack?' He nodded vigorously. 'It would be the trip of a lifetime – for both of us.'

'It certainly would,' agreed Carol. She had refrained from saying 'I told you so' about Norfolk, as it would have been churlish; and they deserved a break: they'd had such a rough time. And she was thrilled at the prospect of them coming; she'd secretly been a little daunted at the prospect of travelling on her own; that was one of the reasons she had asked Lily. 'I'd have to ask Phil of course,' she said, trying to downplay her growing excitement. 'But I can't see it being a problem; he'd be thrilled to see you. And to meet Jack. We'll have to contribute a bit, towards food and housekeeping.'

'Money's no problem,' said Daisy. Then she chastised herself. She had to stop thinking like that: it was Jack's money, not hers. That was the thing with money: they say it changes people, but you never think it'll change you. But she couldn't deny things felt different since Jack had received his windfall. It was a safety net; a huge safety net. It took the pressure off them financially – providing her mum played ball. There was no need for them to work at the moment if they didn't want to. 'So … is that a yes then?' She still felt tense.

'Yes!' her mum squealed, surprising Daisy with a hug. 'Yes! Yes! Yes! I'll go and phone Phil right this second.'

'What did I miss?' asked Lily, surprising them as she returned.

Carol extricated herself from Daisy, wiping a tear from her eye. She suddenly felt very emotional. This was the best bit of news she'd had in a long time. 'Daisy and Jack are coming to America with me,' she said.

*****

And so it was arranged. Phil said he and Trish would be delighted to accommodate the 'young folk' as well. He would get in touch with the girls to see if they could make it over for a weekend, seeing as it was such a special occasion. Carol told Daisy later that evening when they were back home in Norfolk. Daisy was delighted; it was a relief. Jack suddenly felt very nervous at the reality of it all.

And from that moment on, America became an obsession. The distraction of it was part of their healing process. Their future could wait; they'd plan for it properly whilst they were out there. In the meantime, there was so much to organise. This started with handing in their notices: there was no time to waste.

Jack was dreading Chef's reaction. He was bound to take the news personally, even with a month's notice, and make Jack's remaining time there a misery. Jack's hand shook as he handed over the formal letter Daisy had drafted for him. It was all right for her, he thought; she was giving her notice over the phone. 'So, you're finishing just before Carnival Week. Busiest week of the fucking year,' Chef said. 'Fantastic. You taking the piss or what? How am I meant to find anyone before then?' Jack hadn't thought about this, and he felt bad. But what was done was done; he was just going to have to grin and bear it. It was going to be a long month.

Unlike Chef, Hilary thanked Jack for his time and hard work there, and for giving them a month's notice to find a replacement. She told him a week would have done as Jack was paid weekly; he didn't even have a contract. Chef had failed to tell him this, probably out of spite. Jack was more than a little miffed about this: he could have been finished in a week. Hilary would probably have given him a good reference herself: she was the manager after all.

Daisy was on the phone to Alison when Jack got home. She had called Alison to break the news, and they had been talking for quite some time. Daisy looked as if she had been crying: she always seemed to cry on the phone to Alison. 'Wait a minute, let me ask him,' Daisy said. 'He's just got back.' She held the phone to her chest. 'Are you OK us meeting up with the guys after your shift tonight?' She pulled a 'we ought to' face, then whispered, 'I think Tom needs it.'

'What? Have you told them both?' Jack said, presuming Tom was there and feeling a little put out. He'd wanted to give Tom the news himself, but hadn't had a chance to; none of the others had come back to work yet.

'No. Only Alison. Tom's not with her. But she'll tell him as soon as she gets off the phone, she said.' Daisy shrugged apologetically. 'And about tonight.'

Jack felt better that Tom wasn't there, but bad that he would hear it from Alison, not him. They'd grown close and had some great times together. He liked Tom very much. He nodded. 'OK.'

'Good,' said Daisy. 'Thanks.' She lifted the phone off her chest to speak, then quickly put it back again. 'You OK?' A frown crossed her face. Jack looked preoccupied; his face was an open book to her.

'Yeah.'

'OK, speak in a minute.' She blew him a kiss.

*****

That night the gang met up at the Sailor. It was the first time they had seen each other since the funeral. Daisy had already discussed with Jack that she thought they should keep quiet about their plans to leave Norfolk permanently once they had returned from America. She had only told Alison about the open-ended trip and handing in their notice. Jack agreed.

Even so, it was still an emotional affair. Alison had already told Jeanie and Tom, but this didn't stop the girls from crying when they discussed it face to face. The boys managed to hold it together, but only just. Neither of them wanted to be the one who cracked first. Jack found it hard to look Tom properly in the eye, while Tom dealt with it in his own way by cracking jokes continuously. It was as if he was trying to make up for Aitch's absence by being the new Aitch. But he was trying too hard, and everyone noticed. Underneath, he seemed nervous, as if he'd lost some of his bravado and confidence. He looked as if he hadn't been sleeping properly, and his fingers were nicotine-stained and shaking a little as he rolled one fag after another.

As more drinks were downed, conversation inevitably turned to Aitch. It had been too soon to talk about everything at the funeral; too raw and too public. They talked about that night. The agony of not knowing what Aitch's final hours had been like. Not being there for him. The following day when they'd found out. How it had affected them since. They took it in turns to speak, almost as if it was an AA meeting. It was hard. Emotional. And the boys finally cracked, each shedding tears. They'd all been suffering in their own ways.

As last orders were finally called, Mike loudly rang his recently repaired bell. This seemed to snap Tom out of his depressed stupor. He suddenly brightened and took on Aitch's mantle again by announcing he was getting the last round of drinks in, along with some shots – in Aitch's honour.

They all toasted Aitch and sank their shots. It was just like the old days, but with one of their number sadly missing and sorely missed. The Cromer Six were now the Cromer Five. They all vowed to keep in touch more, and to get together again to give Jack and Daisy a proper send off. Maybe even get some smoke in. The night ended with them hugging on the street at kicking out time.

*****

Having broken the news to the gang, focus returned to what Daisy had dubbed 'The Plan'. Everything was falling into place. Jack's passport was being processed; they'd had to get some photos done at the booth in Woolworths. Haslam had been pleasantly surprised to hear from Jack, to hear of their plans and to have a catch-up. He said he would do everything he could to assist them, and to push the paperwork through as soon as humanly possible.

July arrived and the summer rolled on. The anniversary of Daisy's dad's funeral came and went. It was another sad day, but keeping busy and occupied helped. There were ice creams to make for Carnival Week. Being at home more than Jack, Daisy was on a mission. She'd decided to ask the gang if they had any spare freezer space, figuring they needed at least two freezers' worth to start them off. Jeanie, of all people, came up trumps. Her mum had a huge chest freezer in their garage that was barely used; and her mum was usually too pissed or involved with different men, or both, to notice what was going on; she wasn't even going to ask her.

Jack counted down the days of his notice, and ticked them off as if they were a prison sentence. It was a slog, and he was frustrated that he couldn't help Daisy as much as he would have liked. The news that Carol had booked the airline tickets provided a much-needed fillip. An incentive to keep going. They were flying with BA on Wednesday, 22 August, the day after Daisy's birthday, so they could still celebrate with the gang. 'New York,' Daisy squealed when she got off the phone, grabbing Jack. 'It's so exciting!

As July became August, another heatwave hit Norfolk, along with the rest of the UK. It was a real humdinger. Unprecedented. The first week of the month saw road and runway closures as surfaces melted. Railway lines buckled. Hospitals were swamped with heat-related illnesses. The fire services were inundated as fires broke out all over the countryside. There was a spate of drownings as people tried to cool down. Traffic gridlocked in coastal areas as hordes of people made a dash for the beaches. The entire stock of a Liverpool chocolate factory melted. A life-sized waxwork knight at a castle in Essex melted into a puddle. You couldn't make it up.

In Cromer, the holiday season was already in full swing, and the heatwave caused chaos. The town simply couldn't cope. Cars were queueing for hours just to get near to the town. The streets were teeming with people; you could barely move. It was the same story on the beach. The B and Bs and hotels were full. The car parks were full. The restaurant was packed. No one had ever seen anything like it.

It drove Daisy mad that they couldn't capitalise on it all. All those people, all those potential customers. The heatwave had come a bloody week too soon. She had been keeping a beady eye on the weather forecast, and it looked as though the hot spell would fizzle out by Sunday, Jack's first full day off. It was infuriating. Why couldn't it have waited for Carnival Week? Jack, meanwhile, had been sweating his scallops off in a sweltering kitchen, whilst privately blaming Daisy for the fact he was still there. It couldn't have been worse. Instead of seeing his notice out in a sedate, steady manner, he had been rushed off his feet and working longer hours than ever before.

*****

Jack and Daisy's tenure at the Crab's Claw finally came to an end. There was so much going on in the run-up – for everybody – that it wasn't quite the occasion it might have been. The staff were all still recovering from the heatwave for a start, and then there was Carnival Week just round the corner. Jack saw it from the other chefs first hand. There even seemed to be an air of envy in the kitchen, of animosity – probably dripped down from Chef – that Jack was leaving, in effect escaping on the eve of traditionally the busiest week of the year. Whizz was the only exception. Thinner than ever owing to the recent heat and physical exertion – he practically disappeared if he turned sideways – he thrust a four-pack of cider into Jack's hands as a leaving present. ''Ere,' he said in his Norfolk twang, and winked. 'Crack one of these open whils' yer finishing off. You're a good lad and a good chef. We'll miss you.' He punched Jack on the arm. Surprisingly strong. This unexpected gesture meant the world to Jack, brought a lump to his throat, and he thanked him. But the moment was doubly poignant. Jack instinctively looked over to the corner of the kitchen, thinking he would share the cans with Aitch (Chef had already gone; he'd begrudgingly shaken Jack's hand and huffed a 'good luck'), but there was just another young pot-wash lad – a 'Chef de Plungeur' as they were jokingly called in the kitchen – standing in his place. The poor lad was snowed under, surrounded by pots, and Jack's heart went out to him.

'Here,' Jack said, after surveying the gleaming kitchen for the last time. 'You can have these.' He offered him the cans. The lad looked gobsmacked, but pleased – Jack was one of the chefs to him, someone to look up to and respect. He wiped his soapy pink hands on his grubby apron and took the cans from Jack.

'Ah, thanks, chef,' He blushed, grinning. 'Nice one.' It still didn't sit right with Jack, being called 'chef'.

The front-of-house staff were much more demonstrative than the chefs. Led by Hilary, they'd had a whip-round for a joint leaving present – Daisy was also working that night; she'd wanted to be there on Jack's last shift – and got everybody to sign a card for them. The present was a large suitcase, which was such a thoughtful idea and would certainly come in handy. The gang were given the task of handing over the card and present. This was the emotional bit, and more tears were shed; not just by the gang, but some of the other staff too. It was terrible what had happened to Aitch and what the others had all been through as a consequence. They all still felt it. Aitch, no doubt, would have conjured up some practical joke involving the suitcase, perhaps hiding inside it. The place was certainly less colourful without him, and with Jack and Daisy leaving, it felt like the end of an era.

Despite the gang's protestations, especially Tom's, Daisy and Jack couldn't be talked into a boozy night at the pub to mark the occasion. They were both done in for a start. For Jack, his last day had become a finishing line. He just wanted to collapse in a sweaty heap and recover – but he only had a day before the madness of Carnival Week and ice cream selling. He didn't have the energy, and he also didn't trust himself. He didn't have Daisy's willpower: she was single-minded and unwavering in her focus on the week ahead, while he felt like getting hammered, and the last thing he needed in the morning was a banging hangover. They agreed to save it up for Daisy's birthday night on the eve of their America trip. That would be their leaving do.

CHAPTER 22

Running on Empty

The first day of Carnival Week arrived. Jack and Daisy woke up, or rather came round, in bad moods when the alarm went off early. For what seemed most of the night, Daisy had obsessively been going over the next day's logistics – worrying, hoping they'd remembered everything, stressing about the weather. She was beginning to regret the day they had ahead of them; the pressure she was putting them under. She covered Jack with the bed cover again, briefly feasting her eyes on his semi-naked body, before getting up to make a cup of tea.

Loading the freezer into the van without Tom's help was a struggle, even after they had half-emptied it. Then they made the short drive to the town's largest car park, next to the pitch 'n' putt course, a mere two minutes' walk from their home. Daisy reckoned the prime selling spot was right next to the entrance to the pitch 'n' putt. She just hoped they weren't treading on anyone's toes by nicking their pitch, as she'd noticed other ice cream vans parked there. But it wasn't as if they owned the spot. 'The early bird catches the worm' was the way she saw it.

They got set up. Even though it was still before nine o'clock, it was pleasing to see the car park gradually filling. People were clearly worried about not getting a space, and perhaps wanted to make the most of the grand opening of Carnival Week: there were events going on all day, especially for the little ones. The weather was OK – but it was still too early for ice cream.

At around a quarter to ten, an ice cream van appeared as if out of nowhere, and sped into the car park. It almost skidded to a halt when the driver saw their van, and he stopped and glared. Then he drove closer, again a little too quickly. It reminded Daisy somehow of the 'Libyans' scene in *Back to the Future*. There was something aggressive about it, a bit threatening. Jack felt it too; and his hackles immediately went up.

As the van pulled up again, only about ten yards away, Daisy recognised the driver as the one who had stopped and glared at them that day at the car boot sale. Lorenzo's Ices. The man had distinctive black bushy eyebrows, like a pair of wriggling caterpillars, dark stubble and a bald head. 'You two again,' he tutted, as he briefly took in their set-up. 'Playtime's over, I'm afraid, kids. You can't stay: you need a proper permit to sell ice creams here.' Despite the sign on his van, he couldn't have been more English.

The man's demeanour and attitude immediately wound Daisy up. She gave him a withering look. 'Yes. We know that. That's why we've got one.' And she immediately reeled off their trade licence number, which she'd learnt by heart – although she'd anticipated it would be a council officer questioning them, not an irate ice cream man.

The man snorted derisively. 'Yeah, right. Let's see it then.'

'We don't have to show you anything,' Daisy said quickly. 'You're not from the council.' Jack groaned inwardly. Here we go, he thought. Don't bloody antagonise him on purpose. The last thing he needed was a fight. He hated confrontation. Daisy, on the other hand, seemed to thrive on it.

'Look, this isn't a bloody game. It's Carnival Week and this is my livelihood,' the man said. 'So stop messing about, get packed up and clear off.'

'No,' said Daisy. 'We're not going anywhere. We've got every right to be here, just as much as you have. We were here first. Go and park somewhere else.'

Jack groaned again. This was escalating far too quickly. What a start to the day. Desperately, he tried to think of something that would calm the situation, but wouldn't antagonise Daisy. Summoning up his courage, he said. 'Look, we can go and get the licence to prove it. We only live down the road.'

'What, and lose our spot?' said Daisy. 'We're not going anywhere. We're all set up.'

'Well, I'll stay here,' said Jack. He didn't want to, but wasn't going to leave Daisy alone with their adversary.

'No,' said Daisy.

There was a stalemate; a silence whilst the man considered his options. He couldn't physically move them, and the lad looked a bit handy anyway. 'This isn't the end,' he muttered, revving his engine angrily. 'I'll be back.' And with that he sped away.

'I'll be back,' Daisy mimicked. 'Who does he think he is, the Terminator?'

'Jesus!' said Jack, breathing a sigh of relief, but angry with Daisy. 'What's wrong with you? We could have gone and got the licence.'

'We didn't have to,' Daisy said, pulling it from her pocket.

'Oh my God,' said Jack. 'Did you want me to get in a fight? It's all right for you girls.'

'I just don't like bullies, that's all. You know that.' Jack sighed. He'd heard this before. Many times…

As the day progressed, steadily they began to sell ice creams. The irate ice cream man – aka 'Lorenzo the Terminator' – had returned, fairly quickly in fact, which led them to ponder where he had been. But he parked near one of the parking meters without any further confrontation, which brought a smile to Daisy's face. He was in full view, so they'd be able to see how he got on.

By mid-morning the car park was rammed, and there was a constant stream of queuing cars waiting to enter. Most of them circled round and round, then left. Packed vehicles with their windows down. Hot, flustered and disappointed faces. Kids and adults alike. Couples arguing with each other in fractious exasperation. Sometimes unsightly set-tos broke out as two different cars vied for the same spot, beeping horns. Bit by bit, the sheer volume of people turned into sales, building as the day warmed up. The majority of customers were waiting for the pitch 'n' putt: the course only let so many people on at once, so people had to queue. Most were families. And what did they do whilst they waited? Check out the ice cream stall – and buy one to pass the time, or promise their kids one after they'd finished. The location was genius.

By the end of the day, at around six thirty, Jack and Daisy had completely sold out. This was the first time it had happened: a milestone moment. The other noteworthy incident was the arrival of a council official at around midday, who had asked them to produce their licence. So that's where Lorenzo had been earlier, Daisy figured – to report them, the bastard. It gave her great pleasure to produce their licence with a flourish, and to see the official go contentedly on his way. Daisy hoped Lorenzo had witnessed it, but it had been impossible to tell as he was also snowed under, more was the pity.

After packing up and lugging the freezer back into the flat, they plonked themselves down with a well-earned can of cider to count their money. This was the best part of the whole day – what made it all worthwhile. 'Three hundred and fifty-two quid!' said Daisy. 'Our best day by far.'

'That's amazing,' said Jack. 'Could have been even more, though.'

'Really? How come?' said Daisy, surprised.

'We lost two to three decent scoops out of each tub – the ice cream got too soft to scoop from opening and closing the door all day.'

'Really?' said Daisy. 'That's something to think about, isn't it? Add that up and I bet that's about thirty or forty quid. I thought we should have taken more than that for a full freezer...' She took a swig of cider. 'You wouldn't get that with an ice cream cart, I bet: everything's stored in metal tubs behind glass, and in the shade.' Jack gave her a look. 'Just sayin'...'

*****

The next morning Daisy was up and about early again. Wired and on a mission. It looked as if it was going to be another decent day. She was keen to get down to the car park early, paranoid that Lorenzo was going to try and get there before them and steal their spot. But first they had to swing by Jeanie's to restock the freezer.

That day, Sunday, Jack and Daisy worked their socks off and, unbelievably, ran out of stock again. They took a further three hundred and twenty quid; they hadn't had quite a full freezer's worth left after all. But now they had a dilemma, something that Daisy – despite her meticulousness – hadn't envisaged. They were totally out of ice cream. Despite all her wildest hopes and predictions, Daisy hadn't expected to sell their entire stock in two days. Three, maybe, but not two. And now they had to replenish as soon as possible; every day they weren't selling, they were potentially losing up to three hundred and fifty quid, which was crazy. But they had to buy more ingredients first, which meant another trip to the cash and carry. The thought of this was horrendous – and what with the making and freezing of the ice creams, it meant a whole day gone. But they had no choice, not if they wanted to avoid wasting any more takings. Daisy had her sights set on taking a thousand pounds during Carnival Week – this had become her goal.

Somehow, running on empty, they got through the week. As it went on, the weather deteriorated, becoming windy, and sales dropped, especially once Wednesday – official Carnival Day – had passed. On Thursday, when they ran out of ice cream again, they didn't replace it. They simply didn't have the energy. To add to their problems, the van was playing up; it was making an awful squealing noise when they started it up and was intermittently losing power. Daisy figured it was low on oil; she couldn't remember the last time she'd put some in. But they'd achieved their goal. Surpassed it, even, taking a grand total of one thousand, two hundred and fifty pounds – or thereabouts. Way more than their air tickets had cost. They had done it – and without an ice cream cart; that could wait for the next time. If there was a next time. They'd had enough of making and serving ice creams to last for a while, and could now sit back and reap their rewards. Shift their full attention and focus to what awaited them. The next Chapter of their lives: America.

CHAPTER 23

A Pair of Brown Tights

It was less than a week before they were due to fly, and Jack's passport still wasn't ready. Both Jack and Daisy were getting stressed. Especially Daisy. She rang Haslam to find out what the hell was going on. Haslam rang the passport office to chase it up. He got back to her. 'Still being processed, I'm afraid, kiddo,' he said. 'July and August are their busiest times; they've got a backlog. Just bad luck with the timing, I guess. I've requested for it to be prioritised if possible.'

It was hard for Daisy to bite her tongue. Why wasn't it already being prioritised? Hadn't he said he'd do all he could to push the paperwork through? And why wasn't it being processed before Jack contacted Haslam anyway? A year since the deal was struck – the date Jack was eligible for a passport – had been and gone. Perhaps that was all they had meant; that he could apply for one then. She wished to God she had looked into it sooner. But there had been so much going on. And how could they have possibly known Jack was going to need a passport so soon?

'Oh, for crying out loud, Daisy,' Carol said over the phone. 'Why on earth did you give me that date for flying? We could have gone any time after the passport was ready. There wasn't some desperate rush.'

'Because you said you wanted to go in August, we chose the back end of August – a good six weeks after contacting Haslam. How was I to know it would take so long? It's not like I've dealt with getting a passport before… I thought it would be ready for the anniversary of Jack's deal – and it's way past that.'

'Passports always take an age, especially in summer. I'm fuming, Daisy. *And* kicking myself for listening to you. This really should have been sorted out beforehand. I'll lose all that flight money, you know. Or you two will. I'm going regardless. And you also still owe me five-hundred pounds' worth of American dollars.'

Daisy came off the phone and broke down in tears. She felt foolish and stupid.

Two days to go and still no passport. Stress levels had gone through the roof.

Daisy rang Haslam again. Sick of chasing it up – it took forever, and he had more pressing matters to deal with – he gave Daisy the application reference details and the number for the passport office at Peterborough. She called immediately. As Haslam had said, it took ages to get through. Daisy was on hold for a good twenty-five minutes before speaking to someone from the right department; and then they took an age to locate Jack's application. By that stage, Daisy was ready to blow. 'Ah, yes, Jack Gardner, who am I speaking with, please?'

'Daisy. Daisy Jones, his girlfriend.'

'Ah, well, I'd need to speak to the applicant himself, to discuss any application matters. Security, see…' said the snobby-sounding man.

'Oh, for fuck's sake,' Daisy said. It just slipped out.

'I beg your pardon,' the man said. 'We won't tolerate any harassment of staff whatsoever here at the passport office. We're extremely busy, and this is a government building.'

'Sorry, sorry,' Daisy said. 'It just came out. Really sorry. I'll put Jack on. Jack. Jack! Here, you need to speak to them.' She held the phone out, still cursing herself for swearing.

Jack took the phone from her, looking scared. 'Hello,' he said.

'Who am I speaking with please?'

'Jack. Jack Gardner.'

'And can you confirm your date of birth, full address and your application number please.'

Jack gave all the right information.

'Thank you. Right, let me see… Ah, a brand-new passport, I see… requested by Nottinghamshire Constabulary. A Detective Haslam… Yes, well, you'll be pleased to know your brand-new passport has been completed, and is due to be sent out in the next couple of days.'

Daisy was listening. The next couple of days. That was no good. 'Ask them if we can come and get it.'

'What?' said Jack, not knowing who to listen to.

'Ask them if we can come and get it. It's on the way to Mum's anyway. Here, give me the phone.' She took the phone back.

'Hello. Me again. Sorry,' she said, trying to sound calm, despite the sickening panic she felt. 'We were wondering if we could come and get the passport ourselves, collect it I mean, to save it being posted… Bit of a situation, you see… Long story, but we're flying to America the day after tomorrow.' She winced and bit her lip, crossing her fingers.

'Oh, golly,' the man said, softening. 'That's cutting it a bit fine. Erm, yes, yes, that shouldn't be a problem. We get this stuff all the time. I can cancel the post request and make a note that the passport is to be collected. It needs to be signed for, of course…'

Daisy breathed a huge sigh of relief and grabbed Jack's hand. 'Oh gosh. Thank you. Thank you so much. Yes, please do that – don't let it get sent, whatever you do. We'll be there tomorrow. First thing.'

'No problem at all. I'll amend the instruction right away.'

'Thank you,' said Daisy again. 'Thank you so much.'

She collapsed into Jack. A mixture of relief and joy. Why was nothing ever simple?

That night they finished packing. This was Carol's idea. After Daisy had updated her about the passport situation, she had demanded they pack and go straight to hers the next day, rather than returning to Norfolk. She didn't want any more last-minute dramas on the day they were flying. 'And it's your birthday,' Carol had said.

Despite feeling like a naughty child being summoned so she could be kept an eye on, Daisy had agreed. It made sense. But there was one downside: they had to cancel their planned farewell and birthday bash with the gang. Daisy felt awful about this, but wasn't too fussed about missing out. They'd had enough drunken nights at the pub with the gang, and it hadn't quite felt the same the last time they had met without Aitch. It already felt like the end of an era; time to move on. She would miss Alison – but not the other two so much. Surprisingly, Jack felt the same way about it. It was only Aitch whom he had been truly bothered about.

Alison was gutted when Daisy broke the news to her, and she said that Tom would be too. She insisted that Daisy should at least pop round to collect the present they had bought her. It was a sad moment when they finally said their goodbyes. 'Things already aren't the same at work without you,' Alison said tearfully, hugging Daisy. 'We're gonna miss you so much.' Daisy promised they would be back to tell them all about it, and they could postpone their night out until then. This cheered Alison up a bit.

*****

The morning of Daisy's birthday was a bit of a rushed affair; not quite how they had planned it. Jack had bought Daisy a brand-new camera, one with all the 'bells and whistles'; well, he could afford it. He was thrilled with his gift and was so excited about giving it to her. Daisy cried when she received it. It was so thoughtful of him; she'd still been down about losing her camera, and moaning about not having one for their trip. It was perfect. But the main thing on their minds was getting their hands on that passport. What with this and getting the van loaded – double and triple-checking that they had packed everything – the rest of the birthday stuff took a back seat; they could celebrate and relax more once at Carol's.

They finally set off, or rather screeched off, to Peterborough. The noise was getting embarrassing, and increasingly worrying. The van, which had been sitting idle since Carnival Week, had struggled to start again, as if the battery was low. Not taking any chances, they'd topped up with oil. The added stress was the last thing they needed.

Daisy took the journey steadily, trying not to over-exert the van. But despite her best efforts, it continued to act up. Along with the intermittent squealing, there was that occasional loss of power again, a misfiring, when she accelerated. Then, after about an hour or so, a new noise began, a constant ticking sound from the engine. 'Can you hear that, Jack? That ticking sound?' She turned the music down. 'Jack?'

Jack sat up. He'd been staring out of the window, lost in his own private thoughts. As the holiday had approached, he'd become more and more obsessed with the flight – or more specifically by being on a plane. It had become increasingly neurotic. This past week, he'd been looking at planes in the sky, studying them, every time he saw or heard one pass overhead, their white, lingering vapour trails marking their paths. They looked so tiny up there in the blue. Tiny tin cans with wings. And moving so slowly. How did they stay in the air?

'What is it?' he said, straining an ear to listen.

'God knows, but I don't like it. It's been doing it for the last ten minutes or so.'

'Maybe something stuck in a wheel.'

'No, it's coming from the engine.'

They kept the music turned off.

Then, about three-quarters of an hour from Peterborough, disaster struck. There was a loud noise from behind, and then the van lost power altogether. 'Oh no,' Daisy said. 'No. Don't do this now. Shit, shit, shit.' It was a horrible feeling; worse than running out of petrol. Worse still, they were on a long, straight stretch of the A47.

'What's going on?' Jack said, his heart in his mouth.

'It's lost power. Totally. Oh, shit.' The van was quickly decelerating. 'What do I do? What do I do?'

'There,' said Jack. 'Pull in there.' He'd seen a farm track coming up quickly ahead on their side of the road.

Daisy panicked and looked in the mirror. There was a car right up her arse. She yanked the indicator down, braked, then pulled in sharply. But she was still going too quickly. She slammed on the brakes and the van skidded to a halt in a cloud of dust, just before nosediving into a ditch. If it wasn't for the relatively new tyres, they wouldn't have stopped in time. The car behind screamed by with an aggressive and prolonged blare of its horn. 'Oh, fuck off,' yelled Daisy in response.

Then everything fell quiet, except for the on-off click of the indicator and the hiss of passing traffic. 'Jesus,' said Daisy. 'That was horrible.' The van had felt so out of control, coasting like a runaway cart. She turned to Jack – who was breathing heavily, eyes wide. He pulled himself together and reached out to comfort her. It *had* been horrible.

'You OK?' he said.

She leant into him and let out a whimper. 'No.' Daisy sounded more fed up than upset or scared. He let her rest on him for a while. She was breathing heavily. He stroked her hair. Finally, she sat back up.

'I don't believe it. I simply don't fucking believe our luck.

What is it with us?' She turned to look at him, a rare look of defeat on her face. She didn't usually give up. This bothered Jack; made him want to try harder. To help. He let her do too much, and had been too lost in his own world, what with moping about Aitch. Then stressing about the passport and the flight. *And* it was her birthday. He racked his brains, trying to think like an adult for once; a calm adult. He looked out of the window.

'Look. We'll walk up to the farm. Maybe they can help us. They'll have a phone, I bet. At least we're not in the middle of nowhere.'

'Really?' said Daisy. 'Looks like the middle of nowhere to me. There's no garage. No town. We're screwed. And what about the passport? What if the van's had it?'

Jack gulped. He'd momentarily forgotten about where they were going and the tight timescale. He tried not to panic, to be positive and brave. 'Well, it's still early…'

'Good bloody job it is,' said Daisy.

'Well, come on then, there's no time to waste. Let's go.' He began to open his door.

'Wait. Wait, just a minute. Let me gather my thoughts…' She put her fingers to the bridge of her nose, head down. 'Oh God, Mum's going to kill me,' she moaned. Jack waited. He had no answer to that. Daisy took a deep breath and dragged her head back up. 'Right, pull yourself together, Daisy. Think, think. Mum can wait… We'll cross that bridge when we come to it.'

'Exactly,' said Jack. He needed Daisy to be strong. To be herself. 'We'll call a garage, and who knows? Maybe the van can be fixed and your mum won't have to know.'

'Fat chance of that,' Daisy huffed. Did you hear it? Something's gone, something major. I know it.'

'Maybe,' Jack said. 'Maybe not.' He had no clue about cars. Wished he had. 'Come on, let's get going. The sooner the better.'

He was right, thought Daisy. What was she doing, feeling sorry for herself? They needed to get a bloody move on. Think of the bigger picture.

After the gargantuan struggle to manoeuvre the loaded van into a better position – it had been blocking the entrance – they set off on the dusty walk to the farmhouse in the distance. As they walked, Daisy wondered again how it had come to this. That they could have had such rotten luck. She wasn't bothered about the van any more, nor her mother; she just wanted to get that bloody passport.

As they neared the farmyard, two dogs started yapping and barking, quite aggressively, and pacing up and down. Fortunately, they were trapped behind a gate. Great, thought Daisy. She didn't trust dogs. She'd watched *Cujo*, a film about a rabid dog, as a young girl – too young in hindsight; it had terrified her and put her off dogs for life. Having never been allowed pets, Jack merely found them a curiosity.

Amid the outbuildings and barns, farm machinery and clucking chickens, was a stout woman in her sixties, who was hanging out some washing. She appeared mildly suspicious at the appearance of two unexpected visitors, but not altogether unfriendly. By the time Jack and Daisy reached the gate, the dogs were going ballistic and the woman hollered at them. They waited nervously whilst she hobbled over. The sign on the gate read 'DOGS. BEWARE. TRESPASSERS WILL BE PROSECUTED', which made Jack and Daisy feel even more uncomfortable. The dogs calmed a little, but continued to jump up and down.

'Can I 'elp you?' the lady said. She had permed grey hair and a weather-beaten face.

'Yes. Really sorry to bother you,' Daisy said. 'But we've broken down – right at the end of your lane, near the road. I don't suppose we could borrow your phone, could we, please? To phone a garage: we're miles from home. Or from anywhere.'

The lady looked them up and down. There were some queer sorts about these days, folks up to no good. You heard it on the news all the time. It was hard to know who you could trust. 'Where you heading to?' she said.

'Peterborough,' Daisy said. 'To the passport office.'

'Passport office?'

'Yes, long story,' said Daisy. 'We're flying to America tomorrow – we've got our suitcase in the van and everything – you can check. And we've still got to get Jack's passport: we're collecting it from the office.' She hadn't meant to say so much, but it seemed to break the ice. The story was too out of the ordinary to be made up.

'Ah, bless you,' the woman said. 'Poor things, the pair of yer. And here you are, stuck in the middle of bloody nowhere. Well, we can't 'ave that. We can't 'ave you missing a trip to America.' Daisy and Jack sighed with relief as she began to reach for the gate latch. 'Go on! Get!' she shouted, adopting her severe tone with the dogs again, and kicking them out of the way with a welly-booted foot.

She let Jack and Daisy into the yard and the dogs sniffed and jumped round them. Daisy kept her hands well out of the way. 'Come on in, the phone's inside. But I tell yer what. Before you do call anyone, a garage that is – there's one not far from 'ere in Thorney – I'll give my useless lump of an 'usband an 'oller. I call 'im useless, but between you and me he's a dab hand with motors. I wouldn't tell 'im, of course, it would go to 'is 'ead. But you never know, he might save you a bob or two, prices of garages these days.'

'Oh, well, as long as you're sure,' said Daisy. 'We don't want to be any trouble.' She was more worried about how long it would take.

'Nah, no trouble. 'E might as well be good for something. Come on inside, I'll put the kettle on whilst you wait.' She disappeared through a low, open door.

'We're in a bit of a rush actually. The passport and that. But thank you anyway.' Daisy gave Jack a look; she felt rude, but had no choice. They followed the woman inside into a cool, dark hall, then a bright but equally cool kitchen. The dogs scurried past them, pushing against their legs, sniffing them as they went. The kitchen reeked of dogs. Daisy wrinkled her nose.

'Ah, yes, the passport. Silly me. Yer in a rush. Bear with then. Let me find 'im. 'E's out the back somewhere.' She disappeared down another corridor. Jack and Daisy looked at each other again and shrugged; but they both felt anxious.

A minute later, the woman appeared in the large garden at the back that was bordered by a fence, with a field beyond. In the distance, a tractor was working. She hobbled up to the fence and the two of them followed her agonisingly slow progress. A dog tried to sniff and lick Daisy's hand – why did they always come to her? – and she shooed it away, then wiped her hands on her jeans. Yuk. The dog retreated to a fur-riddled basket near the Aga and settled itself. It whimpered and looked at Daisy with sad eyes, making her feel sorry for it. It was quite cute when it was quiet and still.

Meanwhile, the farmer's wife had clambered onto the bottom rung of the fence and was calling her husband, with her hand cupped to her mouth. It didn't appear to be working, and Jack and Daisy looked at each other again in exasperation. They could be on the phone to a garage. Or Daisy's mum. The van was clearly knackered, so what was the point of all this? When the woman waved a flabby arm energetically back and forth, the tractor turned in the field and began to head across to her. 'Thank God for that,' said Daisy.

They felt strangely shy as the husband and wife approached down the corridor. The man appeared first. 'Now then,' he said, with a rural Cambridgeshire twang. 'What's wrong with this 'ere vehicle then? A car is it?' He pulled off his cap and mopped his brow, a typical ruddy-faced farmer in a green boiler suit, a little older-looking than his wife.

'Hi,' said Daisy. 'No, it's a van. A VW camper van – an old one.'

'A camper van, eh? Over this way on 'oliday, are yer?'

'No, they're *goin'* on 'oliday,' the woman cut in. 'To America! I told yer that, yer daft sod.'

'What? In a camper van?' The woman groaned, and her husband burst into a wheezy half-cough, half laugh. It was infectious, causing Jack and Daisy to smile.

'Pay 'im no 'eed,' she said to Daisy and Jack. Then to her husband: 'They ain't got time for your nonsense, they've got to get to the passport office. They're flying tomorrer.' She seemed to shout whenever she addressed him, as if he was a little deaf.

'Flyin' tomorrer! Never been on a plane in mi life,' the man said. 'Never wanted to either. Don't trust the things. Give me a tractor or combine any day.'

'Don't go sayin' things like that, you'll put the fear of God into 'em. Now go on wiv yer and go an 'ave a look at that van.'

'Aye, aye, stop naggin', woman.' He gave Jack and Daisy a twinkly-eyed wink. They were like a double act. 'Keith, by the way, pleased to meet yer.'

'Oh, Daisy,' said Daisy. 'And this is Jack.'

'Pleased to meet yer, Jack and Daisy. Now then, where's my toolbox?'

'In the back of the Lan' Rover, where it always is.'

'Ah, that's 'andy then. Right, out to the yard it is. Let's see what we can do. After you… Come on girls,' he added, calling the dogs, which excitedly hurried past again.

After opening the gate, the man headed over to an open-backed Land Rover in the yard. He let the back tailgate down and the dogs jumped in. Jack and Daisy climbed in the passenger side. The interior of the vehicle was filthy, with caked mud and straw everywhere. They sat down gingerly.

The man started the engine, reversed, then set off over the bumpy yard to the lane. Once through the gate, he stopped and said, 'Do the 'onours, will you?' meaning the gate. Jack got out and obliged. Then they were off down the bumpy lane. 'So, where you pair from then?'

'Nottingham way, originally. But we've been living in Cromer for the last year or so,' said Daisy.

'Cromer, eh? Lovely. My favourite. Bit further down the coast, but I always preferred it to Sheringham. Upped sticks and moved with yer folks out that way, did yer?'

'No, just me and Jack.'

'Ah, just the pair of yer, eh? Brother and sister, is it?'

Daisy laughed and blushed. Jack felt mildly outraged. 'No, boyfriend and girlfriend!'

'Ah,' the man laughed, 'Explains the difference in 'air colour, then. 'E don't say a lot, does 'e?' It wasn't the first time they'd heard this from a stranger. Daisy gave a polite laugh. Jack shifted uncomfortably. 'So, what's wrong with this van, then? Just conked out, did it?'

Daisy filled him in, and the man leant in close to listen, nodding and aahing. 'Hmm…' he summed up.

They reached the bottom of the lane. Daisy had an impending feeling of doom, that this was a waste of time. They got out, and the man took his toolbox from the back of the Land Rover. 'Right, crank 'er open,' he said. 'Let's 'ave a look.' He walked to the front of the van.

'Erm, the engine's at the back,' Daisy said, a little awkwardly.

'Silly me, course it is. Bloody Germans,' he laughed, not embarrassed at all.

Daisy opened the engine hatch and they peered inside. Jack and Daisy hadn't a clue what they were looking for – it all looked filthy and oil-covered. But the old man seemed to know what he was doing. He peered in further and poked around for a second. Then he reached in. ''Ere you go,' he said, extricating something and standing back up. 'Just as I thought.' He had a frayed old rubber belt in his hands. 'Yer fan belt's gone. Knackered.'

'What does that mean?' asked Daisy.

'It means – providing there's no further damage – that it's fixable.'

'Fixable?' Daisy couldn't believe it. She looked at Jack.

'Yep,' the man said. 'Got any tights?'

'Tights?' said Daisy. What on earth was he talking about?

'Aye, tights,' the man chuckled. 'You know, ladies' tights, stockings … maybe in yer suitcase or somethin'.'

What was he, thought Daisy, some sort of old pervert? 'No, I don't have any tights. It's summer.'

'Gets cold in New York, if that's where yer 'eadin' – or so they say.' He laughed again, as if it was all a game. Daisy didn't know what to say, or do. Neither did Jack. 'Don't worry, I'm only messin' with yer.' He could sense he was making them feel uncomfortable. 'I can replace that there fan belt of yours with a strong pair o' tights. Should last long enough to get you 'ome if yer take 'er steady, or at least to Peterborough if that's where yer 'eadin'.'

'Really?' said Daisy. She was astounded – and a little sceptical: it sounded so bizarre, so makeshift, but he seemed to know what he was talking about.

'Yep. So, definitely no tights?'

'No,' Daisy said.

The man sighed. 'Looks like it'll 'ave to be a pair o' the missus's then. More's the pity…' He winked again, causing Daisy to blush. 'Yer can choke a dozen donkeys wi' *them*. Back in a jiffy…'

About ten minutes later, the old man returned with not one, but two pairs of brown tights. They looked a little odd, a little perverse, clutched in his male, work-worn hands. Jack and Daisy watched, fascinated, as he set about his work. It wasn't long before he stood up, clutching the base of his back. 'I can't see any other damage. She topped up with everything else? Oil? Petrol?'

'Yes, everything,' said Daisy.

'Right, fire 'er up and cross your fingers. It's a while since I've 'ad to do this. Leave the 'atch open for now, so I can keep an eye on 'er.'

Jack and Daisy climbed back into the van together; Jack didn't want to be left with the old man. 'Right, here goes,' Daisy said. She was still sceptical: it seemed so unlikely that a simple pair of tights could do the same job as a strong rubber belt. She made sure the van was in neutral, then turned the key, wincing as she did so, not daring to hope. After an initial couple of heart-stopping misfires, the van whinnied into life and began to tick over. They looked at each other in amazement. 'Give 'er a few revs. But gentle, mind,' the old man called from the rear, amongst a cloud of exhaust smoke. Daisy did as he asked, pressing gently on the accelerator. It all seemed OK, nothing untoward. 'Aye, she's good,' he called. They heard the rear hatch slam.

Jack and Daisy simply couldn't believe it. Daisy didn't want to turn the engine off, just in case. Brimming with gratitude, they climbed down. The old man was already putting his toolbox back in the Land Rover, as if what he'd done was the most normal thing in the world, an everyday occurrence. The teenagers watched as he shut up the tailgate, the dogs circling within. He turned to them. 'Thank you,' said Daisy. 'Thank you so much.'

'Yes, thank you,' said Jack shyly.

'Ah, 'e speaks,' the old man laughed.

'Seriously, though, I don't know how we can repay you. You've saved our lives,' said Daisy.

'Well, not exactly. But no problem at all. Don't mention it. Glad to be of service. There's still some use for our generation yet. But do take 'er steady, though. Them tights ain't gonna 'old out forever. And I wouldn't bother stopping at a garage either, not so far from 'ome: they won't 'ave a belt to fit an old foreign van like that in stock; it'll 'ave to be ordered and that could take days.' This was a very good point, thought Daisy. 'So just take 'er steady till yer get 'ome and 'ope for the best.'

'Will do,' said Daisy. 'Thank you so much again. And your wife, thank her too. What was her name? I didn't catch it.'

''Ilda. Been married forty-five years, we 'ave – for our sins.'

'Ah, bless you,' Daisy said. 'Well, I guess that's it, then. We'll be on our way.'

'Guess you will.' They stood there for a moment then, by the side of the A47, feeling a little emotional – for Daisy and Jack because a stranger had been so kind and helpful, and for the old man, well … he'd enjoyed the episode and was sad to see them go. On the spur of the moment, Daisy gave him a peck on his spider-veined cheek. It was his turn to blush, and laugh.

As they climbed back in the van, he stood watching them, clutching his cloth cap. 'Any problems, you make sure you jus' come on back. We'll get yer sorted again somehow. And good luck with that passport!'

'Will do! Goodbye,' Daisy called through the open window, waving as she drove off. The man waved back.

They were on their way again. 'What a lovely man,' Daisy said. 'And couple. We *are* going back there, Jack. On our way back, after America, I mean. To take them a thank you gift and a card or something. I'm not going to forget what they did. Hilda and Keith, wasn't it?' Jack ummed in agreement, staring out of the window, already lost in thought again.

CHAPTER 24

Leaving on a Jet Plane

Miraculously, the tights held out. But it had been an uncomfortable journey. Knowing that the engine was precariously relying on an item of hosiery... It was hard not to picture Hilda's tights spinning round and round all the way home.

But most importantly, Jack was clutching a brand-new navy blue, hardbacked passport as they pulled up at Carol's house. This seemed to have cheered him up no end – for the moment at least. Daisy had kept catching him looking at it, at his name and photo and the strange coloured patterns inside, smiling a little. It made her smile too. And, God, was she relieved. Surely they could settle into their holiday now and enjoy the rest of her birthday... She fancied a drink.

Daisy turned off the engine, sat back and let out a huge sigh. What a journey. They looked up at the house. Carol was already opening the door to greet them, waving and smiling excitedly. They waved back. 'Let's not tell her about the van just yet,' Daisy said. 'I can't be doing with any more hassle. Not right now. We'll tell her when we're away. Maybe when she's drunk.'

They got out and Daisy went over to greet her mum, whilst Jack retrieved their large suitcase. 'Happy birthday!' Carol said. 'All OK? You got the passport all right?'

'Yep, all done and dusted,' Daisy said.

'Thank God for that,' Carol said, putting her hand to her chest, clearly relieved. She gave Daisy a hug. 'Happy birthday, darling.'

'Thanks,' said Daisy.

'And the van's been OK? You said it had been playing up a bit.'

Great, thought Daisy, pulling away. Straight in there. 'Erm … yes and no … kind of a long story.' She headed inside. 'Got any cider?'

*****

The big day finally arrived. Departure day. Lily was dropping them off at the airport. Daisy held onto Jack's hand all the way there, fully aware of his anxiety about the flight. Jack was pale and quiet. He had been all morning. His stomach was in knots. Absolute knots. And he'd kept having to go to the toilet. The closer they got to the airport, the worse his anxiety became. The sky was increasingly full of planes. Lower, bigger, closer and louder. He got his first sighting of a take-off, or its final stages anyway. The ascent, the climb. How did something that big, that clumsy and heavy, make its way into the air? Why didn't it just drop out of the sky? Or what if it lost a wing? Lost power? He'd heard the stories of aeroplane crashes. They happened all the time, and there was no way you could survive. A sickening plummet to the earth, like those dreams he'd had as a child, falling out of a tree or off the roof of a house. That old familiar vertigo feeling. Then the horrific impact. The shattering and screeching and compacting of metal and glass. Then a ball of flames, an inferno. He shuddered.

Daisy had butterflies too, but unlike Jack, they were butterflies of excitement. Flying had never bothered her. Carol was nervous in an excited way, chattering the whole way to the airport. She hadn't flown much, only a handful of times, and certainly never a long-haul flight. She'd never liked the turbulence.

When they arrived at Heathrow, it was heaving with cars, buses and people: it was still the summer holidays. After some rigmarole locating the drop-off point, and everyone getting stressed, they finally pulled up alongside dozens of other cars and taxis. Jack felt as if he was glued to his seat. Was it too late to back out? Daisy gave him a kiss, patted his leg, then practically pushed him out of the car. The planes were louder than ever.

They heaved their luggage from the boot, said their goodbyes to Lily, who was feeling a little jealous that she wasn't going too, and walked inside. It was cavernous, echoey and full of people. Different colours and races. Different accents and languages. Luggage everywhere, and hustle and bustle. They made it through check-in and security without any dramas, and Jack endured it all – the people, the waiting and queuing – in his usual detached way, blocking it all out and doing what he was told when prompted. He watched their brand-new suitcase disappearing on a conveyor belt. Where had it gone? What if it was put on the wrong plane? Daisy kept hold of his hand. She was used to this now, but Carol less so: checking in was stressful enough without Jack adding to it.

On the way to the departure lounge, they passed through fragrant shops selling perfume and alcohol, chocolates and huge teddy bears. Carol and Daisy lingered for what seemed like an eternity, stopping and looking at things, knowing they had time to kill. Jack was impatient, just wanting to get the flight over and done with. Daisy bought a couple of films for her new camera.

And then they had to wait in the sprawling departure lounge. Jack stood at the windows, watching in morbid fascination. The planes looked huge on the ground. Simply huge. Jack couldn't believe it. People were tiny in comparison, and there were little trucks and buses darting about. Stairs on wheels. People entering and leaving planes. Suitcases being loaded and unloaded. Jack tried to spot theirs, but it was impossible. Too many planes, too many trucks, too much luggage. And then there was the taxiing of the planes, negotiating the marked paths like giant cylindrical buses with wings – steered by tiny men in uniform, only just visible through the cockpit windows.

The closer it got to departure time, the more Jack's nerves built up. 'Ooh, I think that's ours,' said Carol. She pointed to a huge white plane with a dark blue belly and tail-fin, 'BRITISH AIRWAYS' painted on the side. Daisy squeezed Jack's hand in reassurance, and excitement. But Jack's stomach dropped. It was bigger than most of the others, and to him there was something menacing about the shape of it, which resembled a great white shark.

'I think I'm going to be sick,' he said.

Daisy rushed after him to the toilets. Carol rolled her eyes. Great, she thought. This is all we need. Why didn't Daisy say he was terrified of flying? Mind you, she should have guessed: he was terrified of everything, it seemed.

After what seemed an age, they finally boarded the plane, Jack still pale and shaking. The plane was even bigger up close. Colossal. The warm breeze ruffled their hair as they queued on the stairs. The roar and whinny of the planes taking off was deafening, intimidating. And then they were inside.

Everything went quieter. And then Jack was hit by a new anxiety: his old friend claustrophobia. He hadn't really thought about this; he'd been too preoccupied with the mechanics of the plane, the bulk of it – and crashing. But here he was, on the verge of being trapped in an enclosed space, for how long? Eight hours? With no way of escaping. No way to say 'I want to get off'. A head-spinning panic and new wave of nausea hit him again. Where were the toilets?

Clutching their hand luggage, they shuffled down one of

the aisles, trying to locate their seats. The sheer size of the interior became more apparent. It was jaw-dropping. There were two main aisles and three rows of seating, all with three or four seats. And this was just the downstairs. To Jack's amazement, some passengers were heading up a small flight of stairs to another level: a top deck, like a bus. He'd had no idea there were stairs on a plane. Jesus, how did this thing lift all these people? What if they were too heavy? And what if all the heavier people sat on one side? Would they make the plane tip over?

All this was going through his head as they finally found their seats. Daisy showed Jack the overhead lockers and told him to put his rucksack away. Hands shaking, he did as he was told. 'Would you prefer the window seat?' she asked, not knowing if this would be better for him or not.

'No,' said Jack. He didn't want to see them take off, to see the ground disappearing. And what if he needed to dash to the toilet? Where the hell were they? He loitered in the aisle.

'Guess I'm the window seat then,' said Carol, also feeling nervous; she had forgotten that flying could make her feel that way. She shuffled sideways to the window seat and plonked herself down. Daisy sat down next, a little miffed at the seating arrangements, but not saying anything. Out of them all, she had most wanted the window seat; she liked to see the plane take off and to be able to look at the scenery. Jack plonked himself down, sitting with his head down and eyes closed, trying to block everything out. Despite it being a non-smoking section, the stale smell of cigarette smoke was prevalent. And people were still boarding in their droves.

To take Jack's mind off things, Daisy showed him how to buckle and unclip his seatbelt, and how the folding tray worked. There were quite a few things to explore and distract him whilst they waited. Telephones built into the seats in front for a start – but who would use them? Businessmen maybe?

Daisy found some strange headphone things – they had a set each – which were long and rubbery and resembled doctors' stethoscopes. They plugged into a hole in the seats. 'Ah! For the TV. Look,' she said to Jack, pointing to a big screen on a dividing wall in front of them. 'Hopefully they'll show some movies.' Jack hmphed in response. There was an in-flight magazine to peruse, and the crew came round with meal-request forms. Daisy couldn't find a vegetarian option and had to ask.

The stewardess smiled awkwardly. 'I'll see what I can do.'

After a while, the pilot of the plane started to speak, and everyone hushed to listen. Captain Plum-in-his-Mouth or something; he sounded really posh. He asked everyone to take their seats as soon as possible, so the cabin crew could prepare for take-off. Jack gulped. Then the captain ran through their flight time, weather conditions and headwinds. Once everyone was seated, various members of the cabin crew appeared in the aisles to go through the flight safety procedure. Jack listened as if his life depended on it. Why were they talking about crashing and water and life rafts, for fuck's sake? Chutes and blow-up vests and lights and whistles. Jack hadn't even thought about that – crashing into the sea. What if it was shark-infested? Oh, God! Daisy, who had heard it all before, was barely listening. She was more bothered about the air stewardess who was standing just a few feet in front of Jack, acting out the instructions so close you could smell her perfume. She was annoyingly slim and pretty – albeit with too much make-up – in her navy-blue outfit and pencil skirt that clung to her. Daisy hoped Jack didn't fancy her.

And then it was time for take-off. There was a whirring, humming noise as fans came on. Then there was an unexpected and heart-stopping lurch as the brake was released and the plane began to slowly move forwards. Daisy put her hand on Jack's to reassure him. A groaning sound came from outside, and Jack jumped. 'Just the wing-flaps,' Daisy said. The plane continued to wheel towards the runway. It seemed to take an age. Finally, it stopped. 'This is it then, honey,' Daisy said. 'We're about to take off. The plane will go really fast for a bit, *really* fast, but it's all normal, so don't be alarmed.'

'Oh, God,' Jack moaned, closing his eyes in preparation. The whining sound of the engines started, getting increasingly louder and more high-pitched. Then, just as Daisy had warned, the plane was suddenly propelled forwards at a terrifying speed. Faster and faster. Jack clutched the ends of his armrests, hands like claws, knuckles white. He could feel himself being pressed against his seat, a weight on his chest, his life in the hands of a pilot and an unstoppable machine. And as the plane hurtled on, Jack saw his life flash before his eyes, as if he was about to die. But it was in flick-book form – something his sister had taught him when he was younger: drawing a stick man on consecutive pages in the corner of a notepad, then flicking though the pages to make the man move. From earliest memories, through childhood, to everything with Daisy – in the blink of an eye, a matter of mere seconds. Then there was an unexpected and alarming shift of the plane's wings, a groaning sound as the plane took off, struggling to bear the weight. Jack began to say a prayer to himself, silently chanting it over and over. His eyes were closed, but he was aware they were in the air. It felt different, and the noise of the wheels on the runway had stopped. There was a dreadful swaying and bumping as the plane fought for altitude, but still that sense of pressure. They were leaning backwards, too far backwards, the nose of the plane tilted towards the sky. Jack groaned involuntarily. The ascent seemed to go on forever, accompanied by heart-stopping bumping and buffeting as they climbed through the clouds. When would it end? Is this what flying was like? And why had his ears gone funny?

Eventually, the plane began to level out and the bumping

stopped. A few minutes later, a beeping noise echoed around the cabin and an air stewardess spoke over the tannoy: 'Ladies and gentlemen, you can now remove your seatbelts…' Jack heard a collective sigh of relief and a clicking of seatbelt buckles. He became aware of Daisy squeezing his hand. 'It's OK,' she said. 'That's it, take-off out of the way. You can relax now.'

'Hallelujah,' Carol said.

Relax, thought Jack. He'd just gone through one of the most terrifying ordeals of his life – and now he had to spend eight hours trapped on a plane with hundreds of other people, somehow – God knows how – hovering thousands of feet above the earth. If the plane lost power during that time, they were dead. Plain and simple. So, no, he couldn't relax…

He opened his eyes. It was bright in the cabin. He turned to Daisy, who was looking at him with a mixture of pity and amusement. 'You OK?' she said. 'Well done. Honestly, you can relax now. That's the worst bit out the way.' She didn't want to tell him about the landing. She leant across and kissed him.

'You needn't be doing that all the way either,' Carol piped up. But when Daisy looked at her she was smiling, clearly relieved. Jack looked about him, trying to gather his thoughts. Behind them, the sound of sparking lighters could be heard, followed by puffs of smoke as people lit cigarettes. The smell briefly made Jack want a spliff. And a drink. No chance of that; they weren't old enough. Great – eight hours on a plane without a drink. Hold on, though: Daisy was old enough…

When the cabin crew came round with their trolley, Carol ordered a gin and tonic. She needed it, and she was on holiday now. To Carol's surprise, Daisy ordered one too. Carol clucked, but she could hardly say anything; Daisy was eighteen after all. Nineteen now, in fact. The stewardess asked Daisy if she wouldn't mind showing her passport to prove it, and Daisy was happy to oblige. Then, when no staff were about, Jack and Daisy shared the drink, gulping it down between them.

Settling into the journey, Daisy scanned through the in-flight magazine to discover it looked as though there were three movies being played on the flight – all of them blockbusters or new releases. But which ones you got looked like pot luck. Soon, the trolleys came round again and both Daisy and Carol ordered another gin and tonic. Jack ordered a soft drink this time, so it didn't look suspicious. The alcohol went to their heads a little – it must have been the altitude.

The first film started, and to most people's surprise it was the recently released *Pretty Woman*. Murmurs of appreciation rippled up and down the plane as they stuck their headphones into their ears. 'Ooh, I went to see this at the Curzon with Lily,' said Carol. 'It's ever so good. Julia Roberts is fantastic. Lily was drooling over Richard Gere, of course. I preferred him in *An Officer and a Gentleman* in that uniform.'

Daisy tutted. Typical. 'Want to watch it?' she said to Jack.

'OK,' said Jack. There was nothing else to do, and it might take his mind off things for a while.

They plugged in their headphones and settled back to watch the film. It was entertaining, and funny. For the first time, despite a few scary bumps of turbulence, Jack managed to forget where he was for a while. Amusingly, Carol nodded off before the end: must have been the gin and tonics. Daisy had to wake her up when the main meal came round. This was a chicken dish, served with sides of potatoes and veg. Three times Daisy had to remind them she had ordered a vegetarian meal. Jack and Carol – and most of the plane – had finished their meals completely by the time Daisy got hers. Chicken chasseur, minus the chicken, but with a few extra vegetables and potatoes. She could have eaten one of the regular meals and just left the chicken.

After the food had been cleared away, Jack and Daisy stared out of the window for a while. It was the first time Jack had felt brave and relaxed enough to do this. Sometimes they were amongst clouds; other times over a sparkling sea. It was such a strange, alien feeling. And scary. Where the hell were they? Another film came on, but they weren't fussed about watching it – and they were both feeling drowsy after another G and T. It was hard to fight it, so they butted their heads up against each other and, lulled by the drone of the plane, drifted off to sleep.

The last third of the flight dragged. When they saw America for the first time, the coastline approaching on the horizon, it was a significant moment and a huge relief. Jack and Daisy looked at each other in wonder. They watched the land get closer and closer until they were actually flying over it. It was hard to fathom that this was really the United States of America. They'd done it. Jack felt like crying. But first they had to land.

Despite the landing being a little bumpy, it was nowhere near as bad as the take-off. Even so, Jack gripped the arms of his seat tight at every buffet of turbulence, and his eyes were wide with terror when the wheels first bumped down hard and the plane suddenly braked. But Daisy assured him it was all normal. If it hadn't been for the trauma he was clearly suffering, she would have been in stitches at his over-reaction. Then very quickly, it seemed, the plane came to a complete halt. Jack let out a deep breath and said another little prayer. He could now *truly* relax. They'd made it. Defied nature, it seemed. He felt proud that he'd dared to do it, and got through it. There was nothing America could throw at him that would be worse than that plane journey.

'Thank God that's over,' said Carol, echoing Jack's thoughts. 'I wonder if Phil's here yet.'

CHAPTER 25

Uncle Phil

Walking into the airport of a foreign country for the first time, being on foreign soil, was an experience that Jack would never forget. It started with the accents. The voice on the airport speaker system, so very different to his own and anyone's he had ever heard, except for on TV. And the airport staff that greeted them were all friendlier, smilier, more tanned, healthier-looking, their teeth whiter, their voices louder. 'Welcome to New York!' And they all said 'Hey' rather than 'Hi' or 'Hello'. The plane had been on time, so despite having to wait an age for their luggage, Uncle Phil was patiently waiting for them as planned in the arrivals lounge. As an ironic joke, he was holding up a sign saying 'JONES FAMILY', like the taxi-cab drivers do.

Carol laughed, then burst into tears as they scurried towards each other and hugged. It was all very embarrassing for Daisy. She had forgotten Uncle Phil was a fair bit older than her mum, and he looked it, with an outdated mullet hairstyle and matching silvery moustache (something her dad had sported for a while in the late '70s, before wisely shaving it off). Daisy had also forgotten – or never noticed – how colossal he was. Both upwards and outwards. He was a huge man, and Carol looked tiny in his arms. There were tears in his eyes as they parted and looked each other up and down. 'Look at you, gone all grey,' she said.

'Gee, thanks, sis,' he said. 'Great to see you too.'

'Sorry,' Carol laughed. 'I just mean, it's been so long. Too long…' She stroked his arm and let out another sob. Oh, jeez, thought Daisy. This really is embarrassing. And then it was her turn.

'Daisy!' he boomed. 'All grown up. Come here!' He grabbed hold of her, and gave her an over-enthusiastic ursine hug of sickly-sweet aftershave that almost masked a faint whiff of BO. Daisy was thankful when he released her. 'And this must be the boyfriend, Jack. How you doin', fella? Pleased to meet you.' He reached out a huge, meaty paw and gave Jack's hand a good pump. 'Well, this is exciting, isn't it?' he said, finally letting go. 'Welcome to the good old U S of A. How was the flight?' It was so strange to hear his American accent. And how loud he was.

'Oh, not too bad really,' said Carol. 'Dragged a little, but otherwise fine.'

'Ah, that's good. So, you guys all set? We've a bit of a drive ahead of us, I'm afraid – four hours or so.' Jack and Daisy looked at each other, both thinking the same thing. Another four hours of travelling. They'd only just got off the plane. They hadn't been expecting this, and Daisy wished her mum had warned her.

'Yep, all OK, I think,' said Carol.

'All righty then, let's go.'

*****

Uncle Phil's car was a huge double cab pick-up truck that seemed to be very high off the ground. It took some climbing into, and, trying to be sociable, Daisy remarked on this. 'Yup, we get some pretty bad winters up there in the Keystone State,' Phil answered.

'Where do you live exactly?' asked Daisy. She was a little embarrassed at not knowing – it was something else Carol hadn't told them.

'Bradford County, right up north. A quaint little place called Asylum,' Phil laughed, buckling his seatbelt. 'Or Asylum Township, to be exact. Asylum Township, Bradford County, PA.' Asylum, thought Daisy. Interesting name. 'Famous for the French Azilum – about all it's famous for. You kids learn about the French Azilum at school?' Uncle Phil adjusted his mirror slightly so he could see Daisy. She shook her head.

'Never heard of it,' said Carol.

'Guess that's why they call it Pennsylvania's best kept secret. A little bit of American history for you English folks, then, courtesy of yer Uncle Phil... French Azilum was a settlement built specifically for fleeing French aristocrats during the bloody French Revolution – so they didn't get their heads chopped off, basically. The queen was meant to end up there apparently – Marie Antoinette: they even built a grand house for her, La Grande Maison. But she never made it – probably because she got her head chopped off. But that's all gone now; all of the original buildings are. But there's a neat little museum and other bits. Really gives you a feel for what it was like back then. We'll go there. Really worth a visit whilst yer in town. All very rural, of course' – he pronounced 'rural' without the middle 'r', almost like 'rule' – 'set right next to the Susquehanna River.' Jack and Daisy looked at each other again. It sounded amazing. Just what they'd been hoping for: a little bit of 'Real America' and its culture. 'Right, you guys all set?' Phil asked. That expression again. 'Let's go.'

They set off from the airport and soon hit the freeway. This in itself was jaw-dropping. Driving on the other side of the road seemed so unnatural. And the freeways were so wide – with multiple lanes in both directions, separated by central reservations – sometimes high up, and sometimes looping round in circles like asphalt spaghetti. God only knew how you figured it all out. The hard shoulder was a wide lane in itself, littered with debris – burst tyres, car parts, rubbish and roadkill. And as for the road signs, these were simply huge – as tall as houses – probably so people could see them better. But Uncle Phil seemed to know where he was going, which was reassuring. He said 'rout' to rhyme with 'out', instead of the English 'route' – more fascinating American pronunciation. And she noticed there was no gearstick, or not a normal one. Instead, there was a stick by the side of the steering wheel that he flicked with a large hand. Daisy still couldn't get over the size and bulk of Uncle Phil. His presence seemed to fill the large cab.

'So … fill me in on all the news. What's going on across the pond?' he said. 'How's Mom doing?'

'Mom!' said Carol. 'It's "Mum", remember? I can't get over how American you sound. My own brother.'

Phil laughed. 'You've heard me on the phone.'

'I know, but it's different hearing it face to face.'

'Must be Trish's influence,' he said. 'Wait till you hear her – she's from down south.'

Carol caught up with her brother, whilst Jack and Daisy continued to take in the scenery, to take in America, in wide-eyed wonder. The radio was on low and it was fascinating to hear American voices coming out of it, but unfortunately no tunes Daisy recognised at all. There seemed to be more adverts than songs – and again they were brash and loud. As she watched the multitude of cars passing, most of them huge and square and wide, the song 'America' by Simon and Garfunkel popped into Daisy's head. The lines about counting the cars on the New Jersey Turnpike and looking for America. It was a strange and wondrous feeling.

Eventually they left the freeway and joined a smaller road; it was still bigger than UK motorways and had more lanes. This road passed through actual towns. Curiously, some of them had population counts on their signs. What was that all about? How did they know? What if someone died or was born? They couldn't go adjusting it every time, surely? Daisy made a mental note to ask Phil. In between towns the road signs were replaced by billboards. Giant billboards on stilts. They were everywhere. And the nearer to the towns they got, the more of them there were, advertising everything it seemed. From giant candy stores (so many candy stores), to lawyers and doctors, to places of worship, shouting that 'JESUS SAVES!' amongst other things. There were even drive-thru banks with huge dollar signs on the billboards. Everything was 'drive-thru', it seemed. What the hell was a drive-thru exactly? There were radio stations, carpet showrooms and car lots advertised. Motels. Supermarkets – so many supermarkets – their names all ending in 'mart': Quikimart. Hypermart. K-mart. Walmart.

And then there were the restaurant billboards… These were constant: it was restaurant overload. Adverts for every cuisine under the sun, and all with huge, garish photos or images. Steak-houses with cowboys on horses, or even cows or herds of cattle. Yuk, thought Daisy. How is that appealing? Seafood restaurants with monstrous crabs or lobsters. Chinese restaurants… Burger joints… Jesus, the number of burger joints, all accompanied by pictures of huge, colourful, juicy burgers. McDonald's of course, Wendy's, Dairy Queen, Burger Chef, Burger King. Daisy had heard of Burger King, but it was still relatively new in the UK. They'd just replaced the Wimpy in town with one. Here they were everywhere.

And the billboards worked. Eventually they got to you, ground you down and made you feel hungry. It was no surprise when Phil said, 'You guys hungry or what? Want to grab a bite soon? Break up the journey a bit, stretch yer legs…'

'Suppose we could stop for something,' said Carol. 'You kids hungry?'

Jack was. He always seemed hungry. And Daisy hadn't exactly been satisfied on the plane. 'Yeah, OK,' said Daisy. It would be good to soak up a bit more Americana.

'Great. Let's give it another fifteen minutes or so, then we'll be about haff-way. Burger OK?'

'Ooh, how very American,' said Carol. It came across a little disparagingly.

'Doesn't have to be,' said Phil. 'It's the quickest and easiest, 's all.' He secretly wanted a burger.

'No, a burger's fine,' said Carol, although she wasn't really a burger fan – not unless she'd made them herself.

'Will they have a vegetarian burger?' asked Daisy.

'Vegetarian?' said Phil, as if he'd never heard of such a thing.

'Daisy doesn't eat meat,' explained Carol. Again, somewhat disparagingly. 'Pain in the bloody arse.'

'Mum,' said Daisy, and Phil laughed.

'Hmm… I'm not sure about a vegetarian burger. I've certainly never *heard* of such a thing. How about fish? McDonald's do a fish one.'

'I don't eat fish,' said Daisy.

'Oh. Maybe some fries and a shake then?'

'They thicken their shakes with chicken fat,' said Daisy.

Phil looked at Carol. 'See what I have to put up with,' she said.

It was getting dark as they pulled into a McDonald's drive-thru. The glowing yellow arches vied for attention amongst a plethora of lurid blinking neon and blinding white: 'COLD BEER' and 'TACOS'. What time was it? thought Daisy, looking at her watch, which was still on English time. To her amazement, it read two o'clock. Two o'clock in the morning. How was that possible? No wonder she felt a bit out of it; it was a good job they'd slept for a while on the flight. This was the first time she'd really thought about the difference in time zones. It was like time travel. They'd set off at about four p.m. on an eight-hour flight, yet landed at around seven o'clock. How strange. It would be the middle of the night back home now, but around nine o'clock here.

'Hey folks, I'm Stacey. What can I get y'all?' the lady in the window said. It was so strange ordering like this, a novelty, none of the English contingent had experienced a drive-thru before.

'Hey, Stacey,' said Phil. 'Can I have a large Big Mac value meal with a Coke, please? And then a separate cheeseburger, a large fries and an apple pie on the side.' Carol looked round at the kids. No wonder he was the size he was.

Stacey didn't bat an eyelid at this order. 'You certainly can,' she said. 'Anything else for you guys?'

'Guys?' said Phil.

'Oh, I don't know,' said Carol, getting all flustered and put on the spot. This was all new to her. 'You two order first.'

'Oh, you guys English?' Stacey beamed. 'I love your accent.'

'Erm, yes,' said Carol, blushing further.

'Yep. All the way from Nottingham, England,' Phil added.

'Oh, my gosh! Notting-ham, England!' She pronounced it Notting-ham, with the emphasis on the 'ham'. 'Robin Hood. Is he real?'

Daisy groaned on the back seat. Jack found it entertaining and amusing, hearing the girl and her accent.

'He *was* real – or so they say – but he's also very dead,' Carol said, suddenly sounding very English and rather stuffy. How had that happened?

The girl laughed, 'Oh my gosh, I just love your accent,' she said again. 'You sound just like the queen.' They all found this highly amusing.

After they had all ordered food (Daisy settling for a Filet-O-Fish burger, even though it went against her principles) and the girl gushing again over the English accents, Phil paid for the meals. 'That's gonna be ten dollars and fifty cents exactly, please,' Stacey said. It was strange being charged in another currency and seeing the notes that were handed over. Jack and Daisy couldn't wait to spend some dollars themselves.

'Thank you kindly. And that's for you, Stacey,' Phil said, handing over an extra couple of dollar bills. 'Keep the change.'

'Aw, thank you so much. Y'all enjoy your meals, and enjoy the rest of your evening. And just holler if you need anything.'

'Will do,' said Phil, pulling off. 'Now, *she* was more Southern.'

He parked the pick-up and they unpacked their respective meals. 'Now if it's OK with you guys, I'd like to keep this stop-off our little secret,' said Phil, before taking a huge bite from a burger. 'In other words, don't tell Trish. She'll kill me.' They all looked at each other in wonder; clearly, he had health problems – and was sweating as he ate. The meals were salty and good, annoyingly so in Daisy's case. She hadn't planned on enjoying the burger so much, and vowed it would be the last time. A one-off.

Once they'd finished, Phil insisted they clear every scrap of rubbish – or 'evidence' – from the truck to put in the bin. He hadn't been joking. It made them wonder how many times he had done this, and what else he kept from Aunt Trish. Unbelievably, instead of getting out of the truck to walk to a bin, he drove over to one instead, and posted the rubbish through the window – which he left open for a bit as they set off, probably to get rid of the smell.

A few minutes into the journey, and Phil opened up another somewhat surprising and candid line of conversation. 'Now, while I've got you guys alone, there's something else I want to discuss before we get home. No big deal or anything.' It already sounded like one. 'It's about sleeping arrangements.' Jack and Daisy looked at each other, wondering where this was heading. Straight to them, they surmised.

'Go on,' said Carol.

'Trish is, how can I put it … a little old-fashioned in her way of thinking sometimes, a bit *Christian* – not that there's anything wrong with that – we all have our moral codes, our standards… I blame her Puritan upbringing.' Great, thought Daisy, a God-botherer. 'But, anyways, long story short, there was some 'discussion' over the young folks sleeping arrangements. You'll be pleased to know it's all been sorted now – or at least a compromise has been reached, one that will suit all concerned, I hope…'

'Go on,' said Carol again, fearful of where this was heading, worrying that Daisy would be in a mard with her for the whole trip. She really wished her brother had brought the problem up sooner, over the phone.

'You see, our girls never had fellas over, not to stay anyway – and certainly not in the same rooms. Trish was very strict about that. Her house, her rules. And it caused a fair few fights, let me tell yer – between me and you, it's probably one of the main reasons the girls flew the nest so early. So, what with young Jack and Daisy coming over, Trish has had, how can I put it, some confliction of mind, I guess. Not just from the moral standpoint, but with the girls coming back to visit…'

'I can totally understand that,' said Carol. 'Consistency and all that. So, what's the upshot? Spit it out, bruv.'

It was so weird for Daisy to hear her mum talk like that. But, yes, for fuck's sake, Uncle Phil, spit it out. They were all on tenterhooks.

'Separate beds in the largest guest room,' he said. 'Single beds.'

'That's fine,' said Daisy.

'Oh,' said Carol, expecting a fight. 'That's that sorted then.' Daisy had been fearing worse, so this solution was OK. They certainly wouldn't be sleeping in both of them. The second the lights went out and the door was closed… What was Aunt Trish going to do, a nightly spot-check? All this made Daisy wonder about her, a little wary of what else she wouldn't agree with…

It was pitch-black when they finally arrived at the house, Daisy and Jack having nodded off for the last part of the journey. The place in front of them, all lit up, looked huge, and appeared to be in the middle of nowhere, almost like a ranch. And to Jack's intense pleasure, there was a veranda to sit on, complete with a porch swing. He couldn't wait to see it properly in the light of day.

Aunt Trish greeted them at the door. Physically, she couldn't have been more different from Phil. Older still, she was a small, slim, raisin of a woman, sun-wrinkled and swarthy. She had an excessively puckered-up mouth, as if she'd been weaned on a gherkin, and pronounced bow legs, as if she'd spent too long riding horses – which was indeed a hobby of hers. This unfortunate affliction didn't help her stature.

Despite her appearance, and the sleeping arrangements, Aunt Trish couldn't have been more lovely and welcoming; she also remarked on how much she loved the new arrivals' English accents. As Phil had said, she had a much more Southern accent than he did. They were all shown round the ground floor, which was sprawling but homely. There were a 'den' and a 'basement', which Daisy loved the sound of. So American. And then they were shown upstairs to their bedrooms. Phil struggled with Carol's luggage, sweating and panting, and Jack carried his and Daisy's. When they came to Jack and Daisy's bedroom, Trish made herself scarce. It was amazing, with wooden floors and big sash windows. There was fresh white bed linen, towels on the single beds and fresh flowers in a vase. They had the added bonus of an en-suite bathroom. It was like staying in a hotel.

When they came back downstairs, Daisy made a point of thanking Trish for the little touches in the room and commenting on how lovely it all was. She nudged Jack. 'Yes, thank you,' he said shyly.

'You're very welcome,' Trish said. 'I've made us all some

cocoa.' When her back was turned, Uncle Phil gave Jack and Daisy a wink, as if to say 'well done'. The cocoa was the best Jack and Daisy had ever tasted, creamy and chocolatey and sweet. There were home-baked cookies to dip in it as well – but not for Uncle Phil. They drank it at the huge kitchen table, and Daisy felt as if they had stepped into *The Waltons* or *Little House on the Prairie*.

Conversation was dominated by events in the Middle East, something that Phil clearly felt passionate about. Saddam Hussein had not long invaded Kuwait and was currently parading Western hostages on TV, refusing to let them leave the country. He was also threatening to invade Saudi Arabia, which would give him control of sixty-five per cent of the world's oil supply. America, more than any other country, had taken umbrage at this, and had deployed tens of thousands of troops, planes, battleships and heavy artillery to stop it happening. 'Operation Desert Storm,' said Uncle Phil. 'See if our boys can rough those Eye-Rackis up a bit. S'all we need, though, what with this recession beginning to bite. Price of oil has doubled. Wall Street's panicking.'

This was all very dull and uninteresting to Daisy and Jack; it didn't seem to affect them in any way. They had no idea what a recession was. It was a relief when bedtime was announced. They made their way upstairs and, after brushing their teeth, collapsed into bed (just the one), totally exhausted. The unpacking could wait.

CHAPTER 26

The Patch

For once, Jack woke before Daisy. At first, it was hard to figure out where he was, and why he and Daisy were practically on top of each other. And then he remembered, and a ripple of excitement spread through his stomach. America. It had been a challenge, sleeping in a single bed together, and a few times during the night he'd been in danger of falling out. But he didn't mind waking up snuggled so tightly. They didn't have much choice. It might get a bit trying after the novelty had worn off, but for now it was OK. Good job they were slim.

Trying not to wake Daisy, who was still out for the count, Jack got up and padded over to the bedroom window, eager to see what was outside. He pulled back a curtain in anticipation. It turned out their bedroom overlooked the rear of the property, rather than the front – it had been hard to keep track last night – so he could see a huge expanse of back garden that looked as if it continued round the side of the house. A badminton net was set up, which looked like fun. This surprised him, though: he couldn't imagine Daisy's uncle playing badminton. The bottom of the garden was bordered by what looked like a stream and a small wood. Jack couldn't wait to explore. Beyond was the countryside, split by a serpentine river – probably the funny-named one that Phil had mentioned. It was glistening in the morning sun. It really did look as if they were in the middle of nowhere, which suited Jack down to the ground. It was a fine day. A fine day in America. He wanted to pinch himself, and took a deep breath, feeling very fortunate. Already, he could feel his cares ebbing away.

Breakfast looked delightful. Aunt Trish had really gone to town – or so they presumed. Surely they couldn't eat like this every day? There were home-made pancakes, the type they would call Scotch pancakes or drop scones back home. Waffles, eggs, bacon, toast, maple syrup, marmalade, something called 'pop tarts', whatever they were, juices, both apple and orange, and cereals. Coffee on tap from a percolator jug. It was endless… If it carried on like this, they would be the size of Uncle Phil before long. 'This looks amazing, Trish, thank you – and, my, so much of it,' said Carol.

'Yeah, you guys are gonna have to visit more often. I never get this treatment any more,' Phil said, answering their unspoken question. Trish gave him a smack.

'It's *this treatment* that's got you into hospital and the state you're in,' she said. 'So go easy, big guy.'

'Hospital?' said Carol, concerned.

'Aah.' Phil waved a big paw dismissively, as if he didn't want to talk about it.

'I'll fill you in later,' said Trish. Then mouthed, '*Diabetes.*'

Oh, thought Carol, concerned. She'd heard of it, of course, but didn't know any details.

Then Trish surprised them all by saying, 'Before we start, if I may, I'd just like to say a little grace. Don't worry! I don't do it very often, but this is a special occasion, our first proper meal together.' Jack and Daisy looked at each other; they hadn't expected this. 'Lord, welcome our English guests to our home and bless this food. Amen.'

'Amen,' said Phil, then cleared his throat, awkwardly.

'Amen,' said Carol and Daisy together. Daisy kicked Jack's leg under the table.

'Amen,' he said.

'Thank you,' said Trish. 'See, that wasn't so bad, was it? Now, let's eat.'

Thank God that was over, thought Daisy. She'd heard of Americans saying grace and seen it on the telly, but never experienced it in real life. It was like being back at school. Hopefully it wouldn't become a regular thing.

The food was delicious. And despite Trish's warning to 'go easy', Phil appeared to be in his element. Boy, could he pack it away. The bacon was crisp and smoked, barely warm, and served in a separate pile. Jack followed Phil's lead: the way to eat it seemed to be with your fingers; although Carol stuck to a knife and fork. Even Daisy was tempted, but there was enough to be going on with without it. Aunt Trish was also surprised that Daisy was a vegetarian, and this formed most of their breakfast conversation.

It was decided they would do a big shop that day to stock up on things the guests were used to or liked. 'Have to head up to one of the biggies on Route 6,' Phil said. 'Not much to offer locally. Towanda's yer nearest town, few bars and shops and that, but no large grocery store. Still, it's worth a look round...' Jack and Daisy couldn't wait to sample the bars.

After breakfast, the visitors were keen to go outside and explore, to see the house and grounds properly. 'Let me get this lot cleared up and I'll give you the tour,' said Trish.

'Oh, we'll help,' said Daisy.

'You don't have to do that,' said Trish. 'You're guests.'

'We want to,' said Daisy. 'It's the least we can do.'

'Let them do it,' said Carol. 'And count yourself lucky: they never wash up at home!'

'"Wash up" means "do the dishes" in England,' Phil pointed out for his wife's benefit, who was American born and bred.

'Hold on, I'm confused,' said Carol. 'What does it mean here?'

'To wash up,' said Trish. 'As in washing your hands … like "go wash up before dinner".'

'Oh… I never knew that,' said Carol.

Daisy did, as she'd heard it on *A Streetcar Named Desire*. This made her feel smug. 'Anyway,' she said, 'that's simply not true. Don't tar me with Lily's brush. We always help wash up – wash the pots – when we visit.'

'Visit?' said Trish. 'Now *I'm* confused. Don't you live at home any more?'

'No. Jack and I live in Norfolk, in a flat on our own.'

'A flat on your own? I had no idea,' said Trish. 'Why didn't you tell me this, Phil?'

'You never asked,' shrugged Phil, picking up the last bit of bacon.

After 'washing up' in their en-suite, Jack and Daisy headed downstairs for the grand tour. Unable to find Trish, they stepped outside onto the veranda. It was lovely, spanning pretty much the width of the house. And the porch swing, tucked in the corner, looked so inviting, surrounded by what looked like climbing honeysuckle. Heaven. They leaned on the rail to survey their surroundings. The property really was stand-alone. It had a long, private driveway, and must have been set in a good few acres. To their right were two double garages and plenty of parking space, and to their left and in front were fields, all neatly fenced. In one of the fields were a couple of horses, one smaller than the other, and behind this what looked like a stable block or barn. There wasn't a main road or another property for miles. Just that meandering river.

They heard the porch door open behind them. 'There you both are.' It was Carol.

Trish followed her out. 'You ready?' she said.

They were given a comprehensive tour of the grounds. The

property was called The Patch, and it really was huge – and lovely. Trish introduced them to the horses, Peppermint and Buddy. Carol showed an interest, even saying she wouldn't mind a ride whilst she was there (Daisy couldn't imagine her mum riding a horse at all). She and Jack kept their distance, both a bit wary of horses, especially Daisy. She'd had a bad experience with one when she was younger. She'd gone to feed it in a field, giving it an apple. But as she walked away, the horse had followed her, nuzzling into her back, probably thinking she had more food. The faster she walked, the more the horse trotted after her, butting her. Its strength had been terrifying, practically lifting her off her feet. She knew if she ran, she'd probably get trampled to death. By the time Daisy reached the gate to the field, she was in tears, and she cried all the way home.

More interesting, to Jack and Daisy at least, were all the home-grown vegetables and fruits. Raspberries, strawberries, lettuce, squash, pumpkins. There was even a patch of fresh herbs, or 'urbs' as Trish pronounced it. It was all very impressive. Trish explained this was more her thing than Phil's, her way of getting more fresh fruit and veg into his diet.

'I love the pumpkins,' said Daisy. 'They look amazing.'

'Yeah, lovely,' agreed Carol. None of them had seen pumpkins growing before.

'Oh, you should see them come Halloween. We holler 'em out and line 'em up on the porch. They look real neat,' Trish said. 'Stick a couple at the bottom of the lane, too.'

'Yeah, I bet,' said Daisy. She could picture them all lined up on the veranda, glowing a fiery orange in the dark. She really hoped they would be still around to see them.

'Of course, we don't get many trick 'n' treaters out here now,' Trish continued. 'Not since the girls have grown up and moved away, but we used to. They'd arrive in their trucks and cars. The girls'd sit on the porch, clutching their bags of candy, watching out for the headlights. Families and friends would all pile out. It was a real occasion. Hot pumpkin soup and pumpkin pie…' Trish looked wistful for a moment, as if she missed those days. Daisy had always wanted to experience a proper American Halloween, like in the movies: everyone dressing up, going from house to house – without the escaped, knife-wielding madman on the loose of course – and now she was too old for it. 'Yeah, they grow up so fast. But you miss doing those things. Expect it's the same for you, Carol?'

'Yep, they certainly grow up fast,' said Carol, tactfully not voicing her feelings on how the true origins of Halloween had been forgotten thanks to American commercialism.

CHAPTER 27

Guns 'n' Booze

Tour of the grounds over, Uncle Phil, Carol and the kids set off in the truck. Aunt Trish stayed behind: she had chores to do apparently. The scenery was stunning. For Daisy, it was like a cross between Wales and what she imagined the Amazon Basin looked like: trees and endless greenery, verdant valleys and mountains. And then that river. It really was something, clearly forming the township's north-east boundary, hugging its curves like a snake. Their soundtrack for the journey – or the backdrop to Phil's American drawl – courtesy of a cassette tape, was a singer Daisy hadn't heard of, called Tom Waits. He had a gravelly American voice, and the song 'Ol' 55' suited the journey perfectly. Daisy was impressed.

Houses were few and far between, and mainly built in the same style as Phil's – clean white clapboard under a neat, grey, tiled roof. Most had farmland attached. A church they passed was built in the same style, so different from an English church. It was all white wood, clean-looking, which gave off an air of purity – with a bright red front door and a bell tower atop its peaked roof. Phil told them there were some Amish communities in Bradford County, the largest on the east side, where there was also an Amish school and church. He then had to explain what the Amish were, about their culture and how they dressed. From time to time you came across them on the roads, travelling in their horses and buggies. The English folk were all intrigued and hoped to spot some.

The highlight of the journey for Daisy was the big, yellow school bus that passed them. It was straight out of the movies – most memorably *Ferris Bueller's Day Off*. Daisy squealed and pointed it out to Jack. Phil found this hilarious: it was just a school bus. But for Daisy, it was like spotting one of the Big Five game animals on safari. Also on her list of American icons, pretty much all of them from movies, were yellow taxi cabs, station wagons and 'cop cars': she'd spotted these three already on the way back from the airport. Jack had loved seeing the cop car; it had reminded him of *The Dukes of Hazzard*. A traditional American mailbox had been ticked off the list too, as Uncle Phil had one at the end of their lane. Daisy hoped she'd soon be seeing a brown paper grocery bag – first encountered in *E.T.* and noticed in virtually every American movie since; Daisy had been dying to bring her shopping home in one her whole life. It was the same with eating from one of those takeaway Chinese food cartons they had, like in *The Lost Boys*. Everything she knew about America seemed to be from films. The list went on…

The grocery store, as Phil had called it, couldn't have been more different from grocery stores back home – small village shops that sold fresh vegetables and maybe a few tinned goods… This was a giant, out-of-town supermarket located with other retail outlets and eating establishments, all surrounding a vast car park. The supermarket itself was the biggest they had ever seen. A K-Mart. It even dwarfed the cash and carry, which was crazy – and the variety… You name it, the store sold it; it was like a dozen different shops all under one roof. There was a clothing section for a start. Since when did a supermarket sell clothes? And some of the clothes were huge. Daisy held a medium-sized jumper against

Jack, and it was more like a dress. But she also spotted some Levi jeans that were ridiculously cheap; she would be buying a few pairs of those. Lily would be so jealous. There was a hardware section, a stationery section, a gardening section – selling lawnmowers, for Christ's sake. A huge toy section. A huge confectionery and candy section that was about ten times the size of a normal sweetshop back home. And here there were two confectionery marvels – one was Pennsylvania's famous Hershey bar (America's favourite chocolate bar), and the other the famed Snickers bar. Snickers had recently caused a bit of a furore back home in the UK, making headlines when Marathon bars were renamed Snickers in July, in line with America and elsewhere. Everyone had been getting precious about it. Daisy had heard rumours about sightings of these new Snickers bars, but hadn't seen one herself; the shops were still trying to get rid of old stock. Yet here they were in their hundreds.

But most shocking of all was a section that was openly selling guns and ammunition. This was simply jaw-dropping. Guns! In a supermarket!

As for the food, the variety was endless. And everything was bigger. Giant milk cartons that must have held six to eight pints. Loaves of bread that looked twice as long as British ones. Huge bags of crisps – or 'potato chips' – about four times the size of a normal pack. Giant pizzas. The cereal selection – a huge wall of choice. The one thing Daisy couldn't find, though, was 'proper' cheese in a block, something that was a mainstay of her diet. All she saw was strange plastic-looking orange cheese slices in cellophane wrappers and, even worse, cheese in tubes and spray cans, like squirty cream. Yuk! What was that all about? 'Sorry, Daisy, we don't really do blocks of cheese out here...' said Phil. Great. What was she meant to live on? She opted for the cheese slices.

And then disaster struck.

'Just gonna grab some cider,' Daisy said, heading over to a tall fridge full of chilled booze.

'Whoa! Easy there, Daisy. No, you don't,' said Phil loudly. 'Alcohol's off limits, I'm afraid. Unless you wanna get slapped with a huge fine and me shot.'

'Eh?' said Daisy, 'I'm eighteen. Nineteen, in fact.'

'Don't matter. It's twenty-one here in Penn State – and pretty much every other state too,' said Phil.

'Mum!' said Daisy, outraged. 'Why didn't you tell us this?'

'Oh, sorry, love. I just forgot, I guess…'

'Just forgot! Great, what are we supposed to do now?' She looked at Jack, who was dumbstruck – and mortified, more so even than Daisy.

'Well, we'll just buy it for you, so stop stressing. It's not the end of the world,' said Carol.

'Uh, uh,' said Phil, shaking his head. 'No can do, I'm afraid. You can't drink it in the house. Or anywhere, for that matter.'

'What?' said Daisy.

'Oh, come on, Phil, don't be such an old fuddy-duddy,' said Carol. 'Trish again, I presume?'

'No, seriously,' said Phil. 'I'll get fined; *you'll* get fined; the kids'll get fined. In Pennsylvania, even in your own home, it's illegal to knowingly allow your child, or any other minor, to consume alcohol. We've got some of the strictest alcohol laws in the whole of the States. Crazy, I know. Dates back to the prohibition era or something… I'm on boards and things – a councillor: I can't risk it. Sorry, Carol. Sorry, kids.'

'Great,' said Daisy, aware she was probably coming across as disrespectful, but unable to help herself. 'Looks like it's cold turkey for us then.' It was a huge blow, and she felt like crying. It was as if the whole trip had turned sour already. She felt for Jack more than her. Jack had no idea what the hell turkey had to do with anything – Daisy was vegetarian for a start. All he knew was that he was gutted. *And* they didn't have any smoke.

What were they going to do for the whole trip without some form of escape, without some form of high?

There was an awkward silence. They stood, mid-aisle, surrounded by American people and voices. Phil cleared his throat. 'It's only for a few weeks,' he said. 'Surely you can go a few weeks without a drink?' No one answered. Phil turned to Carol. 'Are these kids alcoholics or something?'

*****

The strained atmosphere remained in the truck on the way home. The alcohol revelation had burst the American bubble for Jack and Daisy. They had been planning on staying a lot longer than a few weeks. What were they going to do without a drink? It just wasn't normal for them. Carol felt guilty. Although not so dependent on alcohol herself, she wouldn't like to come on holiday, especially a trip of a lifetime, and not be able to unwind or celebrate with a drink. She'd known that drinking in bars was outlawed until you were twenty-one, but she'd had no idea about the strict drinking laws in one's own home. They seemed so draconian – and exacerbated by how unbending Phil was being. If it was her, she'd let them have a beer or two. Surely there was no harm in that. Who was going to know? She bet a lot of parents did. No wonder the girls had moved out so early. But whilst they were staying under his roof – his and Trish's – Carol wouldn't have dreamed of going against their wishes. But it was a difficult situation. Phil, meanwhile, was still trying to justify himself, explaining how even for a first offence kids lost their driving licence as well as being fined. Carol turned to the back seat, but her empathetic smile fell on blind eyes. Jack and Daisy were holding hands, staring morosely out of the window. Carol wished there was something she could do…

Back at the house, Jack and Daisy immediately retreated upstairs to lick their wounds. Somewhat surprisingly, their beds had been pushed together. That was a turn-up for the books.

Maybe there was hope for alcohol yet? They plonked their prized brown paper grocery bag down on the bed with them, its lustre somewhat dulled. In it were their purchases – a few little novelties, but mainly junk food and snack items that they had paid for with their own American dollars (they now had change in cents!). Hershey bars, Nerds, Life Savers, pretzels, Cheese-its, M and Ms, Tootsie Rolls, Twinkies, chocolate milk, root beer… Daisy had seen Phil drinking root beer and had always wondered what it was like; clearly there wasn't alcohol in it. They'd planned on spilling their booty out on the bed and going through it, pigging out. But neither of them was in the mood for it now. Instead, they lay down together and cuddled, Daisy with her head on Jack's chest. Neither of them spoke at first, both still trying to get their head around things. There must be a way, there always was, thought Daisy. She didn't easily admit defeat. Think, think… They couldn't buy alcohol themselves and didn't know anyone who could. Then a thought came to her. 'Hey, maybe mum will still buy us some booze,' she said. 'Behind Phil's back. I think she's feeling guilty…' Jack didn't say anything. He wasn't so sure. 'Yeah, I reckon she would. If we lay it on thick and really plead.'

Jack thought about it some more. 'I don't know. And even if she did – which I doubt – where would we drink it? It's not like there's a lock on our door.'

'Not in the house, silly. It would be too risky. But, I don't know, we could go for a walk or something: the grounds of this place are huge. There's that stream – and the wood. And beyond that, God knows what. The fields go on forever. It's just countryside.' Jack's heart started to race and his brain ticked over. This could be the answer – providing Carol went along with it, of course. It would be like the old days back home, sneaking out with a rucksack full of cider. 'Yes, this could be it, Jack. The solution. We can go on a picnic or something, or just a walk. Every evening if we want. Screw 'em.'

'But what if they find out? What if we get caught? By them or the police? Didn't Phil say you could lose your driving licence?'

'We're not gonna get caught by the police out here in the middle of nowhere: I haven't seen a cop car since the journey back. We'll just have to be careful, that's all.'

Still feeling the after-effects of travelling across time zones, they promptly dozed off.

*****

They were woken about an hour or so later by a knock on their door. 'Hey. You guys OK in there? I've fixed us some soup for lunch.' It was Trish.

Daisy quickly roused herself. 'Er, yes. Fine, thanks. Sorry, we fell asleep.'

'Oh, no worries. Just come down as soon as you're ready. I'll keep it warm on the stove.'

Bless her, thought Daisy. She was sweet. 'OK. Thanks, Trish. We'll be right down.'

The soup was delicious. Home-made 'tomaydo and baysil', as the Americans pronounced it, made from their own produce. Trish had baked some bread to go with it, a whole-wheat bread, which was equally scrumptious. The kids had vaguely registered the enticing smell of baking when they returned home, but had been too preoccupied by other matters. To wash it all down, there was a huge glass jug of cloudy home-made lemonade.

'Mmm, this bread is delicious,' remarked Carol, speaking for everyone.

'So is this lemonade,' said Daisy. 'Thank you.' She had wanted to thank Trish for the beds being pushed together, but thought it might be best not to bring it up.

'You're welcome, dear,' said Trish.

'Do you always bake your own bread?' asked Carol.

'Not *always*,' said Trish. 'But as often as I can. American shop-bought bread – the sliced white stuff – is, well, how can I put it, atrocious. Tastes like plastic. They put so much junk in it. One of the many culinary things we fall down on, I'm afraid…'

They carried on eating their soup. Daisy could feel her mum watching her and Jack, probably trying to gauge their moods. Well, good, she thought. This would help their cause. They just had to choose their moment to ask, and sooner rather than later.

Phil, in contrast, seemed to have forgotten about the whole alcohol conversation already. He was more interested in Jack and Daisy's jobs back home: the restaurant, what kind of food it served. Unfortunately, he directed most of his questions to Jack; a mistake, but he wasn't to know of Jack's reticence with strangers. But Jack did his best, and Daisy helped as usual – even Carol did, who could tell when he was struggling. This was a bit annoying for Daisy in this instance: it wasn't as if her mum knew what went on at the restaurant.

But Uncle Phil and Trish were intrigued by it all, so much so that Phil – in his typical bombastic style – suggested, even demanded, that Jack and Daisy should show off their culinary and hospitality skills by hosting an all-English supper during their stay. 'I know. How about this coming weekend when the girls are over?' he suggested.

'Oh, Phil. You can't expect Jack and Daisy to cook for everyone. They're the guests. Besides, I thought we were doing a barbecue; we've got the steaks in and everything,' said Trish.

'I know, but they're here all weekend. We could do both. And Jack and Daisy'll enjoy it – a chance to show off their skills. Something really traditional, I reckon. Really *English*. The girls'll love it. Get some bunting up. '*God save our gracious Queen, God save our noble Queen*!' he began to sing in a rich, baritone voice. 'What do you say, guys?'

'Oh, Phil. You don't half get carried away,' laughed Trish.

Jack, meanwhile, had gone as white as a sheet and had stopped eating, spoon poised halfway to his mouth. He felt as if he was going to be sick. Daisy was also horrified at the prospect. The pressure of it all. 'Erm…' She didn't know what to say; how to say no. Phil and Trish had been so hospitable.

Trying to read their silence, Phil said, 'We'll pay for it all, of course, so you don't need to worry about that.'

Carol came to their rescue. 'Oh, you don't need to do that, Phil. We want to contribute whilst we're here. I won't take no for an answer. But I think it's more the cooking for everyone – it might be a bit daunting, especially when we'll only have just met.'

'I agree,' said Trish. 'How about we do it one night for us instead? And only if you young folk want to, if you're comfortable with it. It *would* be nice to sample some of your delicious British cooking. I've never been to Europe. Nor the girls. Always wanted to…'

'OK,' said Daisy, relieved. 'Yeah, that would be better. Wouldn't it, Jack?' She turned to him. He was still pale.

'Erm, yes. Yes, I suppose…'

They all laughed. 'You can cook, can't yer?' said Phil, clamping a huge hand on Jack's shoulder, causing him to flinch and blush.

'Yes, he can cook,' said Daisy. 'He's amazing. Especially puddings.'

'I can vouch for that,' said Carol. 'Their ice creams are to die for.'

*****

With lunch and the unwanted scrutiny out of the way, Jack and Daisy were finally set free and allowed to retire to the 'den', aiming to watch their first American TV. Daisy had nipped upstairs first to retrieve their bag of goodies. Before switching the TV on, she cracked open her root beer, sniffed it, then took a swig. She pulled a face. 'Yuk! It tastes like TCP.' Not expecting this, she offered the bottle to Jack. 'Try it,' she said.

He too winced at the taste. 'How can anyone drink that stuff?' he said. Daisy was right: it did taste like TCP, a bottle of which had been kept in the bathroom cupboard back home. His sister had administered it to him from time to time when he was little. Under duress, squirming and wriggling usually. Bittersweet memories…

'I've no idea. Phil loves it.' Despite Daisy's aversion to the root beer, she persevered with it, wincing comically every time she took a sip, hoping she would get used to it.

American television was another astounding experience. The TV was huge, for a start – the biggest they had ever seen. But it wasn't that, it was the number of channels. Unlike the four back home, there were dozens and dozens; there must have been fifty. They couldn't believe it. Shopping channels, which they'd never seen before, news channels, sports channels, documentary channels, religious channels. And the adverts… These, like the ones on the radio, were brash, intrusive and constant. Burgers, pizzas, jewellery, perfume, you name it. Then local ones – lawyers, furniture shops, corny car salesmen in cheap suits – 'Hi, I'm Dan from so and so…' And again, religious ones. The kids were starting to get a feel for just how big a part religion played in America. There were even phonelines, as if you could pick up the phone, dial a number, and speak directly to the big guy upstairs himself. A hotline to God.

They spent ages channel-hopping in wonder and amazement. It was a whole different world. Eventually, they settled on MTV: another novelty. But it was all mainly mainstream stuff. Roxette's 'It Must Have Been Love' – from the *Pretty Woman* soundtrack. Some warbling woman called Mariah Carey, singing 'Vision of Love'; Perhaps she was looking in the mirror when she wrote it – she certainly appeared to love herself. Slightly better, there was a fair bit of rock on there at least. Jon Bon Jovi had just released his first solo single, 'Blaze of Glory', accompanied by a typically OTT video. It was nice to see 'Enjoy the Silence' by Depeche Mode still getting some airtime. And then a brand-new song – 'hot-off the press,' said the enthusiastic spiky-haired, perfect-toothed presenter – by some white wannabe American rapper called Vanilla Ice. 'Ice, Ice Baby'…

Carol came to join them. 'You guys OK?' she said, smiling. 'You enjoying yourselves?'

'No,' said Daisy, munching on a Twinkie. She hadn't forgotten their aim, the bigger picture, and wanted to get straight in there with the portrayal of hardship.

'Oh. Why? What's wrong? The cooking of the meal? Sorry about that. Phil gets a bit carried away sometimes…'

'No, not that.'

'What then?' said Carol.

'You know what.' Daisy wouldn't look at her mum, just carried on munching her Twinkie and staring at the giant screen. Jack felt uncomfortable, but he could see what Daisy was up to, and a lot was riding on it. He privately admired her forthrightness. He would never dare to say half the things she did. Especially with adults.

'Oh, the alcohol…' Carol had temporarily forgotten about it.

'Sshh,' said Daisy. 'They'll hear.'

'Don't shush me, young lady,' Carol said. 'Or embarrass me.' Jack shifted uncomfortably again. 'There's nothing I can do about it. I'm not–'

Daisy cut her off. 'Mum, *please*! We'll discuss it later. In private. Come into our room before you go to bed tonight. We'll talk about it then.'

Carol tutted and rolled her eyes. 'Gordon Bennett, Daisy. *Fine*. But I don't know what you expect me to do about it. Rules are rules.'

*****

That night Carol knocked on their bedroom door as requested. She was in her dressing gown. The teenagers were in bed. 'Come in,' Daisy said.

'Hi. Sorry.' Carol crept in sheepishly, but loitered in the entrance.

'Mum, close the door,' Daisy said.

'Honestly, all this covert nonsense...' She closed the door quietly. 'Ooh, this *is* a lovely room, isn't it? And you've got an en-suite, you lucky so and so's.'

'Yeah, the room's lovely,' said Daisy.

'And Trish's pushed your beds together now. That was lovely of her, wasn't it? Must have been a big thing for her to do...'

Daisy didn't answer. She could see what her mum was trying to do, get in there first with how wonderful and accommodating their hosts were being. 'Sit down,' she said, gesturing to the bed. Carol perched awkwardly on the nearest corner. 'Mum, you've got to help us.'

Carol sighed and rolled her eyes. 'I don't know what you expect me to do...'

'Just listen for a start.'

Carol gave her a look. 'Don't push it, Daisy. Watch the attitude.'

'Sorry.' Antagonising her mum wasn't going to help. 'It's just, this situation ... this alcohol situation ... there *is* something you can do.'

'Like what?'

'Buy it for us.'

'I knew that was coming... How? *Where*? You can't drink it here. Not at the house.'

'We won't. We're not that stupid. We've got it all planned out.'

'Why doesn't that surprise me?' Carol tutted.

'Just hear us out.'

'Hear *you* out, you mean. I can't hear Jack complaining.'

'This is *for* Jack. For both of us. He's just too polite to say anything.'

'Go on then, spit it out. This grand plan. But I'm not promising.'

'OK… We go into town, the one just down the road, just the three of us – say we've got to do some shopping or something, or maybe just to have a look round. And you buy us the alcohol. Then we pack it into one of our rucksacks – secretly of course, somewhere out of the way and private – and then we go on a picnic or walk or something, Jack and me, that is, not you, and Phil will be none the wiser.'

'But it's so underhand – and illegal. What if we get caught? Me? What kind of mother would I look like? To the police *and* to Phil. He'd never forgive me.'

'We won't get caught,' said Daisy. 'We just need to be extra careful, that's all. Do the handover out of town or something, out here in the sticks; we're not going to do it in the middle of the high street in broad daylight.'

'Handover? Can you hear yourself? What if a passing car sees us? Or what if Phil wants to come with us into town? Have you thought about that?'

'He can't. He won't. We'll say we're picking some bits up for this special meal, some secret ingredients, say it's all a surprise.' This had just come to her: she was quite proud of it. Jack was impressed. She seemed to have everything covered, as usual.

'I don't know, Daisy…' Carol ran her hands through her hair. 'It's just so … *underhand*, so deceitful … after all they've done for us.'

'Well, what they won't know won't hurt them, will it? Better for them that we're not involving them. That way they can't get in trouble. We're doing them a favour.'

Carol laughed. The lengths her daughter went to to get her own way. 'I think once we're back in England, you ought to embark on a law career, young lady,' she said. 'Or better still, politics…' The only thing Daisy hadn't said was 'Dad would do it', her go-to weapon if all else failed. But Carol was already losing the fight: she was too tired to argue, and Daisy was an irresistible force. She got up from the bed. 'I'm not promising anything, so don't pressure me about it. Let me sleep on it. See how I feel tomorrow, and I'll let you know.'

'OK. Thanks, Mum.' Daisy got out of bed and gave Carol a hug and a kiss, a rare thing these days. The dutiful daughter.

'Thank you,' said Jack.

'Goodnight, both of you. See you in the morning.'

'Night, Mum. Love you.'

Carol rolled her eyes. 'Love you too.'

'Night,' said Jack.

Carol slipped out and closed the door. Daisy immediately turned to Jack. 'Yes!' she cried, but quietly. 'High five.' She held up her palm, getting the American bug – when in Rome and all that.

'Eh?' said Jack.

'High five. Slap my hand.' Jack slapped her hand. 'One of my finest performances,' she said. 'I think it's in the bag.'

CHAPTER 28
The Handover

'So, you guys wanna visit the French Azilum today?' said Phil, buttering some toast. They were all sitting round the table for breakfast, another lavish affair. Trish seemed to enjoy laying on food and the hosting. But surely she couldn't keep it up every day? At least they hadn't had to say grace this time.

Jack and Daisy looked at each other, groaning inwardly. They were dying for some time on their own to explore the area surrounding the house. They weren't used to having adults around all the time: it was suffocating. Piling into the truck again and visiting some stuffy old museum in the middle of nowhere hardly sounded appealing.

Carol came to their rescue. 'I think we were going to head into town today – the local one – have a look round and grab a few bits.' Jack and Daisy tried to hide their surprise and delight. This sounded promising. Very promising.

'Oh. OK...' Phil sounded put out. He seemed to enjoy being a tour guide and entertainer. 'Well, like I say, there's not a great deal there. Just a few shops and bars... But I can run you in, show you around, introduce you to a few folks; everybody knows everybody – especially me.'

'Oh, that's OK. I think we're going to walk: it's not far and I fancy a stroll. Could do with the exercise. Thanks, anyway,

Phil. And we can do the French Azilum another day – I really want to see it. Sounds fascinating.' Go, Mum! thought Daisy. This'll put him off. He doesn't seem to like walking anywhere.

Again, Phil looked a little put out.

'Well, there you go dear. There's no escaping me now,' Trish said, putting a hand on his arm. 'You can help me around the place for once. The barbecue needs cleaning for the weekend – I always tell you to do it once you've used it, it's so much easier – and the stables need mucking out,' she laughed.

Phil let out a miserable 'humph'. 'I can do the BBQ,' he said begrudgingly.

'And I can help you with the stables when I get back if you like,' said Carol. She felt guilty, and wanted to make Phil feel better. It could be her punishment, her penance for being such a lying, deceitful, no-good, law-breaking sister.

'Oh, you don't need to do that,' said Trish. 'You're on holiday. Here to relax, not to become a farmhand.'

'No, honestly, I'd love to help out,' said Carol. 'Earn my keep!'

*****

And so it was arranged. Courtesy of Carol, Jack and Daisy got their wish – a means of escape and, if all went according to plan, alcohol supplies. They were already feeling they owed her big time. Again.

It was a lovely, warm day as they negotiated the winding country lanes to the small town; it was a fair bit further than they'd envisaged. Just vacating the property's grounds took nearly ten minutes. But they were enjoying it being just the three of them again for a while. 'Can you hear that?' Carol said. 'The cicadas?' It was a chirping, cricket-like noise coming from the fields, but much louder, almost like the buzz of electricity cables.

'Cicadas? I thought they were crickets,' said Daisy.

'They're like crickets. But the American and rest of the world version,' said Carol.

'Ah, I never knew that. Yeah, you hear them in films, especially American films.' It really did hammer home that they were on American soil, as did the surrounding fields that were bulging green and gold with typically giant American corn plants. Straight out of *Children of The Corn*, thought Daisy – another Stephen King film that had terrified her as a child.

After about half an hour, they reached the outskirts of the small town. 'Right, you two, make yourself scarce. I don't want you anywhere near me. You're not even coming into town with me.'

'But, we want to see it,' said Daisy.

'Tough,' said Carol. 'Do you want some booze or not?' This was the first time she had acknowledged this was actually going to happen. 'We'll be coming in again, no doubt, so you can wait. Don't look at me like that. Seriously, Daisy, I'm not comfortable with this at all and don't want you around. It'll look too obvious – a grown woman with two teenagers buying cans of beer or whatever during the day. One of them with a rucksack on his back. There could be a police station in town.'

'Fine,' said Daisy resignedly.

'What do you want anyway? And I'm not buying much. You are *not* stumbling back into the house pissed.'

'Mum, we're not going to get pissed. Drunk.' She looked at Jack and shrugged. 'Just a few cans of cider, I suppose? A four-pack.' Jack nodded. 'And some chewing gum – for after.'

'I'll get mints. Chewing gum's too obvious,' said Carol; it was as if she was starting to think like them. 'Anything else?'

'Erm … no, I think that's it.' They already had some of their American snacks in their rucksack – as they intended on going for their 'walk' straight afterwards – and were still full from breakfast. 'Oh, actually, some lemons. I'm gonna try making some lemonade like Trish's – she's going to show me how.'

'How many?'

'Dunno. A bunch? Sorry, I couldn't resist.' (Everything seemed to be a 'bunch' to the Americans.)

The witticism fell on deaf ears. 'Ten?' said Carol impatiently.

'Yes, ten's fine. Thank you.'

'I must be mad,' Carol said, and toddled off.

Jack and Daisy looked at each other, both feeling a little guilty at roping her in. It was a ridiculous situation. They spotted a bench where they could wait, both feeling a little glum, a little frustrated. A station wagon trundled past, the driver eyeing them a little too closely. 'I can't believe we're not going to see the inside of an American bar,' Daisy said. 'I had visions of us shooting pool in a smoky pool hall with a jukebox on, or sitting at a long bar, having shots poured for us out of those bottles with the metal nozzles.'

'Don't forget I'm only seventeen,' Jack said.

'True,' said Daisy. It was so easy back home, so different. No one really gave a shit. 'Seventeen,' she said. 'Such a child...'

'Get lost!'

'You are! Technically.' And they laughed. But it did feel slightly different now Daisy had turned nineteen.

Eventually, Carol returned, looking stressed and her face flushed. She was carrying a brown paper grocery bag and kept looking behind her, as if she'd been shoplifting. It was almost comical: talk about drawing attention to herself. 'Jesus, Mum. What did you do, buy the whole store?' said Daisy.

'Well, I didn't want it to look obvious, did I? I had to buy other things.'

'Good point,' Daisy said. 'Did you get it OK?'

'Yes, I did. Now don't mention it again till we're well out of town.' She looked around, but the street was still clear. 'Come on, let's go.'

They walked away quickly, Carol clutching her groceries. It wasn't until they were back on the country lanes that she slowed down a little and relaxed. 'Here, take this,' she said to Jack. She'd been struggling with the bag. 'These things really aren't made for walking with. Why don't they give them handles?' Jack took it from her.

'Did you get the mints?' asked Daisy.

'Yes, I got the mints.'

'And the lemons?'

'Yes, I got the bloody lemons.'

'Thanks. What else did you get?' Daisy tried to peer into the bag, curious.

'A pint of gin for me. That's what they call a half-bottle out here, apparently.' Carol joining in with the Americanisms made them all laugh,.

'Did you really?' said Daisy.

'Yes. And some tonic. I bloody need it after that.' They all laughed again. It was nice to hear her relaxing. 'And I'm borrowing one of your lemons, too – I've been dying for a G and T since I got here. They don't seem to drink at all, do they? I certainly haven't been offered one. I'd have felt guilty drinking in front of you two anyway, with you drooling at it. Now I won't. Just hope Phil doesn't label me with the alcoholic brush too.'

'He won't,' said Daisy. 'Everyone deserves a drink. Maybe Phil'll have one at the weekend when the girls are over. A *real* beer, not that disgusting root beer stuff. How old are the girls, anyway?' She was nervous about meeting them.

'Ooh, now you're asking. They'll both be well into their twenties now. Haven't seen them since they came over all those years ago, that Thanksgiving we did for them. Gosh, how time flies.'

As they walked, Jack enjoyed giving his biceps a workout, carrying the shopping bag first on one arm, then the other – he was missing his weights. Maybe there was a gym somewhere. It wasn't long before the house became visible in the far distance, the wood they could see from the house coming up on their right-hand side. There was a convenient field-gate to jump over and thick bushes they could hide in. It was the perfect place for the handover. The wood looked like private property, but at least that meant there wouldn't be anybody about.

Making sure no one was looking, Jack vaulted the gate with the rucksack, then Daisy passed him the grocery bag. He disappeared behind the hedge with them both. 'Don't forget the mints,' she called.

'Keep it down!' hissed Carol.

'Ready,' whispered Jack, a few minutes later.

'All clear,' said Daisy. 'Leave the rucksack there.'

Carol tutted. Not for the first time, she couldn't believe her life had come to this. Jack passed the grocery bag back to Daisy, and she passed it to Carol.

'Right, see you later, Mum. Skedaddle before you blow our cover. See you back at the house.' And with that, Daisy clambered over the fence. Once safely over the other side, she said, 'Will you be OK?'

'Yes, I'll be fine. The drive's just round the corner.' The bag was lighter without the cans. 'See you in a bit – and be careful. Don't go trespassing and don't get drunk.'

'On two cans of cider?' said Daisy.

'Car coming,' said Carol suddenly. 'Go!' And she quickly walked away.

Daisy and Jack hid behind the hedge until the car had passed, then listened out to make sure it wasn't stopping – some kind of weirdo like Ted Bundy on the prowl. It didn't. They were on their own. 'Come on, let's go,' said Daisy.

The wood was easily accessible via the field. It was on a bit of a slope, leading down to a stream. Inside, it was dark and cool. Jack was in his element. Even though the wood was very small, more like a copse, it felt like old times exploring it with Daisy. He could feel his heart racing. Despite it only being midday, he was really looking forward to a cold can of cider.

They made their way through the trees and down to the stream, which was babbling musically. Speeding up, they laughed like a pair of kids, spooking a plump, tawny-coloured bird that startled them in its desperate flight for escape. 'Jesus,' said Daisy. And they laughed some more. When they reached some tall boulders by the brook, they leant against them, catching their breath. 'Cider?' said Daisy.

'In a minute.' Jack had something else on his mind. It was the situation, the excitement, the privacy, the danger. He dropped the rucksack at his feet, pressed himself against Daisy and kissed her full on. It took her by surprise, but felt good, and she responded. It was intoxicating, kissing in America, amongst the tall rocks and the smell of the pines. Jack kissed her more urgently, bringing his hand up to caress her. Daisy breathed heavily and could feel him hardening against her. 'Jack, stop, we can't.'

'Why not?' he carried on, kissing her neck, driving her mad.

'Because we can't. Oh God, Jack, stop!' But she wasn't even convincing herself. It was too late. They both wanted it. It was the first chance they'd had. To be free. The moment was right. To do it in America for the first time. She began to unzip her jeans. Jack had his hand inside the front of them, in her pants. Then he spun her round to face the rock. Daisy pulled her jeans down and leant against the rock. Waiting as Jack unzipped himself. And then he was in her. Like that, from behind. Her hands on the rock. His hands on her hips.

It didn't last long. And afterwards they were laughing uncontrollably, quickly pulling their clothes back up. 'Shit, Jack. I'm in a mess,' said Daisy, and they laughed some more.

Finally, they sank down, still breathing heavily, to sit amongst the rocks, their backs against them. 'Good job I brought some tissues,' Daisy said. '*Now*, do you want some cider, you naughty boy?' She looked at him, flushed, then rummaged around in the rucksack. She pulled out the four-pack and inspected the cans. 'Hmm, American cider.' Her mum had done well; they were tall cans, which would last longer. She offered one to Jack. It was still nice and chilled from the shop. 'Here goes then. Cheers,' said Daisy.

'Cheers,' said Jack. Their cans fizzed and hissed delightfully when they popped them open. They took several gulps. The cider was good: flavoursome, cold and dry. 'Aaah,' said Jack.

'Better?' said Daisy.

'Much better.' They took another swig, then inspected their cans again. Neither of them had heard of or seen the brand before.

'I hope Mum got back OK,' said Daisy. 'God, I hope she didn't hear us.'

'She was long gone,' said Jack.

'I can't believe we just did that,' Daisy giggled.

'Me neither.'

They were quiet for a while, then became aware of the rush and trickle of the stream again. 'Do you fancy a wander? Take our cans?' said Daisy.

'Yeah,' said Jack. 'Why not?'

They made their way down to the water. The main source of the rushing sound was a natural dam of rocks to their left that the stream negotiated before it calmed to a placid trickle. They sat where the stream was relatively clear and still. Over the other side, they could see daylight and the gently sloping fields that led back up to Uncle Phil's property. It wasn't possible to see the house. So much the better.

They drank their cider in peace. It was lovely down there, if a little cool, with the tinkling notes of the stream and the dappled rays of sunlight. 'You know the only thing missing?' said Daisy. 'Music.'

'Yes,' agreed Jack.

'Be amazing down here, away from everyone. We could come back here; this could be our spot. Maybe we could get a little speaker from one of the big supermarkets and plug it into my Walkman.'

'Yeah, that would be good.'

'So, how you feeling about this meal that Phil wants us to do?' It was the first time they'd had a chance to talk about it properly. 'You thought about it?'

'Not really.' He had, but wanted to sound casual. He'd been racking his brains, trying to think of what he could cook: he was desperate to impress.

'I nearly died when he suggested we cook for my cousins as well.'

'God, me too.'

'It's gonna be weird seeing them after all these years. I hope they're not pretty. You'd better not fancy them.' Daisy gave him a shove.

'Don't be stupid!' He shoved her back. It was crazy how she always seemed to worry about these things. If only she knew… 'A chicken dish, I reckon,' said Jack. 'Everyone loves chicken.'

'What about me?'

'Ah, good point. Why do you have to be bloody vegetarian? Such a pain in the arse.'

'Because I'm special, that's why…'

'Well, you can just have the potatoes and veg. They'll be special.'

'Gee, thanks…'

'Nah, only joking. I'll think of something. But, yes, chicken breast with dauphinoise potatoes – the ones at the restaurant are amazing. Some nice green veg, like asparagus and French beans and that. And maybe wrap the chicken breast in some Parma ham or something, and serve it with a nice sauce…'

'That all sounds lovely, Jack, but you're forgetting one thing.'

'What?'

'It's not typically English, or British even. Sounds more

French to me. They wanted something traditionally English. That's the idea.'

'Oh.' Jack looked glum, a bit at a loss. 'Well, I don't know then. I can hardly cook fish and chips – they wouldn't have a fryer big enough – and it's boring.'

'No, but you're thinking along the right lines. How about a pie? That's nice and British.'

'A pie? That's boring too.'

'It doesn't have to be. You could do individual ones, make them look more fancy. How about your cottage pie? Now that's to die for – and *very* English.' She had loved his cottage pie before becoming vegetarian; she missed it.

'Could do, I suppose…' He made the one they did at the restaurant, the one he had tried the first night he had worked there. 'Like I say, just seems a bit boring, that's all.'

'I think that's what they'd prefer,' said Daisy. 'They strike me as pie people, rustic and that, farmhouse cooking… You can still do all your nice veg. And how about going to town on the pudding instead? Really present it nicely. Wow them…'

Jack was starting to like the sound of it. Now he needed to think of a dessert. He drained the last of his cider and looked at the can longingly; he'd drank it far too quickly and was considering having another one. One was never enough.

Daisy read his mind. 'You can finish mine if you want; I've still got half left. Here.' She passed him the can.

'You sure?' He felt bad.

'Yeah. Bit early for me, I think. And we ought to save the other two for tomorrow, really, or whenever – we can't keep asking Mum to go to the shop.' Jack took a swig and then looked at the can glumly. She was right.

'And I know just the place,' he said, snapping himself out of it. 'Come on.'

'Oh, OK.'

He got up, and Daisy followed him to the edge of the

stream, where it was shallowest. It reminded Jack of the brook back home. He crouched down and plunged his hand into the water to test it. It was cold, very cold in the shade, and he gasped. But so much the better. He felt his way along the edge of the bank a little, searching for the perfect spot. Then he found it, an overhanging clump of bright green grass, with a hollow underneath. 'Here, pass me the cans,' he said.

Daisy pulled them out of the rucksack and passed them to him. He plunged them into the water, rummaged around for a second, then tucked them underneath, muddying the water a little. 'Perfect,' he said. 'This is going to be our fridge. No one's gonna find them here.'

'Come here,' said Daisy, smiling and pulling him to her. 'I love you.' She kissed him.

'Love you, too. Here.' He offered her the last of her can.

She drained it. 'Shit,' she said. 'What do we do with the rubbish? We can't take the empty cans back to the house – and I'm not just chucking them away.'

'I know. We'll flatten them. Like Aitch used to do.' It was the first time he had mentioned or thought of Aitch in days. That was remarkable. It felt strange. *And* he'd spoken of him in the past tense. He felt guilty, but knew he shouldn't. Maybe he was healing.

Jack stood the cans up straight, then stamped on them, just as Aitch had, reducing them to a flat, crushed disk that would be easy to hide in a crisp packet or something before being disposed of.

'Shall we see if we can find a place to cross?' said Daisy. 'So we can head straight up to Phil's the other side?'

'Yes, good idea,' said Jack.

They wandered further up the stream in the opposite direction to the road; and, sure enough, before long they found a decent crossing point. The water was shallower still and there were some useful stepping stones. Despite this, trying to traverse them after the strong cider was another matter. Both of them lost their balance at different points and nearly fell in. Safely over, they negotiated a small wire fence and then headed up a sloping field. To their pleasant surprise, the roof of Phil's house soon came into view. They looked at each other and smiled. It was going to be strange looking out of their bedroom window later on at the wood and the stream and trying to figure out exactly where they had emerged – and where their cider cans were stowed. Daisy spotted the horses in the field to their right. The smaller, more dappled, one was Peppermint. This reminded Daisy. 'Ooh, mints,' she said, reaching for the rucksack. 'Before we forget.'

CHAPTER 29
Biscuits and Gravy

The next morning, Saturday, Phil decided they were going to have breakfast at a local diner, rather than Trish cooking for them all again; she had enough to do with the girls coming over that day. True to form, she stayed at home when the rest of them set off. This seemed to be a thing. Either she preferred it that way – a homebody – or Phil was a bit sexist and figured it was her place. Daisy was undecided, but was starting to feel a bit guilty about it.

The diner wasn't far, no more than a ten-minute drive, situated alongside the busy main road that led to the K-Mart but in the other direction. It was a highway, not a freeway, apparently – all very confusing. Had they been awake on the journey from the airport, they would have noticed the diner: it was well situated, clearly signposted and lit up. Despite this, somewhat surprisingly, the large car park was fairly empty, and there was a large 'FOR SALE' board on display.

This didn't dampen Daisy and Jack's excitement one iota: they couldn't wait to sample a proper American diner and practically leaped out of the truck. According to the garish pink neon lettering, the diner was called 'The Happy Grill' – not the most inventive or inspiring of names. The diner was long and low, like a large railway carriage without wheels, and it looked a bit tired, with peeling paint and weeds around the door. It was hard to see in as the windows were steamed up. A sign hanging on the front door said 'SORRY, WE'RE OPEN'. Daisy thought this was ironic genius. 'This place used to be heaving,' Phil said. 'Gone a bit downhill now, but Mikey still whips up a mean omelette.'

A bell rang as they entered. Immediately, they were hit by an unpleasant haze and the stink of fried food. Not the best impression. 'You'll get used to it,' said Phil, as if reading their thoughts.

'Be right with you,' a harassed-looking middle-aged waitress said, whizzing by with a couple of plates.

'No problem, Di, we'll just grab a booth,' said Phil.

The waitress turned her head, and her face brightened. 'Well, hey there, stranger! Didn't see yer there with yer folks.'

Phil laughed his big laugh. 'And I thought I was your favourite.'

Di cackled, waltzing off.

Phil gestured to a booth – one of many empty – and they all went to sit down. He practically took up the whole side of his bench, hemming poor Carol in next to the window. 'Shame about this place,' he said in a hushed voice – for him. 'Di's lovely, but she's just the manageress – and she's lasted longer than most. What this place needs is some hands-on owners – and some investment. Folks who live and breathe the place. Work here. Get their hands dirty, you know? Get to know the regulars. That's how Joe ran it; he was the previous owner. 'Simply Joe's', it was called. But locals called it 'Amish Joe's' – affectionately of course. He wasn't orthodox, but Amish nevertheless. The place was heaving. He used to do this mean dish called scrapple – a traditional Pennsylvanian dish, a bit like meatloaf. Used to pan-fry it and dish it up with eggs. They used to come from miles around for Joe's scrapple. Of course, the new lot took it off the menu, along with all the other favourites. Suicide! Took all his pictures off the walls, too. The history of the place: Joe with a few famous faces … actors, boxers, a politician or two… They all passed through here back in the day. This stretch of road used to be called "The Golden Mile". People used to drop in just to see Joe. For the banter. And the food of course, it was to die for. But he kicked the bucket, unfortunately.'

'Oh dear,' said Carol. 'What from?' It was hard to get a word in edgeways with Phil.

'Heart attack. Dropped down dead, just like that. Skinny fella too. Not a scrap of meat on 'im, always running around. Anyways … where was I? Oh yeah, then this foreign lot bought it. Or more accurately murdered it. Had grandiose ideas about creating a chain to rival the biggies – the McDonald's, the Dairy Queens – they've got another one up Sayre way, near the New York border. Happy Grill, for Christ's sake. More like Unhappy Grill. That's what the locals started calling it. They stayed away in their droves – boycotted the place. They've got through manager after manager, cook after cook, always understaffed. You never knew who you were gonna be served by. Hence the state it's in now. Like I say, Di does her best, but half the time she's rushed…'

'Hope you're not spreadin' malicious gossip about me, Mister,' said Di, appearing with four huge menu cards and a big smile. She was wearing a yellow and white waitress and pinny combo, with a matching hat. A big Happy Grill label was stuck to her bosom with her name on it. She handed out the menus; they were a little tacky to the touch.

They all thanked her. 'Oh, my,' she said. 'You folks are all English! Or Australian. Don't tell me!' She held her palms out. 'English!'

'Yes,' they all said and laughed. How could she get an English accent mixed up with an Aussie one?

'Oh my. English. You didn't tell me you had English

relatives, Phil.' She gave him a playful whack with her order pad. 'Especially such attractive ones. I love the colour of your hair, darl,' she said to Daisy.

'Thank you,' blushed Daisy.

'And where *you* bin hidin'? We ain't seen you in months,' she said to Phil.

'Gotta watch my calories these days, I'm afraid. This is a rare treat for me now.'

'Well, we'd better *make* it a treat then, hadn't we? You folks all over here visitin' then or what?'

'Yeah,' said Carol. 'I'm the little sister from across the pond.'

'Gosh. How exciting. And these two gorgeous things are your two?'

'No, just Daisy. Jack's the boyfriend.' The second time this had happened recently.

'Oh, I'm sorry. Course you are. Handsome boy.' Jack went bright red. 'Now then. Can I get you folks some refreshments whilst you peruse the menu? I'd normally give the big "Happy Grill" spiel with you being strangers an' all – "Hey, I'm Dianne and I'm your waitress today, bla de bla de bla" – but Phil knows very well who I am, so I'll spare y'all.'

They all laughed. Di seemed nice. A people person.

'The usual for me,' said Phil.

'One regular coffee, one root beer,' said Di. She scribbled it down on her pad.

'Just a tea for me, please,' said Carol.

'One tea. I think I've got some left, but I'll have to check,' said Di.

'Left?' said Carol.

'She means hot tea – with milk and sugar,' Phil explained to Di, laughing.

'Oh my. Of course you do. You're English. My apologies – can't remember the last time I served hot tea. I'll do you some hot water out the still, bring it all over.'

'Tea here means iced or cold,' Phil said to Carol.

'Aah…' Carol and Daisy said together.

'And for you young folks?'

'Erm… tea for me as well, please,' said Daisy. 'Hot tea.' They all laughed.

'Another hot tea… Thank you, darl.'

'Me, too,' said Jack, blushing again. 'Hot tea. Thank you.'

'You're so very welcome, sugar – gosh, so polite, all of you. So English.' She beamed, seeming to be enjoying the novelty. 'So we've got one regular coffee, one root beer and three *hot* teas. All good?' They all nodded. 'Comin' right up then. Y'all have a good look at the menu whilst yer waitin' – we're out of waffles and the meatloaf, I'm afraid, and there are no specials to speak of just yet.' She leant in to Phil, cupped her hand to her mouth, then whispered, 'Bo's on.'

'Oh, great,' said Phil. He looked genuinely put out. 'Where's Mikey? He always works Saturdays: that's why I brought the folks today.'

'Off sick. He's got the flu.'

'Great,' Phil said again. 'That's the omelette out then. Last time Bo fixed me one, you could bounce it off the walls. Well, he'd better be on form today – tell him Phil says so – and that I've brought my folks from England.'

'I shall personally give him a kick up the backside myself and pass on the message, sweetie.' She gave her big, unfazed smile and waltzed off.

'See what I mean?' said Phil. 'Never used to be like this – things missing off the menu, second-rate cooks on. You watch, we'll be waiting forever as well.'

'It's fine,' said Carol, putting a hand on his arm. 'Just relax. We're not in a mad rush, and here to enjoy ourselves. I'm sure the food will be fine.'

'That's the other thing,' said Phil, leaning across Carol (squashing her even more) and rubbing a big finger down the steamy window. 'What else this place needs is a brand-new extraction system. Another thing that puts folks off.'

'Yeah, it is a bit stinky,' said Carol. Everyone was starting to wonder why Phil had brought them in at all; all he seemed to be doing was moaning.

'You get used to it, but wait till you're outside again – you can smell it on yer clothes.'

'Hmm, wonderful,' said Carol. 'I've had a shower this morning. My hair is going to stink.'

'Me too,' said Daisy. 'I'm going to have to change my clothes now.'

'That's another reason I don't come here so often,' said Phil. 'Since the … you know … the "diagnosis"'. Trish can smell it straightaway. That and she thinks I'm having an affair with Di.'

The rest of them looked at each either. Judging by the pair's banter so far, they could see why. What if he was?

They all focused on the huge menu. There was so much choice; too much really. It was an all-day menu, rather than a specific breakfast one, with everything you would expect, and much more. Waffles, pancakes, muffins, burgers, fried chicken, omelettes, eggs – eggs with everything. Then some more unfamiliar, more American items that Daisy and Jack hadn't heard of – French toast, club sandwich, sliders… What the hell were sliders? Biscuits and gravy… Biscuits and gravy? What the hell was that all about? Daisy couldn't let it 'slide' without asking…

'They're like baked dough, I guess,' said Phil. 'What you guys would call a savoury scone or something back home. Not a sweet biscuit like you have with your tea. Usually served with meat scraps – sausage, bacon – but in a gravy. Sorry, not a gravy as you know it, but a creamy white sauce flavoured with pepper and stuff.'

'Sounds absolutely revolting,' said Carol. Daisy concurred, but was too polite to say so.

Phil laughed. 'It can be delicious. Trish fixes a mean biscuits and gravy. I won't eat it anywhere else, in fact.'

'It's so hard to decide,' said Carol. 'There's so much choice.'

'Yeah, and none of it vegetarian,' said Daisy. That much had become apparent.

'There's eggs,' said Carol.

'I'm sick of eggs already. I know, I'm going to have a grilled cheese sandwich.' She'd been wanting to order one of those her whole life.

'Will that fill you up?' said Carol.

'I'm gonna have a drink, too – a shake.' She'd been eyeing up the drinks section – floats, sodas, shakes. 'When in Rome, and all that…'

'Yep, if you can't beat 'em, join 'em, I guess,' said Carol. 'I think I'm going to have the BLT. I know it's still breakfast time, but all these dishes make you want something different. I fancy something fresh and a bit crunchy. What you having, Jack?'

'I don't know,' he said. He couldn't decide and it was starting to stress him out.

'Have a bacon and egg sandwich,' said Daisy. 'You love that.'

Just then, Di returned with their drinks on a tray. 'Here we go,' she said, dishing them out, 'Just give me a holler if you want any refills.' She tucked the tray under her arm. 'Right then, you guys all set? What can I get y'all? Ladies…'

'I'll have the BLT, please,' said Carol, thinking that would be it. Nice and simple. She was then bombarded with a dozen more questions: what bread would she like it on – white, rye, whole-wheat, sourdough – how would she like her bacon cooked, if she would like her sandwich with 'everything', what sides would she like with it. Hash browns, fries, curly fries, garlic fries, wedges, mashed potatoes, potato salad, coleslaw… It was endless.

'Grilled cheese sandwich for me, please,' said Daisy. 'On white bread. Just as it is. Nothing else with it all.'

'Me too,' Jack blurted out. 'Exactly the same.' A kind of panic had set in with the pressure of it all.

Di looked up from her pad for a second. 'OK … two grilled cheese sandwiches on white. No sides.'

'And a vanilla milkshake, please,' said Daisy. She hadn't had a chance to order it before Jack butted in.

'One vanilla milkshake.' She looked at Jack with expectant, raised eyebrows to see if he was going to add one to. He cottoned on and shook his head. 'And for you, sir?' She turned to Phil.

'I'll have the haff-dozen sliders with the works.'

'Oh, Bo'll love you for that,' she laughed.

Phil laughed, too. 'Well, it'll keep him on his toes!' What on earth were these mysterious sliders?

'Fries?' said Di.

'Large, cheesy.'

'Large and cheesy. Right, think I've got it all.' She read the order back to them, asked them again if they were all set and needed any refills. Then she waltzed off. It was eye-opening.

Whilst they waited, Daisy took in the rest of the diner properly for the first time. The floor was made up of black and white checked tiles, one of the best features. It was also surprisingly spotless. There was a long counter with lots of stools in front of it; but only a few punters. A glass display case with pies and cakes in it, some of them portioned into mammoth wedges, sat on the counter, together with a till. Behind the counter were all the drinks machines. Music was playing in the background. Daisy searched the whole diner, but couldn't spot a juke box. That was what it needed: an old-fashioned juke box.

The front doorbell clanged again, surprising them all, and more surprisingly still, two police officers walked in. Jack and

Daisy looked at each other. Proper American cops. 'Good day, officers,' said Di brightly, returning from the kitchen. 'Take a seat and I'll be right with you.'

'Mam,' said the officers, tipping their hats, then removing them. Each of them took a stool at the counter, very serious-looking.

'Pair of troopers,' said Phil. 'Not our local boys, I know them.' He seemed to know everybody.

The English lot couldn't help but stare at the two officers. They were both smartly dressed in light grey, short-sleeved shirts with black epaulettes and gold badges on their arms. Light grey hats with black trim. Dark grey trousers with black trim. Black ties. They looked as if they'd stepped straight out of an American TV show. 'Oh, my God,' whispered Daisy. 'Look. They've got guns!' They had, and batons, too. This was a shock. Very sobering.

'Sh,' said Carol. 'And stop staring!'

'All US cops carry firearms,' said Phil casually. 'You have to out here. For protection. Most folks have guns themselves.'

'What, do you have a gun?' said Carol, shocked.

'Sure do,' said Phil. 'Back at the house. A Remington 870 shotgun. For protection, of course. And dealing with the odd wild animal.'

He said it matter-of-factly, but there was a shocked silence all round. America really was something else. And Carol, especially, didn't know how she felt about staying in a house with a gun in it with the kids. Now that she thought about it, that had been one of the reasons Jim and Phil hadn't got on, and why Jim hadn't wanted to visit America. Guns. She seemed to recall a slightly heated debate. Jim had been very anti-guns; even protested about them in the '60s.

'Don't worry, you won't find it,' said Phil, as if trying to reassure them. 'And neither will anyone else. It's well hidden.' Daisy pondered the somewhat skew-whiff way of looking at things: a nineteen year old – technically an adult – couldn't drink alcohol in their own home, but could be in a house with a gun. She bet nineteen year olds could even own guns.

Finally, their food arrived. It had taken a while, too long really, and they were getting hungry and a little impatient. 'So sorry about the wait,' a flustered Di said. Unbelievably, she was still the only waitress, taking orders, making the drinks and preparing the bills all by herself. They all felt sorry for her, so there was no way any of them were going to criticise the excessive wait. 'Two grilled cheese, both on white.' She dished the plates out. The portions were huge. Not one but two thick toasted sandwiches, oozing with gooey orange cheese. They were piled high on the plate and stuck together with wooden sticks, with little 'Happy Grill' flags in the top of them.

Di disappeared and returned with the other two meals. Again, huge plates and portions. The doorbell clanged again. 'Shoot,' she said under her breath. 'Hey folks, take a seat, be right with you. One BLT, and the sliders for you, sir, along with your large, cheesy fries. One vanilla milkshake coming right up … and any more refills whilst I'm here?' she asked again.

'Gosh, no,' said Carol. 'We don't want to be any more trouble.'

'Trouble?' said Di. 'God bless yer, darl. It's my job! And in case you English folks don't know, the refills are free, as standard.' She winked.

'Same again for me, Di, thank you,' said Phil.

'Oh, perhaps just a top up of tea then. Thank you.' said Carol.

'Coming right up.'

'She's a *diamond*,' said Carol, once she had gone. 'So lovely.'

'Sure is,' said Phil. 'But don't tell Trish that.' He laughed loudly, then started coughing. 'Seriously, though, don't worry. I always leave her a big tip.'

They tucked in, and the food was surprisingly very good. Phil seemed to agree. 'Bo's outdone himself,' he commented, clearly pleased and relieved. But Jack, Daisy and Carol still couldn't get over the huge portions. Daisy's milkshake – already piled high with squirty cream and all manner of other sweet treats – came with a separate metal cup and spoon on the side, containing the surplus that didn't fit in the glass. And as for Phil's 'sliders' … these turned out to be six individual smaller burgers in buns. Six! All loaded with different toppings and fillings, and again held together with sticks.

By the time they'd finished, they were all stuffed, except Phil. He asked Di what pies she had on offer. 'Well, we're a bit short again today, I'm afraid – so sorry, honey – it's just what's on the counter… We've got chocolate cream, banana cream, lemon meringue, Key-lime, strawberry and rhubarb, and good ol' cherry…'

'No apple?' said Phil.

'Sorry, hun, no apple.'

'Dang it. I'll have the cherry, then. With cream and ice cream. Thanks, Di.' Carol gave the kids another look. She felt as if she was going to have to say something before long. Her brother was going to kill himself at this rate.

'You're welcome, sugar. Can I get you folks some ice creams or anything?'

'Gosh, no,' said Carol.

'No thanks, we're stuffed,' said Daisy.

By the time they left, there was only a few other customers. The police officers had long gone, tipping their hats as they left – all very polite. Phil insisted on paying again, leaving Di what looked like a ten-dollar tip. No wonder she was so friendly. But she deserved it. 'Lovely to meet you folks, and you be sure to come back again whilst you're staying. I could serve polite folks like you all day long,' said Di.

Outside, the fried-food smell on their clothes immediately

became apparent. This got even worse when they were trapped in the truck. They really *were* going to have to change their clothes and shower again. They wound down their windows. 'Told ya,' said Phil, laughing.

CHAPTER 30

Cousins

By the time the girls turned up at around oneish, it had built into a sizzler of a day, the temperature hitting the mid-eighties. For Daisy and Jack, the nerves had built too, and also for Carol; she was excited at the prospect of seeing her grown-up nieces. None of them knew what to expect of their American relatives. There were a few photos of the girls dotted about the place, family photos, but none seemed that recent.

Everyone was in the garden out the back when they arrived. Phil was busy getting his barbecue set up, a huge pinny tied round his vast midriff, bottle of root beer in hand, sweating profusely. Jack and Daisy were enjoying a game of badminton for the first time: Trish had fished the equipment out of one of the outbuildings. It was fun – the first time Jack had ever played badminton – and also some much-needed exercise after all the excess calories. Thankfully, the net was set up in the shade of the house, out of the hot sun.

'Ooh, that sounds like a car,' sang Trish. 'I'll go and see.' Daisy's stomach somersaulted. She couldn't believe how nervous she felt. More so than Jack for once. They continued to bat the shuttlecock back and forth, as a distraction, and also to appear casual. Jack could have murdered a drink. A cold, alcoholic one. It was driving him nuts.

It seemed to take an age for Trish to reappear. When she did, she was flanked by two tall girls – or young women – who dwarfed her. One was very slim, the older one by the looks of it, the other not so slim. A little tubby, in fact. Daisy couldn't remember which was which. It didn't help that they were both wearing shades. 'Look who's he-re,' Trish said in her sing-song voice, clearly thrilled. 'Come and introduce yourselves, girls.'

'All right, Mom. Calm down already,' said the younger of the two as she was practically shoved forwards. 'Hey, guys, I'm Tara. Pleased to meet you all.'

'Sue,' said Sue, waving a hand. 'Great to meet you.'

Everyone said a big hello. Carol and Phil walked over to greet them. Jack and Daisy followed slowly behind, feeling awkward, still clutching their badminton rackets.

'So lovely to see you girls. Remember me, your Aunty Carol?' She practically squealed and Daisy groaned inside – so embarrassing… It sounded as if she'd been on the gin already. 'My gosh, how you've shot up. So tall!'

'Hey, Aunty Carol,' they said in unison. Their voices were deep, those deep American female voices you get sometimes. They took it in turns to lean down and hug Carol.

'And you remember Daisy?' Carol turned round with her arm outstretched. 'She would have only been little last time you met. Daisy, come here, don't be shy.' Daisy was dying inside; it was as if they were a load of kids on the first day of school.

Daisy and the girls exchanged 'hellos' and Jack was introduced too.

'How about a hug for your old man, then?' said Phil, moving in with outstretched arms.

'Hey, Pops,' they said, hugging him.

'Eww, you're all sweaty,' said Sue, the older girl, releasing him. 'And *clearly* the new diet's going well.' Phil's belly made it hard to get your arms around him.

'Gee, thanks, honey. I thought I'd lost a few pounds,' Phil

said, holding his wobbling gut and laughing. It all seemed a big joke to him.

'Hmm…' said Sue.

'See you've dragged the old badminton set out then, Mom,' said Tara, 'Not on our account, I hope?'

'No-oo… Jack and Daisy have been having a game. You girls used to love it.' There was silence for a second.

'Right, drinks,' said Phil. 'Barbecuing's thirsty work in this heat.' Ooh, this'll be interesting, thought Daisy, pricking her ears up.

'What? You haven't even started cooking yet,' said Trish, and they all laughed.

'Whadya got?' said Tara.

'Well, there's plenty of home-made lemonade – Daisy made it,' said Trish.

The girls groaned and rolled their eyes. 'So, she's got you on the lemonade wagon already,' joked Tara.

Daisy blushed and laughed. She'd enjoyed making it earlier: her contribution to the day. But clearly it was a running joke.

'And there's beers too,' said Trish.

'And gin,' said Carol.

'Erm, I'll go with the lemonade,' said Sue. 'See how Daisy's measures up to Mom's.' God, boring, thought Daisy. What a waste of being able to drink.

'It's my recipe still,' said Trish.

'I'll have a beer,' said Tara. 'Hope they're nice and cold.' That's more like it, thought Daisy. Clearly, they were both over twenty-one. Lucky so and sos.

'Of course,' said Trish. 'Chilled and ready.'

'Yeah, turned into a hot one, hasn't it?' said Phil. 'Perfect barbecue weather. I'll have a beer, too, honey. Sounds good.' Mmm, the plot thickens, thought Daisy. So he does drink sometimes then…

'Kids?' said Trish, turning to Jack and Daisy. This made

them feel even more like children. Why was she even asking? It was lemonade or lemonade.

'Lemonade,' they said resignedly.

'I'll come and help,' said Carol. 'Leave you young 'uns to get acquainted.' She had a guilty and sympathetic look on her face, clearly feeling for Jack and Daisy.

'Talking of barbecues, I need to go and check on it. Yes, you young folks sit yourselves down and get to know each other a little… We'll catch up in a second, girls, great to see ya.' And Phil waddled off with his spatula.

'No pressure then,' said Tara sarcastically, acknowledging the awkwardness of the situation. Daisy and Jack relinquished their rackets, and they all sat down to chat. Sue, being the eldest, led the way. 'Lovely to meet you both finally. How you finding it, stuck out here in the middle of Hicksville with the olds? Glad you came?' They all laughed.

Daisy fought her shyness to reply. The girls were quite intimidating somehow. Their voices, their accents. The way they were impenetrable behind their sunglasses; it made Daisy feel exposed and scrutinised in comparison. And there was just so much of them. Physically. Their hands were huge. She cleared her dry throat, could feel her heart in it. 'Yes, it's lovely. Really enjoying it. Phil and Trish are lovely too.'

'God bless you for a liar,' Sue laughed. 'You don't have to be polite. You can bad-mouth them, we won't mind. Go on, get it off your chest!' And they all laughed.

'No, really. They're lovely,' said Daisy.

'Sorry, but I've got to say this,' said Tara. 'That accent. Am I right?' she turned to her sister. 'It is *adorable*.' Daisy blushed. What was this with their accents out here? Why was it such a thing? Mind you, she was just as bad with them.

'I know,' said Sue. 'Carol Vorderman!'

'Yes,' said Tara, 'So posh and proper. So *English*!'

Carol Vorderman, thought Daisy. What the hell? 'So, you get *Countdown* out here then?' she said.

'Hell, yeah. Watch it every day,' said Sue. 'You Brits get so embarrassed when a rude word comes up. It's hilarious. But Carol's great – so clever and sophisticated.'

'Right. Your turn, Jack. Go on, say something – just for us. Make our day,' said Tara. Oh gosh, poor Jack, thought Daisy. She immediately felt his leg start to tap under the table.

'Aw, look, you've gone and embarrassed him now,' said Sue, smacking her sister. 'He's gone bright red, bless him.'

'Sorry guys,' said Tara. 'It's just such a rare thing out here, an English accent, but lovely to hear.'

'That's OK,' said Daisy. 'We love your accents, too. And all the American stuff. That's what's been so great. Seeing it all. Such an eye-opener. Hasn't it, Jack?' She really needed to bring him into conversation, but naturally. Not put on the spot like some performing monkey.

Jack cleared his throat, too. 'Yes,' he said. 'Really good.'

Tara and Sue put their heads together and sighed at Jack's voice, 'Aw!' they said in unison.

'Word of warning, Daisy. The girls are gonna *love* him out here,' said Tara.

Daisy laughed awkwardly. Great, she thought. That was all she needed. 'So, where do you guys live?' she said, keen to change the subject.

'New York,' said Sue. 'Together, unfortunately.'

'Hey,' said Tara.

'Really?' said Daisy. 'Wow. That's amazing.'

'Yeah, I tried to escape, but she followed me,' said Sue.

'Well, you shouldn't have left me out here with the olds then, should you? I just couldn't hack it any longer. Joking aside though, it *is* Sue's apartment – she earns all the money – I'm just the scrounging lodger.' They all laughed.

'Gosh. New York, though,' said Daisy wistfully.

'You never been?' said Sue.

'No. Well, only to the airport – we flew in there – but this is our first time in America, both of us. We haven't seen any of the sights or anything. But we'd love to whilst we're here.' Shit, thought Daisy. Hope that didn't sound like dropping a hint.

'Ah, well, see how it goes. How long you here for?' said Sue.

'Not sure yet. We haven't got a return ticket. Maybe even a month or two if Mum gets her way. She was planning on staying a while and making the most of it, visiting a few places.'

'Really? Well, why not? We'd love to have you over, wouldn't we, Sis? Show you the sights,' said Sue.

'Oh God, that would be amazing,' said Daisy, not knowing if she meant it or not.

'Sis?' said Sue.

'Sorry, I'm still taking in that accent…' Tara was leaning in with her head on her sister's shoulder. They were clearly very close.

Sue shoved her off. 'Pack it in,' she said.

'Sorry, yeah, it would be great, we'd love to. How old are you guys anyway?'

'Nineteen, but only just,' said Daisy. 'It was my birthday the day before we flew out actually.'

'Oh, well, belated Happy Birthday then,' said Sue.

'Yeah, congradulations,' said Tara. 'And you, Jack?'

'Erm, seventeen,' said Jack, embarrassed, feeling so young compared with everyone else.

'Aw, bless,' said Sue. 'You don't look it. I'd have taken you for at least eighteen.'

'Hey! Do you guys pardy?' whispered Tara, hunching forwards.

'*Here we are*,' called Trish, announcing her return with the drinks across the lawn.

'Sorry?' said Daisy.

'Shit. You know, *pardy*…' She clenched her thumb and forefinger together, pressed them to her lips and sucked, still hunched forward.

The penny dropped for Jack and Daisy. She was saying 'party', but meant 'smoke'. As in marijuana. They couldn't believe it. They nodded and Tara winked. 'Later,' she whispered.

'*Sshh*.' Sue gave her another dig and she sat back up.

'Well, don't y'all look like you're getting on like a house on fire – thick as thieves already,' said Trish, appearing next to them with a tray, a large jug of cloudy lemonade on it and some glasses. 'What y'all whispering about? Moaning about the oldies, I bet.' Carol, who was standing behind her, laughed too loudly. Everything she did was embarrassing today.

'Jack and Daisy have been singing your praises actually, Mom, you'll be pleased to know,' said Sue.

'I don't believe a word of it,' Trish said.

'Oh, I'm sure they have, Trish,' said Carol, 'The hospitality has been wonderful.'

'Aw, well, bless you for saying that, Carol, it's been a pleasure to have you, too. Phil! *Beer*!' she hollered. Such a big voice for such a small woman. 'Stop poking that there fire and come and get it whilst it's cold – won't be for long in this heat. And in case you didn't know, yer two daughters have driven all the way out here to see you.'

'All right, woman. I'm comin'. Quit yer hollerin'!'

They ate. They drank. They baked in the hot sun. They got to know one another better. The girls were lovely. Very down to earth; friendly and easy to get on with. They got Phil to rig up a music system to liven things up a bit. They played a few games of badminton doubles with Jack and Daisy, rotating the teams to keep it fair. Even Carol and Trish had a go, but not Phil. Jack and Tara made the most successful pairing, peeving Daisy slightly – especially the way she kept high fiving him. She was definitely the most outgoing, the bubbliest of the two girls, possibly because she was the youngest. Or maybe it was because she was the only one drinking. Trish had warned her a couple of times to 'take it easy'. Sue still hadn't touched a drop.

It was early evening. The shimmering sun, paler and less fierce now, had floated right across the big, blue bowl of Pennsylvanian sky. The shadows on the lawn were stretching. An alcohol- and food-induced collective stupor seemed to have descended, and there was a lull in proceedings. Phil looked as if he was dozing, a baseball cap covering his face. Trish and Carol weren't much better. Jack and Daisy were getting restless, sick of sitting there without a drink; they could have easily slipped away upstairs, but it would have been rude. As if sensing this, Tara cleared her throat. 'Right, I think Jack and Daisy need a bit of a stroll, a break from the olds for a bit. It's like a nursing home round here.' Jack, who was suffering the most, immediately pricked up his ears.

'Charming,' said Trish.

'What? Pop's practically snoring. Sue? You coming?' Tara said.

'Yeah. I'm up for that,' said Sue. 'Be nice to have a wander, see some of our old haunts.'

'Well, don't go too far. I'm gonna fix some supper soon. And once that sun goes down, it soon starts to cool,' said Trish.

'We won't. Ready, guys?' said Tara.

Jack and Daisy couldn't believe their luck. They were both hoping the same thing; that this was Tara's plan to sneak them away for a smoke. They were starting to think she'd forgotten. Even though they'd been off the gear for a while, the thought of a smoke seemed like Heaven. The fact that Tara had her bag with her – she hadn't let it far out of her sight the whole day, even taking it to the loo with her on several occasions – boded well. It was a hippy-looking bag, brown suede with tassels and coloured flowers. The more they got to know her, the more of a hippy bohemian type she seemed. Sue, on the other hand, seemed more strait-laced.

They set off in the direction of the horses and fields, down towards the woods. Jack was thinking about his cider – picturing it sitting there waiting for them, chilled in the stream. He was hoping they would get a chance to retrieve it. The girls seemed cool; he couldn't imagine them having a problem with this, especially if they were going for a smoke. It was strange being alone with them. Two tall American girls, practically strangers, but somehow familiar already. When they reached the field, the horses trotted over to stand at the fence. 'Hey, Bud; hey, Peppermint,' said Tara. 'How ya doing?' The girls petted the horses, which were huge up close. The horses responded, snorting and snuffling. 'I ain't got anything for you. You missed me, girl?' Tara said to Peppermint.

'D'you ride, guys?' Sue turned to ask Jack and Daisy. They were both keeping their distance.

'No, we don't,' said Daisy.

'Come on 'n' pet 'em, they won't hurt,' said Tara. 'Especially Peppermint. She's a right softie, ain't ya, girl?' Jack and Daisy looked at each other. It felt awkward and rude not to go over. Tentatively, they gave the smaller horse a token pat and stroke on the nose. It was weird for Jack to feel that short, bristly hair underneath his hand, the warmth. He was so unused to animals, especially petting them. He'd never been to a zoo or a farm. Daisy could sense the fear-inducing strength of the horse, and they were careful to keep their hands away from its prominent teeth.

Petting time over, they continued towards the wood. Jack and Daisy were both trying to figure out where they'd emerged from, and where their stash was. The girls continued in a straight line, seemingly heading for a specific place. 'Look!' said Tara as they neared the wire fence. 'They still haven't fixed it.' She pointed to a sagging section of fence, with the wooden poles either side leaning inwards.

'It was probably us that did it in the first place,' said Sue, laughing. Jack and Daisy hadn't noticed this the other day, as they'd exited a little further along. It was on both their minds to tell the girls they had already been there; they were going to have to if they wanted to get their cider.

'Now this,' said Tara, 'is where me and Sue used to come to get away from the olds.' She clambered over the fence.

'And to hang out with our friends,' said Sue. 'Mine anyway – Tara didn't have any! After you.' She gestured for Jack and Daisy to go next.

'I did too. Screw you!' said Tara, laughing. 'I even snuck a boy down here once.'

'You didn't!' said Sue.

'Yep. Chet Brubaker, lived at the farm up the road. Folks still do, I reckon.'

'You little slut,' said Sue. 'Mom would have gone ballistic.'

'I know. Rebel, eh?' said Tara.

It was fun listening to the girls banter, as if their true personalities had come out away from their parents. They stood in the woods. Hidden. Tara had unzipped her bag and was rooting around in it. 'Now this, my English cohorts, is where the magic begins.' Jack and Daisy expected her to pull out some smoking paraphernalia, or maybe a ready-rolled spliff. But it was a small bottle of spirits. Vodka by the look of it, about half the size of Carol's bottle.

'Old habits, eh?' said Sue. 'Guess that's why you kept disappearing to the toilet.' She didn't seem surprised at all. 'Yer gonna get caught one of these days, I tell yer.'

'Haven't yet,' said Tara. 'And you've been telling me that since I was sixteen years old. Don't blame me, blame Penn state and its ridiculous alcohol laws. Here,' she said, unscrewing the cap. 'I'm figuring you guys need this more than me. You wanna hit?' She offered the bottle to Daisy. Not wanting to appear square, but against her better judgement, Daisy took a swig. The spirit burned and went straight to her head. It tasted gross and she winced.

'God, that's strong,' she said, coughing a little. 'Sorry.' She passed the bottle to Jack, still pulling a face.

'You get used to it,' Tara said. 'But I've got an even better trick for you whilst you're here – if you're partial to a drink or two that is. Home-made lemonade. It's perfect. Stick a shot or two in your glass when they're not looking, or even better whilst you're in your room. You'll be amazed the opportunities you get if you look for them, like when the olds are outdoors, riding the horses, off the property, or even in the lounge or on the porch. They don't stay up late any more – and once the sun goes down, my friends, that's prime vodka time.'

'Christ, Tara, you're gonna get these guys shot. Not everyone's an alky like you,' said Sue.

'Just sayin', is all. Trying to help them out. You *do* drink, don't you?' said Tara.

'Yeah,' said Jack rather loudly. The spirit had gone straight to his head. 'We've got some cider stashed in the stream down there.' He couldn't help blurting it out. As if he was trying to impress, Daisy thought.

'Really,' said Tara. And the girls burst out laughing. Jack passed Sue the bottle, but she declined, passing it back to Tara.

'You see,' Tara said, holding the bottle up. 'Folks after my own heart.' And she took a swig. 'I remember *exactly* what it was like living here under their rules, so I feel your pain – but even I didn't think of storing cans in the stream. Genius.' And she shoved the bottle back in her bag. Jack beamed, pleased with himself.

'Where did you get cider from?' asked Sue, curious. 'They never usually have it in the house.'

'Mum,' said Daisy. 'She got it for us from the shops.'

'Aunty Carol!' said Tara. 'Oh my God, what a dark horse. Go, Aunty Carol!'

'Oh God, please don't say anything, whatever you do,' said Daisy, panicking. 'She'd kill me. We really had to talk her into it. Your parents don't know.'

'God, no. Of course. We wouldn't dream of it,' said Tara.

'Just surprised, that's all. Wish our parents had been that lenient. You're lucky.'

'Yeah, guess so,' said Daisy.

'Right, let's go and find this cider, then we can sit down for a smoke,' said Sue. 'I take it that's why you've dragged us out here.'

'Of course,' said Tara. Yes! thought Jack.

After crossing the stream, they retrieved the cider, which was still in situ and pleasantly cold. Jack found the spot easily and appeared to be in his element, Daisy thought, having the girls to impress. Or was it all just in her head? Why did she even think these things?

Then Tara led the way to what she called her 'regular spot'. As it turned out, it was the sheltered location that Jack and Daisy had discovered the other day, between the tall white boulders and pine trees. The very same place where they had 'done the deed'. Jack and Daisy exchanged glances. It was strange for Daisy to sit with her back against the rock again, knowing what had gone on. It turned her on in a way, thinking of their little secret.

Tara already had a spliff rolled; she had a few of them, in fact. Small ones, sealed in a little plastic bag, in a small purse along with a lighter. She lit the spliff. It seemed ages since Jack and Daisy had smelt that smell. Unlike their spliffs, however, Tara's turned out to be pure weed. No tobacco at all. Perhaps that was why it was smaller than the spliffs they rolled back home. She called it a joint. The weed they called pot.

They passed the joint round. For Jack it was bliss – sitting there amongst the rocks with Daisy and these American girls, these new-found friends, as the sun began to set and the smoke drifted up amongst the pine trees. The heady combination of the cider and the weed; he hadn't felt that dreamy release in a long time. Or so happy. Not since before Aitch died. The only thing missing, as Daisy had said before, was music. And this was the topic of conversation for a while. Music and their tastes, and the difference between American and English music; the Billboard chart and the UK Top 40. Daisy came alive. In her element, she displayed her knowledge of the subject, but was also fascinated by the girls' tastes. They bonded over a mutual love of the Smiths. 'God, I just *love* those miserable English bands,' laughed Sue.

As another joint was passed round, their guards dropped further and conversation descended into a candid silliness, mainly involving the different terms Americans and the English had for things. Even Jack joined in. Biscuits. Sneakers. Faucet. Jello. Pants. 'What, that's underwear?' said Tara.

They took it in terms asking questions and taking the mickey. 'What's the crack with the Royal Family?' 'Is it always foggy in London Town?' 'No, and nobody calls it "London Town",' said Daisy.

Jack plucked up the courage to ask why American chickens' eggs were white, something he had noticed. But even the question had them all in hysterics. 'Why, what the hell colour are yours?' Sue responded, crying with laughter. It even got a bit rude, with Tara asking what their name for a 'Johnson' was.

'What the hell even *is* a "Johnson"?' said Daisy.

And then Jack nearly spat his cider out when Tara shifted her backside, saying, 'I've got a rock sticking right into my fanny.'

Feeling braver, Daisy mentioned that Americans couldn't pronounce their r's either. As in mirror, rural and all right. They dropped the middle syllable. In response, the girls tried, but couldn't stop doing it. 'Oh my God! We can't pronounce our r's. Why can't we do it?' They tried and tried, saying the words slowly and over-emphasising them until they were all crying with laughter.

Before long, it started to get dark. 'We'd better be getting back,' said Sue, always the more sensible one. 'Mom will be getting stressed.'

It was surprisingly light as they emerged from the wood and negotiated the trodden-down fence. The moon and the sun were both up, the sun only just. 'Right,' said Tara. 'One last thing before we head back.' And she rummaged in her bag again, pulling out some sort of spray; it looked like a miniature deodorant can. 'Get in line and open your mouths,' she said.

'Ah, the famous breath-freshener spray,' said Sue.

'You really have thought of everything,' laughed Daisy.

'Years of practice,' said Tara. 'Which reminds me, before bed I'll show you where to stash your vodka – or whatever your choice of liquor is: I've got the perfect spot.'

'The loose floorboard in the guest room,' said Sue.

'Correct. Now, get in line and open wide.'

'Oh, for Christ's sake,' said Sue. They all lined up, Sue a good head or so taller than Jack or Daisy.

'God, I feel like a midget standing next to you,' said Daisy.

'And you make me feel like a freak. I'd rather be your height, trust me,' said Sue. 'Ow! You squirted it in my bloody eye.'

'Well, you should have stayed still,' said Tara laughing. 'And yes, me too. I'd much rather be your height, Daisy.'

'Really?' said Daisy. 'Why?'

'Guys don't wanna know with really tall girls like us. It's like we don't exist,' said Tara.

'Yeah, and forget wearing heels,' said Sue.

'Gosh, I'd never thought of it like that,' said Daisy. 'And I'm sure it's not true.'

'Oh, it is. I blame Pop,' said Tara. 'I mean, look at Mom, she's like a hobbit.' And they burst out laughing.

'What do you say, Jack? Tall or small girls?' said Sue.

'Yeah, Jack, you're a guy,' said Tara, standing wide-legged with the spray-can poised in her hand.

Jack, who had been feeling a little out of his depth with all this female conversation, gulped and blushed. He didn't know what to say. Daisy felt a little breathless waiting for his answer, a little tense. 'Erm … never really thought about it,' he said. 'I just like Daisy, I guess.' And he shrugged.

Both the girls squealed. 'Oh my *GOD*! Where did you get this one from, Daisy? He's *adorable*. Are there more like him in England?' said Tara.

Daisy laughed, feeling warm inside at his answer. 'Nope. Not that I know of. And I found him on a bus – but that's a story for another day.'

'Oh, no! You can't say that, then leave us hanging. Come on, tell us,' said Tara.

'No. It really is a story for another day,' said Daisy.

'Boo,' said Tara. 'Right, we'll hold you to that. Now open wide.' Tara bent her knees to concentrate and sprayed in Daisy's mouth, her hair hanging in front of her face. There really was a hippy element to her; a bit Joni Mitchell but with a few extra pounds. The spray was cold and hot at the same time on the back of Daisy's throat, but minty and not unpleasant. 'Jack,' Tara said. Jack dutifully opened his mouth and she sprayed inside.

It was nice seeing the warm yellow lights of the house in the distance as they made their way back. All around them, the cicadas were chirping in the fields again. 'You really do forget how rural it is out here don't you, how quiet,' said Tara. 'Rural. Rural. Goddamnit.' This had them all in hysterics again. Tara really was a character, a bit of a kindred spirit. She would have fitted in well with the gang.

'Right, quit yer squawkin' now, everyone. Remember to act normal,' Sue said as they reached the back garden. The adults had cleared up and gone indoors.

'Yeah, nobody say rural or anything,' said Tara. Jack and Daisy sniggered.

'Tara-May, seriously, pack it in now,' said Sue.

'*Hey*!' the girls called as they stepped into the kitchen.

'There you are, you lot,' said Trish. 'Was startin' to wonder where you'd got to. Close the screen door, you'll let the bugs in.' A moth was batting around the ceiling light. Trish was busy as usual, laying out yet more food on the kitchen table.

'Where's the others?' said Sue.

'Oh, Aunty Carol and your pop are in the lounge, looking at old family photos and reminiscing. I think your pop's a bit drunk. And Carol.'

This turned out not to be a bad thing. It was genuinely funny to see Phil a bit tipsy, and it also meant they weren't scrutinised too closely – it reminded Jack of his father when he was drunk. Once supper was eaten and cleared out of the way, the parents were yawning and ready for bed. The younger ones were left to their own devices, just how they wanted it. After saying goodnight, they retired to the porch, with a pack of cards and a jug of home-made lemonade. 'Special' lemonade. They made for the end of the veranda with the porch swing. Next to it, against the wall of the house, was a cushioned bench, and between them was a low sort of coffee table. It gave the feel of an outdoor lounge. Jack and Daisy sat in the swing seat. Amazingly, it was the first time they had used it. And it was a revelation. They sat and rocked gently, sipping their drinks and inhaling that sweet, nostalgic smell of the clinging honeysuckle.

Jack and Daisy introduced the American girls to Shithead, and they declared the game 'awesome' and 'neat', saying they were going to take the game back to New York with them. But eventually, they began to tire: it was time to call it a night. They were all a little tipsy, even Sue, so it was a good job the older folks were asleep. Everyone agreed how great it had been to meet. The girls reiterated their offer to Jack and Daisy of a stay in New York, which was so exciting. There were drunken hugs all round.

Upstairs, whilst Tara was showing Jack and Daisy where to stash their vodka (trying, but failing to be quiet), the sleeping arrangements became evident. 'Sue! *Sue*!' she hissed. 'Come and look at this.'

'What?' said Sue. 'You'll wake everyone up.'

'Look! In the same room *and* beds pushed together.' Jack and Daisy looked at each other uncomfortably.

'Well I never,' said Sue, clearly surprised, but not angry as Tara was.

'I know. Don't worry, guys – you haven't done anything wrong. But I'm gonna have this out with the old bat tomorrow,' said Tara.

'Well, don't cause a scene, it's not worth it…' said Sue. Tara didn't answer. 'Tara. Please…'

Jack and Daisy went to bed feeling a little uneasy. It had been an unfortunate end to what had been a very memorable day.

Chapter 31

Strike!

By the morning, Tara appeared to have calmed down a little. It was either the alcohol wearing off, or she was just heeding her sister's entreaty for peace. But she still brought the matter up at breakfast, albeit in a fairly non-confrontational way. At first…

'So, mother dear, I see you've relaxed your stance on young people sharing a bed with each other…'

'Tara,' said Phil immediately in a serious voice, the most serious he had sounded so far; it was unexpected and a bit of a shock.

'Don't worry, Pops, I'm not gonna make a scene.'

'Good,' said Trish. 'We've got guests.'

'Well?' said Tara.

'Well what?' said Trish. She stopped eating. 'I knew this was going to be a problem… Anyway, you shouldn't be snooping around in other people's rooms.'

'Snooping around? This used to be my home. And I put the emphasis on *used* to be. I was saying goodnight to Jack and Daisy was all.' Everyone at the table was feeling a little tense, wondering where this was heading.

'Your mom and I thought it would be more comfortable, the decent thing to do, to allow Jack and Daisy to stay in the large guest room with the en-suite whilst they were here,' said Phil. 'Seein' as they're fixin' to stay a while, helps with the bathroom situation too. That's all…'

'I can understand that,' said Tara. 'But it's all just so – you know…'

'Go on, say it,' said Trish.

'Hypocritical,' said Tara.

'There we go. I didn't put them in the same bed, Tara…'

'You might as well have. We were never even allowed boys in our room, never mind stayin' over. And you know the arguments that caused.'

'Sorry about this, folks,' said Phil; he seemed a bit embarrassed.

'I know, but that was different,' said Trish.

'Different? How? I just don't get it. Please explain to me how it's *different*.'

'Jack and Daisy are guests, for a start. They're not *my* children. And furthermore, they've been living together for some time, over a year. Clearly, they're sensible' – Daisy, Jack and Carol tried to hide the complicit guilt on their faces – 'and Carol's perfectly OK with it, so me keepin' them apart ain't gonna change a thing, other than make their stay an unhappy one. I was just tryin' to do the right thing, Tara. Believe it or not, I always have.'

Feeling guilty, and desperate to try and defuse the situation, Daisy said, 'We don't have to stay in the same room; it's really not a problem.'

'God, *no!*' said Phil, Trish and Tara, all at the same time.

'I love the fact you guys can sleep together,' said Tara. 'It's sweet. How it should be. I just wish we'd been granted the same privilege and trust, is all.'

'Well…' said Trish. 'Maybe next time you girls are goin' steady with a fella, properly steady – not some flavour of the month, fly-by-night cowboy – then maybe you *should* be allowed to share the same room when you visit; if you visit. Maybe I've been too strict too long, set in my ways; and for that I apologise … but I've always had your best interests at heart, both of you girls, I promise you. I didn't want you makin' the same mistakes I did, that's all…'

'Well, hallelujah for that,' said Sue, breaking the tension. 'Did I tell you I was seeing someone?'

'*What?*' Phil and Trish said together.

*****

Breakfast and serious discussions out of the way, Phil finally talked everyone into visiting the French Azilum place he'd been mentioning. The girls had rolled their eyes and groaned. 'I don't know what your obsession with that place is, Pops. Every time we have someone to stay, you drag 'em out there,' said Tara.

'It's part of our history, that's why. Our heritage.'

'Erm, weren't you born in Derby?' said Sue. 'Derby, England.'

'Oh, can it,' said Phil.

The girls asked Jack and Daisy to travel with them, which was nice; it made a change. Sue's car was a fairly sporty number. New-smelling, with a fold-down hood. It made Daisy wonder what she did as a job; clearly, she wasn't short of money. It was fun driving along with the top down, the wind rushing through their hair; Jack and Daisy had never been in an open-top car before. 'Rush Hour' by Jane Wiedlin came on the radio, and Sue turned it up. Daisy loved the song, and all the girls sang along.

The French Azilum site was interesting, but not that interesting – as there wasn't a great deal there. The land was mainly flat, next to that big old snaking river, with a few signs and commemorative plaques, stone overlooks and monoliths dotted about. All the original log cabins on the site had long been dismantled for firewood by the thrifty settlers. They found this out at Laporte House, the main tourist centrepiece and home to the Azilum museum. Daisy took the opportunity to get used to her new camera; it had been sitting untouched in their suitcase.

In the car journey on the way back, Tara suggested they should go bowling after lunch – 'something that's actually fun'. Jack and Daisy thought this sounded a great idea, as it was something else she and Jack had never done. They broached this with the parents over lunch, who insisted on coming with them. They thought it sounded fun too, and didn't want to miss out. The girls groaned. Apparently, Phil took his bowling very seriously. He was on a team, and even had his own ball.

As usual, it seemed, they had to head out of the township again for the bowling. As they hit the busier main road, they passed the diner. Shame about that place, thought Daisy. Despite the smell, she'd enjoyed the experience and wanted to go back. The waitress had been lovely.

Going to a ten-pin bowling alley was another all-American experience for Jack and Daisy. The place was big and noisy. They had to swap their shoes for bowling shoes, which was an unexpected and traumatic experience for Jack. They looked silly and didn't fit properly. He felt foolish in them, clumsy and clown-like. Phil had to talk the guy behind the desk into letting them have seven people on one lane as they wanted two teams; the maximum guideline was six. A couple of dollar bills pressed into the guy's hand seemed to help with this – Phil knew him, of course…

Not only did Phil have his own bowling ball, which he'd brought with him – the thing was purple and shiny and weighed a ton (he called it the 'mauve marauder') – he also had his own bowling glove, which he squeezed onto his hand. He was so confident of winning that he said he would go with Jack and Daisy – just the three of them – against the other four. The total score won. 'Besides,' he said, 'one guy's worth two gals, ain't that right?' He slammed a weighty hand down on Jack's shoulder and squeezed. Jack grimaced an awkward smile in response.

'Oh, you're gonna pay for your outdated sexism, Daddio. Bring it on. Losers pay for the drinks,' said Sue.

'You're on,' said Phil, roaring with laughter. The enthusiasm was infectious and everyone was in high spirits, Carol was giggly, and the girls kept hitting each other and squealing, as if they'd regressed ten or fifteen years. How old were they? Daisy kept forgetting to ask. Jack was the only really nervous one; he didn't want to let Phil down. But first he had to learn how to bowl – and the only way to do that was to watch.

Fortunately, the ladies' team went first: the 'Pink Ladies' as they'd called themselves, from *Grease*. Uncle Phil had named his team the T-Birds in response. Sue was up first. Like her dad, she seemed to be quite serious about it, taking her time to set up her throw. She had long levers and a big back-swing, so she rattled the ball down the alley at a fair old pace. Straight down the middle, in fact. A strike, straight off the bat. Sue whirled round with a clenched fist. 'In your face, old man!' The ladies went wild, jumping up and down and high fiving each other. Tara jumped on Sue's back, nearly knocking her flat on her face. 'Jesus, Sis, you're killing me,' Sue gurgled in a strangled voice. 'You need to cut down on those New York cheesecakes.' They couldn't stop laughing. Trish and Carol were also in hysterics, acting like kids. It was all highly amusing, yet a little disturbing for Daisy to witness.

Phil was up next. 'Right, let's see if the master of disaster can quieten these cacklin' women-folk. Stand back, my friends, yer usin' up my oxygen: this bull needs plenny of room.' And he did, what with his sheer size and his considerable run-up; but he certainly looked as if he knew what he was doing. First, he clutched his bowling ball to his chest like a stolen baby in a strange, cupped, hook-like grip; then, approaching the bowling line at pace, he let the ball go with a flourish, following through with his arm, his right leg flicking out behind him. It was surprisingly graceful and stylish for such a large man. The ball looked as if it was heading off to the right, then about three-quarters of the way down the lane the vicious spin bit in and it reverted to dead centre, hitting the middle pin as if he had it under remote control. It looked for all the world like a strike, but one pin was left wobbling and remained standing. 'Gosh-darn it,' he said. 'Too central. It's got to be just off.' The girls were hollering in delight again. Phil ignored them, sweating, nodding his head and waiting patiently. What for, Jack wasn't quite sure. Then the 'mauve marauder' popped back out of the ball-return machine. Jack hadn't noticed the first ball coming back with all the commotion over the strike. The machine reminded him of the suitcase conveyor belt at the airport. Phil picked up his ball, clearly not wanting to use any of the others. He then took his time, repeating his routine to a tee, and dispatched his ball again, picking off the remaining pin and sending it flying. It was a great shot, and he made it look so easy.

The ladies booed and hissed theatrically. 'Well done, Uncle Phil,' said Daisy. He high fived both Jack and Daisy – they loved their high fiving, the Americans – but more seriously.

'Hey, guys, how we all doing today? I'm Patsy.' They all turned. A girl on roller skates in a sparkly T-shirt and shorts combo was standing with a pen and pad in her hand, smiling broadly. She had plaited pigtails, braces on her teeth and a lot of make-up on.

'Hey, Patsy,' all the American folk said, as if a waitress on roller skates in a bowling alley was the most normal thing in the world.

'What can I get you folks?'

'Erm, I'll have a large root beer, thanks,' said Phil. Textbook. 'Guys?'

'7 Up for me, please,' said Sue. 'Medium.' Tara and, surprisingly, Carol both ordered beers. Carol really seemed to be enjoying herself, and Daisy had to stop herself from privately berating her mum for it. It was lovely to see after all she had been through with Dad. Tara was asked to show some ID. Again, this seemed totally normal procedure. Daisy and Jack had to order sodas as usual. It was so galling.

'And can I get you guys any snacks? Hot dogs? Chips?' the girl said.

'Well, it'd be rude not to – especially since these guys are gonna be payin' for them,' Phil said, chuckling.

'Christ, Dad, we've just eaten,' said Sue.

'Just tryin' to bump up your drinks bill is all,' he said. 'We'll have a large popcorn – sweet – some buffalo wings…'

'Phil, no,' said Trish.

'All right, scratch that. A large popcorn, some salted pretzels and some chilli peanuts to share – that should do us.'

'All righty then. You guys all set?' said Patsy. They all nodded. 'Great. Comin' right up then.' And she skated off.

By the time it was Jack's turn, he still hadn't got a clue what he was doing and felt painfully self-conscious. Especially in those stupid shoes. Daisy felt for him; he looked so awkward. But Daisy and Phil both gave him encouragement; and he did OK. More by luck than judgement, he managed to knock down seven pins. No strike or spare, but at least he didn't get a gutter-ball. He was high fived again by his fellow teammates and sat down, relieved it was out of the way.

Halfway through the game, Tara spotted an old friend on the other side of the alley with another group. 'Oh my gosh, it's Ruth,' she said. 'Sorry, guys, I've got to go and say hello.' Tara approached the other group, who were about the same age as her; and a couple of them greeted her with hugs. They chatted for a short while, then Tara and one of the girls, presumably Ruth, disappeared to the toilet together.

Everyone used the opportunity to have a breather and graze on some of the snacks. Phil also used the opportunity to give Jack and Daisy some pointers, a little bowling technique lesson; he was amazed when he heard they had never been bowling before. Tara returned, looking happy. 'Sorry, had to use the john. That was some old friends from high school. We still keep in touch.'

'How's Ruth?' said Trish.

'Yeah, good. Just lost her job, though. Reckons it's this recession…'

'What does she do?' said Sue.

'Works up at the construction place, junior marketing exec. Or did!'

The bowling game resumed, and by the end the 'T-Birds' had won by some margin. Phil's consistency and experience paid off: he was deadly accurate and only failed to get a strike or spare once, making up for Jack and Daisy's shortcomings – although they had improved considerably under his guidance. Having really enjoyed themselves, they had decided to come back for a game on their own, without everyone watching. In comparison, despite their promising start, the 'Pink Ladies' had got worse rather than better – possibly because of the beer, with Sue being the exception here and clearly the best player. They grudgingly accepted their loss and Trish said she would 'pick up the check'. 'Oh, so that means I'm still payin' then?' said Phil.

On the way back in the car, Tara surprised Jack and Daisy. 'I've got a little something for you,' she said, unzipping her bag. 'Two things actually.' Sue was trying to see what she was up to, and the car swerved a little. 'Jeez, keep your eyes on the road, Sis. You tryin' to get us killed?' said Tara. She plucked something out of her bag, then turned to Jack and Daisy, leaning between the front seats.

'Oh, for Christ's sake,' said Sue, checking the rear-view mirror.

'Look what yer cousin Tara's got for ya.' She was dangling what looked like a little bag of weed between her thumb and forefinger. Jack and Daisy couldn't believe it.

'Seriously, Tara, quit waving that thing around and sit back down,' said Sue. 'You'll get us arrested.'

'Chill, dog,' said Tara, stashing the bag away. She turned back to them, sunglasses on, the wind blowing her hair about. 'Seriously, though, I got it off Ruthy for you. But that's not all. Here.' She passed Daisy a piece of paper. Daisy unfolded it and Jack leant in close. It was a phone number: an American phone number and a guy's name, Dewey. 'That's Ruth's brother. He's the guy around here apparently – and still in high school. I told her about you guys and how long you're out here for, told her you were cool, and she was happy for you to give him a call should the need arise, if you know what I'm sayin'. This is how the kids round here get by without liquor. How *I* used to get by, anyway. Or get high, should I say. Most of the high school kids are at it, so you might even get to meet some. But if you *do* get any more whilst yer out here, smoke it or ditch it before you fly home. Do *not* take it back on the plane with you. I'd never forgive myself. Oh, and use a payphone. There's one in town. Make sure you've got some quarters. Do *not* ring from home.'

Jack and Daisy didn't know what to say. They thanked her profusely; it could make all the difference. Tara really was a star. And they were thinking the same thing. Plenty of long walks ahead…

Not only had Tara come good for them, but she also insisted on swinging by the local liquor store to get some rolling papers, saying they were hard to come by – and even though Daisy was old enough, sometimes you needed a state or federal ID to purchase them. 'A baggy of pot without any papers is no good to anyone,' she said.

They pulled up in town and the rest of them waited in the

car while Tara went inside. Unlike Carol, the girls didn't seem to have any qualms about the youngsters being so close to the store. But Jack and Daisy both still felt nervous.

'Goddamn hick-town,' said Tara, returning to the car and closing the door forcefully. 'They didn't have any.' Despite this, she was clutching a brown paper grocery bag that she stashed by her feet. 'You'll have to have mine,' she said. 'I've got some in my bag.'

'God, no, we couldn't,' said Daisy.

'No, it's fine. Seriously. We're heading back tomorrow. I've still got a couple of Js rolled – we can have another tonight if you guys are up for it – and I can get more papers back in the city. Back in civilisation. You'll have to ask this Dewey kid to supply you some if you're runnin' short. I'm sure he'll oblige…'

That night for supper, despite Trish's protestations but at the girls' request, they had takeaway pizza for dinner. Phil was acting as if all his Christmases had come at once. 'As the Lord is my witness,' said Trish, 'once the girls go back tomorrow, Mister, you're back on the veggies.'

'I've still got Jack and Daisy's English banquet to come yet,' Phil protested. 'And Labor Day!' Banquet? What on earth was he expecting? thought Daisy. And what the hell was Labor Day?

The pizzas took an age to arrive. They'd come from a fair distance. Phil had paid extra for the honour – they'd done this before. And when the pizza delivery guy arrived at the door – Daisy loving how American it felt – the pizza boxes were simply huge. A stack of them, all seemingly two feet square. Phil tipped the delivery boy generously. He didn't look much older than Jack and Daisy, and called Phil 'Sir' when he tipped his baseball cap in thanks.

The pizzas were enormous: cheesy and greasy, but delicious. Jack had never had a takeaway pizza before, and neither had

Daisy, so it was something else ticked off the seemingly endless American bucket list. Daisy had margarita, Jack had pepperoni and Tara, oddly, had tuna and sweetcorn – which she called 'tuna-fish and sweetcorn', pronouncing it 'tooner'. Who'd have thought a pizza like this even existed? Sitting round the table, Phil filled the girls in on Jack and Daisy's English banquet. 'They're doing the whole nine yards, appetisers and everything,' he said.

'Gosh-darn it,' said Tara. 'I wish we were sticking around.'

'Well, I did suggest that,' said Phil, shrugging.

'We thought it might be a bit too much for them, cooking for everyone,' explained Trish.

'Sounds amazing, though,' said Sue. 'Whadya dishing up, guys? Any ideas yet?'

'That would be telling,' said Daisy, making them all laugh. 'We want it to be a surprise. But we've got a pretty good idea now, though, haven't we?'

Jack nodded shyly. He was pretty much there with his menu. Inspired by Trish and her home-grown produce, he was going to make soup, which was nice and easy, a cottage pie with some exciting veg – again, what was growing in the garden – and then for pudding a chocolate tart, as he knew Baz's recipe off by heart, with vanilla ice cream – he'd spotted a small machine in Trish's kitchen. Now that he'd got to know the girls and felt comfortable with them, he was kind of wishing he was cooking for them too.

'Ah, you can tell us later then,' whispered Tara, leaning into Daisy. 'We won't tell.'

The discussion moved on to the restaurant back home, and what Jack and Daisy's plans were now they'd handed in their notices. This was one thing they hadn't given much thought to: America had been all too new, all too consuming. 'Hey, maybe you should buy that diner for sale out Route 6 way,' said Tara. 'And you guys could run it – Jack in the kitchen, Daisy out front.'

'Now there's an idea,' said Phil. 'We went there yesterday. Such a shame about that place.'

'God, yes,' said Sue. 'Can you imagine? The locals'd love it. English owners – their accents – it'd be such a novelty.'

'Probably would, too,' said Phil. 'Especially if they were properly hands on. That's what that place needs.'

Trish rolled her eyes. 'If I had a dollar for every time I'd heard that. Why don't you just buy the place and run it yourself, dear?' she said.

'Yeah, Pops. Or better still, buy it for Jack and Daisy to run – can't be more than a hun-red grand – that's peanuts to you.' They all laughed.

'Hun-red grand?' said Phil. 'It ain't worth haff that, state the business's in. I'd like to see the books, put it that way.'

'Whoa, slow down,' said Carol. 'You lot trying to kidnap my daughter and keep her out here or what? She doesn't need any more silly ideas put into her head. What she needs is to knuckle down with her education.'

'Hear, hear,' said Trish. 'Kids need a proper education.'

Jack and Daisy said nothing – they hadn't had a chance – but they'd been listening in amusement. As for silly ideas being put in Daisy's head, it was a bit late for that – they already had been.

*****

The girls left the next morning. It was a surprisingly emotional affair for all concerned. Carol was the worst; she probably wouldn't see the girls again – or not on this trip anyway. She was blubbing and this set Trish off, too.

Jack and Daisy felt emotional, too. Despite the girls being somewhat older – twenty-three and twenty-five as it turned out – they had bonded with them so well, had so much fun. The previous night they'd been for another walk to the rocks by the stream and had another smoke, then returned to the veranda for more 'special lemonade' and cards. Before bed, Tara had handed over the weed and rolling papers, telling them to stash everything under the floorboard; it reminded Jack of the set-up in his old room. The girls wished them luck with their English meal and reiterated their invitation, 'Give it a few weeks or so, then call,' said Sue. 'We'll show you the sights.' Jack and Daisy felt ripples of excitement in their stomachs. This sounded amazing.

Before leaving, Phil insisted on taking photographs of them lined up on the porch. Daisy thought this was a fab idea and grabbed her camera too. She'd been taking quite a few snaps, trying to master all the settings. Giving Daisy one last hug before getting in the car, Tara whispered, 'Check under the floorboard in your room. There's another little surprise.'

Then they all waved the girls off, the sports car with its top down leaving a trail of dust on the long lane out of the property. Both of the girls had their sunglasses on again, their hair blowing out behind them, music on, waving and whooping. The place sure was going to be quieter without them.

Once they'd gone, Jack and Daisy immediately made their excuses and rushed upstairs. Closing the bedroom door, they cracked open the loose floorboard. There, lying next to their smoking stuff, nestled in the dusty alcove, was a pint of vodka, the same size bottle that Carol had bought, and a little note: 'ENJOY. SEE YOU GUYS IN NYC! X'. Tara must have bought the vodka from the store the previous day, but God knows when she had managed to sneak it in. Must have been that morning. Jack and Daisy looked at each other. She really was a star and had set them up good and proper. For the foreseeable anyway…

CHAPTER 32
Food for Thought

With the distraction of the girls out of the way, their stay – in the sense of a vacation – resumed. The day-to-day routine they had fallen into was interspersed with sightseeing trips. Now they had been there for getting on a week, they wanted to spread their wings. The Patch and surrounding area were lovely, so picturesque, but as Tara had pointed out it was so rural. Everything of note was several hours away – it all looked so much closer on the map. 'Welcome to America,' Phil said, shrugging. 'That's why we fly everywhere.' They all wanted to point out that this statement was negated by the airport being nearly four hours away.

One day, they all piled into the truck – even Trish – and after Phil had topped up with 'gas', they set off for Philadelphia: a proper American city, about three hours away. Phil told them proudly that it was famous for Independence Hall, where the Declaration of Independence had been signed and where the famous Liberty Bell rested. There were cobblestone streets and other historic buildings, including the Ben Franklin museum. But better than all this – in Phil's (and Daisy's) opinion – a trip to the city provided the opportunity to see his beloved 'Phillies', the city's famous baseball team, play at the Veterans Stadium. Phil had checked the schedule, and the Phillies were playing at home to the LA Dodgers that very day. Better still, the match was in the evening – which left the rest of the day free for sightseeing. 'A swell way to finish up,' Phil said.

The baseball stadium was simply vast, and despite being only about half full, was a sight to behold in the evening sun. The atmosphere was electric, with the echoing noise from the crowd quite intimidating. Jack couldn't help but notice that a lot of the fans looked overweight. Mobile vendors were working the stadium, trudging up and down the long stairs with metal boxes strapped round their necks. 'HOT DOGS! HOT DOGS HERE! COME AND GET YER DOGS!' 'ICE COLD BEER!' They were wearing brightly coloured polo shirts, shorts and baseball caps, some of them with shades. Daisy had no idea the hot dogs would be sold in this way – she'd imagined a stall or a cart, like at Glastonbury. She cajoled Jack into ordering one (there was no such thing as a veggie dog) just for the photo opportunity. Of course, Phil had one with all the trimmings.

Phil tried to explain the vagaries of the game and some of the baseball terminology – the plate, the pitch, curve-ball, foul-ball, infield, outfield – it was all bewildering, and so was the game; but Daisy *had* heard of a home-run and a strike. Jack hadn't a clue. Unfortunately, for Phil at least (the rest of them couldn't have cared less), the Phillies lost 5–1. Whether this was an especially bad loss or pretty normal was anybody's guess. But all in all, it was another memorable experience for the tourists.

*****

Trish had dug Tara and Sue's old pushbikes out of the outbuildings for Jack and Daisy. They were still in pretty good nick – just needed the tyres pumping up and some new batteries putting in the lights. The bikes provided some much-needed transport and independence. They were perfect for exploring the surrounding countryside, and also for nipping to the local shops. Carol was relieved: she'd been feeling a little guilty at how isolated the property was for the teenagers; they couldn't keep asking Phil for lifts.

Thrilled with their new transport, Jack and Daisy headed into Towanda to purchase some supplies for their English supper, items that weren't already at the house. Mince, more eggs, cream, chocolate. It gave them a wonderful sense of freedom to be away from the adults and cycling along the country lanes – it reminded Jack of when he'd first found his sister's bike. And, just like home, some of the hills were killers.

The day of the supper arrived. Jack and Daisy spent all day preparing it. They were a little nervous, but it wasn't as if they were cooking to order for dozens and dozens of people. There was no mad pressure or urgency, except to do a good job. And they'd chosen their menu well. It was nice to be busy, to have something to occupy them. Jack was enjoying the cooking; he'd all but lost interest back in Norfolk.

Under his instruction, Daisy was given the basic tasks, such as peeling and cubing the potatoes and prepping the veg. He joked that he was the head chef and she was his commis. Daisy didn't mind this at all; in fact, being ordered around by him really turned her on. She kept saying 'Yes, Chef!' or 'What do you want me to do with this again, Chef?', licking a spoon or holding a dubious-shaped vegetable suggestively.

The large farmhouse kitchen was a hive of activity, filled with the delicious, pungent and varied scents of cooking and also the sound of music emanating from Trish's radio-cassette player. Daisy had brought a few tapes with her, and neither of them could cook without music. Jack had a tea-towel draped over his shoulder as usual, so Daisy copied him. The adults found everything quite intriguing – especially Phil and Trish – and they wouldn't stay out of the kitchen. 'Ooh, what's this?' or 'What is that you're preparing now, Jack?' Trish nosily peered into pans and bowls. 'Ooh, I haven't seen that thing in action in years,' she remarked, pointing to the whirring ice cream machine. 'How exciting!'

Phil was more interested in trying things before they were finished, running a fat finger around a bowl or loitering with a spoon, like an overgrown child hoping for the cake mix bowl to lick out. He made appreciative noises, then said something like 'Keep up the good work, folks', and wandered off humming, with an impressed look on his face.

Jack and Daisy took it all in their stride. The nearest Jack got to being stressed was over the setting of the chocolate tart. This had to be cooked just so, then removed from the oven with a bit of a wobble left to the mix; overcook it, and the mix shrunk and cracked. And he wasn't used to Trish's gas oven. But everything seemed to go without a hitch, and the tart set up nicely.

The table was laid and set, decorated with glasses and napkins. Everyone was waiting, the food was ready to go, and Jack and Daisy had pinnies on ready to serve. Placing the soup in front of everyone was the first time Jack got real nerves; it was having to wait for their verdict. But he also felt a sense of pride. Daisy went round the table, serving the wine – begrudgingly omitting their own glasses – with a white serving cloth draped over her arm.

Trish insisted on saying grace before they got stuck in; it was another special occasion. And then, carried away by the occasion and to everyone's utter shock, Phil said, 'Oh, heck. You kids pour yourself a splash of wine. It ain't gonna hurt just this once. I can't imagine no law-enforcement officers will come knockin' on the door at this time o' night – and we'll hear 'em first if they do.'

Everyone was gobsmacked, especially Aunt Trish. 'Mercy me,' she said. 'I never thought I'd see the day.'

Carol beamed from ear to ear. 'Aw, thanks, Phil,' she said,

leaning across to peck him on a bushy, rosy cheek. She was flushed and teary-eyed. Jack and Daisy were astounded: it was the gesture more than anything. Phil suddenly went up in their estimation.

The soup was devoured to murmurs of appreciation and promptly declared delicious. Then the individual cottage pies – the main event – were brought steaming to the table. There were more 'oohs and aahs' as Jack and Daisy dished them out, golden and crispy-topped, garnished with leaves of flat-leaf parsley plucked from the garden. Not to leave her out, Jack had gone to the trouble of creating a vegetarian version of the pie for Daisy, omitting the mince and replacing it with butter beans and more veg.

'My oh my,' said Phil, wiping his chin with a napkin. 'No offence, darl, but I've never tasted pie like that in my life. And the gravy!'

'None taken,' said Trish. 'I agree. It is *simply* delicious. So flavoursome.'

'Do all English cottage pies taste like this?' said Phil.

'Trust me, no,' said Carol. 'At least mine never do. Well done, Jack – and Daisy. This really is superb.' She was very proud of them. Jack and Daisy blushed.

'Talk us through the vegetables, Jack – so interesting and so much flavour,' said Trish. 'You're gonna have to leave some of these recipes for me. Maybe then Phil will take more of an interest in eating them.'

Jack suddenly felt shy. He wasn't used to discussing his recipes with anyone – other than Daisy, of course. 'Go on,' Daisy said, squeezing his hand to encourage him. 'Start with the spinach.' They all waited patiently. Phil and Trish were starting to get used to the fact that Jack was shy, painfully so; unlike their own two children. Jack swallowed the last of his wine and cleared his throat.

'It's creamed spinach,' he said. 'With a little garlic and nutmeg – and seasoning, of course.'

'Nutmeg,' said Trish. 'I knew there was some sort of spice in there. It works so well – and that hint of garlic.'

'Mmm, it's lovely,' Carol said.

'And what's in the cabbage?' said Phil. 'How the hell d'you get it to taste like that?' He couldn't get enough of the gravy, liberally pouring more of it .

'Smoked bacon,' said Jack, gaining confidence. 'Stock and fresh sage – from the herb patch.'

'It's a revelation,' said Trish.

'I love the roast squash,' said Carol. 'Kind of sweet but savoury at the same time. With a hint of heat.'

'Cayenne pepper,' said Jack. 'A little garlic and plenty of seasoning again. And the asparagus is, well, just asparagus, finished with a squeeze of lemon, butter and plenty of black pepper.'

'This is not *just* asparagus, it's divine,' said Trish.

Daisy beamed at Jack, her face filled with love and pride.

They had a break for dessert, to give everyone's stomachs a bit of a breather and for Jack and Daisy to get most of the pots out of the way. Trish protested that she wanted to help, but Daisy wouldn't let her. 'Those two are *angels*,' she said to Carol, returning to the table. 'You're very lucky: my two would have left the pots – take after their father – and they certainly wouldn't have cooked for us like this.' Phil got up to put a Glen Campbell record on, and they all had a bit of a singalong to 'Rhinestone Cowboy', the older folks drinking their wine, whilst the youngsters dried the dishes.

Then the dessert was served. Jack was most proud of this. Pie was pie to him, but a dessert could be a work of art – and this certainly looked it. A glossy, mud-coloured wedge of chocolate tart, beautifully presented with an ivory ball of vanilla ice cream and plump raspberries sitting on top and heart-shaped bursts of raspberry coulis adorning the plate.

'For once, I'm speechless,' said Phil. Having already

devoured the tart, he was practically scraping the pattern off the plate with his spoon.

'Me too,' said Trish. 'That's possibly the finest meal I've ever eaten in my life.'

'Just amazing,' said Carol. 'You can do this more often back home.'

Jack and Daisy both had lumps in their throats.

'You've got a talent, son,' said Phil. 'Seriously. You'd make a killing up at that diner. They'd come from miles around for grub like that. Just like the old days.'

'Oh, don't start in on that again,' said Trish. 'What do you think they're gonna do? Emigrate out here, just so you can eat yourself to death?'

'Yeah,' Carol laughed. 'It really would be the death of you! Sorry, I shouldn't laugh.'

'What a way to go, though,' said Phil. 'But why not? They're young. No ties from what I hear … nothing to lose… I'd invest in 'em on the strength of that meal alone. Great lookin' girl like Daisy out front…' Daisy blushed.

'Oh, Phil,' said Trish.

'Just sayin'…' he shrugged, rocking back in his seat. 'I've got money to invest burnin' a hole in my pocket. Been lookin' for somethin' for a while…'

Carried away by the moment and the praise, Daisy blurted out, 'So have we. Money, that is. Lots of it. Well, Jack has anyway.' Oops. Jack couldn't believe what she was saying. She wasn't seriously considering it, was she?

'Really?' said Phil.

'Yeah. We've run our own ice cream business too.'

Carol tutted. 'Oh, for Christ's sake, Daisy… See what you've started?' she berated Phil. 'It wasn't exactly a business, was it?'

'It was. We bought produce, made a product and sold it at a profit. That's a business.'

'Sounds like a business to me,' said Phil.

'We made nearly four hundred quid some days,' said Daisy.

'I'm impressed,' said Phil. 'There's a lot more to you young folk than meets the eye. I'm starting to realise that.'

'You don't know the half of it,' muttered Carol under her breath.

'I think you've all had too much wine,' said Trish. 'And possibly gone mad at the same time.'

'Food for thought, that's all,' said Phil. 'Food for thought. We'll discuss this further when your mother's not around.' And he gave the teenagers a wink, still rocking back on his chair, his hands interlaced over his huge belly. Jack and Daisy laughed.

'Shush now,' said Trish, smacking him. 'Now, who wants coffee?'

CHAPTER 33
A Recce

From that night on, the idea of the diner wouldn't leave Daisy. It became her new obsession. This was how her brain worked. She and Jack spent most of their time alone together talking about it, during the day on their walks and late into the night in bed. In the dark, with their heads still spinning a bit from a drink and a smoke – that weed was strong stuff, especially smoking it neat – the idea really came alive, became tangible. They'd come out here to plan their next move. Maybe this could be it. What else were they going to do? Everything seemed so dull and unappealing. But the idea of a business – running a business, being her own boss – seemed so stimulating and exciting. She must have got this from her dad: he had the same entrepreneurial spirit, was a self-made man. She loved the figures side of things too.

They decided to visit the diner again, but without Phil this time. Daisy had been wanting to go back anyway, and now she wanted to see how she felt about the place – the good and the bad – without Phil's influence. Maybe to put the idea to bed one way or another. Perhaps it was a stupid idea, a pipe dream. Even though Phil had lit a fire in Daisy the other night, he hadn't mentioned it since – perhaps it had been too much wine talking. It was Labor Day weekend – a big deal in America by all accounts – and Phil had been preoccupied with planning it; mainly which sports he was going to watch. They were going to have another barbecue on Monday, officially Labor Day, to celebrate.

Jack and Daisy set off on their bikes. It was a bit of a trek to the diner – the furthest they had been – but what else did they have to do? Whilst they were out, they were going to take the opportunity to call Dewey, the weed guy – to kill two birds with one stone: their stash was all but gone. They stopped in Towanda to locate the phone box, and found it tucked away against a wall on Main Street. Unlike red English phone boxes that stood out a mile, the payphone was a small rectangular hood housing a phone set on a stand, all made of dull silver metal. It still looked kind of cool, though. A sign read 'LOCAL CALLS. 25 CENTS'. Daisy was looking forward to feeding some American coins into the slot; they made such a satisfying sound in the movies.

She pulled out the note with the number on it and picked up the receiver, holding it out to Jack. 'Right, you can do the talking.'

'Why me?' said Jack.

''Cause you're a boy. He's a boy.'

'So?'

'That's how it works. I deal with girls, you deal with boys.'

'But I don't know him and I don't know what to say.'

'Well, neither do I. Say who you are and introduce yourself – but make sure it's him. Don't go blabbin' to his parents or something.'

'You do it,' he said, handing the receiver back. 'I'll mess it up.'

'Oh, for Pete's sake.' She took the receiver, fed some coins into the slot and began to punch in the number. It began to ring. Daisy began to feel a little nervous. After about four rings, the phone was picked up and a boy's voice said, 'What's up.' It was a deep, mature voice, which threw Daisy. And why was he asking what was up? She hadn't even spoken.

'Erm, hello. Is that Dewey?'

'Who wants to know?'

'Erm, my name's Daisy. I'm Tara's cousin from England – she's friends with your older sister.' His sister's name went right out of her head. Shit, shit, shit! 'We met her at the bowling alley the other day; well, Tara did. She spoke to your sister – Ruth – and she gave us your number in case we needed it.'

'Needed it for what?'

Again, Daisy was thrown. She felt flustered and didn't want to say anything incriminating out loud. 'Well, you know – "should the need arise",' she said, quoting Tara. 'This *is* Dewey, isn't it?' She looked at Jack.

Suddenly, the kid burst out laughing, right in Daisy's ear. 'Sorry, I'm only messin' with ya. Oh my God! You are *so* English! Ruthy said you might call.' Daisy let out a huge sigh of relief and looked at Jack again. 'Not gonna lie, I was expectin' a dude, though. You got a boyfriend, don't ya?'

'Yes, Jack, he's right here.'

'Ah, thought so. Interesting…'

'I'm Tara's cousin, that's all. Not Jack. So we thought it would be best if *I* call…'

'Nah, that's cool…'

There was silence for a second. Daisy had never ordered weed over the phone before, neither of them had, so it was difficult to know what to say without saying it outright. 'Sooo … we were wondering…'

'Yep,' he said, cutting her off. 'That's cool.'

'It is?'

'Yep.'

'Cool,' said Daisy.

'What you guys doin' tonight?'

'Tonight?' That was unexpected. 'Nothing, I don't think.

No plans. Have we, Jack?' She wanted to bring Jack into it, to prove that he existed. It almost felt as if she was getting chatted up.

'No,' said Jack, a quizzical look on his face.

'You wanna come to a pardy?'

'A party?'

'Yes, a keg-pardy at a friend's. And a bit of a smoke, of course.'

'Oh gosh,' said Daisy. 'I don't know about that.'

'So English...' the boy said again. 'Love it.' There was another pause. 'Well?'

'Hold on,' said Daisy. She put her hand over the receiver. 'He's asking if we want to go to a party.' She shrugged. Jack shook his head firmly, his shyness and anxiety immediately kicking in. 'But what about the stuff?' said Daisy. 'How do I say no?' Jack scuffed his shoe on the ground, non-committal. Why did everything always have to be so complicated? Daisy was thinking the same. 'Hold on,' she said again, but to Jack this time. Then to Dewey, 'Will there be other girls there?'

Dewey laughed again. 'Oh my, you're crackin' me up, Princess Di. Yeah, there'll be other girls there. A few anyway. It's no big deal: a few of us guys hanging out, a few girls, having a smoke, no more than ten or so. My buddy's parents are away for the weekend. Thought you could hang out for a bit whilst I sort you out, that's all.'

'OK. Where?' said Daisy. She looked at Jack. He was looking none too pleased. She made exasperated eyes back at him as Dewey gave her the address.

'You cain't miss it,' he said. 'Towanda ain't a big place, as you've probably already fig-yered. First right after the bar and grill on the corner, then Nate's house is on the left about haff-way down the block. It's got a big ol' RV with a flat tyre parked out front.'

'RV?' said Daisy.

374

'Recreational ve-hicle.' Daisy tried not to laugh at the exaggerated pronunciation. 'You know. What you guys would call a motorhome, I guess.'

'Ah,' said Daisy. 'Got it. Great. Oh, and what time?'

'Any time after eight's fine.'

'Great. See you then. Thanks a lot, Dewey.'

'No problem at all. See you later.'

Daisy hung up. 'What was I meant to do?' she said, turning to Jack.

'Say no.'

'What, and then not get the stuff?' Jack said nothing, still scuffing the ground with his foot. 'You can do the talking in future,' Daisy said. 'In fact, you need to get used to doing a lot more talking in general, buster. Especially with strangers. You can't run a diner without speaking to people.' Daisy immediately regretted this outburst; he couldn't help his fear of strangers, his anxiety – it was his upbringing. 'Look, we'll just say a quick hello. Maybe have a quick toke for decency's sake, then get straight out of there. OK?' Jack nodded. Daisy went over and kissed him, and nuzzled his nose a bit. Then they got on their bikes. 'He called me Lady Di,' Daisy said.

*****

Arriving at the diner, they parked their bikes in front of one of the big windows where they could keep an eye on them – if they could see through the condensation. That really needed sorting: it was so off-putting. What with the smell as well, no wonder folks stayed away. But on the plus side, if the extraction was sorted as a priority, the only way would be up.

Approaching the entrance, Daisy went into 'business mode'. It almost happened naturally. She looked at everything through the eyes of a potential customer and proprietor. The peeling paint on the windows and doors all needed stripping and redoing. The weeds, the patchy gravel, both needed addressing. She pictured welcoming pots of fresh flowers and plants out front, some bursts of colour. Mum could help with that. That ironic sign on the door 'SORRY WE'RE OPEN' could stay. She liked it: it tickled her for some reason. Sadly, it was too close to the truth, though. The doorbell clanged as they entered. Did they want to keep that? It gave the place the feel of an old-fashioned high street shop back home, rather than a diner. If the place was heaving and fully staffed, they wouldn't need it.

The fried food smell and haze hit them again. It just wasn't good enough. The last thing people wanted was to leave with their hair and clothes stinking, or even to eat in such an environment. She wondered how much it would cost to fix. Di looked up from behind the till. 'Well, howdy there,' she said, instantly recognising them. 'Welcome back! How you both doin'? You enjoyin' your vacation?' A couple of customers at the counter turned round to see whom she was talking to.

'Yes. Lovely, thanks,' said Daisy. It was so important to remember customers, she thought. Di was a pro. *She* could stay. Wonder if she came with the inventory?

'Aw, I'm so pleased to hear it. We haven't scared you off yet then?' she laughed. 'Where's the big guy? Not with you today? Or your mom?'

'No, just us today,' said Daisy.

'Well, take a seat, darlin's, anywhere you like. I'll be right on over with some menus.'

The two old guys at the bar watched with interest and wonder as the English teenagers sat down, as if scrutinising an alien species.

Jack and Daisy chose the same booth as before. But this time Daisy sat facing the other way, so she could see more of the diner. That reminded her: she needed to visit the loos to see what shape they were in. Jack watched as she reached into her rucksack and pulled out her journal that doubled as a notebook. 'What have you brought that for?' he asked.

'To make notes, of course.' She opened it on the table and began to scribble with a biro. As always, Jack was silently amazed to watch her at work. He ran his finger down the wet window, as Phil had. Then, trying to think like Daisy, he tried to spot where the kitchen was, hoping he could peer into it, to see how big it was and why the extraction was so bad. He spotted a door behind the counter, presumably the kitchen, but it only had one small, cross-hatched window in it that he couldn't see through.

'All righty then,' said Di, appearing with two menus and that big smile. 'I'm so pleased you came back.' Daisy put a napkin over her notes. 'Been wonderin' how you folks been getting' on.'

'Really?' said Daisy.

'Yes, really. It's not often we get English folks in here, especially such polite ones. Y'all been doin' some sightseeing?' Daisy filled her in on what they'd been up to. 'Oh, I just love Philly,' she said in response. 'And I could listen to you talk all day long. Now, what can I fix you lovely people to drink?' They were both thirsty after the bike ride, and ordered sodas. 'Comin' right up,' said Di. She then went through her spiel about the items and specials they hadn't got or had run out of, being as apologetic as the previous time. It must get very tedious and embarrassing, Daisy thought. As soon as Di had gone, she made more notes.

Di returned with their drinks, and after she had taken their food order (two grilled cheese sandwiches again), Daisy asked, as casually as she could, how business had been. 'Oh, much the same really. Quiet. A lot of folks is away, on account of it being Labor Day weekend.' She looked a little sad for a moment. 'Although we did have a coach party in yesterday. Just turned up and pulled in. Caused chaos, I tell yer. I wish they wouldn't do that. Who just turns up with a coachload of old folks without giving some warning? Of course, I was on my own…' She tutted and looked sad again. A little tired. God only knew how she had dealt with that, Daisy thought. She deserved better. 'They was out of state, of course. The local boys always give me a heads up – or at least used to. Used to get heaps of them, back in the day – coaches – but then we had the staff to deal with it. Just drive on by now – knowing they'll have to wait too long, I guess. Honk and wave an' tip their caps at me through the window as they're passin'.' What a waste of potential revenue, Daisy thought. She would make a note of it.

'How long you been here, Di?' Daisy said. 'Worked here, I mean.'

'My gosh, now yer askin'. Must be getting on for five years now all in all. Used to be a waitress, you see, then a year or so ago – when the last manager quit, one of many – they just promoted me. Just a title is all, though, if you ask me. Same hours – longer in fact – same pay, more stress. I must be mad,' she laughed. 'Yes, nearly five years… How the time goes… Anyway, listen to me prattling on about my woes. Let me get your food on the go. You poor things must be starvin' after yer bike ride.' She didn't miss a trick. '*You* don't say a lot, do yer, handsome?' she said to Jack as she took his menu away.

Jack thanked her and blushed. 'He doesn't,' Daisy laughed. 'I keep telling him. Oh, can I keep mine, please?' she said, meaning the menu. 'I just wanted to have another look.'

'Bless him. Just shy is all. And sure, sugar. If you want anything else, just holler. But if yer gonna change yer mind, then hurry up. Mikey'll be spittin' his pacifier out.' And she waltzed off, laughing.

Daisy immediately made more notes before she forgot them. Her brain was racing. Then she looked up. Jack was looking a bit sorry for himself. 'Come round here next to me, "handsome"', she said, patting her booth seat. It had unsightly holes in it, and the foam stuffing inside was visible.

'I want your opinion on the menu. Your ideas. You're the chef extraordinaire.' Jack came round. She gave him a peck on the cheek, then they studied the menu together, from top to bottom – making notes on what they'd keep, what they'd get rid of and what the menu was missing. It was a useful exercise.

Before long, Di returned with their sandwiches: quicker than last time. Maybe the best cook was back on. Mikey, was it? Or perhaps it was because it was so quiet. Perhaps that was why Di was so chatty today, too, even more so than before. Daisy couldn't help but take advantage of this. 'What's the most popular dish on the menu?' she asked. 'Or dishes. What do people tend to go for?'

'Oh.' Di sounded surprised. 'A lot of questions today, young lady! Yer not fixin' to buy the place or somethin' are you? You and yer Uncle Phil?' And she let out that cackling laugh of hers. Shit, thought Daisy. Was she being that obvious? She wasn't used to this stuff.

Daisy laughed in response, but she didn't want to lie. 'Oh, we're just interested, that's all. We work in a restaurant back home, you see – or did. Jack's a chef.'

'Really?' said Di. 'Well, I never. How interesting! Not a drunk one, I hope, like that guy off the TV – Floyd isn't it? Keith Floyd. He's so funny. Always seems haff-cut. But very entertaining. And so English!'

'Yeah, my dad likes him. Liked him…' said Daisy.

'But, in answer to your question … hmm … don't sell a huge amount of anythin' at the minute is the plain truth.' Di cocked her head towards the menu. 'The omelettes always go, we serve a few of them… Depends on the time of day, really. Later on, it's the burger and the club, I guess…'

'And is there anything that doesn't sell at all? Like, none?'

'Gosh. Ev'rything. It's awful really. Always chucking stuff away. Cryin' shame, all that waste. End up takin' stuff home m'self – and the chefs do. Saves buyin' dinner, I guess …

about the only perk o' the job. But, that's why we ain't doin' the specials of late, just don't seem worth it, just more stuff to chuck away. But then that stops folks comin' in, so it's a vicious circle. There's too much on the menu, really…'

'I agree,' said Daisy. 'If you don't mind me saying, it *is* a large menu.'

'Don't mind at all, darl. Sounds like you both know yer stuff. Right, if you guys are all set, I'll leave you to it. Enjoy your food.'

They thanked her and she waltzed off, humming. All very interesting, thought Daisy.

Once they'd finished their sandwiches, they got up to visit the loos before leaving – Daisy insisted Jack did too, to see what the Gents were like. Only thing was, they couldn't see them anywhere. Nor any signage. 'You all right, darl?' Di said, seeing them standing there, looking confused.

'Toilets,' Daisy said. 'Sorry. Where are they?'

'If I had a dollar for every time someone asked me that,' said Di. 'Round the corner, far right-hand corner. I've been askin' for better signs ever since I became so-called manager o' this place.'

Bet she has, too, thought Daisy. 'Thanks, Di.'

To Daisy's big surprise, the Ladies was actually OK. In fairly good nick: out of keeping with the rest of the place, like the floor. The equipment too – the drinks machines and all that – seemed fairly new and in good order, probably because they hadn't been used much. 'Well?' she said to Jack. He was waiting for her.

'OK, I guess,' he said. 'A bit smelly.'

'Ugh, yuk. Shame. The Ladies is OK.' She knew she wasn't going to get a definitive answer out of a man: Jack's 'OK' probably meant they were gross.

They settled their bill at the counter. Learning from Phil, and wanting to, they left Di a huge tip – about twenty-five per cent. She deserved it and they felt so sorry for her. 'Oh,

goodness. You don't have to tip me that much, darl. Here!'
And she tried to give a couple of dollar bills back.

'No. We insist,' said Daisy. 'Just hope things pick up for you today.'

'Well, ain't you just the sweetest,' said Di. 'Thank you. And you be sure to say hello to yer Uncle Phil for me. Enjoy the rest of your Labor Day weekend.'

'We will. You too,' said Daisy.

'And go easy on them pushbikes!'

*****

All the way back, Daisy couldn't stop thinking about the diner. Despite its lack of customers – and the smell – there was something about the place. A charm, a homeliness. And Di. She made you *want* to tip her. Want to go back. Daisy thought they would make a good team. Imagine it with great food too, with Jack in the kitchen. And a bit of advertising or marketing – letting people know it had changed hands; getting it back on the map. The place needed that juke box, too. Daisy hadn't spotted one anywhere: a traditional, retro one. Like off *Back to The Future* or *Grease*. It would really change the feel of the place. And what about some outside seating? If people see a place looking busy, it draws them in. Like Aitch had said, 'Business creates business'. Like the wheels on her bike, Daisy's brain was whirring round. They needed to talk to Uncle Phil; to see if he'd been serious or not. She thought they could afford to buy it themselves with Jack's money, but she was getting ahead of herself; they couldn't get an advance on more than half the money before he was eighteen anyway. How much did a run-down diner cost? It was a huge risk doing it on their own. What did they know about running a business? A proper business. Rates and insurance and accounts and all?

As they cycled up the winding drive, a bit of a slog after a long bike ride, they spotted the adults in the horses' field.

Amazingly, both Carol and Phil were on horseback, trotting round the field, with Trish in tow, looking tiny and apparently giving them instructions – Carol, anyway. She was on the smaller horse, Peppermint. They presumed it was Phil on the other one – as there weren't that many men around who were his size, but it was hard to tell as he was somewhat bizarrely dressed as a cowboy, ten-gallon hat and everything. The adults spotted them and waved, the cowboy removing his hat and brandishing it above his head. Yep, it was Phil. The kids waved back, then stopped to watch. Seeing her mum riding a horse was a bizarre sight for Daisy, and an amusing one. They heard Phil shout 'G'won! Giddy up!' and he spurred his horse into life. Showing off, probably.

'Hey, don't say anything about the diner just yet. Tell you why in a bit,' Daisy said to Jack.

The horse's hooves made a fair old thump on the ground as Phil approached, but it was a satisfying sound. 'Woah, there; easy, boy,' he said, pulling sharply on the reins and slowing the horse. As with the bowling, Phil looked surprisingly agile and impressively deft in his control; he had probably been a good athlete in his youth. The horse slowed to a steady trot, snorting and breathing heavily. No wonder, they thought, carrying all that weight. Phil was breathing heavily too, his face flushed and sweating, and he removed his hat to mop his brow. He really had gone to town, with a pale blue chambray shirt with tassels and shiny tips on the lapels, denim jeans, tan leather gloves, cowboy boots and a big, shiny-buckled belt. Daisy found it funny, but Jack secretly thought the outfit was wonderful. It gave him flashbacks to his childhood, when he'd been obsessed with John Wayne and Westerns and cowboys, had wanted to be one. 'Well, howdy there, partners,' Phil said.

'Well, howdy there yourself, cowboy,' Daisy said in response. And they all burst out laughing.

'Yeah, don't mind the outfit,' said Phil. 'I don't ride that often these days, but when I do, I like to look the part.'

'Well, why not?' said Daisy tactfully. 'Very swish. And you certainly look like you know how to ride.'

'Well, thank you kindly. I'm not too bad. But Trish puts me to shame. She goes like the wind.'

'Look at you,' said Daisy to her mum, who had made her way over with Trish at a more sedate speed. Carol was flushed and beaming, with a riding hat on. It made her look like a young girl, and she looked as if she was enjoying herself again.

'I know,' said Carol. 'Can you believe it? I haven't ridden in years, not since before you girls were born. It's so exhilarating. You ought to try it. And Jack!'

'Oh, God, I don't know,' said Daisy. 'I'd probably fall off and break my neck.'

'Ah, not if you take it steady, you won't. That's all I'm doing. She's a darling, aren't you?' Carol said, patting the horse's neck. It was all so strange for Daisy.

'Where you guys been anyway? Anywhere special?' said Phil.

'Not really. Just getting to know the area, that's all,' Daisy lied. 'These bikes are a godsend.'

'Well, I'm glad they've come in useful,' said Trish. 'They've only been sitting there in the shed since the girls left. They've got no room for them in the apartment. Expect there's not much call for a pushbike in New York City anyways.'

'True,' said Daisy. 'Right, we'd best be getting back up to the house. Could do with a drink.'

'There's a jug of lemon iced tea in the fridge. I made it special for the weekend. Try it with some chipped ice, it's lovely. So refreshing,' said Trish.

*****

They were back in their room, sitting on their beds with the window open slightly to let in the breeze. The days seemed to be warming up. They tried the lemon iced tea. Neither of them had had this before. It had always seemed an odd concept to Daisy – and Jack had never even heard of such a thing. But it was a revelation: robustly flavoured, but sweet, lemony and refreshing. The liquid was an appealing dark honey colour. The light from the window shone through it. There had been lemon slices and mint sprigs in the jug too, giving the whole thing the appearance of Pimm's, something Daisy's mum and dad had drunk in summer when Wimbledon was on. The mint imparted a subtle extra flavour. 'What d'you reckon?' she said.

'Yeah, it's nice,' said Jack. 'Refreshing.'

'Isn't it? God, imagine serving this at the diner. I bet it'd go down a storm. "Aunt Trish's Lemon Iced Tea – a secret recipe!" People love stuff like that.' She needed to write it down.

'Yeah,' agreed Jack.

'Hey, imagine it with vodka in it,' said Daisy. 'Now, there's an idea. Almost like a cocktail.'

'Now, that *is* a good idea,' said Jack. 'That could be our new drink. We ought to try it – secretly, of course.'

They sat back on their beds, propped against their pillows, sipping their iced tea as the net curtain flirted with the breeze. Times like this were the magic moments in America: time-slowed and amber-dusted afternoons.

'Hey, why didn't you want to talk to Phil about the diner?' Jack asked. 'I thought you'd be dying to. I thought that was the idea.'

'I am, but I was just thinking about tonight. We've got to go and get the stuff, remember. And I've been thinking about it. I don't even know how we're going to escape as it is – without us engaging Phil in some lengthy discussion about the diner as well. You know what he's like: once he knows we're really interested, that'll be it for the night. Then Mum'll get involved, too… So I thought we were better off waiting till tomorrow.'

'Yeah, good point,' said Jack.

'And I mean, where are we even gonna say that we're going

tonight? At that time in the evening? We can't just keep saying we're going on bike rides or walks, especially if it's getting dark. And what if we have to stay for a bit to have a smoke?' Jack looked at her. 'Just saying. It'd be rude not to. Especially if we want to get some more at some point. Our clothes are gonna stink for a start. Again. Mum doesn't even know I smoke. How we gonna get around that one?'

Jack pondered this for a moment. She was right. Again. When they used to smoke at the Love Shack, they used to come out stinking. 'Well, what if we go later? Much later? Sneak out when everyone's in bed.'

'God, it's a bit risky … and what if we get caught – or locked out?'

'I know. But I don't know what else we can do. They normally head up around nineish, and we get left on our own then. Just hope these sports don't go on too long.'

'But what about Mum? She doesn't always go up that early. And I don't like lying to her either. Sneaking out.'

'Dunno… Well, for all she knows, we've gone for a late-night stroll – on the premises. We normally stay on the porch till late anyway. I mean how long we gonna be out for? An hour? Another reason not to stay too long.'

Jack was making sense, thought Daisy. If they did tell her mum, get her involved, she would only want to know where they were going, why and with whom. How they'd met them and when. She'd probably wait up for them – and then she would smell them. 'OK,' she said. 'Just hope this "keg-pardy" is going on till then. It's gonna be about ten-thirty by the time we get there. Good job those bikes have got lights. Guess they need them round here. And what even is a keg party anyway?'

'Search me,' Jack shrugged.

*****

Later that afternoon, their plan hit a major snag. They found out from Phil that the culmination – and highlight – of his day's sports marathon was a Phillies game that was starting at nine-thirty. Talk about timing. He even asked if they wanted to watch it with him. They politely passed, but it proved a problem. There was no way they could wait until that had finished – judging by the game they had watched, it would last for several hours. They had no choice but to sneak out – with any luck whilst he was still engrossed in the game – and then creep back upstairs afterwards; at least the lounge was nowhere near the stairs. If they did get sprung, they'd just have to say they'd gone for a stroll.

CHAPTER 34

Our Man in Towanda

Dewey's appearance dashed all Daisy's preconceptions. Judging from the phone conversation – his cocksure, laid-back demeanour – and the fact he was peddling dope, she had drawn the conclusion that he was a townie, or whatever the equivalent was out in rural America. Was it a jock? Popular. A bit of a poseur. A wide boy. Full of himself. Smart, trendy clothes, and into mainstream or dance music. Daisy had pictured one of those guys off the American TV shows and films – neat quiffed and gelled hair, one of those two-tone college jackets with the big initials stitched on them. Skinny, pretty, barbie-doll cheerleader girlfriend…

With the baseball game already started, Jack and Daisy made their escape the minute Carol had retired for the night, saying goodnight to her on the porch. But the clock was ticking, and they raced to Towanda on their bikes. As they stood outside the door of the property they had been directed to, they were feeling very nervous. It was strange and daunting to be invited to a house-party full of strangers – in your own country, never mind a foreign one. The house itself was modest, unremarkable, nothing to write home about – unlike some of the houses they had passed: huge, fancy and imposing properties, some of them old-fashioned and slightly Southern

387

in style. Jack and Daisy were starting to get to know the town a bit now. The phone box. Main Street. The handful of shops. The gas station. They had passed a gun club, whatever that was, and a bar or two – one of them very busy: it was Saturday night after all. They heard loud music and the crack of pool balls from within – just what Daisy had been hankering after. That snapshot of small-town America. And, as Dewey had said, Towanda was a small town.

They rang the doorbell and waited. They could hear faint music from within. No one answered. Jack and Daisy looked at each other. They knew it was the right house: that RV was on the drive. Daisy pressed the doorbell again. After another minute, the shape of a person approached the door. This was it. Jack and Daisy held their breath.

The door was unlocked, then it opened a crack and a girl's head poked out cautiously. They hadn't expected this; nor for her to be Asian. She was pretty, with long, perfectly straight, jet-black hair. 'Oh. Hey,' she said. 'Come in.' And she opened the door properly. She looked and sounded a bit spaced-out, probably stoned, and had a plastic cup of beer in her hand. She was wearing black drainpipes and Doc Martens, a black T-shirt with a long-sleeved white sweatshirt underneath. Almost 'gothy' in a way. This wasn't a bad start, thought Daisy.

'Thanks,' Daisy said. And they walked in.

'Woah,' the girl said. 'You're, like … English?'

'Yeah,' laughed Daisy shyly.

'No way,' the girl said. 'I didn't think I'd seen you around. You here for the pardy? You know Nate?' She seemed amazed, and to have woken up a little.

'No, Dewey actually. Is he here?'

'You know Dewey?'

'Er, yes. No. Sort of. It's complicated. He asked us to meet him here.'

'OK…' She dragged it out in her American drawl. Then

she stood there, trying to take it all in. 'And you're, like, English too?' she turned to Jack.

Daisy was starting to lose her patience a little. The girl was sounding drunk and spaced again. Before Jack could answer, she said, 'Yes, he's English, I'm English, we're both English. Is Dewey here? We're in a bit of a rush, you see…'

'Shit. Yeah, he's here. We're all in the basement. We've got a keg. Come on, I'll show you the way. Oh, wait, let me lock the door again. Nate'll kill me… Right, follow me.' They passed a kitchen, littered with snacks, bottles and pizza boxes, and headed down the hall to a door that was ajar. The music, which was getting louder, was coming from behind the door. The girl opened the door to reveal a set of stairs. The familiar smell of marijuana smoke hit them and the music got louder still. Daisy recognised it as Hüsker Dü, a heavy band she loved, which was again surprising and promising. With their hearts pummelling in anticipation, Jack and Daisy followed the girl down the stairs. 'I hope you guys pardy,' she said over the music.

That expression again. 'Er, yes,' Daisy said.

'Good job! I'm Ash, by the way. Nate's girlfriend.'

Before Daisy could introduce herself, they had rounded the bottom of the stairs and were in a dimly lit basement. Through a fog of smoke, a raft of teenage faces, girls and boys, stared at them, like rats in a sewer. Most of them looking monged out. Some of them were sitting on a tatty old sofa in front of a TV; some were standing around. Daisy and Jack both gulped, their hearts beating even harder. Jack lurked behind Daisy. 'Dewey. Your English friends are here,' Ash shouted.

'Shit!' said one lad, standing up. He was holding a bong – like Aitch's. 'Here,' he said, thrusting it into the hands of the guy next to him. The speaker had long, straggly hair, a little bit greasy, and was wearing baggy jeans and Converse boots, a short-sleeved blue and black checked shirt with a Nirvana sweatshirt underneath. Chains linked his jeans pocket to his belt. He had a piercing in his nose. 'Turn the music down,' he shouted.

Panicking, the guy nearest the stereo went one step further and bounced the needle off altogether, making an ugly scratching sound as the music suddenly stopped. 'Shit! Sorry!' he said, embarrassed.

'I said down turn it down, not off, you doofus,' said the Kurt Cobain wannabe. And then there was silence, save for some sniggering, as everyone stared at Jack and Daisy again, some of them looking a bit shy. 'Dewey!' the guy said, hitching up his jeans and approaching them to shake hands. The music started up again, albeit at a lower volume.

'Daisy,' said Daisy, shaking his hand.

With every ounce of courage within him, Jack stepped out from behind Daisy. 'Jack,' he said shyly, unable to meet Dewey's gaze as he shook his hand. Strangely, someone somewhere whistled at the sight of Jack. It happened quickly and there was a lot going on, but Daisy registered it nonetheless. Maybe it was in response to Jack's body. He was wearing a fairly tight T-shirt, and at first glance none of the guys looked like him. The whistle sounded male at least.

'Woah, you guys are English? Awesome,' said the guy holding the bong. He, too, stood up to shake hands. 'Nate,' he said. Jack and Daisy said hello and shook his hand. He was wearing a Sonic Youth T-shirt, which was cool in Daisy's eyes. These guys obviously loved their music.

'Dude, I told you they were English,' said Dewey.

'No, you didn't,' said Nate.

'I did! Dickwad!' Daisy couldn't help but laugh. It felt to her as if they'd stepped into a real-life version of *Bill and Ted's Excellent Adventure*. But she was already starting to relax. These guys seemed harmless; she could see herself getting comfortable here. 'This is Nate's place, by the way, not mine. His folks are out of town. Woah, I already told you that, didn't I?' He slapped his forehead.

'Yeah, you did,' Daisy laughed again.

'Give the girl some space, dude,' said Nate, taking over. 'Come and sit down. Clear a space, guys, give them some room.' Some of the kids stood up, amongst a rattling of plastic cups. There was smoking paraphernalia littered everywhere.

'Oh, no, you don't need to do that,' said Daisy. 'We can't stay long anyway. We kind of snuck out, you see.'

'Rad,' said Nate. 'You've got to have a beer whilst yer here, though – we got a keg!'

'Yeah, I can see,' said Daisy. They were practically sitting around it, like a metal deity with a pipe and a tap sticking out of it.

'Here, sit down.' Nate ushered them to the end of the sofa.

'Thanks,' Daisy said to the girl next to her who had budged up.

'No problem,' the girl said. 'I love your accent. And your jean-jacket. Donna, by the way,' she said.

'Hi, Donna.' It was hard to keep up. And 'jean-jacket' was a new one. But it was nice to be away from everyone's scrutiny.

'Get these guys a beer, someone. Scotty, pour 'em a beer – and someone get rollin'. You did lock the door again, didn't you, Ash?'

'Yep,' said Ash.

There was an awkward silence as the guy called Scotty dispensed two plastic pint glasses of beer, whilst everyone watched. 'Look at his hands shakin',' someone said. 'There'll be more on the floor at this rate.' And they all burst out laughing.

'Yeah. Hope you like froth,' someone else said.

'Will you guys shut the fuck up,' Scott said, reddening as he felt the pressure. And they all cheered.

'Butt-boy bites back!' someone said, and they all broke into hysterics again.

'Here,' Scott said, thrusting the beers into their hands.

Daisy felt sorry for him. He reminded her of Brian out of

The Breakfast Club. 'Thanks,' she said, giving him a warm smile. He blushed further and scurried off.

'Thanks,' said Jack.

As Daisy thought of *The Breakfast Club*, Donna said to her, in a totally bizarre coincidence, 'Has anyone ever told you you look like Molly Ringwald?'

'Yeah, I was thinking that,' one of the other girls agreed. 'I love your hair.'

Daisy swallowed some beer. It was cold and good. 'Ah, thanks. And, no, they haven't.' She blushed.

'And she sounds like Sandy off *Grease*,' one of the guys said.

'Yes!' someone else cried. It was so strange being analysed in this way – and compared with people – but Daisy was almost getting used to it. 'Sandy and Danny! That's you two!' They all laughed, but good-naturedly. There were some high fives heard.

'Wait, wasn't she Australian, though?' someone said.

'Who, Sandy?'

'No, the actress, what's-her-name?'

'Olivia Newton-John,' said Daisy.

'Yeah, that's her.'

'Man, she was smoking hot! Especially in those leather pants at the end,' said Nate.

'Oi!' said Ash, smacking him.

'Had to sew her into them apparently,' another lad said.

'Jesus, you guys,' said Donna.

'Yes, I think she's half-Australian, half English,' someone said.

'They sound the same to me,' Ash said.

'Yeah,' someone agreed.

Feeling braver after a couple of gulps of beer and unable to help herself, Daisy said, 'What is that? That's the second time someone here's said that Australians and Brits sound the same – and I just don't get it. They couldn't be more different. I mean, it's not like Americans and Canadians…' Daisy knew this would get a rise, and it did. Americans famously hated hearing they sounded the same as Canadians – even though they did, in her opinion. More good-natured banter followed, but Daisy's joke had really broken the ice. A couple of spliffs were lit and the party resumed.

'What's your deal anyway, dude?' Nate said to Jack. 'You look like yer gonna punch someone's lights out.' And a few people laughed again. Jack reddened and Daisy braced herself, hoping this wasn't going to go the wrong way.

'Easy, Nate. He might just punch yours out,' someone said.

'Yeah, someone give him a joint quick. This guy needs to relax a bit,' someone else said.

'Don't worry, we're only messin' with yer,' said Nate. 'Great to have you guys here.' Then he turned to the guys with the spliffs. 'But seriously, though, you guys got mortgages out on those Js or what? Spread the love, bros. Show a bit of American hospitality. We've got company here. English royalty!' Two joints were passed to Jack and Daisy, and everyone watched as they inhaled.

'There we go,' said Nate. 'That's better. Deep breaths…' He adopted a yoga pose. 'Let it all out…' This made Jack laugh, and he coughed out smoke. 'Yes! We've broken him!' And everybody laughed. He stood up and held his hand up for Jack to high five him. 'You're all right, buddy. Let me get you another beer. Yer a thirsty boy.' Jack had already necked his drink. 'Yer not driving, are yer?'

'No, cycling,' said Jack.

'Yeah, we're on bikes,' said Daisy.

'Bikes? Jeez, you guys really are old school rebels. Sneaking out from the olds on yer bikes!'

'Where have you come from anyway? Hold on, how do you guys even *know* each other? *Dewey*!'

Dewey, who had been busy rolling another spliff, lit it and blew out the smoke. 'Now that would be telling. They're just some overseas customers of mine is all. Spreading my operations over the pond. Ain't that right, Jack?'

'Yeah,' Jack laughed, feeling a whole lot better after the smoke and a beer. Like Daisy, he was starting to relax a little. He had no need to be threatened by these guys. They reminded him of the gang back home in a way. He could imagine Aitch fitting in so well. He would have had them in stitches by now, Jack thought sadly. If only he could banter like Aitch.

'Jerk,' Nate said to Dewey. 'Seriously, how do you know 'em? Here you go, buddy. Swap ya.' He passed Jack another beer in exchange for the spliff.

Dewey explained, and the night went on. More drinks and smoke were had and more banter was exchanged. Mainly the British–American thing – as with Sue and Tara. Jack and Daisy were starting to feel a bit like performing guinea pigs – 'Oh, just say this for us.' And mind-bogglingly inane, but genuine, questions, such as 'Are Britain and Europe the same thing?' This was Ash. She was either stupidly stoned or just plain stupid. Jack and Daisy didn't mind, though; the language difference seemed to be a mutual fascination.

Despite the good time they were having, and how well they had fitted in, Daisy had kept an eye on the time. She'd also stuck to just one beer. They'd already been there an hour, too long really, and they'd got to cycle home. She was starting to feel stressed and it was time to go. 'Sorry, guys, but we've really got to go,' she said, standing up.

There were groans and protests all round, which was nice, but Daisy held firm, apologising. Jack stood up a little more unsteadily. He'd managed to put away three beers in an hour and the lads had been impressed. 'I'll show you out,' said Dewey. 'And we'll sort out what you really came for.' He gave them a wink that was way beyond his years; in contrast to the bum-fluff moustache and fine blond whiskers on his baby face.

They all said their goodbyes. The Americans seemed genuinely sad to see them go, telling them to come back again. Jack and Daisy were a little sad too. It would have been nice to hang out a little longer.

Back upstairs, Dewey took them into the kitchen and asked them how much they wanted. He reached into a large back pocket of his baggy jeans and threw four different-sized bags of weed onto the counter. 'Ten-deal, tenth, an eighth and a quarter, take yer pick,' he said. 'Bigger you go, the more bang for yer buck you get – we *can* go bigger, of course. Not sure how much you guys were fixin' to buy, you didn't say…'

'No, sorry, we hadn't really discussed it ourselves. Had we, Jack?' Daisy put her hand on his arm. 'What do you reckon, baby?' She wanted him to make the decision in front of Dewey. Besides, it was always him that dealt with this stuff back home.

'How much for the quarter?' Jack said, putting his finger on the bag.

'Normally thirty bucks. But I'll do it you guys for twenty-five – call it a first-time discount.' They didn't know if this was just sales patter. He had slipped back into slick 'Phone Dewey' again. 'Besides,' he added, 'between you, me and that-there fridge, I think the guys got a real kick out of you. You can come back any time you like. Reckon you'll be good for business.' Great, thought Daisy, bartering tools now. Don't ruin it, Dewey, she thought; she was starting to warm to him. 'Nah, only kiddin', it's been great meetin' you guys,' he said, saving himself. 'A real blast.'

Jack didn't have a problem with the price. It was not dissimilar to back home. 'Yeah, twenty-five's fine,' he said, and pulled out some notes. For a brief second, he had an out-of-body experience. Here he was in a kitchen in America. Him. Little old Jack Hemsley from up on Bunny Hill. Who'd never even stepped out into the real world until he was sixteen. Yet here he was. Not only striking a drug deal, but paying for it in American dollars. How had his life come to this? It all seemed so surreal. What would his sister think of him now? What would his *father* think of him?

He felt his hand being tugged. 'Jack?' It was Daisy. He'd zoned out for a second.

'Sorry, yeah, here you go,' he said.

Dewey took the cash, and handed over the bag. 'No problem at all, buddy. Been there m'slf. Happens to the best of us. That there's good shit.' He held out his fist for a pump. Used to it from Tom, Jack obliged. Dewey did the same to Daisy.

'Thanks, Dewey,' she said. 'Oh, and thank your sister for setting this all up – you've been a lifesaver.'

'Sure will,' he said, unlocking the door. He popped his head out, looking both ways. 'Clear. Can't be too careful.' He let them out. 'Catch you guys later. Any time. You've got my number. Best get back down there; that keg ain't gonna drain itself.'

Jack and Daisy laughed and said their farewells. They heard the door being locked behind them. And then it was just them and their bikes and the night. 'Here, give me that bag,' she said.

'Why?'

'I'm gonna stick it in my purse and keep it zipped up. They mustn't smell it in the house.' Jack handed it over. 'We'll stick my purse under the floorboard and keep the window open a bit. And we don't open the purse unless we're away from the house. Got it?'

'All right,' said Jack. 'Shit, we forgot to ask for more papers.'

'Shit, yes,' said Daisy. 'Well, too late now. I'm not knocking on the door again. We've got a few to last… We can always call him at some point. I don't want to smoke too much anyway. I want a clear head. We've got to talk to Phil tomorrow.'

They wheeled their bikes down the drive to the street before mounting them. Despite having lowered her seat as much as possible, Daisy struggled to get on, and she tottered slightly after the smoke and beer. 'Shit,' she giggled. 'At least we can't get done for drink-driving.'

'No: drink-cycling, though,' Jack said, getting on his bike. He'd never ridden a bike stoned before. They set off through the town, passing the bars and the nightlife.

'So, what do you reckon then?' Daisy said as they cycled along.

'About what?'

'About that lot. They were funny.'

'I guess so,' said Jack.

'Yeah, I reckon we might have found ourselves a new gang out here,' Daisy laughed. 'I want a basement. It's so cool!'

And then they were out of the town. The streetlights disappeared and they were whizzing down the country lanes, their lights probing the way. It was an exhilarating feeling, cycling stoned and drunk in the dark. A summer-scented breeze caressed their hair and faces. The indigo night was astir with nocturnal conversation and the buzz-saw throb of the cicadas. A creamy slice of moon promised not to tell on them. But their nerves soon returned as they reached the driveway. They dismounted and turned their lights off, pushing their bikes up the lane. One of the horses whinnied, as if welcoming them back. 'Sh!' hissed Daisy. Instead of heading straight up to the house, they skirted round the back to deposit the bikes in the shed. Thank God Phil and Trish didn't have a dog – or a security light. Stealthily rounding the corner of the veranda, Jack had paranoid visions of Phil sitting there in the porch swing, waiting for them and cradling his shotgun; worse still, mistaking them for wild animals. Or Carol standing there, thin-lipped with her arms folded, asking where they'd been. The whole thing reminded him of his nights sneaking out to see Daisy.

But the porch was empty and the light was still on. The same went for the kitchen when they crept inside and locked the door. The house felt uncomfortably hot after the fresh air, but had a welcoming, familiar smell. A homely smell. Biscuity. Daisy put her finger to her lips, then they quickly tiptoed across the kitchen and into the hall. From down the hall, the loud racket of a baseball game was still in full flow. They looked at each other, then shot upstairs to their waiting beds. The Patch was already starting to feel like home.

CHAPTER 35

The Pitch

The whole family had just returned from church in Phil's pick-up truck. Yes, church.

Phil had sheepishly asked the visitors the previous day if they would mind accompanying him and Trish. She traditionally went on Labor Sunday, as she did on most significant dates. 'It would mean a lot to her,' he said. 'Sorry.'

So they'd all piled into the truck in their Sunday best (or smartest clothes) and made the short trip to a pretty Methodist church not far from the French Azilum site, near the river.

'So, what d'you reckon? Has our local pastor converted you all?' said Phil as they entered the kitchen. He was in a good mood; the Phillies had won the previous night.

'Oh, quit it,' said Trish. 'You may mock, mister, but there's a lot of relevance today, a lot to be said for traditional Christian values. Holidays ain't all about stuffin' yer face in front of the TV, watching sports, barbecues and consumerism. They're about family time, charity, bakin' a pie for a neighbour, reflection… I think Pastor Carmichael summed it up very well. I certainly feel relaxed and contemplative. I love the change of the seasons Labor Day represents: the end of the summer and the herald of the coming fall…'

'Jeez, you're even startin' to sound like him,' said Phil.

'Well, I thought that was very eloquent,' said Carol. 'And I for one enjoyed the experience. A day or two in church a year never hurt anybody.'

'When do you ever go to church?' Daisy scoffed.

'I do,' said Carol. 'Christmas time, anyway…'

'Well, here's my church,' said Phil, opening up the giant fridge, basking in its yellow light, Christ-like, with outstretched arms. And they all laughed. He grabbed himself a chicken leg and began to tear into it, shutting the fridge door.

'Lord, give me strength,' said Trish.

'Right, don't know about you folk, but all that righteousness has worn me out. I'm gonna see how Mac's gettin' on at Flushing Meadows.' said Phil. 'And the Phillies are on again later. Yippee!' He was like a big kid. Trish threw a tea towel at him, and he caught it, laughing.

Daisy picked her moment – whilst Phil was in such a good mood, and before he disappeared. 'Oh, Phil, we were wondering actually, me and Jack that is, if we could have a quick chat with you about something.'

'Ooh, this sounds serious,' said Trish.

'Yeah, sure,' said Phil, a little surprised. 'What's up? Shoot.'

'If this is about that diner idea, Daisy, forget it,' said Carol. She knew they'd been to visit it again, and Daisy had been scribbling away in her notebook – a tell-tale sign she was up to something if ever there was one.

'Mum!' said Daisy. 'For Christ's sake.'

'For Christ's sake what? You're not emigrating to America, I'm telling you that now.'

'Why not?' said Daisy.

''Cause I said so, that's why not. Honestly, it's one thing after another with you. It was bad enough you moving to Norfolk. And look how that turned out. Now America. You've only been here five minutes. No wonder I'm turning grey.'

'Nobody said anything about emigrating. *You've* come up with that. We just wanted to chat, that was all.'

'Humph,' said Carol. 'I'll be in the den if anyone wants me. Watching crap and eating Twinkies.' She grabbed a pack off the side and stomped off.

'Well done, yer big lump,' said Trish.

'Me?' Phil said, shrugging and brandishing his chicken leg, his beard shiny with grease. 'What have I done?'

'You know what. All that talk of the diner the other night…'

'I just said they'd go down a storm there, that was all.' He looked at the kids, shrugging again.

'Go and have your chat,' she said. 'But do it out on the porch. I've got dinner to prepare. And don't go putting any ideas in those kids' heads. And wipe that grease off yer chops.'

*****

'Your mom always that uptight?' said Phil, out on the porch. 'She never used to be when she was younger. Quite the opposite, in fact. Was always the wild, headstrong one – the rebel. You remind me of her actually, Daisy, 'cept you're prettier.'

Daisy smiled a thanks. 'Only since Dad died,' she said. 'She *has* changed. Kind of like she's trying to take on the parental burden for both of them or something.'

'Yes, that makes sense,' said Phil. 'Such a sad business all that.' He looked serious. 'He was a good guy, your dad, and I'm sorry for your loss. Far too soon…'

'Thanks,' said Daisy, suddenly feeling emotional. Jack put his hand on hers.

'Look,' said Phil. 'I ain't here to break up the family' – Daisy had heard something like that somewhere before – 'Sounds like you and your mom have been through enough. And Lily. How is she? She closer to Tara's age? I can't remember…'

'Twenty-one,' Daisy said. 'And she's, well, Lily.' She shrugged.

Phil laughed. 'You guys get on?'

'Sometimes,' Daisy said, non-committally.

'Ah, one of those, eh? Anyways, I meant what I said. You *would* make a killing up there at the diner, young ambitious couple like yourselves, Jack's food – jeez, I've never tasted anything like it – but maybe somewhere in the UK might be more suitable. Somewhere closer to home, closer to your *mother*. I'd still consider backin' you, or going fifty-fifty if, like you said, you've got some money of your own to invest. You never told me how come or how much: I ain't pryin', and it can wait, just interested's all. And if you've got some decent ideas of course, a concept...' He nodded to the journal Daisy was clutching on her lap.

'Really? You'd invest in us?' said Daisy.

'Be happy to hear you out,' he said, opening his palms.

Daisy suddenly felt shy and young and foolish, opening up her journal with band stickers on it. Childlike. A sudden crisis of confidence. 'Well ... we liked the diner idea,' she said. 'We went back up there yesterday.'

'Really?' said Phil.

'Yeah. Di was on again.'

'Not surprised,' Phil laughed. 'Bless her. She deserves better. So wasted there. As things stand anyway.'

'That's exactly what we said,' said Daisy, brightening and sitting up. 'We'd want to keep her on; she's an asset. She knows the place inside out, the day-to-day running, the accounts, the suppliers – and she's amazing with the customers.'

'You're starting to sound like a business owner already,' Phil said. 'Go on!'

Buoyed by this, Daisy took the bull by the horns. She told him all their observations from the other day. All her notes. Her revamp ideas. The outside seating area. The extraction. The retro jukebox, the toilets. The signage. The potential for coaches. The advertising. The marketing. Sponsoring a local sports team or something – Phil loved that idea. And the more she talked, the more Phil sat up and began to take notice. It was infectious, and, unable to help himself, he started throwing his own ideas into the ring. Like bringing the scrapple back for some of the old regulars and making a big deal out of it. Getting it in some of the local papers and magazines – he said he knew some of the editors. Maybe even some of the food guides. Do a press release about the change of ownership.

Daisy went through their menu observations, bringing Jack into the conversation; how the menu was too big and there was too much wastage. Which dishes they'd get rid of and which they'd keep. Maybe they'd do a signature burger. Maybe even pizzas – something that was missing from the menu – but in a proper wood-fired pizza oven, so people could see it. Make a real feature out of it. And vegetarian choices – like a veggie burger... Phil listened intently, but then threw them a curveball: 'Your ideas are great, guys, and I agree with most of what yer sayin'. But I think you're coming at this all wrong.'

'Really? How come?' said Daisy, disappointed.

'Think about it... waffles, pancakes, burgers, pizzas – we're overrun with that stuff. You've seen the signs. Pizza and burger joints are two a penny – one on every corner. They line the highways out here. Everyone wants to be the next chain, the next success story – but you can't compete with the big guys, and few do, or make it at all. What this area needs is something different – something that stands out from the crowd: a destination. And I've got just the thing...'

'What?' Jack and Daisy said, intrigued.

'Wait for it ... English food.'

'English food?' said Daisy.

'Yeah. Traditional English grub – like Jack's cottage pie. We Americans brought you burgers, you bring us this stuff – your bangers and mash, your fish 'n' chips. I dunno – your steak and kidney pies...'

'What, and you think that would work in a diner?' said Daisy.

'Hell, yeah. But maybe you don't call it a diner, maybe you call it a pub – pub grub – or an inn. Yes, an inn. Something that conjures up olde worlde England. Your old schools and colleges. Shakespeare. The royal family – Charles and Di, Andrew and Fergie – Americans love all that crap.'

Jack and Daisy looked at each other again, this time with wonder on their faces. Phil might have hit upon something. Something big. This was beginning to get exciting. Really exciting. 'Full English breakfast,' said Jack shyly.

'Yes,' said Phil. 'You don't get much more English than that.'

'And suited to a diner,' said Daisy, putting her hand on Jack's leg. 'But you can order it all day. An all-day breakfast, like our signature breakfast.' She loved the idea of signature dishes.

'Roast beef and Yorkshire pudding,' said Phil. 'It's as English as they come.'

'But only served on a Sunday as a special,' said Daisy.

'Yes!' cried Phil. 'Families with their kids, and grandparents. Word would spread and you'd have to start booking.'

The screen door opened. It was Trish. 'I can hear you lot inside. What are you getting all excited about?'

They looked at each other guiltily, as if they'd been sprung. 'Are you gonna tell her, or am I?' said Phil.

No one answered.

'Oh, jeez,' said Trish. 'I'll go and get Carol. And her gin…'

*****

The conversation didn't go well. And that was an understatement. Carol broke down in tears when she heard they'd been discussing the diner as a real possibility. They didn't even get a chance to give her the spiel about all their ideas. 'Why is someone always trying to steal my daughter away from me?' she sobbed. 'Why are you always trying to leave me, Daisy, your own mother? First your dad, and now you.'

Although this had come across as a little dramatic – Jim hadn't exactly left her, he'd died – the raw display of emotion was still upsetting for Daisy, and a little awkward for everyone else. Phil felt guilty and was taken aback – he'd had no idea these feelings ran so deep. But how could he? It wasn't as though they'd kept in proper touch. He hadn't made the trip over for the funeral, for example.

'I'm not always trying to leave you, Mum – and I'm certainly not dying.' She put her hands on Carol's. 'Just trying to live my own life, that's all; make something of it. Surely you want me to do that? You're always telling me to do that.'

'Yes, but not on the other side of the bloody world. Why does it have to be America? Why not somewhere local? Norfolk's bad enough. I never see you as it is. This would be the final nail in the coffin. It would break up the family for good. I'd never see you from one year to the next. And what about when you have kids? My grandkids. I'd never see them either, and I couldn't bear that.'

Daisy couldn't help but laugh at this – despite the gravity of the situation. 'I don't think you have to worry about being a grandma just yet, Mum. I'm only nineteen and Jack is seventeen. It's the last thing on our minds. Anyway, you could move out here too. We could all live together, maybe? The house is already on the market…'

'Yeah. That's a great idea. Come out here too,' said Phil. 'We'd love to have you.'

'Oh, now that would be swell,' said Trish.

'Oh, I couldn't! Daisy knows I couldn't. As much as I'd want to, what about Lily? What about Grandma? Your *mother*, Phil! Who's going to look after her in her final years? The idea was to move closer to her, not further away.'

True, thought Daisy; she'd never do it, not whilst Grandma was still alive. 'Well, maybe when she's popped her clogs, then.

We might be ready for some kids about then.' It was Daisy's attempt at a joke, to lighten the mood, but it went down like a lead balloon.

'That's a terrible thing to say,' Carol said.

'Sorry,' said Daisy.

'I'm going back inside,' said Carol, wiping her eyes and getting up. 'I can't talk about this any more. Not right now. I want to phone Lily – you've just reminded me. I want to know what's been going on with the house.'

Daisy got up and gave her a hug then Carol and Trish disappeared inside.

'Well, guess that's that then,' said Phil. He felt really bad, and figured he was in the doghouse – with his sister and his wife. Although Trish did seem to be warming to the idea a little.

'Not necessarily,' said Daisy, surprising him – and Jack. Daisy loved her mum, of course she did, but why should she share her problems? And she knew that if her dad was alive – and the two of them had discussed it – he would have talked her round, and said to Daisy, 'Go for it kiddo. Go make a difference in this world!' And this knowledge, more than anything else, was enough to push her guilt to one side. Daisy wasn't giving up just yet.

CHAPTER 36

A Cri de Coeur

September rolled on and the weather continued to warm up; so much for the onset of fall. The days drifted past slowly. But that was fine. Some days Jack sat on the porch, with nothing better to do than to watch the sun cross the sky, as he'd done as a child – trying to work out the time by it. He hadn't done that in ages. Daisy continued to work on Carol. This was something she was used to, but not on this scale. Although the diner idea was up in the air, Daisy's vision and enthusiasm were undimmed. Quite the opposite. She and Jack continued to discuss it and to work on the menu, focusing on their 'concept', as Phil had put it. They thought his idea was genius.

Wise to Daisy's unsubtle manipulation techniques, Carol retaliated with her own diversionary tactics, hoping that given time the diner idea would just go away. She tried to get everyone to focus on the next sightseeing trip, 'Something that everyone seems to have forgotten about,' she said. 'Our real reason for coming out here.' She'd singled out Niagara Falls as being next on the agenda, which made sense, as it was no more than a four-hour drive. Save for New York – also on her list – everything else was so far away; and none of them were quite ready for another plane journey yet. Carol was even making noises about going to New York with Jack and Daisy, booking herself into a hotel; she'd barely spent a dollar yet. Despite the stifling thought of this – how were they going to smoke for a start? – Daisy began to consider agreeing to it, to get her mum on side.

Sometimes at night, under the ruse he was staying up to watch a ball game, Phil would secretly slope out to join Jack and Daisy on the porch, to ask how things were going and if Carol was softening. He also wanted to throw ideas around, so excited he couldn't stop thinking about their plans. Having discussed it with Trish, Phil reported that she thought the English grub idea was a winner too. 'What's that workman's lunch thing you guys do back home? With the bread and pickles and cheese?' he said.

Daisy laughed. 'Do you mean ploughman's lunch?'

'Yeah, that's it. With the apple. So English! But you could serve it with meats too – like cold cuts of ham, maybe chicken legs – and on a big board.' Daisy laughed and gave him a look; it was always about the meat with him. 'And a vegetarian version too, of course.' Phil was starting to come round to Daisy's idea of vegetarian options. It was forward-thinking, moving with the times.

The three of them really got to know one other on those warm, sticky nights, and it was good. Almost a routine. One night – to their amazement – he even brought out a cold bottle of beer for each of them. They couldn't believe it. 'Don't tell Trish,' he said. 'And keep an eye out for any headlights.' Feeling more comfortable around Phil, Jack finally filled him in – when pressed again – on how they had come by his windfall, and also its stipulations; that Carol was the trustee and so on. Without going into all the details, he said his father had died and he was the only remaining child. Therefore he'd inherited the family property, which had then been sold. 'Dreadful business,' Phil said. 'Turned out all right in the end for you, but dreadful business nevertheless. Money cain't bring 'em back. Really sorry, buddy.'

In turn, Phil seemed to have no end of anecdotes. And he seemed to know everybody. It soon became apparent how useful this could be. 'I'm on the town planning team, so nothin' like that should be a problem.' 'I got a buddy in construction.' 'I got a lawyer acquaintance, who specialises in visas…' He was starting to sound like Marlon in *Streetcar*.

As the days went on, Carol started to soften, possibly appeased by the Niagara Falls trip they were organising for the following week. Phil had too many 'commitments' before then to set an entire day aside. Daisy and Carol were shelling some beans for Trish at the kitchen table one afternoon. It was a lovely fall day, perfect and tranquil, the kitchen awash with butter-coloured light. The radio was on, playing country songs. Carol was humming to one she knew. 'Well, this is nice,' she said, acknowledging the rare time on their own together. There had been a delivery of winter hay for the horses – Phil had said they always bought at this time of year before the prices shot up in October – so Jack was helping him and Trish shift and store it. He'd jumped at the chance: a much-needed physical workout.

'Yeah,' said Daisy. She'd been distracted whilst shelling by thoughts of Jack in action, wondering if he had worked up a sweat and taken his T-shirt off. 'Mum, can we talk…'

Carol groaned, as if annoyed that her peace, her happy head space, was being disturbed. She carried on shelling beans. Pop, pop. Daisy waited. A song ended and an advert came on. She was about to say 'Mum' again. 'It's just so sudden, that's all,' Carol said. 'This whole hare-brained scheme. I mean, it's preposterous – we've only been here, what, three weeks. And you've already decided you want to up sticks and move out here? Even for you, this one *really* takes the biscuit.'

'It's not a hare-brained scheme, Mum. You haven't even let us tell you about it properly yet. Phil's come up with a great idea.'

'Phil,' she said. 'He should know better. Influencing you kids like this.'

'He's not influencing us. He's just seen an opportunity, that's all.'

'Yeah, an opportunity to steal my daughter away from me. Don't think I don't know about your secret little meetings out on the porch at night. I can hear you upstairs, you know. Well, Phil, anyway.'

'It's not like that at all, Mum. I'm nineteen. I have my own mind.'

'Huh. Don't I know it! Well, he must be mad. Does he know your track record? Like I do? Your *mother?*'

'Track record?' said Daisy.

'Yes. You flit from one thing to another. Only five minutes ago, it was Norfolk and an ice cream business. How long's it going to be before the novelty of this one wears off? What then? Or what if you and Jack fall out? Again. You can't just hop in the van and drive a couple of hours home. You're on the other side of the world, Daisy. Without support. Proper support of family. Your family. I don't think you've thought the reality through at all.'

'I have. And me and Jack aren't going to fall out. I love him. We love each other.'

'Oh, please,' said Carol.

'It's true. And as for the ice cream business – this is just an extension of it. But bigger and better – an actual premises. We can make and sell our own ice creams at the diner. And that's just one of a hundred ideas.' Daisy's eyes lit up, and she put her hands palm down on the table. 'Mum, I've never felt so excited about something. This just feels like, I dunno, destiny. Like my life's been leading up to this moment. Look at the timing of it all. Me and Jack were done with Norfolk – which was kind of foisted upon us anyway. Our year's up at the flat. We've quit our jobs and are looking for a new challenge. A new chapter. It just feels like this is it. But *our* choice this time. Mine and Jack's. For better or for worse.'

Carol had stopped shelling, and was looking defeated, as if she was going to cry again. 'I just feel I've got no control with you any more, Daisy, no control at all. Not without your dad's support. You don't listen to a word I say.'

'Mum…'

'Don't say it.'

'It's true, though. I'm sorry, Mum, but it is. He would have wanted me to.' Carol burst into tears. 'Oh, Mum, come here.'

Daisy came round the table to hug her mother, and she sobbed in her arms. 'I just can't bear the thought of it,' Carol said. 'You being so out of reach, so far away. The thought of it makes me feel panicky and sick and claustrophobic.' This set her off again. 'I feel so lonely sometimes, Daisy. I miss your dad, I miss him so much.' And she convulsed with violent sobs. Daisy felt so sorry for her mum that she began crying too. They hadn't done this for ages; held each other and cried. Not like this. Not this close. Probably not since Jim had died.

'I do too, Mum. So much…' They stayed like that for a while, just holding each other and crying. Eventually Daisy pulled away. 'You can still visit us out here – I've been thinking about it. It's only a plane journey away, and you can do that once a year – twice if you wanted to. You can afford it now. And look at our time in Norfolk – just saying, so don't take offence, but we've been there a year and you haven't visited us once…' Carol didn't answer; she was still sobbing, albeit more softly. 'Or you could stay out here for three months at a time, spend a good part of the year out here, swap between the two. Phil will always put you up, you know that…'

'If we're still speaking, that is.' But it sounded as if she was calming down.

'Course you will be,' Daisy said. 'And I'd love you to hear me out, to hear our ideas…' She stroked her mum's hand, but she pulled away, still not quite on side. 'Please, Mum.'

'Go on then,' she sighed. 'If you must… But get me a gin first. I need one.'

'OK,' Daisy laughed.

'See, this is what you do to your mother. Drive her to drink!'

Daisy made her mum a G and T and poured herself a lemon iced tea – it was so tempting to slosh some gin in it. When she sat back down with the drinks, she excitedly began to fill her mum in. Carol listened, and despite being impressed, she tried not to show it, merely sipping at her drink. 'So, what do you reckon?' Daisy said when she'd finished. 'Say something, Mother! Don't you think it's an amazing idea?'

Carol paused for a minute. 'You forgot cream teas,' she said, a little sulkily.

Daisy laughed. 'Shit! Sorry. Yes! Cream teas!'

'And afternoon teas. On stands. Cakes and tea and sandwiches with the crusts cut off – it's as English as it gets.'

'Mum, you're a genius,' said Daisy, and leant over to kiss her.

At that precise moment, the screen door opened and the other three burst in, looking hot and dusty and dirty and sweaty. Jack was bringing up the rear.

'Ooh, what's going on here, pray tell,' said Trish. 'A bit of mother and daughter bonding?'

'Something like that,' laughed Daisy, and sat back down. Carol said nothing; she still had the hump with Phil and wanted him to know it. 'Mum's just come up with a great idea actually – for the diner.'

'Ooh, this sounds promising,' said Phil, plonking his giant frame down in a protesting chair. 'Jeez, my dogs are pooped.'

'Cream teas,' said Daisy, catching Jack's eye with a look that conveyed, 'She's coming round.'

'What's a cream tea, exactly?' said Trish – American through and through. 'Sounds like tea with cream in it – no offence, Carol.'

'It's a fantastic idea is what it is,' said Phil. 'Very English. Conjures up holidays in Devon and Cornwall when we were kids. Remember, sis? Mom and Dad?'

'Yeah,' said Carol. 'Mum and Dad would always have a cream tea at some little café, maybe by a harbour or quayside, where we could crab and they could keep an eye on us.'

'Yeah, and they'd always have the same argument – no, two. One, which do you put on first, the jam or the cream, and two–'

'Whether it was pronounced "scoan" or "scon",' finished Carol.

'Exactly,' cried Phil, slapping his knee in glee.

'I haven't the faintest idea what you two mad people are going on about,' said Trish. 'You still haven't said what a cream tea actually is.' They all laughed and explained. It was a relief all round that the two siblings were reminiscing and getting on again. Things had been a little fraught of late.

'Hey, what about puddings?' said Phil, always animated and excited when it came to food. 'Had any thoughts on them, guys?' It was a relief for him to be able to talk about it in the open at last.

'Yeah, we have,' said Daisy. 'Puddings are Jack's forte. We were thinking ice creams, maybe his chocolate tart, Eton Mess…'

'Now there's a British one,' said Carol. 'I love all the old classics, the nursery puddings, as they're called, your jam roly-polys, your spotted dicks…' This raised a few sniggers.

'Yeah. Your English school-dinner puddings. Hell, I miss all that stuff. Can still remember them now…' said Phil. 'And all with lashings of custard.'

There was silence for a moment, as they all pictured puddings.

'I don't know how you even think you're going to make this happen,' said Carol. 'I mean, what makes you think Jack and Daisy can just come and settle here? Live and work here? Surely it's not that simple. Won't they need a visa?'

'Oh, yeah, they will,' said Phil.

'He says so casually...' said Carol.

'It's all right, I got a lawyer buddy. He specialises in that stuff.'

'Great,' said Carol. 'Sounds like you've got it all figured out.' Phil looked sheepish. 'You've already spoken to him, haven't you?'

'Phil!' said Trish.

'I just made some initial enquiries, s'all,' said Phil. 'Sounds like they might need a green card at first or something. Relatives already living in the US can sponsor family members apparently. Be easier if they were married, but we can arrange that.'

'Oh, give over,' said Trish. 'Now yer just talkin' hogwash.'

CHAPTER 37

Options

'Here you go,' said Daisy, slapping down two sheets of paper in front of Phil. 'A proposed menu, along with a brief outline of our concept. We've thrown a few American crowd-pleasers in there, too – milkshakes and burgers and the like, just in case.' Phil had asked them to come up with something as he'd got a meeting with his bank manager that day. Daisy had been working on the menu on Phil's home computer, a luxury she didn't have at home. The other thing Phil had requested was a rough list of any costly equipment they thought they might need – in the kitchen or otherwise; the outside seating and juke box, for example – and any significant predicted maintenance and structural alterations, like the Gents. Daisy had summarised her notes, but it was hard to be exact without doing a detailed tour of the place, especially the kitchen.

'All righty then, let's have a look,' said Phil. He put his half-moon glasses on to read the menu.

'We haven't decided on a name yet, but were thinking maybe simply Jack 'n' Daisy's or The Highway Inn,' said Daisy.

'I *like* the Highway Inn,' Phil said. 'Classy.'

'And all the descriptions need adding, of course – what everything comes with.'

'Sure' said Phil.

The proposed menu read as follows:

MAINS

BANGERS 'N' MASH

BUBBLE 'N' SQUEAK

FISH 'N' CHIPS

TOAD IN THE HOLE

JACK'S COTTAGE PIE

STEAK 'N' KIDNEY PIE

LANCASHIRE HOTPOT

PLOUGHMAN'S LUNCH

SIGNATURE DISHES

THE FULL ENGLISH – OUR SIGNATURE BREAKFAST

HIGHWAY INN BURGER – OUR SIGNATURE BURGER

HIGHWAY INN VEGETARIAN BURGER

SCRAPPLE – A TRADITIONAL PENNSYLVANIAN-DUTCH DISH

SPECIALS AND OTHER STUFF

HOME-MADE SOUP OF THE DAY

ROAST BEEF AND YORKSHIRE PUDDING (SUNDAYS ONLY)

EGGS ON TOAST – HOWEVER YOU LIKE 'EM!

CREAM TEAS

AFTERNOON TEAS

PUDDINGS

JAM ROLY POLY AND CUSTARD

ETON MESS

HOME-MADE ICE CREAMS
BREAD AND BUTTER PUDDING
APPLE CRUMBLE AND CUSTARD
SPOTTED DICK AND CUSTARD

DRINKS
TEA
COFFEE
MILKSHAKES
SOFT DRINKS (POP)
AUNT TRISH'S HOME-MADE LEMONADE
AUNT TRISH'S ICED TEA
ALCOHOL? BEERS/WINES?

Phil laughed at the 'Aunt Trish' mentions. 'She'll love that,' he said. 'And I think it's fantastic. Well done. Simple, honest grub… Not too crowded a menu… It's making me hungry just reading it. You even remembered the scrapple!'

'Yeah. Thanks.' Daisy blushed. 'Jack helped too, of course.' She was pleased and proud of the menu. She'd never done anything like it before.

'And alcohol's an interesting thought. Do diners sell alcohol?'

'Well, if people were having main meals – pies and that – I guess they'd be wanting a pint or a glass of wine to wash it down with,' said Daisy. 'I know back home they would – and we're supposed to be an inn after all.'

'It's a good point, actually,' said Phil. 'We'd need to apply for a licence, of course. Might have to be in my name…' He scribbled a quick reminder on the second sheet, then let out a sigh. He took off his glasses and rubbed the bridge of his nose. 'There's so much to think about, isn't there? We haven't even discussed the finance side of things – ownership-wise, I mean. There's plenty of options. But I guess we'll have a clearer picture of things once I've ran it all past Bob – he's my bank manager. Just hope he buys into the idea. I can't take you guys in with me as well, can I? I suddenly feel nervous.'

Despite some initial reservations from Bob because of concerns about the ongoing recession, Phil's meeting went well. He came back chuffed to bits. He could easily borrow up to three times what he reckoned they'd pay for the place. And the diner had been on the market for the best part of a year, which would work in their favour. The loan could be secured against the house, which they already owned outright. 'Bob reckoned we were onto a winner,' Phil said. 'Loved the menu and concept. Said he'd be out there himself with the family and would help spread the word, once we were up and running. I told him to keep it under wraps for now. If word gets out that I'm looking to buy the diner up on Route 6 – Joe's old place – it'll spread like wildfire *and* the phone won't stop ringing. We don't need that just yet; it'll push the price up.'

With Phil's preferred anonymity in mind, they viewed the diner as potential purchasers when it was closed for business. They all went along – Carol and Trish too. Daisy took her notebook, feeling professional and grown up. Jack took a keen interest in the kitchen, which was a shock at first: how small and dirty it was compared with the Crab's Claw: like a galley kitchen, narrow, with a bank of equipment on each wall. Daisy reminded him that he might be working on his own, to start off with at least, and a smaller kitchen was better suited to this. Less charging back and forth. Running a kitchen on his own was going to be a new thing for Jack, and it seemed a little daunting, to say the least. He stood there, trying to picture it…

'Ugh,' Carol shuddered, when they checked out the Gents.

'Pongs, doesn't it?' said Trish.

'Just a bit. Needs a damn good clean. The whole place does.'

'All needs ripping out in here if you ask me,' said Phil. 'There's nothing worse than poor facilities at an eating establishment. They tell you how the business is run.'

'The Ladies is fine,' said Carol. Everyone agreed.

All in all, the viewing went well. Other than a drastic deep-clean, there was nothing obviously or structurally wrong. And picturing themselves running the place had been exciting for Jack and Daisy. Daisy couldn't wait to get started.

'Of course, we'll be getting a proper survey done 'fore we commit to anything,' Phil said to the selling agent.

'Of course,' the rep said. 'There's someone I can recommend.'

'Oh, that's fine, I've got a conveyancer acquaintance. I'll give him a call,' said Phil. Jack and Daisy looked at each other, trying not to laugh. 'Thanks for these,' Phil patted a document wallet holding the past three years trading figures, 'and for the tour. We'll take a look at the fig-yers, have a chat and hopefully be in touch.' He shook the man's hand. Phil had been very serious throughout the viewing, very business-like; it was quite intimidating.

*****

After supper the next day, they had a summit meeting at the kitchen table. The porch door was open to let some air in and Trish had a fan going; it was a close night. The gravelly voiced Tom Waits was on the stereo. Phil's choice. Daisy was really beginning to like him. He would always remind her of that time.

'OK. Me and Trish have been doing some talking,' Phil said, leaning his meaty arms on the table and intertwining his large hands. He was perspiring as usual.

'You have,' Trish cut in, and they all laughed, Jack and Daisy a little nervously. It had been an anxious wait.

'Now, as I said before, I've been looking for an investment opportunity for some time.'

'A hobby, you mean,' said Trish.

'Are you gonna let me speak already or what, woman?' said Phil, and they all laughed again. 'You've got your horses, ain't yer? It's my turn.' He took a deep breath. 'Seriously, though … we're happily retired now, comfortable – more than comfortable – got regular money still coming in, pensions, savings, interest on savings and what-not. And now this potential loan offer on the table – never use yer own money, that's always been my motto. So finance isn't an issue. Add into the mix Jack's considerable sum – should he care to use it down the line – and, well, the world's our oyster. We could have that diner…'

'Inn,' cut in Daisy.

'Thank you for reminding me, yes, inn, cleaned up, revamped, refurbished – so shiny you can see it from the New Jersey Turnpike. All yer extra equipment, Daisy's juke box, outside seating, the works. Then there's the advertising money to think about, the initial cashflow whilst things take off…' Daisy's stomach fluttered at the thought of it all. 'It's just how we want to play it, that's all – ownership-wise, I mean – and to my mind there are several options. This is why I think it's important you're privy to all this, Carol. Especially considering you're Jack's trustee. It'll be up to you to help guide the young folk – if we *are* to go through with it – and help them make the right decisions.'

'I wouldn't count on it,' said Carol. 'Daisy tends to do exactly as she pleases these days.'

'Mum!' said Daisy.

'It's true. But go on anyway… I can but try.'

'OK. Option one. Utilising Jack's money – I can lend him the required amount if everything goes through before he's eighteen – we pay for the diner and all related costs fifty-fifty, the other haff from me, and run it as an equal partnership. All profits would be split fifty-fifty.'

'But how's that fair?' said Carol 'Firstly on Jack – he's putting fifty per cent of the money in, swallowing up his inheritance. And then if it's a success, how's that fair on Daisy? They'd both be working equally hard, throwing themselves into this thing, but Jack would be coining it. And does that mean Jack would technically be Daisy's boss? I can see trouble ahead with that one.' Jack and Daisy looked at each other worriedly. This wasn't sounding simple.

'That's a good point,' said Trish.

'Look, I'm not saying any of these scenarios aren't without their drawbacks. I mean, is Daisy putting some money in an option? Like a three-way split?'

'No,' said Carol quickly. 'No offence, but it's too much of a risk in my opinion.'

'Gee. Thanks for the vote of confidence, Mum,' said Daisy.

'OK. Well, we can come back to that one,' said Phil, ignoring Carol's comment. 'Jack being a minor might be an issue too; it might have to go in Daisy's name, for example, which again is complicated. Like I say, we'll come back to that one. Moving on… Option two is for me to put all the money up for the place myself, along with all the refurbishing costs, and then, on top of an initial start-up fee, Jack and Daisy would rent or lease the premises from me, kind of like a franchise – all drawn up properly, of course. This way, the bulk of the financial risk is on me, but the actual business would be theirs. Being a businessman myself, I wouldn't want to miss out, though – especially considering all the investment – so I think some sort of fluid, percentage-based rent would be the way to go: the monthly or quarterly rent would be based on turnover. And this would be beneficial to both of us. You guys have a quiet month; you have the reassurance that your rent stays low. Business is booming or takes off like a rocket, and we all win.'

'That sounds quite fair,' said Trish.

'Yes, I agree, a much better arrangement,' said Carol.

Poor Jack, a lot of this was going over his head – and he was starting to struggle. It was too much to take in. Daisy was only faring slightly better. She wasn't au fait with all this finance talk, but she was starting to see what a shrewd businessman her

Uncle Phil was. No wonder he had done so well for himself. It was reassuring, but scary at the same time. 'And the third option?' said Carol.

'Similar to option two,' said Phil. 'But Daisy and Jack only manage the place and I pay them a salary. No up-front costs. They'll still treat it like their own business; it'll be in their interest to. I wouldn't want to see them miss out either – would hate it, in fact – they'd be the ones working their butts off. So we could have a variable salary, based on profit not turnover, or a set salary with a monthly or quarterly bonus, again based on the equivalent period's profit. This would probably suit them – not me – better than the variable salary. If they had a slow month, for example, or an unexpected outlay that hammered their monthly profit, they'd still get paid the same salary regardless. It would be me that would take the hit.'

'Or option four,' said Carol, 'we just forget the whole idea.'

'Mum!' said Daisy again. 'Stop being so negative. It's stressful enough as it is.' And it was. So much to think about. Talking in such detail had really hammered home what they were letting themselves in for. Contracts. Legal documents. Reliance on profits… It had all got very serious.

'I know,' said Phil, speaking for everyone. 'It's a lot to think about. But I'm just trying to give you all as much information as I can, to be as fair and transparent as possible. It's important that we come up with the right set-up; something that works for all parties concerned. But I'm also very keen to do the right thing by you young folks.'

The meeting broke up. Carol and Trish disappeared off to bed, and Phil said, 'I'll leave you guys to chat. But don't stress. Sleep on it all. You've got days to decide yet. And this whole thing won't become legally binding for months and months anyway. Try to remember this is all good news. It's been a good day. Exciting stuff. Goodnight.'

'Thanks, Phil,' said Daisy.

It was a relief to be on their own, not just so they could

talk, but because they were both dying for a drink. And when Phil was safely in bed, the vodka came out. It was cooler out on the porch. 'So, what d'you reckon?' said Daisy. 'A lot to take in.'

'Yeah,' said Jack. He felt strangely subdued.

'I like option three best,' said Daisy.

'Which one was that?' He'd lost track by the end.

'Where we just manage the place, but get a percentage of the profits.'

'Why that one? Surely it's the least money for us – and it wouldn't be our business.'

'I know. But it's also the least risk. I mean, what do we *really* know about running a business? It sounds terrifying. This way, we can work our way in. Learning how to do it – in effect running the place ourselves – but without the financial stress and pressure. And Phil mentioned the word "lease". Dad would turn in his grave.'

'Guess so,' said Jack. 'I know one thing, and I'd been thinking about this – I've been thinking about a lot of things actually – even before Phil gave us his options. I'd been stressing, I guess, about the thought of using all my money, *losing* it all.'

'I'm sorry, honey,' Daisy said. 'I had no idea. I know I get carried away with stuff… I'm sorry, I didn't mean to worry you.'

'It's OK,' said Jack. 'And I'd have done it if you'd wanted me to – all of it. Whatever it took.'

'It's so sweet of you to say that,' she said. 'But I never would have wanted to. Not if you didn't as well. I don't know what I've done to deserve you. Come here.' And she gave him a big hug, resting her head on his shoulder.

'Stop it – you'll make me cry,' Jack said. He was in an emotional mood: it was probably all the stress. 'Anyway, it made me think – all this talk of the diner and my money. The longer it's gone on, and if it's really gonna go ahead, us moving out here – there's probably something else I'd rather do with my money.'

'Really? What?'

'Buy a property.'

'Really?' said Daisy. 'What, out here?'

'Yeah,' said Jack. 'Why not? You know it's always been my dream to live in America – I told you when we first met.'

'You did.'

'And, I mean, look at this place.' He gestured at the house.

Daisy followed his gaze and laughed. 'I don't think we'd get something *this* size! But I tell you what, properties are well cheap out here – about half the price at home. I've seen them in Phil's paper.'

'Really?' said Jack.

'Yeah.'

It felt good to talk, to get it all out in the open. And talking about it made it seem more real. 'Can you imagine?' Jack said. 'Having our own place out here? Not this big, of course, but this type of house. The white clapboard, the porch, the swing, the garden. It's everything I've ever wanted…'

'I know. It's crazy.'

'We'd want our own space anyway if we lived out here. We'd see enough of Phil at the diner, I'd bet. And we'd soon start getting on each other's nerves. But imagine having our own place – to smoke, to *drink*, for crying out loud. Without having to sneak around. Without Phil's rules. To … what was it you used to call it? "Get them coloured lights going" again, without anyone listening…'

'Yes!' Daisy laughed. 'Oh my God, you're so right. It *would* be amazing.' Their own little place… 'And it looks like we've got a new gang out here – Dewey and Co.' She laughed again. 'Our own supply of stuff… I'd bet they'd sort some booze out for us if we asked. I bet they've got older brothers and sisters. There's Ruth for a start.'

'Yeah,' said Jack. 'I bet they would. Hey, if we have alcohol at the diner, maybe we could swipe it from there. It'd be our stock. Our profits.'

'Well, depends on the arrangement. It could be Phil's too, remember. But I'm sure the odd bottle of wine wouldn't go amiss. Hey, maybe you can learn to drive out here. Imagine that. We'd have to get a car. We'd have to. An American car. Something classic. Like a Plymouth. Imagine that!'

Jack had no idea what a Plymouth was. But yes, learning to drive would be exciting. Scary as hell, though…

'And we've got our trip to New York to come,' said Daisy. 'I can't wait for that. It's nice to know we've got the girls fairly close by, people we know and like – *relatively* close by anyway.' They were quiet for a moment. Thinking about it all. Their futures. 'So I guess that's settled, is it?'

Jack gulped. 'Looks that way,' he said.

'I'll let Phil know in the morning, then – option three it is. And option one is *not* an option. We're gonna have to break the news to Mum as well, poor thing. Let's just hope we get the bloody place after all this stress. The sooner Phil puts an offer in the better.'

'Yeah,' said Jack. And he put his head on hers.

He'd meant what he'd said. He would have put all his money in if it was what Daisy had wanted. He'd do anything for her. She said how lucky she was to have him, but he saw it the other way round. He'd be lost without her; couldn't imagine going through life without her. Wouldn't want to. Everything he wanted to do, it was with her. Every day was an adventure. Sometimes a whirlwind, admittedly, but a wonderful, exhilarating whirlwind. He couldn't control her and had no desire to. He'd also meant what he'd said about doing some thinking. Something Phil had said had stuck in his head.

CHAPTER 38

An Unguarded Moment

It was the following evening. The screen door slammed. Jack looked up from the porch swing; he'd been lost in thought, lulled by the back and forth motion. Daisy appeared on the veranda clutching two tall glasses, closing the door with her hip. A splash of bright colour in her cotton gingham check dress; the one she'd worn on Midsummer Night's Eve. In another lifetime. Another world away. Jack had no idea she'd even packed it.

Everyone else had retired to the lounge. They'd not long finished a celebratory meal, hence Daisy's dress. Phil had even cracked open a bottle of champagne, letting the youngsters partake again; he seemed to be getting softer and softer in that respect, treating them more like adults.

That morning, over breakfast, Jack and Daisy had told everyone of their decision. A thrilled Phil had wasted no time in putting in an offer for the diner. Later that day, it was accepted. He'd got his wish, at nearly half the asking price. And Jack and Daisy had got theirs. Carol had cried; she was emotional all night. Understandably so. There seemed to be no turning back. 'Don't worry about all the visa stuff,' Phil had said. 'There's a way around everything. And I got friends in high places.'

'He's not joking,' said Trish. 'He could probably get you a hotline to the White House if you asked.'

Daisy walked over to join Jack. Her dress swished as she walked. It still fitted her perfectly, except clinging to her belly a little more. Her hips swayed. The ice clunked in the beaded glasses. Her feet were bare on the wooden floor. Already a little tipsy, Jack couldn't take his eyes off her: he could smell her perfume, a sweet-scented and gift-wrapped package in the form of a girl. His girl. God, I love you, he thought.

'Here,' she said, passing him his drink and blowing a damp curl away from her mouth. Like the glasses, her forehead was a little beaded with moisture, her hair clinging to it slightly. It was so humid. A proper Indian summer evening.

'Thanks,' he said, taking his drink and taking a sip. Special lemon iced tea. She was taking a risk with everyone still up. God knows how she managed to get away with it.

Daisy plonked herself down on the porch swing, and it rocked again, their drinks sloshing slightly. 'Oops,' she said. 'Well, chin, chin.' And she held her glass out to his. They clinked them, their eyes meeting briefly.

They settled down and surveyed the expanse of land off to their left; the long driveway. The seclusion, the isolation was comforting. A peach sun was setting. Dusk was imminent. One of the horses whinnied, and the cicadas were in full voice.

'They're so loud tonight,' said Daisy. 'Maybe it's the heat.'

'Yes, like they're in competition. They put our crickets back home to shame.'

Daisy laughed. They sat there for a while, sipping their drinks. Daisy, as always, did most of the talking – even more so than usual. Jack was quiet. Thoughtful. His drink was going down too fast. Daisy's had gone to her head too. In a rush, she'd overdone it with the vodka.

'You OK?' she said.

'Yeah,'

'What a day, hey?'

'Yep,' said Jack.

'Can you believe we're actually doing this? I keep wanting to pinch myself. I mean, it's all just happened so fast.'

'I know.'

'It's almost as if it's happening to somebody else, not me. Not us. This opportunity – it's the kind of thing you can only dream of when you're growing up… I wonder what the kids at school would make of it. Me ending up in America. Be green with envy, I reckon.'

This was hard for Jack to relate to. He had no idea what kids at school thought. The gang, maybe. Be interesting to know what they'd make of it all…

'You sure you're OK?' said Daisy. 'You're not having second thoughts, are you?'

'No,' said Jack.

He necked the last of his drink, and placed the empty glass on the floor, next to the swing. Then he looked at Daisy. Intently, but shyly. She met his gaze. 'What?' she said. 'Why are you looking at me like that?'

He took her glass from her, placed that on the floor as well, then took her hands in his. Daisy was confused. 'What?' she asked again. The smell of the honeysuckle was everywhere, mingled with her perfume. Some sort of heaven, thought Jack.

'Daisy. Marry me,' he said.

ACKNOWLEDGEMENTS

A huge thank you (again) to PC 2397 Jon Stevens for his invaluable help with all police matters.

Julie Memmory for all stuff pertaining to wills and inheritance.

And last but not least, Mr. Jim Barrett, Asylum Township resident, for helping me bring that little corner of America to life.

Forever indebted to you all.

About the Author

Despite being a full-time chef, Adam Longden fulfilled a lifelong ambition when his debut fiction novel, The Caterpillar Girl, was published in October 2016.

Seaside Skeletons, the much-requested sequel to The Caterpillar Girl, was released in 2019, as was a separate novella, Eva: A Grown-up Fairy Tale.

A self-confessed music, book and film addict, Adam draws heavily on his own experiences, influences and surroundings when bringing his books and characters vividly to life.

Adam resides in the East Midlands, where the majority of his books are set.

www.adamlongden.com

OTHER BOOKS BY ADAM LONGDEN

The Caterpillar Girl

Seaside Skeletons

Eva: A Grown-up Fairy Tale

All available from Amazon

Printed in Great Britain
by Amazon

22073724R00238